FIRE DANCE

Tor Books by Ilana C. Myer

Last Song Before Night
Fire Dance

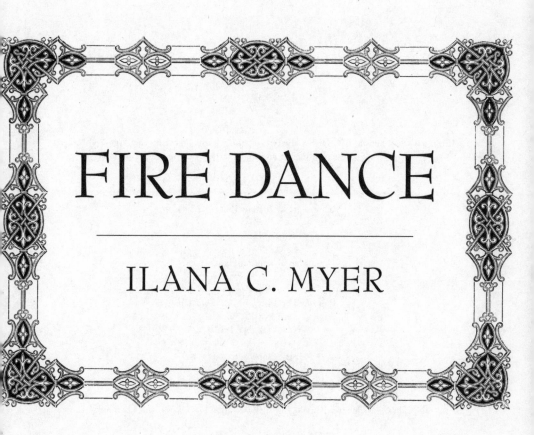

FIRE DANCE

ILANA C. MYER

TOR

A Tom Doherty Associates Book
New York

This is a work of fiction. All of the characters, organizations, and events portrayed in this novel
are either products of the author's imagination or are used fictitiously.

Map by Jennifer Hanover

A Tor Book
Published by Tom Doherty Associates
175 Fifth Avenue
New York, NY 10010

www.tor-forge.com

Tor® is a registered trademark of Macmillan Publishing Group, LLC.

The Library of Congress Cataloging-in-Publication Data is available upon request.

ISBN 978-0-7653-7832-3 (hardcover)
ISBN 978-1-4668-6104-6 (ebook)

Our books may be purchased in bulk for promotional, educational, or business use. Please
contact your local bookseller or the Macmillan Corporate and Premium Sales
Department at 1-800-221-7945, extension 5442, or by email at
MacmillanSpecialMarkets@macmillan.com.

First Edition: April 2018

Printed in the United States of America

0 9 8 7 6 5 4 3 2 1

In memory of my grandmother

Elly Teitelbaum

whose love of the arts opened worlds to me.

KAHISHI

NORTHERN MARCHES

■ ALMYRIA

Iberra River

MARAVA DESERT

MAJDARA

Gadlan River

MARABAG

ZIRTAN

SERGOVANA

KARSHISH

JEDDA PASS

MEROZ

TANZIN

ISLANDS
OF
PYLLANKARIA

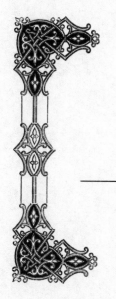

PART I

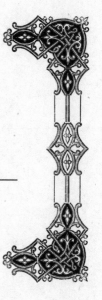

CHAPTER
1

THE storm that had raged two days, tearing at the willow trees along the shore and stirring shrieks of indignation from the ospreys, was at last swept out to sea the morning Archmaster Myre was found dead. He was in a chair by the window of his chamber, wrapped in a cloak, eyes turned toward the sea. The mark of the Seer black around his eye as if it had been set aflame. Perhaps that was what happened when a High Master died, the student who told of it to a crowd of others suggested, looking awed, a first-year boy of thirteen. In her corner, silent, Julien Imara thought it a strange story.

It was a morning of quiet after the long tumult of the storm. As the winds departed, they bore away the soul of a Seer.

In the dining hall shortly after sunrise the students were assembled. From the rose window above the high table a spear of sunlight sliced the length of the room, blinding the students who looked up. The Archmasters sat in great chairs at that table, the largest chair at the center gaping empty. In a voice that quavered, Archmaster Hendin announced the cessation of lessons for the next week. The poets in Vassilian—those who already had their rings, who had gathered in that northern castle to study the recovered enchantments—had been summoned to Academy Isle. Rites of burial for an Archmaster must be observed with rigorous adherence to law. For a High Master, all the more. Such a thing had not occurred in nearly thirty years. To the students, the reign of Archmaster Myre had seemed eternal as the oak groves and rock of the Isle itself.

As Julien observed it all she felt like a sparrow perched on a window-sill, peering into a space where people fretted and wondered among themselves. She did feel regret for the loss of Archmaster Myre, whose voice, for all his years, had resounded with force in the raftered halls. In his bearing he had been noble as any king. It seemed impossible that such a presence could be snuffed out. Become a corpse in a chair, gazing sightless at the water he had not crossed since his youth. His window offered a view past the forbidden boundary, to darkened woods on the mainland shore.

Julien often thought of leaving. It was a possibility—to return home, allow that she had erred in coming here. That she was ready to become useful. Perhaps even marry. Her mother would sniff, and her father's eyes would scan past her shoulder; but she would be home in familiar rooms, sun and olive trees at the window, her sister embroidering beside the hearth. There would be the bedchamber with the furnishings she'd had since birth, the mirror with its hairline crack, the dolls, a shelf of books. By contrast, the halls and galleries of the Academy with their elaborate ceilings massed in shadow were impervious, would never hold evidence of her. The library that extended in caverns beneath the castle would bide its secrets another year, another century; it mattered not.

At home were fewer ways to fail.

Two other girls were in the Academy besides Julien Imara, but they had no interest in becoming poets. Miri and Cyrilla were youngest daughters of lords who had too many daughters. These lords saw an opportunity in Lady Amaristoth's directive to the Academy to take girl students—for which the Crown would pay. The girls chafed at the sur-roundings and dull lessons, anticipated eventual rescue in marriages. Some of the boys at the Academy were lords' sons—this, too, presented an opportunity for the girls' future. But that was not enough of a draw for most to send their daughters to this cheerless isle. In the eight months since the Academy had begun to take girl students, there were only the three. And all too old—at fifteen, Julien should have been in her third year, not the first.

She had seen the Court Poet once, from a distance at a festival. A slight woman who held herself erect, a banked fire in her eyes. Her mark of the Seer a gleam like silver thread. When Julien thought about her reasons for coming here, to the Academy, Lin Amaristoth was at the heart of them. For the first time it was planted in Julien's mind that there might be possibilities for her, out in the wider world. Perhaps even in the capital, in Tamryllin. To be a woman with a straight spine and formidable presence, instilling awe in those surrounding.

Possibilities that seemed a joke when Julien caught sight of her own reflection in a glass. That was one advantage of the Academy—there were few mirrors, and no one saw her. She could imagine herself as she pleased, at times. Deny what she knew.

This was a place where it was possible to lose oneself in a variety of ways—in the maze of the library, in halls of historic carvings, in tower gardens overgrown with hedges and weeds. Yet it seemed to Julien no matter how lost she became, she could not escape herself.

Without lessons that day, she wandered. The students maintained a hush out of respect for the dead—when they remembered. The older ones, who were permitted outside the grounds, went out to the woods to enjoy the absence of rain. Others practiced at harps or huddled in groups in the dining hall. Julien sought the quiet places. In the chapel she came across one of the Archmasters kneeling at the altar of Kiara, head bent towards his chest. She could not see who it was; the lines of his body evinced genuine grief. She passed the Hall of Harps, saw some of the older students using ropes to hoist a new pillar in place alongside the old. Archmaster Myre's harp would be displayed.

In lessons she had learned some of the history of the Academy and its customs. Archmaster Lian delivered the lectures in a level intonation that lulled many young first-years to sleep, invoking names, events. Wars. Julien's eyes grew round when he told of the siege of the Academy carried out by King Eldgest centuries ago; of poets sacrificed to torture or the sword. The spell of the Seer Davyd Dreamweaver that had changed everything—driven the enchantments from the world to appease the king. And Darien Aldemoor, who had given his life to change it all back. It was said the Court Poet, Kimbralin Amaristoth, had accompanied Darien in the Otherworld. None knew what they had seen.

The wall carvings in the Hall of Harps were old as the castle. There were hundreds, and each different. One might show a knight on a horse passing into the mouth of a creature with enormous teeth, his lance upraised; another a crowned woman who ran a sword through the strings of a harp. Yet another, a dancer with a torch in each hand, wild hair like snakes. There were disputes among Archmasters, through the years, whether these carvings arose from a language of symbols, now lost, or were mere decoration. In time, theories had accumulated. Julien could spend hours with a candle in hand, staring at the carvings, discovering new images each time.

Some nights she wandered the halls, explored intersecting passage-ways. No one had caught her yet. The Archmasters prohibited what they referred to as "mixing," so the girls' rooms were in a different wing from the other students. It wasn't boys Julien was after.

In the night, she could pretend. That she was slender and regal, a mark of the Seer around her eye. That the immensity of the place and its secrets belonged to her. No one knew this castle as Julien did, she was sure. At night it became hers.

It was dusk, the sky stained violet above the dark arcade of trees when she saw lights. She was standing at the window of a crumbling tower and spotted them below, yellow and casting bright ripples on the water. She watched. The lights were lanterns, affixed to boats. The poets from Vassilian were coming.

"So you're chosen." A mild tone, possibly amused. Dorn Arrin couldn't tell, not without seeing his friend's face, and it was nearly dark. They sat at the window of the room they shared, and watched the boats come in. Night was growing. By now the line of red in the western skies had turned cobalt, and on the water they saw the lights.

"You make it sound important," Dorn said. "Instead of a bloody inconvenience."

Etherell Lyr laughed. Now Dorn could imagine his grin, the shake of his head. "An inconvenience." He didn't seem put out as Dorn had feared ever since they'd been informed of the choice. Being among those selected to sing at the High Master's funeral rite was an honor worthy of recounting to children and grandchildren—should Dorn ever be so reckless as to have any. Most of those chosen were poets arriving from Vassilian. Though at twenty, Dorn Arrin and Etherell Lyr were in their last year of the Academy—very nearly poets, themselves.

It was true Etherell didn't work as hard as Dorn did at lessons, nor was his singing as remarkable. Etherell had a winning voice, diamond-clear, like a prince in a pageant play. He relied on charm. A lord's son had less need to invest effort in success. Without the benefit of such a background, Dorn knew whatever he himself accomplished would need to be on his terms. He would not return home to an apprenticeship in bookmaking if he could help it. Songs would be his bread and wine.

"Yes . . . an inconvenience," Dorn said. "Singing all the night until dawn."

"If I understand it right, you'll be spending the hours before that in prayer and fasting," said Etherell. Now Dorn knew for certain his grin was merciless. "I'll be sure to keep you in mind tomorrow at dinner."

"All the same," Dorn began, hesitated. They so rarely spoke of serious matters. "All the same . . . It's a damnable thing. About Myre."

"He was old, wasn't he?"

"You don't find it strange?"

"What?"

"His mark."

For several moments Etherell was quiet. From the window they heard distant shouts—the men from Vassilian pulling ashore. The students would be expected in the dining hall to greet the guests.

At last Etherell said, "I don't know. I thought that was something the tadpole invented. For attention. You think . . ."

"You know what I think." Dorn was grim. "Who knows what Myre got himself into . . . what sort of *enchantments* he was playing with? We were better off before all that flummery. When music was music, and words were words. And those who wanted power planned to live off the court like leeches, or wield a sword someplace. Leaving the art to itself."

"You've said it often enough." As ever, Dorn's fuming left Etherell untouched. Dorn often felt unkempt, crude, beside him. He was always too aware of his origins. Yet his path to the Academy had begun in his father's workshop, where as a child he had spent late nights poring over manuscripts by the light of sneaked candles.

But now his friend pursued a different line of thought. He leaned forward, grey in the twilight. "In autumn we'll have our rings. Dorn Arrin, what will you do?"

The question took Dorn aback, then sank in his stomach like a rock. *What will you do?* The voices outside had faded. Now all they heard was the murmur of waves, the call of an owl as night fell; sounds that made the peaceful backdrop of their lives. Though if Dorn were honest, he didn't know much of peace. Only his studies, and the words he wrestled by candlelight in the Tower of the Winds, at times kept torment at bay. A reason, perhaps, that he excelled at his studies.

"What will I do?" He was pleased with the tone he managed, a balance of whimsy and cynicism. "I will take to the road and sing. And hope for a meal and a bed at night. Perhaps the last poet to live that way, it's true." That came out more melancholy than he'd intended. Hastily he added, "And you?"

"I?" Etherell reclined in his chair. "I believe I will take up hunting."

"You're far too lazy." What Dorn would never say was: *Come with me.* He had seen his friend's face when something irritated or disgusted him; the way it froze into pure perfection of form, without expression. Dorn never wanted that face turned his way; there was no wit or art he had against it.

Meanwhile Etherell had stood, lit a candle. His face serene in its light. "We should go downstairs," he said. "They're here."

DINNER was a great affair, with food more festive in honor of the poets who had come, led by Piet Abarda. There was meat, wine, and speeches—these last barely audible to the girls at the far end of the table. Julien gathered that the next day would be dedicated to the mourning rites for Archmaster Myre, culminating in a night of song by the fifteen poets who were chosen. Dawn the following day would mark the final rite, when the High Master would be set adrift to sea.

Piet Abarda was a lithe, dark-haired man with a confident stride. There was something smooth about him, she thought. When he expressed grief for the passing of the High Master—his teacher—it was with controlled sophistication. The poets of Vassilian were under Piet's guidance, if not exactly leadership; he was in service to the Court Poet, reported to her through Valanir Ocune. Many poets, long finished with their studies, had gathered at Vassilian since the return of the enchantments.

Students whispered among themselves that Piet Abarda had a pet demon that rose from the Underworld at his command, and for this reason Julien was disinclined to believe any of the stories she had heard of Vassilian. What she saw were ordinary men, mostly young, dressed in the formal grey of the Academy. There was no telling, from the look of them, if they consorted with supernatural creatures—demonic or otherwise. But she doubted it.

At the conclusion of the meal, one of the final-year students was asked to sing for the company. Tall and lank so he appeared awkward, his shaggy hair nearly hid his face. But with dignity he stood, allowed a silence to fall before he began to sing. His voice was deep. The ballad he chose was a lament for a hero's passing, a warrior of long ago. No emotion stirred in the student's angular face, but Julien felt an impulse to weep. When he was done, the emptiness where the music had been seemed a tangible thing. Archmaster Hendin rose and bowed in his place at the high table. "Thank you, Dorn Arrin."

SHE thought of her sister that night, when she couldn't sleep. Though she felt sorrowful for Archmaster Myre, the mood stirred in her by Dorn Arrin's song came from a different place. There were times when Julien was forced to admit that however accustomed she might become to this castle and its warren of hallways—however expert in its secrets— it would never be home. The Archmasters didn't want the girls here and ignored them in the lessons. Catching on to this, the boys ignored them, too. The Court Poet might be able to force the girls' admission; their acceptance was another matter. It would be reasonable, perhaps even wise, to leave. Julien was here by her own choice, rather than that of her parents. She could exercise that choice again.

But in the house of her birth, of her childhood—which had mostly been happy, despite everything—Julien was not welcome unless she could meet certain expectations. If she could forget the desire that had brought her here.

Her younger sister Alisse had understood. Content to spin and sew, Alisse was the only one who knew her sister's heart. Who had said once, smiling, "You are meant for a different life." Though they looked alike—short of stature and rounded, with brown curls and eyes—that was the only similarity between them. Most of Julien's clothing had been sewn by her sister. Alisse favored embroidered hems, buttons of onyx and pearl, on dresses that enfolded Julien in protective warmth. But Alisse would soon be married and sent to another home.

These were thoughts Julien tried to avoid. She spent hours in the library combing through the scrolls and books. Practiced the harp until her fingers ached. Yet sometimes the draft that rilled through the castle in long sighs was like a question. Or else it was in the evening call of the whip-poor-will: *Where is home?*

When it was very late she knew she wouldn't sleep. She crept from her room out to the hall, where moonlight seeped through apertures. At the end of the hall a staircase rarely used, a narrow spiral in the dark, with cracks and gaps she knew by heart. When she reached the ground level, Julien made her way to the entrance hall, which opened onto the Hall of Harps. She liked to visit it at night: to be alone with the sacred objects, the wall carvings in candlelight. But tonight she heard voices coming from one of the meeting chambers nearby, saw light under the door.

Alisse might have said something cautionary, in that moment, about the perils of curiosity. The peril was real—there was nothing imaginary about the birch rod the Archmasters used to administer discipline. And there were other punishments, worse ones, that Julien had only heard hinted at.

She thought quickly. There was a small passage that cut past that chamber on the other side, connected it with the kitchens. There she would be less exposed than if she lingered in the entrance hall. Making her way to the kitchens first, she snatched a biscuit, which would give her a pretext for wandering if she was caught.

From the kitchen she found the passage, a corridor of doors—most of which were used only by servants. The glow beneath one of the doors lit her way as she pressed against the wall. Across from her, a leering face carved in the stone stared back. The Mocker. It was everywhere in this castle, along with other faces. The King. The Mourner. The Goddess. And of course, the Poet. Faces half-melted into the stone, that saw everything.

She heard Piet Abarda first. "He is hardly cold, and you speak of this?"

"Delay is a pastime for lovers and fools, it is said." A voice she knew, one of the Archmasters. She struggled to recall the name. Kerwin, that was it. The youngest of the Archmasters, she had never liked him, though Cyrilla and Miri thought him handsome with his trim black beard and broad shoulders. "Lord Abarda, if we can depend on your support, you will not regret it. Whereas if not . . ."

"Threatening me, Archmaster Kerwin?" said Piet. "Do you forget I have the ear of the Court Poet?"

"None could forget," said Archmaster Kerwin. Julien now recalled why she disliked him—he always seemed to be sneering. His voice became oily, what perhaps he imagined as persuasive. "You are in a unique position, Lord Abarda. So much power and prestige . . . yet so precarious. Your protector is not looking our way at this time—is preoccupied with politics in Kahishi, as it happens. Here is an opportunity much nearer to hand."

"So far you've presented me with no opportunities, only threats," said Piet Abarda with scorn.

"If that is how it seems, I apologize," said Archmaster Kerwin. "I will only remind you that a time is coming to . . . choose. And to make matters more interesting, I know which Seer has been chosen to complete the ten."

Complete the ten. Death had reduced the Archmasters to nine.

"Surely, Valanir Ocune . . ."

"You see, Lord Abarda. You are not acquainted with the way of things. Valanir Ocune may be hand in glove with the Court Poet, but that is no advantage. Once it might have been. Not anymore."

"What will you give me?" A note of defiance from Piet even as he gave in.

"Surely you know." Archmaster Kerwin sounded as if he were smirking. "What could Lord Abarda want, other than his high position? And yet—he is not a Seer. The Court Poet has lavished him with importance, yet has not seen fit to give him that power. And there is power in it now, Piet Abarda. After tomorrow night, there will be even more."

A hand on Julien's arm made her jump. She whirled, terrified that an Archmaster had discovered her. Found herself staring into the surprised face of Etherell Lyr, which inspired a different sort of terror. He was holding a candle and looked at her with puzzlement. "Julien Imara, is it? What are you doing here?"

"They'll hear us," she whispered, inclining her head towards the door. He nodded and walked with her down the hall. All clear thought had left Julien's head, and she could only think how silly she looked in the prim high-necked nightrobe sewn by her sister, with lace at the cuffs. Etherell Lyr was a fantasy for all the girls, with his golden hair and eyes bluer than the forget-me-nots that bloomed on the Isle in spring. Julien was furious with herself, with the banality of such thoughts. She had not gone so far as to compose a poem about him, but had thought about it—which was bad enough.

"What are *you* doing?" she said when they were out of earshot, summoning irritation as a defense.

"I was hungry," he said, unperturbed. "I see you were too."

"You know my name," she said. Regretted it instantly.

"Yes," he said with a quizzical smile. "Well, good night. I think you had best go to bed."

"Wait—Etherell, what do you think is happening?" It felt odd, presumptuous, to say his name. They had never spoken before.

"Lots of things." He sounded patient. "That's the way of it, in places where power resides. Julien, you are not powerful yet, won't be for some years. Stay out of it now. When you're ready, well." He laughed. "Good night. I think I'll get one of those biscuits."

She turned with a sigh, back to the dark stretch of hallway. Heard him say, "Julien."

She turned back, and her throat caught. His expression had become stern, like a lord about to mete out judgment. "You're fortunate it was my path you crossed tonight," he said. "Try again, you may not be so lucky. There are dangers here."

"You mean . . . like Maric Antrell?"

He surprised her by smiling. "You know, then. That's good." With a jaunting step, even a slight hum as if he was off for a picnic, he ambled down the hall and into shadow. She heard a door shut. And then all was quiet in the hall.

Julien sought her room. She felt a chill, as if the wind had got inside her robe. Of the final-year students, Maric Antrell—talented, handsome, with auburn curls—was among the most admired. And most feared. Julien had seen Etherell face down Maric and his friends in defense of Dorn Arrin. But not before the boys had broken one of Dorn's fingers. They were wealthy, noble—untouchable, though that was supposed to be against the rules. Archmaster Hendin might occasionally have sharp words for them . . . as had Archmaster Myre. But the others seemed not to see.

Julien had thought such dangers well beyond her. She was no one. Invisible. But the recollection of Etherell's stone gaze unnerved her. She shivered under her blankets for a time, as the air crisped with the dawn. A blackbird nested in the eaves began to sing.

Stay out of it now.

She had lived in this place eight months, thought she knew its ways. With one death everything had become strange. The skies were light by the time Julien Imara fell asleep, into a chasm of dreams that resounded with the song of Dorn Arrin, lamenting. A great soul was gone from the world.

CHAPTER
2

WHEN he arrived it was from rain, the first of spring. Before him the palace rose through fog, the same clouded grey as the sky. Behind, the great bells of the Eldest Sanctuary had begun their tolling of the hour, marking it noon. The Seer spurred his horse through a side gate, was welcomed by attendants. From a long distance he had come.

"The Court Poet is in audiences all day." An attendant, intoned with a note of false regret.

"She'll see me," said Valanir Ocune.

A bath was offered, which he declined, though he did submit to an escort to chambers where he might change his clothes. He had not ridden south for seven days through almost continuous rain to be delayed by formalities. It weighed on him what could be happening at the Academy now, in his absence. "Where is she? The Court Poet," he asked one attendant, a boy. "Has she been informed I am here?"

"She has," the boy said smoothly. "I am to escort you to a midday meal. The Court Poet is concerned for your health."

"My—" Valanir could scarcely find words, but saw the boy's face was blank. "Tell her I will eat when it pleases me. No, I'll tell her—where is she?"

He took to the halls barely as soon as the words were out of the boy's mouth. He would find Lin himself. Annoyance was growing into something like anger. He had ridden in haste to get here, with barely a stop on the way, not even pausing to pass time with the friends who would have

welcomed him as a guest. One in particular, an aristocratic widow of slender form and heavy, silver-threaded red hair gathered at the top of her
head in a braided crown, would have been a great solace to Valanir after
his interminable time on the Isle. Wit made all the more alluring by a
melodic voice. She lived by a vineyard on the outskirts of Tamryllin.
Letters she'd sent to the Isle teased, incessantly, with references to
pleasures taken in the course of years. She did not mind that he wandered, and that he had other women. That was the way of it with poets.

It would have only added a day to his journey if he'd made the detour
to her estate in the outlying valleys. One day. Instead he'd come gallop-
ing as fast as he could for the good of the realm and the clearly ungrateful
Court Poet. Through torrents of rain, no less.

As far as he could gather, Lady Amaristoth was in council with rep-
resentatives of the guilds. He also knew these men petitioned the Court
Poet for various favors and ordinances nearly every day. To let them cool
their heels for once would have done them good.

When he arrived at the council chamber to which the attendant had
directed him, it was empty. Another attendant was there to tell the Seer
with fervent apologies that the Court Poet had only just left, was sched-
uled to take the midday meal with lords of the council. It was unclear
where the meeting would take place—whether it was in the solar or in the
Green Chamber, which was in a different wing of the palace altogether.

The situation was beginning to remind Valanir of a farcical ballad. He
would rather have been composing such a ballad instead, from the prospect of a manor house that overlooked a vineyard cupped in hills. After
he and the vineyard's lady had collaborated—alternately in her bed, on a
couch, even the carpeted floor—on new points of discussion for correspondence. Instead he was here, in this palace and the responsibilities it
brought, waiting for the Court Poet to deign to acknowledge him.

The Seer was in a passage that led to the Green Chamber, after he'd
had no luck in the solar, when he heard a voice behind him cry a greeting.
"Not exactly the man I expected to see, but a surprise I welcome," said
Ned Alterra. He looked well, Valanir thought with some pleasure; he
liked the boy. After they'd exchanged pleasantries Valanir said, "I am
here to see her—Lin. It's been uncommonly difficult finding her."

"I imagine she's busy," said Ned with an apologetic air, as if the
fault were his somehow. "I was just here for a meeting of the council.

My father thought I should come. But if we're to speak of it . . ." Glancing around, he motioned the Seer to join him in the shadow of an alcove. Beneath an arch of ornate scrollwork a bench was carved in the wall, but neither man was inclined to sit. Beyond, a marble colonnade made a stately procession down the hall and wound around a balustrade to the upper levels. It seemed to be empty, though one never knew in the Tamryllin palace who might be listening. In an undertone Ned said, "We've had word from Kahishi—they are beset in the north by attacks. King Eldakar requests financing for a campaign."

"Attacks from whom?" said Valanir Ocune, a sinking in his stomach. Seven days he had journeyed, but events had moved faster. He had hoped to arrive ahead of the emissaries from Majdara. He would barely be in time to talk to Lin. If he could find her.

"The King of the North, he calls himself," said Ned Alterra. "In Kahishi he is named the Renegade."

"I know the man," said Valanir.

"*Know* him?"

"It has been a long dance between the Renegade and the court of Majdara. He was not always in disfavor . . . though he was never trusted," said Valanir. "There has always been distrust of the Fire Dancers."

"The Fire Dancers, exactly," said Ned. "King Eldakar suspects them of using . . . magical means of attack. He wishes to consult with Lady Amaristoth in person."

"You mean . . ."

Ned's clear gaze seemed to see through to his thoughts. "She has agreed to go."

HE saw the glint of a jewel at her throat. Lady Amaristoth had risen from her place at table, a goblet uplifted as she smiled at one of the delegates from Kahishi. Her place at the king's right hand. They were seated with the delegates at the head table on a raised dais. Valanir Ocune sat below, with the Tamryllin lords who dined here tonight.

Briefly the Seer and Court Poet had exchanged words in the dining hall. She embraced him with a smile brilliant as the jewel she wore and as she stepped away, looked amused. Her hair was twisted in silver combs atop her head, a court fashion.

"I must speak with you," he had said, holding in check his anger. She had deliberately avoided him all that day. The anger was, in a way, comforting; it distracted from the emotion coursing beneath it, which was shock. With anger at least he had some measure of control.

She had nodded, diamonds in her ears reflecting sparks like ice. "Soon." And then was at the head table, a ring of light from lamps and gold plate surrounding her as she made welcome the lords and delegates. Extending her hand like a gift, to be kissed each time.

These men knew who had the king's ear. Harald relied on his Court Poet more than on his chancellor, just as in the time of Nickon Gerrard.

Valanir Ocune watched and wondered. Was she angry that he had absented himself from Tamryllin for so long? She could not know what was happening at the Academy . . . what he believed was happening.

He remembered their last meeting, in autumn of the previous year. The conversation had been strained. She had seemed a world away even while clasping his hand in farewell. And now she had consented to go to Majdara without seeking his counsel, even though no one in Eivar was better versed in the court of Kahishi than Valanir Ocune.

Old man, perhaps she grows away from you.

It would be natural, he thought, if she sought to assert her independence. Lin could hardly forget it was Valanir who had put her forward as a candidate for Court Poet. Who had made her Seer. If her purpose was to demonstrate where power lay, he would readily concede.

Still he recalled the hard glitter of her smile and wondered.

There is too much at stake now, he wanted to tell her. *We cannot be at odds.*

On the dais Lin Amaristoth turned to one of the delegates and laughed.

A NOTE came for him close to midnight. Valanir Ocune was at the desk in his chamber, composing by candlelight. So she knew his habits. The bearer of the message, one of the smirking boys Valanir had come to detest, waited to escort him. They were in their petulant way striking—perhaps she had begun to take lovers. Last he had seen her, Lin had seemed clenched in herself with enforced solitude. Hedged in responsibilities, some private griefs. He only understood some of them.

She was seated at her desk when he entered, poring over a scroll. At the sound of his footfall, looked up. "I thought you'd be awake," she

said, and dismissed the servant. They were alone, then. Valanir had wondered if this time he would only be permitted to see her under guard.
He had been many times in this room. Tonight, he was struck by its
simplicity. She was Court Poet, and of House Amaristoth, yet the harp
by the window was the only object of great value. Above her desk hung a
painted landscape: mountains on a moonlit night, hues of violet and black
melting into mist. He wondered what that landscape meant to her.
Whether it was her origins, or the Academy—nexus of her desires. Or
both.

She had not desired the honors and responsibilities that came with
this room. Those had been his doing.

"Thank you for seeing me, lady," he said.

Lin laughed and rose. She had changed her dress. This was black, and
high-necked, almost to the chin. A belt of silver links clasped her waist.
Valanir felt stirrings of recognition: Lin almost resembled her mother.
Now her smile in the dining hall was like a breath down his neck from
the past, and for the first time the Seer felt fear. He had only seen Ka-
linda Amaristoth once, twenty years ago. He was then a poet of thirty-
two years of age, and without a care. He had ventured into that castle
with a light heart, imagining there was nothing he didn't know about
people and the world.

As it happened, he'd been wrong. And had never forgotten the lesson.

"I'm impressed, truly, that you'd thank me at this hour," said Lin,
and motioned him to a couch while she sat at the one opposite. "I'm sure
you've heard of my imminent journey. Perhaps you have advice?"

He could not tell if she mocked him. "No advice," he said, seating
himself across from her. "Only what I may share of my experience."

"An experience of years," she said. "I'd be a fool to discount it. But
first tell me why you are here."

"Two things. The first, and most urgent, is about Majdara," said
Valanir. "I had hoped to get here before their messengers did. The situation in the Kahishian court is . . . delicate, Lin."

"Please explain," she said. "I see this is going to be interesting. I'll
pour us wine."

"I've had word from a friend," he said as she handed a cup to him.
"Zahir Alcavar. He is some years younger than I, but already First
Magician in the court of Majdara. It was with his help that I learned

what I needed of Kahishian magic to defeat Nick Gerrard. They know of such things in Kahishi—of spirits in lower realms. They believe there are seven dimensions of earth. We reside at the highest. What Nick summoned was from one of the lowest . . . a creature of hell. We could never have stood a chance without Zahir's help."

"So we owe our lives to this man," she said. "You had word from him—how?"

"He is a Magician," said Valanir Ocune. "Zahir suspects this war . . . that there is something at work. That someone near King Eldakar is responsible."

"A traitor at court."

"Yes. It must have been Zahir Alcavar who suggested summoning you, Lin. He doesn't trust anyone in the Zahra. Not even his fellow Magicians. Something is going wrong there, though he didn't say more to me. Probably he dared not—these connections over a distance can be spied upon."

She was expressionless. "So I am to go and root out this traitor," she said. "Is that what you believe I should do? Why you rode here in such haste?"

"So you knew."

"*Erisen,* we are linked," she said. The Seer's mark around her eye had caught the moonlight in netted strands. "I am not yet sure what that is good for, but I did know you were coming. I knew the moment you arrived."

"And avoided me."

She shrugged. "What is the purpose of your visit?"

Anger twinged, but he restrained it. "My purpose," he said, "is to prevent your going. Despite my friend's wishes. Every instinct tells me you would be walking into danger. I offered to go in your place, but . . . King Eldakar does not welcome me in his court. To him I represent the court of his father. They only want you."

For a while she was silent. Her face slanted away from his. At last she said, "It means much. That you came all this way, with thoughts of my safety. I am grateful."

Gracious words, lacquered in formality. Nonetheless: "Of course I thought of your safety," he said.

"That was one thing that brought you here," she said. "What was the other?"

He temporized by drinking some of the wine. In his mind, the Academy was a knot. There were parts of it he would not share yet, even with her. He said, "The other was to keep you apprised. Lately I've sensed—almost a hostility towards me from the Archmasters. They hold meetings in secret. I can't be sure if it concerns the Crown or not, but I thought you should be aware." He tried to meet her eyes. "It's why I haven't been here since last year," he said. "I wanted to come. I fear what might happen while I'm not there."

"Yet concern for me drew you out," she said, with an arched eyebrow. "Couldn't you have sent a message?"

"There is no one I would trust with such a message."

Lin seemed to consider. As she bent her head, a curl escaped the combs to caress her cheekbone, lent her face a softness. "I must go, you know," she said. "To refuse would imperil our alliance with Majdara. More than that . . . I want to go."

"Do you now court death, Lady Amaristoth?" This half in jest.

The sideways curve of her lip was like a crack in glass. She said, "Death has courted me for years now." Then smiled, and crossed the room to him with the light steps of a girl.

THAT morning she had cornered Garon Senn against a woodshed. Despite the dawn chill they were both perspiring. The air humid with the promise of rain. He had raised his sword arm to deflect her blow, too late to stop her locking her blade's edge with his. She slid her blade down until the point reached his chest—and stopped. As they broke apart, he called out, "Now that you have me against the wall, I'm sure that's all for today. Don't you think, my lady?"

Lowering the practice sword, lips relaxing from her teeth, Lin Amaristoth had to laugh. A grizzled warrior who had been halfway around the world before he had found his way here, to become the court of Tamryllin's master-at-arms, Garon Senn was not awed by anyone, not even the Court Poet. She, in turn, accepted that a former mercenary captain was unlikely to ever learn the smooth ways of court. "Done, then," she said. "Maybe I'll let you beat me tomorrow."

"I insist on it," he said with a grin.

Heading for her rooms and a bath, Lin Amaristoth felt as if weights were settling on her, one by one. Mornings with Garon Senn were the few occasions she was unequivocally herself. The instinctual space that opened in her when she had a blade in hand—a space that had taken shape in childhood—admitted nothing else. Not even the soul of a dead Seer.

As Lin bathed in scented oils, a female attendant read out the day's agenda. Delegates from Kahishi—yes. She'd had word ahead of time what it was about, what they wanted. She knew what she would say. Then there were the inevitable meetings with the guilds, with courtiers. That was the weave of the court of Tamryllin—equal parts urgent and ridiculous, too fine to disentangle.

It left little time for music. But her dreams being what they were, she seldom slept; and nights were hers. Lin would rise sometimes in the dark as if the harp had called to her. She would perch by the window with the instrument in her arms, her gaze out to sea. There was no way to know if the songs were hers, or if Edrien Letrell channeled his words through her, from the dead.

Art was, had always been, a gift that took her by surprise. She could no more know its source than see the wind. And all the more so now. Lin Amaristoth supposed she could believe as many poets did, that it was the goddess Kiara who provided the gift of music. But faith, for her, was difficult.

Nights were when she most felt him with her. Almost she could believe if she turned she would see him hunkered in the shadows beside the bed, moonlight catching the mark on his eye. The sigh of the water below like the sound of his thoughts. If she slept, she would be swept into his memories, the heartbreak and pleasures of his life, his art. Or else into the recurring dream she had just begun to understand.

So she gave her nights to music instead.

Music could take her away from memory for a time. But it also returned her there. It recurred in her memory: the night Darien Aldemoor had done what he'd done. When she had cut her own wrists so he would not kill. With all the force of will that was in her she'd said, *"Let me do this."*

To Lin it had made sense to give her life, a thing broken and twisted, to preserve the innocence in him. Not thinking ahead to the logical next step: in consenting, he lost that innocence.

And then had died for her. Every day with its dealings in petty politics and the whims of an idiot king had been purchased at that cost. The world would never know the music Darien could have drawn from the growth of years. Not know the full extent of his art.

No wonder, then, that she sought Garon Senn most mornings. Lin wondered what he knew. His black eyes were flat and inexpressive even when he laughed. She had presented him with a ruby earring that he wore at court, displaying her favor. Lin thought he was loyal, but would have preferred to be sure.

There were few ways to lose herself to thought, or memory. Perhaps that was why she seldom allowed her mind to rest. Even in the bath, she was already at work, her mind fixed ahead on what her strategy would be with the delegates from Kahishi.

It was when maids were pouring new hot water into the tub from silver ewers to wash her hair that Lin suddenly sat upright.

"What is it?" one girl asked, with a fearful look.

Lin stretched back into the embrace of the heated water. "My old friend and teacher will be here soon," she said, and did not mind that it sounded cold.

THE day had passed much as expected: the Kahishian delegates had told a tale, elegantly phrased, of the terrors facing them in their northern marches. Lin Amaristoth and King Harald had received them in a private audience. She had listened with narrowed eyes to their account of attacks on villages, raids carried out by warriors clad in white, the battle gear of Fire Dancers. Of these, Lin knew little: only that they were a people who lived in the mountains of northern Kahishi and refused Kahishian rule. There had always been enmity between the Fire Dancers and the royal house.

Lin knew what the sharper of the lords of the council would think: the situation still amounted to minor skirmishes, not a true war. And while Eivar could hardly refuse a request for aid from its powerful ally, it was strange that the famously opulent Zahra could not deal with common brigands. With the aid of his viziers—who commanded armies in their own right—King Eldakar had the capacity to assemble a force known throughout the world.

But then the delegates began to speak of magic. Another detail to which Lin had been alerted ahead of time. Their leader, a greying man with a clever face by the name of Tarik Ibn-Mor, had said, "King Eldakar requests with all possible speed the presence of Lady Kimbralin Amaristoth to advise him in this matter."

Harald had immediately objected. "The Court Poet doesn't leave our side."

The Kahishian had allowed his eyes to flicker to her, the Court Poet, at the king's side. Restraint there, it seemed to her. "I myself am of the Seven, the Magicians of the Tower of Glass," he said. "Yet King Eldakar wishes to consult with one who defeated a demon, returned the magic to your land. He cannot be swayed from this." Lin thought his tone hinted at an attempt to sway. She hid a smile.

"We must confer with the council," she'd said to Tarik Ibn-Mor. She already knew how events would proceed: Harald would object, along with the lords who were currying favor. She counted on support from those who were stronger, and sensible, such as the lords Alterra. Everyone must agree, ultimately, that the unbalanced relationship between Eivar and Kahishi afforded no choice. Eivar could have been conquered a thousand times by the armies of the east, if not for the beneficence of Kahishian kings throughout the years—and their esteem of poets. They even generously overlooked the Eivarian worship of what they considered false gods. Their own deity, Alfin—the Thousand-Named God—had for centuries been a rallying cry in wars from Kahishi to Ramadus and the lands between.

Truly, there was no refusing Kahishi anything they might ask.

"My lady," pressed Tarik Ibn-Mor, "we must return to the Zahra in a matter of days, if it pleases you."

She had inclined her head, unblinking. A hiss of suspicion from Edrien Letrell surfaced in her mind: *Magicians*. She said, "Soon enough, you shall have your answer."

WHEN she faced Valanir Ocune that night it was with the awareness that he was most likely angry. All throughout that day she had felt the nearness of him—not with the intimacy that Edrien Letrell imposed upon her; rather like a melody played in a distant room. She had toyed with him today. It was the first time she had done any such thing. Since his last visit she had grown older in all ways. It was a loss, she reflected as she met the Seer's eyes. But she could not feel it as a loss, couldn't grieve. Perhaps that was a part of it.

His eyes as she crossed the room were wary. And if she felt infinitely older now, it seemed to her he didn't show his age—his face barely lined, his features fine. She'd had similar thoughts upon meeting him in that tavern, when he was passing as a Seer named Therron, a summer that seemed long ago. As if life's griefs washed over him without penetrating . . . as if there had been no griefs at all.

She realized how she, in turn, must seem to him. *The lady in her castle.* So much an Amaristoth.

Not what she'd intended for the shape of her life. Not what Darien had intended for her, either, when he'd traded his breath for hers.

Valanir stood when she did. As if they were on formal terms. She advanced with slow steps. He watched her advance with a bewildered paralysis. As if he stood in the path of an avalanche. "Lin—" And stopped, when she reached out to touch the side of his face. For a long time she had wanted to do that. It salved an ache in her, but created new ones.

"Sit," she said, a command. He had barely done so before she was on him and around him on the couch, her mouth to his. The heat of him against her, his immediate response, like warm wine.

After what seemed a while, Valanir pulled back to look at her. The color had risen in his face, his gaze heavy-lidded and languorous. But it was with seriousness that he said, "Lin—is this what you want?"

"Shut up," she said, and put his hands to her breasts. Even through her dress his fingers moved expertly, and soon she had lost control of her voice. She paused to laugh at herself. "It's been a long time," she said.

"I want to hear that sound again," he said, and slid a hand under her skirts.

Rain had begun to beat against the windows. The lamp burned bright. As she writhed and cried out, Lin felt exposed in its glare. She wouldn't meet his eyes. He was murmuring in her ear, things she had never thought to hear him say.

The words, more than the manipulations of his hands, wore at her defenses. What she most strove to avoid throughout the days and nights by means of a blade, the council chamber, and the harp, was assaulting her. The recurrent dream that plagued her nights—its meaning, she had only recently begun to understand. Always it was the same: A man crouched in the corner of her bedchamber, between a chair and a towel-rack, crying. Always he had his back to her, but still she knew him. Darien Aldemoor, head buried in his hands.

Lin moaned in a different note, halfway between grief and a plea. Though she still wouldn't look at the Seer's face, she gripped his hands. Valanir seemed to understand, shifting his weight beneath her. Soon he was inside her and thoughts were gone.

The rain was drumming more gently some time after, when they both lay still. Thunder a muttered portent in the distance. Valanir was still beneath her, her face between his hands. She had given up trying to avoid his eyes. He said, "You seem surprised by something. But it is you who surprised me."

"You said you've . . . thought of me." Referring to the murmured words in her ear.

"That should not surprise you, lady." His hand drifted from her face to the fastenings of her dress. "May I?"

Together they stood. He was behind her, untying her dress. There had been a time when she would have shied from letting him, anyone, see her. She thought of the lamp and exposure and thought, *So be it,* and lifted her chin, as if in defiance of an enemy.

But there was only Valanir Ocune, who said, inexplicably, "You break my heart," and lifted her up. She felt terror for a moment, at being helpless, but it passed. He carried her to the next room and her bed, where dark enfolded them; she could see little more than the mark of the Seer on his brow and the light it reflected in his eyes. Gently he parted her legs, and then at the foot of the bed, knelt between them. Thunder was shattering the night as Lin filled the dark with raw, lost cries.

Later they slept, and for once her sleep was dreamless. When she woke it was before sunrise. She slid from bed into a velvet robe. The rain had ceased, banks of clouds breaking to admit grey streaks of light. The sea a darker grey. Seagulls glided in wind above the water. Without turning she said, "That was better sleep than I've had in a year. Thank you."

"Come here," he said.

She turned to face him, but did not advance. As if thoughts that crowded her mind fixed her in place. Valanir Ocune lay on his side, the mark of the Seer faded. His eyes clear as if a haze had been scrubbed from them.

"Who are you, Lady Amaristoth?" His tone was wistful. "Word comes to me you imprisoned a poet for satire."

"Three nights," she said with a dismissive gesture. "His song was a stain on my honor. And the king's. I could not allow it." The poet had more than suggested the Court Poet ensnared King Harald—in enchantments, and elsewhere. It was crude and not very clever. Some lordling who would not amount to much as a poet. "He was unharmed. The point made."

Valanir sat upright. "Do you want to talk about last night?"

The stillness of the room, the half-light, made it all seem unreal to her. As if it could evaporate like one of her dreams. She looked out at the water again. "I do not ask anything of you."

"Nor I of you," he said. "That isn't why I asked."

Through mists she could see the docks. Boats. She said, "I have to tell you something."

"You *were meant to die*," the wizard had told her. He was not what she had expected. She had thought he would be old, and smell of incense. Neither of these were true. His beard was black, his features weathered but not aged, eyes showing sorrow beyond his years. His robe and cap were white linen, his one ornament an amulet of silver worked in filigree.

She had sent for him precisely because he was from far away, from a land with no ties to Eivar. Even so it was a risk. So many would have been happy to oust her on a flimsier pretext than this. Court Poet, and a woman, who had enforced changes at the Academy that many resisted. They would never forgive her for the girl students, or for being forced to take orders from Valanir Ocune.

The enchantments of Eivar held no remedy for her. Valanir had told her there was no cure for the spell of Darien Aldemoor, which had intertwined another man's thoughts and memories with hers. Which seemed to grow stronger by the day. She had placed her hope in a far-off magic, its practitioners who had developed their art over the course of centuries.

The wizard bade her sit, recited an incantation in his language as he waved his hands once, twice, three times in a circular motion around her head. She was shivering. For once Edrien Letrell's thoughts were quiet within her, which oddly had the effect of making her feel abandoned and more afraid.

"It was a deep spell," said the wizard at last. "You sheltered within you a soul from the Underworld."

"My friend—the man who cast the spell—did not know what he did," she said. "We had been without enchantments for so long. He didn't know."

The wizard took her hand. The sadness in his eyes grew more pronounced. He said, cradling her hand, "A body cannot give shelter to the dead, even for a little time, and still live."

"But I am needed here," she said, stupidly.

He said, "I have no doubt." Lin Amaristoth thought, in her shock, that he probably had a good singing voice. Of all things, she had not been expecting this outcome. There was nothing he could do. He would not accept her offer of gold. He did take the gift of a horse for his journey home.

A SILENCE. She pressed her forehead to the glass, its chill a relief. Behind her, he said, "How long?"

"He thought I might have a year," she said. "Or less. No one can know."

Another silence. Then she heard a rustling behind her. After some moments, felt his hand on her arm. "Look at me," he said. She turned her head. He had hastily dressed, though his shirt was open at the chest. Her eyes lingered there a moment, but the rigidity of his stance forced her gaze upward. She had never seen Valanir Ocune so angry. "I won't let this happen," he said.

She drew back. Before his rage she felt flat, listless. "You'd said there is nothing to be done. Now we have confirmation." She drew a breath. "I must apologize." The words came as if they were stones that she hefted, one by one. "I thought . . . I was . . . no more to you than a game piece. Last night you showed something else. I've made this more difficult for you. I swear I didn't mean to."

"You thought that." His voice seemed nearly to break. "What, then, did you want?"

Now she could meet his eyes, almost with a smile. "You."

This time it was he who turned away, with great strides. But soon returned as if drawn by invisible cords, his hand passing over the side of her face, the nape of her neck. Sunlight made his eyes too green, implausible. Lin knew she was trying to hold the memory, in its smallest details, as day broke at her back.

"I only regret the time we did not have," he said. "And that you didn't know your own power. Two sorrows I have so far. I won't allow a third and worst, from losing you."

Lin caught his hand at her neck as she would a weapon. "Give thought to a successor," she said. "A Court Poet who will live long enough for our work to be complete. Perhaps it should be you." She shook her head when he began to speak. "Think about it while I am away." Her grip on his hand tightened. "It was you who taught me to put the needs of this city before my own, Valanir Ocune. Let me go."

CHAPTER
3

SMOKE made a blue mist in the pavilion and smelled of ambergris. Faces shifted from shadow to lamplight and back, as in a masquerade; but finery, embroidered and jeweled, made for a continuous whirl. The dishes that arrived from cookfires outside were richly spiced and inventive, their scents mingling with the incense. Beside Lin Amaristoth an exquisite woman with gold earrings was laughing, perhaps more loudly than was proper; Rihab Bet-Sorr, young queen of Kahishi. King Eldakar, his queen, and their retinue had honored the Court Poet of Eivar by riding out from Majdara to welcome her and hold this banquet. The pavilion, long and nearly as high-ceilinged as a dining hall, was erected in a poppy field just a week's journey from the Zahra. Later, after there had been sweets and music, they would retire to beds of silk in small pavilions hung with velvet for warmth.

Lin had never seen the like. She had slept roughly all through the journey from Eivar and not really minded. The mountain pass had offered brisk air and the colors of spring. Her only complaint of travel was the space it left for thoughts. In the absence of meetings and affairs of state her mind was free to wander; and as ever lately, the paths it took were misted, as if with fog or unshed tears. Nights by the fire, she could not bring herself to sing. She had brought paper and ink for the journey, filling sleepless nights in her tent with study and composition. Almost Lin could not admit to herself how much she desired just one more thing, nurtured one hope: that she might produce a song that would last.

There was very little time.

Her retinue was escorted by Magician Tarik Ibn-Mor and his men. It was a journey made tense by Tarik's obvious opposition to his own assignment. For now, Lin could only guess at the reasons, guessed they had little to do with her personally. She avoided speaking with him, though they sat together at mealtimes. One time, when they sat at the fire, the Second Magician had said to her, "Valanir Ocune made you Seer?"

There was contempt in his voice. Perhaps this was the source of his grievance—a dislike for Valanir Ocune? In as neutral a tone as possible, Lin had replied, "He did." It was as public a fact as could be. A scandal, in some ways. It was not in the usual fashion that Seers were made. Archmaster Myre had never forgiven either of them.

Though there was only firelight to illuminate that clouded night, still she could see the Second Magician's glance downward, at her hands. "I see your mark, when the moon is out," said Tarik. "But I also see something else. You have no ring. Even poets who never attain the rank of Seer have this, the sign that they have completed the studies of the Academy. Yet not you? Not the Court Poet? It seems . . . remarkable."

Lin reclined on cushions that had been placed for her beside the fire. "The Archmasters choose a gemstone according the poet," she said with a shrug. "They have not yet chosen one for me."

Tarik's sharp, clever face looked more interested now than malicious. "That seems to me odd," he said. "A division between Academy and Crown that cannot bode well."

"We have our divisions, it's true," said Lin, looking him in the eye. "But King Harald supports me. If the Academy wishes to have their small demonstration of resistance, I may as well allow it. Ultimately it is the Crown that reigns." She then found a reason to speak to a guardsman, on the other side of her, and afterward take her leave for bed. The lack of a ring—a thing even the meanest of poets received—was a reminder all her days that she was not like other poets. Lin thought she had succeeded in dismissing Tarik, diminishing his rudeness, but still . . . he had not missed the mark.

In the course of the journey the Second Magician had sent word to the Zahra—no doubt through his particular methods—that they were close. She was surprised when King Eldakar sent word of his plan to ride out to meet the Court Poet at the border and host a banquet in her honor.

It seemed a strange thing to do in time of war, but the hospitality of the Evrayad dynasty was famed. And Lin had been duly impressed as, reclining in the field of poppies with her attendants, she watched as the wave of silver and red that was the king's guard advanced. Their ceremonial armor—compared in Kahishian poetry to mirrors—caught the sun, edged in the red brocade of their cloaks. Their crest a falcon, gold on red.

It was armored thus that forces led by Yusuf Evrayad had conquered in Kahishi. It had not been so long ago. Eldakar's father had come from Ramadus and united the squabbling Kahishian provinces, made them his. What was once a land ruled by a handful of petty kings had, over decades, grown strong beneath the dynasty of Evrayad. Now those kings were viziers, leaders in their provinces who owed allegiance to one king.

It was Yusuf who had been a friend to Valanir Ocune, a patron of his work, granting him years of hospitality in the Zahra—the magnificent palace he'd built in Majdara, the capital.

His son Eldakar was another matter. Valanir could tell Lin little about him, save that he'd been a boy when last he'd seen him, and seemed withdrawn, quiet. Unlike his father in all ways. Perhaps the most distinctive thing Eldakar had done so far, in his short reign, was marry the wrong woman.

Now at the banquet table as she studied the queen's profile, the long straight nose, black hair gathered at the nape in a jeweled net, Lin recalled Ned Alterra's words to her the night before. "*There is a story about her*," he had said.

Lin had sent him into the Kahishian camp to find out what he could. With his innocuous appearance and a mind sharper than most, Ned made an indispensable spy. It was he who controlled Lin Amaristoth's network of eyes and ears in Tamryllin. She had recognized early in her time at court that such practices were necessary; had done her part to discover the identities of those who had once reported to Nickon Gerrard. Ned was the only one in the court of Tamryllin she trusted.

The rest were dubious, even Garon Senn, though she had still included the master-at-arms in her retinue. Garon had good reason to be loyal, for she compensated him generously. Lin valued his agile wits and field experience. She had appointed him her personal guard.

From a night of drinking with guardsmen Ned returned to report to her. Ruddy and grinning, he threw himself on the floor of Lin's tent. Drink brought out something in him that was usually concealed, a crudeness. She could see he struggled to hold it in check in her presence. One reason, among several, that she trusted him. No one would hold Ned Alterra to account for his actions more severely than he already did himself.

Of the queen, he said, "It was a forbidden marriage. Eldakar was to have married a princess of Ramadus, to cement an alliance. Instead he jeopardized everything and married a slave girl."

"So this Eldakar Evrayad," said Lin abruptly. "Is he an idiot?"

Ned tried to hide a smile. "It's hard to say. The common view is she bewitched him. He came upon her singing beside a stream in the palace gardens. They say he had her that same night, which is possible—she was a slave. But now, it seems, she holds the reins to him."

"What do you think, Ned?" She valued his thoughts over rumor.

"I think we should observe a while," he said, drawing his knees up to his chest like a thoughtful boy. "It does suggest there may be more to the coming war than bands of Fire Dancers."

"You think they may be backed by Ramadus." A kingdom said to be magnitudes more complex, more splendid, than nearly anywhere else. Eldakar Evrayad's father had come from Ramadus, an army at his back. Lin didn't know the particulars of his claim to Kahishi; the spiderweb of bloodlines and dynasties in the east were a field of study in themselves.

"The Ramadians have reason to hold a grudge," Ned assented.

Lin was silent. If true, this would have repercussions for Eivar; it would have to. All this imbalance, even havoc, because of a woman singing in a garden.

She remembered the words of Valanir Ocune about a suspected traitor in the Zahra. Then Ned: *She holds the reins to him.* Was this the answer?

"There's more," Ned said then. His voice barely louder than the hiss of Lin's tent fire.

"Tell me," she said.

What he told her next was imprinted in her mind the next day at the banquet, when her gaze narrowed on the king, Eldakar Ibn-Yusuf Evrayad, seated beside the queen. A sensitive face, slender hands adorned with rings. Dark eyes long-lashed as those of his wife. He made skillful conversation with Lin from the start, about poets and the works he favored. He was intelligent, unlike Lin's own king. "But now the Academy is given over to new powers," said King Eldakar with solemnity that made him look younger than he was. "Pardon me, lady, but I wonder. Will the art itself be forgotten?"

Lin blinked. "I'm not sure what you mean."

Queen Rihab Bet-Sorr was looking at her, too. She wore a crimson gown, embroidered with peacocks worked in azure and thread-of-gold. She leaned into Eldakar's shoulder as if the two of them were alone. "The songs from your land have given us pleasure, through the years," she said. "But if a man seeks power through poetry, is it yet an art—or a means to an end?"

A slave girl? Already the rumors were showing seams of incredulity. Lin said, "Men have often become poets to obtain power and all that it brings—fame, gold, women of beauty. Little has changed." As she spoke, she felt the words were a knife—towards the king and his queen, she offered the handle; towards the listening presence of Edrien Letrell, the blade. Sometimes she felt at war with him, as she sought to preserve her self. And because he was killing her.

"But it is different now, is it not?" said Eldakar Evrayad. "Surely the balance of power in Tamryllin will change. Perhaps not right away. Here in Kahishi, the Tower of Glass can shape the fate of the king—though it has been our tendency to deny it." He was smiling faintly.

"It is early yet," Lin acknowledged. "But most of our songs remain entertainment—or art. We access the enchantments rarely, at great cost."

"You bested a *laylan*," said Rihab Bet-Sorr. The Kahishian word natural, sweet on her tongue.

Lin nodded. "Yes. But not alone. The Seer Valanir Ocune was with me."

"Did it cost you?" Rihab's gaze seemed open, her question straightforward. Lin recalled that elegant as the queen was, she was also young.

But around the table, others were listening. Lin said, carefully, "We all have paid, in our own ways."

Now Tarik Ibn-Mor interceded. He had sat shrouded in shadow and a cloak, but Lin had all along been aware of his presence, an abiding disdain. His cloak was threaded with silver, so it resembled a fall of water from his shoulders. Water was his element, it was said; he was versed in the mysteries of hydraulics, an art kin to magic, and had worked his spells in the king's gardens. Fountains, Lin was given to understand, were of more than symbolic importance in lands that ran dry. "The powers of Eivar are new, untested," he said. "Our Tower of Glass has stood nearly two-score years. The first school of Magicians, in Ramadus, more than a thousand."

"Yes," said Eldakar, mildly. "And our First Magician, Zahir Alcavar, comes from the school in Ramadus."

Without troubling to disguise his resentment, Tarik said, "A Ramadian leads us. Yes."

Lin sat back, watching. The king's face had gone remote as stone. A man of almost feminine beauty, he resembled a sculpture of the god. It was hard to tell whether he was fearful or angry. Beside him, Rihab Bet-Sorr bit her lip.

Ned's words of the previous night came back to Lin. "There is a widespread belief that Eldakar is weak," he'd said. "That a war in the north would overthrow him. His younger brother Mansur, a battalion leader, is more popular. There is even a tale that King Eldakar is caught between dueling lovers—the queen and Zahir Alcavar, who dominate him for their purposes."

"Zahir Alcavar, really?" Lin had asked, surprised.

Ned shrugged. "For years Zahir and Eldakar were the closest of friends, against King Yusuf's wishes. Some say, more than friends."

There was nothing Lin could say. For all that Valanir Ocune had lived in the Zahra and been guided by the First Magician to a mastering of enchantments, he had told her little of Zahir Alcavar.

There was tension after Tarik's remark, in which he had all but accused the king of weakness. At last it was Rihab Bet-Sorr who spoke. "We have wandered far, it seems to me, from a discussion of poetry. Lady Amaristoth, greatly have we desired to hear a poet of your stature recite. Will you honor us here?"

Before Lin could answer, King Eldakar said, "You must have your harp, of course. As tradition dictates."

Lin waved her hand. "No need," she said. "I thank you." Of late she had no desire to sing. There was the chance if she did, her heart would show. Not only to others, but to herself.

She waited as servants were sent around the table to call for silence.

Burning into her she could feel Tarik Ibn-Mor's glare—*you have no ring*. The expectant gaze of the king and his queen. And all those present— courtiers, soldiers—who may have wondered at the small woman who had been sent to meet the demand for a Court Poet. Lin cast her gaze around the pavilion, meeting each assessing pair of eyes in turn. Some shrank, others looked away; no one held her stare.

Who are you, Lady Amaristoth?

He had sounded as if even then, he somehow knew what was lost.

Where there had been a clatter of dining and conversation, there was now a low sputter from the braziers. But she was not in this tent at all when she redirected her mind. This place was but one link in the necklace-chain of her life. Its forging nearly done.

She had written some lines by candlelight on the journey here. Rough, not very skilled. She cared not what they thought of her, these strange eyes and faces. Lin spoke.

> *A tale was told me of a golden stair*
> *lit with captured stars*
> *that leads to marvels too immense*
> *for a poet's skein of verse.*
> *'Ascend the stair,' comes the fierce*
> *command of poets gone.*
> *Yet those who live, hold back—*
> *desiring that summit, yet knowing, too*
> *it is the end.*

"WATCH her, Ned," Rianna had bidden him a week before. It had been the morning he was to present himself at the palace as a part of the Court Poet's retinue, and depart. She was standing on tiptoe to fix his cloak. Ned knew it was an excuse to lean close and would certainly not resist. He breathed in the scent of her hair, unchanged since he could remember. The fact of his leaving heavy between them.

"You worry for her," he said.

"I'm afraid," she said, and stopped. There was a bruised quality to her eyes, as if she hadn't slept. "Her mother was mad, you know."

"I know."

"Just watch her," she said.

And that night Ned Alterra did, along with everyone in the ban-queting pavilion, as Lin stood at the head of the table. Even in the soft light she was ghostly, but for a spot of color in each cheek—an irregu-larity like a fever that also burned in her eyes. The night before he hadn't seen it, his wits clouded by drink. He had seen a woman whose slender waist was like an invitation. Had flung himself to the floor, at a dis-tance, and kept his eyes on the tent fire or his knees.

The high color in her face and intensity in her eyes did nothing to diminish Lin Amaristoth's desirability. An odd thought—Ned had seldom thought of her as desirable. Perhaps the words she recited held power, whether or not she knew it. She had confided to him that the enchantments of Seers evaded her skill. A weakness to be kept secret, and the Court Poet trusted Ned Alterra with her secrets. Some of them. He was not fool enough to think he knew them all.

Mindful of his task that night, Ned scanned the faces in the pavilion that were turned to Lady Amaristoth. Noted the interested expression of the king, the rapt attention of his queen. And naked disdain from the Second Magician of the Tower of Glass, Tarik Ibn-Mor. He didn't even try to hide it, Ned mused. As if his position were so assured he need not dissemble. But that was almost never true—anyone could fall. It was a part of what made the game exhilarating for some. In his time in the court of Tamryllin Ned had learned much, from watching.

Standing behind Lin, Garon Senn. He was a broad man, and though going grey, seemed hewn of a tougher substance than flesh. His attire the red and black of the Tamryllin palace guard, but the red as accents only; Garon preferred mostly black. Ned could seldom read his expression—a dark beard and shadows cast by the angular planes of his face concealed it. It made sense that Lin would want such a man at her side, but Ned wished he could discover more about Garon Senn. He had been able to confirm little of the man's account of himself, which ranged in distant lands and likely included deeds best left buried. Men who fought for coin were the worst kind. But so far Garon Senn had demonstrated perfect loyalty, as was in his interest.

Ned Alterra had different ideas about loyalty. When genuine, it might come at a price—not be sold for one.

When Lin was done reciting, there was a round of cheers, wine in goblets upraised. The color in her face settled, or drained, as she took a delicate sip from her cup. Her eyes met Ned's for an instant; in a glance conveyed to him amusement, or irony. He wondered why.

He hadn't told Rianna about the time he had come upon Lin in her chambers, playing her harp. She hadn't seen him at first. It had been near dawn and Ned wasn't expected—there was some emergency for which the Court Poet was needed. And so he had gone up, and found her.

And there was something wrong with the scene, though Ned Alterra could not have said, later, what it was that made it feel wrong. Her eyes were closed, her lips curved upward slightly, but her face tensed as if with pain. The music that poured forth made him think of awakening spring, buds trembling on the bough. But it also closed a dark well around his heart. He'd thought if he listened much longer he would fall down that well, never to be seen again.

When she opened her eyes and saw him, in that moment, she had smiled too widely. And then ceased her playing, straightened, addressed him in ordinary fashion. Not as if he'd seen something he wasn't supposed to have seen, or heard. And in time, Ned had come to wonder if it really had been that strange; if he'd imagined it. But some nights, the notes of the music returned to him; Ned would startle awake. He would leave his bed to look at the child, with her fine hair like his own, and stand over her bed awhile. With the sight of her small limbs and rounded face he would try to recall who he was, what was urgent in the present.

He couldn't tell Rianna any of that, though. Yet somehow she must have seen something, or guessed.

"*If she is mad, make her come home,*" she had said. "Ned, she saved my father. Do this for me."

Now in the banquet tent Ned drank. He was loyal to his sworn lady, and to the lady of his heart. He hoped wine might clear any discord between the two, at least tonight.

In her tent Lin Amaristoth lay wakeful, swathed in silk: coverlets and an embroidered robe that had been a gift from the Kahishians. Its caress on her skin like a breath, recalling nights in other beds like this one; soft skin, legs enfolding, cries of surrender. Edrien Letrell had been hosted in palaces of the east. Restless, Lin sat up, cursing under her breath.

A singing, of insects or some amphibious thing, was all that marred the night's quiet.

"Do you require anything, my lady?" Garon Senn, outside the doorway of her tent. He had taken the night watch for himself. His voice like sandpaper, a steadying contrast to silk.

Almost, she solicited his aid in calming her need. She'd seen how he looked at her when they were practicing. But knew the danger and the folly of that road. "Nothing," she said, and the quiet crept back.

She mulled the events of the evening. It was clear already that Valanir had been right—there was something odd at work in the Kahishian court, though she doubted it was complex. The hostility she had felt from the Second Magician was unmistakable . . . he had not troubled to hide it. She had seen King Eldakar take a blow to his honor without retribution or even reply. His wife, Rihab Bet-Sorr, was a political liability, without family or connections to avail the kingdom. The more popular brother was away, at war in the north. It was no wonder someone like Tarik Ibn-Mor saw an opportunity. Perhaps he schemed with the king of Ramadus, promised an alliance through marriage if raised to the throne . . . it fit together almost too perfectly, like a puzzle box.

A bird cried out in the night. Lin didn't recognize its call. She was far from home. The fragrance of poppies blew through the tent flap.

Her thoughts went to Valanir Ocune, who would have returned to the Academy by now. They had spent hours in conversation, and he'd told her all he could of the Zahra. Of his friendship with Yusuf Evrayad, who had been fearsome in battle but harbored a deep respect for the poets of Eivar. The Tower of Glass, Valanir averred, was a wonder to behold. It was there that Zahir Alcavar had helped guide Valanir towards the enchantments of Eivar. Tarik Ibn-Mor he knew less well, though the two were contemporaries; the Second Magician held himself aloof.

Valanir also gave her the name of a contact in Majdara; someone to seek out who might help her find out more about the Fire Dancers. More than that, he would not say. Nor would he say more about the politics of the Academy. The Seer's manner of evading a direct question, Lin thought with some wryness, likely took as much skill as his songs.

He was unquestionably hiding something, but Lin did not try to draw it from him. She was gentle with him those last days, almost solicitous, to compensate for the way she'd misjudged him. Had made use of what she knew from Edrien Letrell of the varied ways to give a man pleasure, their last nights together. That first night she had done no more than take what she wanted. Believing him immune to loss, or love.

The night before she was to leave for Kahishi they had held each other a long time. "How can I persuade you not to go?" he'd said.

She'd smiled into his shoulder. "Do you have any methods left?"

"It's dangerous," he said again. It was a recurring argument.

"I'm dangerous," she said. "And already endangered. There's no use arguing—my mind is set."

"We will most likely never meet again," he said. His first time using this, his last arrow.

"You want to make me weep." She traced his chest with her fingers. "Sing to me instead."

He had, then, until the dawn.

CHAPTER
4

HE arrived to singing. Voices that coiled in harmony, soared upward. They came from the chapel but rang clear in the entrance hall, lent an even greater sense of vastness to that space with its sculpted ceilings, pillars hewn of mountain rock. The sound nearly brought Valanir Ocune to his knees. Twin forces at work on him—memory and realization. He recognized the elegy for a High Master. And was flung back to another night many years prior when he himself had stood in the chapel to sing the mourning rites for a fallen Seer. Someone he'd loved.

Tonight would not be like the last time. His actions and those of a few others had seen to that. There was enchantment in the music now offered upward to the heavens or gods. In truth, Valanir did not believe gods had much to do with it.

He was shaking as he shut the doors behind him. He could not recall his last conversation with Myre, but doubted it was how he would have wanted to leave things between them. The old man had shown a distrust for Valanir Ocune since the latter's student days. A sentiment not wholly unwarranted. Valanir had been a fractious student. He and Nickon Gerrard together. They showed remorseless, relentless disobedience, and talents too brilliant to be suppressed. A figure of iron even in those days, Seravan Myre had not been amused by the combination. Where the High Master of that time was inclined to indulge, Archmaster

Myre had encouraged punishment. Valanir and Nick, the two of them, were cause for dissension in the highest ranks of the Academy.

It made Valanir's task of mediation between Academy and Crown more challenging now. Especially after he'd broken the Academy's most fundamental laws by making Lin Amaristoth a Seer without the consent of the High Master. Such a crime as would have been held against him, had the Academy the right to punish him. But as an agent of the Crown, he was immune.

While Lin had seen Valanir Ocune as a creature of the Academy with a cold view toward her use, Archmaster Myre had believed him motivated entirely by self-interest. In the end, Valanir thought, the old man probably had the truth of it. But there was not much one would accomplish in life if one spent it racked with introspection and second-guessing. The desire that had animated Valanir Ocune to become a Seer, and to delve beyond that, was not one for which he would repent. Desire and art were of a kind.

Desire. He had been too long in that room of subdued light from the east, with its view of the ports of Tamryllin.

I won't let this happen, he had said. They were supposed to have power, a Seer's words.

Valanir Ocune knew he had become vulnerable to introspection as he stood in the foyer, travel-weary. The whole journey he'd been in a daze, even when entertained in the homes of friends. Some who took him in had certain expectations, such as the red-haired woman he'd often visited. He'd made the excuse of illness, and then felt undeserving of her anxious ministrations. He could have availed himself of her comfort, but had not the heart. As if the grey that encompassed Lin's room at daybreak had entered into him.

A shadow crossed towards his in the entrance hall. Archmaster Hendin, looking careworn. "So you're back."

"Too late, it seems."

His friend's eyes widened. "You think . . ."

"A moment." Valanir held up his hand. He crossed to one of the pillars. Felt a rush of relief. "What are you doing, Julien Imara?"

The girl emerged from behind the pillar. She had been sitting, wrapped in grey, on a shelf beneath one of the windows. It had made her seem a part of the stones. She lowered her eyes. "If you please, *Erisen*," she said in her soft voice, "I wanted to hear the music."

"Young woman, you should be asleep," said Archmaster Hendin, though he sounded more tired than angry.

"It is a strange night," said Valanir Ocune to his friend. "Perhaps a difficult one for sleeping." He turned back to the girl, whose eyes were now raised to regard him. Solemn eyes. Chestnut curls pulled back with a ribbon. *What are we doing to these children?* "Am I right?" he asked the girl.

Her gaze was steady. "I learn by listening."

"Do you." He felt a pain, though that may have been occasioned by a rise in the voices nearby, in a melody so familiar it did more than give shape to a new grief; it recalled old ones to him as well. "You remind me of someone," he said. "Archmaster, how does this student in her studies?"

Hendin seemed surprised by the question. "She is capable," he said after a moment. "But does not speak in the lessons."

"Is she encouraged to speak?" Valanir shook his head. "Never mind. I know you do the best you can, Hendin. Mistress Imara, we will speak of this later. Go to bed."

When he had ascertained she was out of earshot, he turned back to his friend. "Tell me how he was found."

"Peaceful," offered Archmaster Hendin. "In his room. But there was one strange thing." He recounted that the Seer's mark had blackened around Myre's eye. "And the others—they are already beginning to talk of who will be next in line. And who will complete the ten. Both they speak of as a given. I dare not protest."

"Go on," said Valanir Ocune.

What Archmaster Hendin proceeded to tell was only somewhat surprising. Valanir had expected Archmaster Lian would be elected by the Masters' council to take Myre's place. Lian was one of the eldest, considered able, but more than that: he was pliable. A contrast to Archmaster Myre, known for his steel resolve.

The tree that does not bend will break.

The other news, about the Seer due to arrive and complete the ten, was less expected. A name Valanir Ocune had not heard in some years. It recalled to him things he had long thought forgotten: memories of his time as a student. Archmaster Lian had been only a year ahead of

Valanir—they had disliked one another on sight. The supercilious son of nobility believed he was owed deference. Yet there was one student at the Academy to whom Marten Lian himself deferred. Serving him as one would a king.

And now that student—now a Seer—was coming back to be an Archmaster here.

It was a great deal to think about. But before he went up to his room, Valanir looked closely at his friend. "Cai." A short sound, Hendin's given name. A weight of memory attached. They'd been friends for so long. "Are you all right?"

Hendin hunched his shoulders. "I will miss him," he said, and turned away. It was unlike him to be so abrupt. They were friends but he still didn't want Valanir to see his grief. When he was gone there was only that song, resounding from pillar to pillar in the entrance hall.

Valanir was lost in thought as he mounted the stairs to his room, the song fading behind him. Whatever happened tonight, thought Valanir Ocune—even if nothing happened—it was unlikely he would sleep. When he arrived at the door to his chamber he stopped. He reached out with his mind in the way Magician Zahir Alcavar had guided him years ago. Nothing. But he checked again after he had unlocked the door, set down his candle on the bedside table and his bags on the floor. The room appeared undisturbed.

He began to change out of his clothing, which was stained and damp. Almost immediately there was a knock.

But as he rose, the Seer relaxed. That particular knock—three raps, a long pause, two more—was familiar. He had devised it himself. "I thought you'd come," he said as he opened the door. "As it happens, I have a new task for you."

THE greatest danger to Dorn Arrin on a night such as this turned out to be neither fatigue nor hunger. Both had dropped away when he found himself tangled in a glory of voices. These were amplified by the acoustics of the chapel. Extended deprivation—hours of fasting and prayer to Kiara—had opened a well of vulnerability in him. From this the music came. As the men stood facing the plinth where their High Master lay, voices merged as one, Dorn felt as if a knife slit him open. None but he saw what it exposed. But standing in the chapel for hour upon hour, pouring himself out in song, he could not look away.

His had been a life too confined, he knew. Years on this rock, far from where real things happened. He had never even visited the mainland against the rules, as the others did some nights. It was forbidden, yet may as well have been tradition. Students would steal a boat and go into Dynmar—for girls, mostly. Etherell sometimes joined them. Most expeditions were led by Maric Antrell, who in many ways led the students of their year. A reason Dorn had few friends.

Yet he felt joined with these men as they sang together; even with Maric, who stood nearby—another of the students chosen. Tomorrow they would be enemies again, with Maric and his cronies finding some way to trap Dorn in a corner. Etherell Lyr would come to his defense, all lordly swagger and skill, and Dorn would seethe with the humiliation. These boys had been trained for combat practically since birth. Dorn knew how to sew a binding.

The most recent incident had been just that week, the night before Archmaster Myre died. Dorn had been late that evening in the library. There was a curfew, but he tended to ignore it, and he pursued an interest of his own. There was an entire genre of songs written after the fall of the Academy and the disappearance of the enchantments. A time known as the Age of Laments. The songs that emerged in those years were ragged with loss. Their powers gone, the poets of Eivar had not ceased to sing. But the wound was fresh, their words like blood.

Dorn leafed through manuscripts of these sometimes. Voices called to him in the pages. Notations preserved the melodies. He would read and in his mind the notes sounded. They produced the feeling in him similar to when he watched the descent of dusk on the Isle from the window of his room, another day slipped irretrievably away.

It was late, then, when Maric Antrell had materialized at Dorn's elbow, like a malevolent spirit summoned. He did not look well, Dorn had thought spitefully; but most of note was his smile: wide and crazed. Light from Dorn's candle was flung up Maric's chin and cheekbones, giving him the appearance of a skull.

"Just where I thought you'd be, book-boy," said Maric. "I like knowing where I can find you. It might be useful."

"I had no idea I so interested you," Dorn said, pointedly turning back to his pages, though every nerve was tensed. "Isn't there a cure for unrequited love? *Enchantments*, of some sort?"

Maric bared his teeth as if to snarl a reply, but just then Archmaster Hendin emerged to light. "I believe, boys, it is long past time for sleep. Especially, young lord, for you." Maric had stalked away, muttering. Dorn had found his hands were shaking as he gathered up his notes. The library had never seemed a place of danger. People like Maric seldom went there for the books. But it seemed they might go there for *him*, if so inclined.

Etherell was becoming concerned for his safety. He had tried to convince Dorn to carry a dagger, offered to teach him to use it. He'd said, "I can't be around all the time."

"It would be tedious if you were," Dorn retorted. Ending that conversation.

Six years they had shared a cramped cell of a room. Dorn was aloof the first year, expecting the golden lordling would disdain a bookmaker's son. But Etherell Lyr allowed Dorn's acerbity to break over him, or it made him laugh. It was his friend's equanimity that convinced Dorn to curb his rages. He tried. Perhaps not hard enough. Rage lingered on the edges of his songs, unspooled in reams by candlelight. It was never enough.

Now was a night for inward wrestling, though so elliptical an act would only return him where he'd begun—to himself.

The Archmasters saw promise in him. There had been offers to tutor him privately, to begin to work towards the enchantments. He'd turned them down. Maric Antrell showed similar promise. Dorn had seen him in hushed conversation with Archmaster Lian in the hallways. The Archmaster had taken the lordling under his tutelage. And of course everywhere Maric went, an entourage of students trailed, finding a natural leader in the broad-shouldered heir to Antrell.

It used to be that few poets even aspired to becoming a Seer. It was an honorific for the most learned, a path to becoming an Archmaster at the Academy if one so desired. But the return of the enchantments had changed all that. Now the Seer's mark symbolized a heightened access to powers of the Otherworld. Thus in just a short span the atmosphere of the Academy had changed, charged with a new aura of ambition. What once had been a study of art, of music, had become something else. The mists on the Isle had not changed, nor the wistful cry of birds at night, but at its heart Dorn thought the place would never again be what he remembered.

A fact reinforced by the sight of Archmaster Myre, dead on the plinth. Their voices entwined in farewell. An ending to something larger than they who had seen far fewer winters than Myre could comprehend.

It didn't matter, Dorn told himself as he sang. In autumn he would have his ring and be free. He loved the Academy and it tortured him, in equal measure. He imagined taking to the road alone. There was no joy in the idea, but a kind of release.

Here was the crux of where music brought Dorn Arrin that night. As if he gazed into a pool of pure solitude and need, and saw his future there. He had always known, in truth; but through song he faced it. *Autumn,* he thought. *Alone, and free.*

LATE that night Valanir Ocune was alone again with only a candle to pierce the darkness.

He thought of his last conversation and knew it added to his tally of transgressions. But was necessary. He would pay one day.

Or would he? So far, it seemed it was others who paid.

How did you capture me, Lady?

A line he'd written years ago. With irony. His heart had been lighter then, the world a banquet spread before him.

His memory ranged across mountains and deserts. Evenings camped with a caravan, listening to lute music as beside the fire a woman danced. A garden inlaid with yellow and blue tile, a fountain centered with perfect symmetry. It spilled into a pool long and slender as a wood beam, green with water lilies. A place where he was received with honor, more than once; where among the roses, as evening fell, they disputed questions of philosophy. A plate of figs passed around, cups of jasmine tea and later, wine. These were simple pleasures; more complex were those to be found in palaces with their costly scents and beds of silk; where occluded desires gave way to more, as in a maze of doors. Valanir Ocune had traveled enough to know that such places, no matter how deep he fell into them, signified but a temporary escape.

He had been much younger when he'd learned that. He recalled disentangling from a strange bed and going to the window to look at the moon. Knowing he was alone. These were lessons for the young.

It was not the role of a poet to escape the demands of life. So Valanir Ocune had always believed. Yet for years he had lived sheltered, cosseted, studying secrets in the Tower of Glass. The prophecies that were forbidden knowledge. One could argue he had done this to prepare for engagement with an enemy. Only in Kahishi could Valanir have learned about the thing that possessed Nickon Gerrard, and how to banish it.

Zahir Alcavar had shown Valanir their magic. Had taken him through portals, where he'd glimpsed dimensions beneath the earth, above the sky. Most of what he'd seen so strange his mind couldn't encompass it; he remembered little. Seven earths and seven heavens the easterners believed in, inhabited by creatures beyond comprehension.

A memory: he'd accidentally summoned one of these beings, one of those nights with Zahir. They'd been in the Tower of Glass, had drunk too much, and he could not recall how it had happened. The creature of green fire that towered over them was what Zahir had later named a djinn.

Despite being half its size, Zahir had shown no fear, darting forward to confront the djinn. Like a lover, he had whispered in its ear. To Valanir's surprise, the reaction of the creature was of sudden agony. It gave a shriek that rattled the glass walls of the tower. Then vanished in a plume of red smoke. Unruffled, Zahir had turned to Valanir and said, "If you call upon one of these, be ready to forfeit your soul." Then laughed. They'd drunk far too much that night, Valanir now recalled. "My guess is you're not ready for that. Not even close."

Valanir was discomfited by the memory—embarrassed; the younger man had saved him. But most of his time in the Zahra had been serene, not like that. Much of it spent in the company of Yusuf Evrayad, the king who had recently died. A complex man, Valanir had thought him; a warrior who tolerated nothing of softness, yet revered the art of poets. Their discussions had touched on questions of power and a fulfilling life—at times, far into the night.

It was one such night in King Yusuf's chambers, when the candles burned low, that Yusuf had confided what perhaps he kept most closely hidden from the public: his disappointment in Eldakar, his eldest son.

"He is a poet," he'd said to Valanir. "An excellent quality in a man, any man . . . Any except a king."

"You have not tested his mettle on the battlefield," Valanir had pointed out. "You send Mansur on campaigns, give him the chance to prove his valor. Not Eldakar."

"For a simple reason," said Yusuf. He had at that time begun to show his age; his face sagged. "If Eldakar goes out to fight, and fails . . . certain conclusions would be drawn. The viziers won't respect him. All I have built—this court, a united Kahishi—will crumble. Better to keep him here. Mansur will keep the name Evrayad burnished bright."

"And win glory his brother might have shared," said Valanir.

Yusuf shook his head. "Eldakar would acquire no glory for our name. Mansur makes conquests, puts fear of our strength in the hearts of those abroad. But I fear for our future, Seer. Sing me a song, now. Help me forget my fears." And so Valanir Ocune had done, that night and many more. That was the nature of their friendship, composed oddly of equality and servitude. They conversed as equals, and Yusuf applied to the Seer's range of knowledge and lore; but it was Yusuf who was king, and conqueror.

Valanir knew Eldakar, a little. Had spent his share of nights in the garden with Zahir Alcavar and the young prince. The three men had recited verses composed in the moment, a waterfall serving as counterpoint. Eldakar, though shy, seemed congenial enough company. Yet now the boy didn't want him at court.

Power balances in the Zahra shifted constantly as light in the depths of a gem. It meant Lin Amaristoth went instead of him, risked herself. Seemed to want to, and that was another worry.

He could hear Archmaster Myre, in one of the last talks they'd had. Frigid as winter's oak. *You have opened the door.*

It was true. Before Valanir Ocune had found a way to defeat Nickon Gerrard, he'd first engaged in blood magic with him. They'd opened that door together. For Valanir it had been an adventure. But for Nick . . . the abyss. That deep well of need that could never be filled.

The mark of the Seer blackened around a lifeless eye. More added to Valanir's tally. How would he pay?

At the end she had met his eyes. *Captured me.*

Verses Valanir Ocune had composed on the trek home—composed

the old way, the oldest way, by heart as he rode through rain—he recited now. In candlelight and with night sounds around him, he reached out.

He was in woods. Scent of wet leaves and pine, salt air of the sea. The Isle, then; *his* woods. A night bird called, then another. As his eyes adjusted, Valanir saw a pavilion of pale and intricately carved wood, lit with torches against the night. Two figures stood in it, a man and a young girl. The man was tall and broad, slim at the waist; the body of a warrior, but he wore a harp. A magnificent face, godlike, blue eyes keen in the firelight. The girl at his side less sure, no less beautiful with a curtain of shining hair.

Around them rose the requiem for Archmaster Myre, that until daybreak would go on. And Valanir Ocune knew that he saw what was to come because the music gave it to him. Those boys and young men with their voices uplifted did not know the changes they wrought, the doors opened. Valanir scarcely knew, himself.

The man and girl did not see him, it seemed; just stood intent on something in the distance, long-lashed eyes a match.

Come on, then, Elissan Diar, Valanir thought. *I'm ready for you.*

CHAPTER
5

HE was crying in her dream, as he did most nights. This time on the floor in the corner of her tent, beside the legs of the brazier. His face hidden in his hands. Lin Amaristoth sat up, buried her own head in her hands. "I think of it, too," she said. "It doesn't help. What is to be, will be." She turned and saw herself in the bed, adrift in sleep. So pale, as if dead already. Yet she was also standing, looking down at his hunched shoulders and golden head. A bright heart brought low.

"We all made mistakes, my love," she said. Then paused, brought up short by the words. *A dream,* she reminded herself. Moonlight through the tent flap, slender as a rapier, split the wall between them. Lin was still. She felt to cross that line would signify the end of something.

Instead she reached out a hand, towards the shaking shoulders of the man who had died for her. Said, "I know you never meant to hurt me."

WHEN she awoke it was still night. As ever when Lin first awoke, she was unsure in her own body and where she was, as if she saw double. There was the tent and its slat of moonlight through the flap, and overlying that, another place and time where the stars were different. Where not as many years had worn on the earth and stones. But to be in two places at once, she found, meant you were not fully present in either. Sometimes she expected even the most vibrant sunlight to pass through her as if she were glass.

Lin supposed this feeling, of not being entirely present in her body, had to do with the way she was fading. That was how she'd come to think of it, like a star gradually winking out of existence—or, if the astronomers of the east were right, into an expanse of rock. Though that took thousands of years. As many mortal lives swallowed within that time as scattered sand.

Viewed that way, a life was nothing. Not even the men who became legends could count for much, when their memory lived only in fragile creatures like themselves.

Lin sat up in bed. She had begun to notice a sound, quieter even than the crickets and the wind. At first wondered if it was another dream. Or Edrien. But as she listened, as the sound merged with the night, it became ordinary. A man's voice, singing. A sound like a chant, melodious repetition.

She draped her blanket around her shoulders, rose from the bed. The blanket was crimson velvet and of surpassing softness, lined with gold silk. Gathered about her it was like a cape, finer than any she'd owned, and less practical. She drew aside the tent flap and stepped out.

Garon Senn had gone. In his stead a pair of guards kept watch—young men, likely terrified of their new responsibilities and of her. They started like hares when she emerged behind them. She permitted herself a smile at this test of their reflexes. Heard them stir uneasily as she passed. But neither dared yet to speak.

Out here, she could hear the singing more clearly, though it was faint. The royal pavilions were camped at the crest of a hill; the sound seemed to be coming from partly down the slope. The tune not one she recognized. It was a song released in circles, without finding resolution. She remembered: the scales of music used here were different.

It did not occur to her to be afraid—the camp was well-guarded. She trod carefully to avoid the poppies, as she understood they were considered sacred—the red ones. Painted with the blood of some martyr of long ago, as their faith would have it. She picked her way around them in the soft earth. Moonlight made dimpled shadows on the grass.

Lin was some paces away when one of the guards timidly called out to her. She straightened as if the blanket were in fact a cloak. As if she was outfitted for a hunt. "Yes?" she said over her shoulder. "I am going to walk a bit. If I have need of you I will call you." She could not have said what compelled her. She was weary, saddened from the dream, and tired of being alone with the image of stars guttering to rock and the grief of a man who had died for her.

In a way she did hunt that night, for she didn't want to alert the singer to her presence. Her footfalls were light on the grass. It brought to mind times past, the excitement of setting out on a night's expedition. She and her brother, clad in leather and fur, armed with bows and knives. Setting the bait—salt poured on the bole of a tree—for the stag that would come. They two comprising a silence more profound than night. All the things each of them thought, and did not say. The hatred and love that could not be disentangled. And now would never be, since Rayen Amaristoth was gone.

But this was an altogether different place, where the air was rich, seductive with poppy scents. Where beneath her feet there was, instead of dirt and twigs, a carpet of grass. And she was not on the hunt to bring down a proud, antlered creature in its home. Not in years had she done so now.

The singing grew near. She spotted movement in the dappled shadow of cypress trees. Later she would recall how she found him, seated on a stone outcropping. His song, as she approached, seemed sad to her, though perhaps she would have heard any music just then as sad. It was in a language she didn't know. Not Kahishian, not her own.

He ceased when a clump of pebbles crunched under her foot. His head turned towards her. She could only see an angular face, framed with shoulder-length black hair. Lin became aware of how she might look—slight, childlike under a blanket. A disadvantage. But it was too late. In Kahishian she said, "That is a sad song. It drew me."

He smiled. She could see that, the gleam of teeth, but it was hard to see more. When he replied it was in her language, and perfectly. "Is it sad?" he said. "It is from my childhood. It goes around in my head sometimes, until I find I must let it go."

"Valanir Ocune mentioned something about music, and you," she said. "He said before you studied magic, you were a musician." The Seer had spoken admiringly of his friend, who had risen from humble origins to make his name in Ramadus, and subsequently the Zahra.

The dark curtained his expression. "You are Lady Amaristoth."

"*Gvir* Alcavar," she said, inclining her head in mock formality. "You are late for supper."

This time he did not smile. "It is a failing," he said. "One for which, thankfully, Eldakar forgives me. The fighting in the north . . . requires my focus. This past week especially."

"Why? What's happened?"

He shook his head. "No real news yet—what I have, I must save for the council. You will be there. Mansur—the king's brother—has been encountering fierce battles. There are—terrible things happening." She saw now that he looked exhausted. "I try to warn the forces where the attacks will come. Still, it is bad. Mansur doesn't have enough men. But all this . . . it can wait until morning. I am here to welcome you, as are we all."

"Valanir intimated that you and I have much to discuss," she said. She chose her words with caution, though she didn't think they were overheard. "As to who you think is . . . responsible."

She felt his eyes on her sharpen. Light-colored, they brought to mind a mountain cat. Something new in his voice when he spoke again. Four words, but they chilled her. "Lady," he said. "You are alone?"

Lin glanced around, behind her. There was a sinking in her stomach. But she raised her chin, met his eyes as if unconcerned. "I am here with my guards and attendants—of course."

He continued to stare. Under his gaze Lin felt fear at first, then the beginnings of anger. It was in response to *his* summons that she had come, after all. Come all this way. She could have stayed in the palace of Tamryllin, with her rooms that overlooked the sea, the daily rituals that gave her comfort. Small comfort, but nonetheless. She could have stayed there, in the time that was left.

Lin realized she had hoped she could rely on this friend of Valanir Ocune with the truth. This man the Seer held in such high regard, who was a Magician of renown. But hearing that cold mistrust in his voice, she doubted that now.

Despite feeling increasingly desolate, she held his gaze. "The fighting in the north concerns me, too, Zahir Alcavar. It is the reason I am here."

No question about his coldness now. "There is a shadow that moves with you, Seer. I see it even in the dark."

Lin's fists closed. But she kept her tone even. "A shadow?" she murmured. "Why don't you explain?"

His tone remained level as well. He had a deep, sonorous voice, such as had been evidenced in his singing. "There are several possible names for what I see accompanying you," he said. "None of them good."

Lin looked down at the man sprawled at her feet. Assessing him not just through her own eyes. "You will need to decide if you are willing to take me as you summoned me, Magician." The last word pronounced like an epithet. That she had come this far, bearing under her burdens, and this was the end of it. Rage filled her like a tide. "I have turned back a *laylan* from my land's destruction. Watched people I loved die. What have you done in your palace, Ramadian? In your tower above the world?" He was silent. He was a court fop, she thought, soft from palace life. Valanir's stories of singing with Zahir Alcavar in the palace gardens began to take on a new light. Of Magicians trammeled in luxury and concentric circles of flattery, safe in their tower. Lin knew these were not entirely her thoughts—what Magicians had she known?—but resolve like iron backed her words. "I will leave if you wish it," she said. Her tone turned soft. "Leave your people to whatever fate Kiara has decreed for them. I shall return to the court of Tamryllin, perhaps write a song about the Kahishian mountains in spring. And then forget them, and if we meet again it will be on the battlefield, or else never. Those are my terms."

Still he didn't speak, his face masked in night. She had not wanted to imperil this alliance but neither could she compromise her honor, which did not belong wholly to her. It was done. Since he was silent, it seemed there was no more to be said. She turned, began to make her way back up the hill. Zahir Alcavar did not call out to her. Nor did he take up the strands of his song again. Silence was all that accompanied Lin in the march to her tent—that, and her ghosts. *Perhaps he will have me killed,* she thought, and almost it made her laugh.

As a child Lin Amaristoth had been taught contempt for *the upstart,* as her family named Yusuf Evrayad; he who had united the splintered provinces of Kahishi and built a mountain palace above Majdara of such splendor it shamed any in the land that had come before. But this was vanity by the reckoning of an Amaristoth, in their fastness of centuries. To their view, the decades-long reign of Yusuf Evrayad was an eyeblink, a hothouse orchid beside an oak. As ever her family concealed their true attitudes—even their nature—from outsiders. Often Kahishian dignitaries were guests of House Amaristoth, especially in summer. Decked in ostentatious scents and finery they came, like tropical birds amid the sparrows of the north. From them, over years, Lin had learned the tongue of Kahishi. She never knew what these visitors with their clattering gold earrings and neck chains thought of the ghostly daughter of Amaristoth, who tended to linger in corners or else near the fire, as if she never could get warm. Doubtless they—strangers to Vassilian who drank chilled gold wine with Lord and Lady Amaristoth and their son Rayen until agreements about ships and caravans and bolts of wool were reached—gave the daughter little thought. Seldom she spoke while these negotiations took place. She listened. Most of her life she had spent listening.

Lin Amaristoth's family hid their poison behind smooth smiles, made use of Kahishian connections by necessity. *Majdara is our gate to the world,* Rayen had once said. It held the keys to trade with the south and east; to the west the seas were uncharted, and no ships sent on exploratory voyages that way returned. Standing at the mountain passes, guarding the coastline, Kahishi also held the keys to Eivar's defense. *Or our defeat,* Lin had thought at the time, and thought it again now, hands tightening on the guardrail as she looked out on the River Gadlan, waters murky green in the shadow of the royal barge. Along the bank ran the walls of Majdara, spiked with battlements and hung with the banners of Evrayad. The sun was high and picked light from the gold-threaded banners, made them gleam with each stir of the wind.

They had ridden three days from the poppy fields and the temple there. Before departing, Lin had stopped to pay her respects to the god, to see for herself what a temple to Alfin was like. It was a small building of adobe, unadorned, but for its domed roof and minaret. As instructed ahead of time, she removed her shoes upon entering, felt cracked tile underfoot. A temple that had not been in use for some time, it was empty this morning. Arches split the half-dark in multiple angles, gave a feel of depth even to this small space. Lin noted that though the god of the

Kahishians had a thousand names, he was without a face: there were no images of him to be seen. In Eivar, even the meanest temple to the Three might have figures, or a fresco, depending on what the community could afford. Artists in Eivar made their livelihood depicting images of gods. Here, the art was without a human subject: intertwining tree limbs made for a frieze along the wall. This was interspersed with grapes hanging from a vine, a lion frozen in the act of stalking a gazelle.

In a corner, the grave of the martyr was an upright slab, his name an inscribed curlicue that had faded. But the bas-relief beneath his name endured: a winged horse. This in their faith represented the journey from earth to the heavens.

Lin had insisted on entering alone, against Ned's protests. She could tell that was a problem for him—she hoped he would forgive her. It was useless for him to try to protect her. *I'm already endangered,* she'd told Valanir Ocune with a wry lightness of tone, in part to set him and his sorrow at a distance. But here in this abandoned temple to a foreign god, surrounded by flowers stained with the blood of a long-ago martyr, Lin could not deny the heaviness in her heart. The place forced her into an awareness of herself. Something in the entrenched silence; in the blades of sunlight, glittering with dust, that cut the shadows between pillars. In the engraved letters, strange to her eye, that ran in flourishing strokes across the wall. Unthinkably old, this place was. Though Ned waited outside, she felt alone.

That evening, following a day's ride, a council was held in the banquet tent. They had set up camp on the banks of the River Gadlan, a watery road that led to the capital. Zahir Alcavar had not, it seemed, denounced her, but he avoided her, too. He was close to the king; her words would have consequences. She wondered if he was biding his time—if they all were. But for what? It seemed as if, for now, the plan was to go forward. As if, bizarrely, they felt an urgent need of her.

Or no, it was Zahir Alcavar who felt a need for her, an outsider to the machinations of his court.

At the council Zahir had stood at the head of the table, at the other end of which sat the king and queen. In between, to either side, sat the courtiers who had accompanied the retinue, whom Lin didn't know yet by name, along with Second Magician Tarik Ibn-Mor. Now Lin could see that Zahir Alcavar was tall and slim-waisted, with skin like copper.

And like copper exposed to days of air and rain were his eyes, vivid blue-green. Silver streaked the hair at his temples; he was, she recalled, some ten years younger than Valanir Ocune. About his waist a sash of gold silk, the mark of First Magician. A hush fell in the tent when he began to speak, to tell of the battles Mansur Evrayad faced in the north. From the Tower of Glass, the Seven could foresee where the Fire Dancers were to attack and send a warning to the prince. It gave him enough time to lead his men to the villages' defense.

It was not enough time to prevent the nightmare that came.

As Zahir spoke, he became impassioned; it was clear that some of this nightmare he had seen for himself.

Lin Amaristoth was flanked on either side by guards and her personal men-at-arms, Ned Alterra and Garon Senn. She had instructed them to remain impassive, no matter what they might hear. Ned knew the Kahishian tongue well, as was customary for a scion of one of Tamryllin's great houses. Garon Senn, commander of Lin's guard, spoke it with crude efficiency by dint of his field experience abroad. Certainly he would comprehend Zahir Alcavar's tale of war.

Zahir's eyes were ringed with shadow as he recounted what he'd seen. "Without purpose, without mercy, the Fire Dancers kill," he said. "They do not seem to have a motive beyond killing—there is no theft. Cattle, even dogs, are slaughtered along with the rest. The last village they attacked, Mansur Evrayad reports that he and his men waded up to their ankles in blood. There were—heads piled in the streets. Women, children—it matters not at all to them."

Eldakar Evrayad cleared his throat. He looked pale. "And you still think it is magic."

The Magician bowed his head. "There is some spell," he said. "The way they appear within town walls or village gates—as if barriers do not exist for them. When they fall, their bodies rot within moments. Not in the natural way of things. It is another horror for the prince's men—the sight and smell of melting flesh. Morale wears thin."

Lin looked at the head of the table where Eldakar and his queen sat. She saw Rihab Bet-Sorr was upright, her expression calm. But her eyes were another story. Lin wasn't sure what she saw there, but she made a note to herself to find out more. She thought there were things that did not make sense in what she had been told of Rihab Bet-Sorr.

Now Tarik Ibn-Mor had risen. He was draped in green brocade bound with a bronze sash, the mark of Second Magician. He sounded harsh, even hoarse, as he said, "There is much here not in accordance with what we know of the Fire Dancers. Their magic has never tended to violence. Previously we defeated them in nearly every battle. Those we lost were due to the uncommon cunning of the Renegade. He has not stirred for years from his mountain fortress—until now. What we must ask now is, *What has changed?* Who is helping them obtain this power? Moreover, what do they want?"

"There is the matter of my father," said Eldakar. He spoke drily. "His breaking faith with the Renegade brought us to this. We could not question Yusuf Evrayad, not on any matter, while he was alive. Now we pay the price for that silence."

"It does nothing to blame your father," Tarik began.

"Perhaps not," said Eldakar. "But it is truth. And truth must be our light to see a way out of this. The Renegade has asked nothing from us—so it must be he wants revenge. You know what happened to the messengers we sent, seeking terms."

For the first time, Lin spoke. Her tone was sharp. "What happened?"

Eldakar eyed her across the table. He looked so young and helpless in that moment, Lin marveled that this man commanded the armies of Kahishi. But of course—it was Yusuf Evrayad who had built those armies, not his son. "Their horses returned bearing the messengers," said Eldakar. "Without their heads."

Lin bowed her head.

"Something is at work here," said Zahir. "Something we don't yet see. As I have often acknowledged, *Gvir* Ibn-Mor. It's the reason Lady Amaristoth has come."

"And that is to our shame," said Tarik, eyes flashing anger. "With respect to the Court Poet, and our alliance with Eivar. We have never needed to call upon Eivar for aid, and should not have done so this time. We have all the resources we need."

"You say that," said Zahir. "Events give the lie to your words. We are no nearer the truth than we were months ago."

"Then why not turn to Ramadus?" Tarik demanded. "They are our equals, if not more. Our neighbors to the west, though they make charming music, make little else that is of use."

"Enough." Eldakar Evrayad had risen from his seat. "This is grievous disrespect to our guest. And foolish, besides. The enchantments of Eivar have returned. What we once knew of them is no longer true. At the very least, it can do no harm to consult the Court Poet in matters that continue to stymie us." He looked to Lin. "My lady," he said, "my apologies for the remarks of Tarik Ibn-Mor. They were uncalled for."

She made a gesture of dismissal. "What I hear him saying, your grace," she said, carefully, as she felt all eyes on her now, "is that the Fire Dancers may not be the enemy." *Either that, or he wants to turn to Ramadus for aid.* If Tarik was working with Ramadus, it was the logical next step. Instill fear in Kahishi, then present the eastern empire as their salvation.

"And would that that were true," said Zahir Alcavar. He appeared haunted, as if scenes of violence still played in his mind. "I am not sure I understand the Second Magician's game here. In our seekings, we have traced the shadow."

"You see shadows," she said. A flat tone, without mockery. Their eyes met.

"It is part of what we do." No anger in him that she could see. A directness. "A Magician of the Tower might see the dark and demons that surround us, that are invisible to the eye. This one comes from the north."

Lin's gaze moved to Eldakar. She said, "Why not attack their fortress, then—in the north?"

"You mean war," Eldakar said shortly. "The Renegade is wily—has built a stronghold of warrens and weapons, possibly enough to outlast years of a siege. It would require most of our forces, leaving Majdara, and the Zahra, unprotected. Of all the counsels my father gave me, the one against doing *that* is most clear in my mind." Eldakar's lips twisted, as if he tasted something sour. His hand clenched on the table. "It's what our enemies are waiting for."

"And yet if we don't," said Zahir, "we lose Almyria."

A silence. Lin knew of Almyria, jewel of the north. The city that, long ago, had been the capital.

"We will send men," the king said. "As many as may be spared. But no more."

* * *

"By sunset we will be there." Ned had joined her at the guardrail. Wind off the water blew back his hair. He had befriended the Kahishian guardsmen, and had come to know before she did what the next stage of the journey would be, the route of the day's ride.

She turned to him. "You are smiling."

His teeth flashed. "This wakens . . . memories for me. Despite that we're in a toy that would perish at sea."

"The seas blooded you," she said, remembering. Her hand found his on the guardrail. "Ned, thank you. For being here." A glancing touch, and then she withdrew; she would not impose her need, her deepening isolation, on Ned Alterra.

He looked at her with sombre eyes. "I am here as long as you require me, my lady."

"I took you from home."

"I have my duty just as you have yours," said Ned, becoming stern. "Say no more of that."

Only Ned was permitted to speak so to her. She turned back to the water. Beyond the green shadow cast by their boat, the river mirrored the sun's glare. Nearer the bank, spindle-legged herons skimmed the surface like intrepid couriers, calling.

"Look." Ned's voice was soft.

She followed his gaze. Beyond the city walls rose the mountain. Piled upon it a layered confection of towers, gold in the late sunlight. There were terraced gardens. Cutting upward through these, a white stairway tunneled under a series of archways that reached all the way to the top. The Zahra looked vast enough to contain several palaces within it, yet all the parts together were harmonious—arches and terraces and tower-tops mirroring one another in their curves. As a contrast, the jagged stairway was of a piece with the terrain of the mountain.

"Do you believe it is as they say, Ned?"

He was looking up still. "I daresay we shall see."

"Yes." She looked around, saw no one within earshot. "You with your tasks, and I with mine." She was thinking of one of the last things Valanir Ocune had told her—the address he had pressed into her hand, in that way he had. "*This person may help you*," he'd said. "Keep it secret. You must find a way to go out to the city alone, without a guard."

She had smiled at this, for it had not sounded much of a challenge at the time. Not after all they'd done. But today, staring up at the proud spear of a mountain overlooking a strange city, she knew there would be more layers to this—to everything—than experience had led her to expect.

She had given some thought to what she wanted of Ned. Not to investigate Tarik Ibn-Mor—she would not send her man after a Magician. The risk was too great. But there were other ways Ned's skills could be of use.

"Your task is to befriend the queen," she said. He didn't react, still watching the water. "It is an odd tale, this slave girl elevated at such great cost to the king—to the kingdom. Find out all you can. Become a friend to her. She strikes me as a woman of few friends." Ever since the council, she had been thinking back to the still, lovely face of Rihab, the way emotions had seemed to flicker through it nonetheless. It might have been horror at the events recounted . . . but it might not.

Now Ned turned to her. His fierce smile was without humor. "You think I'm skilled with women."

She shrugged. "I know it." And was surprised—then amused—that he looked away, blood risen in his face.

IT was drawing toward sunset when a servant approached Lin, summoning her to a private meeting with Zahir Alcavar. Or no, that was not entirely true. *Requesting* her presence. The distinction mattered. She was standing alone at the guardrail, watching the conflagration of the sky. Had sent away anyone who might protect or watch her, tiring after all of that. Of being watched.

Without summoning any guards to her now, Lin followed Zahir's servant to a chamber on deck. The double doors to it were of polished cedar, each gilded with the Evrayad falcon sigil, its beak like a dagger. Lin recalled many a tale of guests summarily dispatched by their royal hosts—an assassin in a bathhouse, a cup of poisoned wine.

There was no dignity in such an end. On the other hand, she didn't know what her end would otherwise look like. Last night she had found herself standing incrementally nearer to Darien as he sobbed in the corner. Lin did not need anyone versed in magic to explain what this meant. In her mind's eye she saw the silver amulet of the wizard swing on its chain: once. Again.

As it happened, no apparent threats waited behind the double doors. There was only Zahir Alcavar himself. He sent away his servant. So against protocol and perhaps good sense, they were alone.

The last of the sun was soft in this east-facing chamber, with bay windows that opened generously to the air and a view of the river. The wood-paneled walls were of the same décor as the doors, the falcon repeated. In place of chairs were velvet cushions of various colors, adorned with thread-of-gold. He motioned her to sit. "If you will."

"I prefer not," she said. "First tell me what it is you want."

He let out a sigh. "I suppose I should not be surprised. I said things to you, when we met, that I shouldn't have. It's why I asked you here."

She nodded. "Good. But not quite enough. There is a pall that lies between us now."

"Distrust."

Her lip curled, grudging acknowledgment of his candor. "Yes."

The Magician looked at her as if weighing something in his mind. There was a vulnerability to him such as he'd shown in the council meeting, when describing the atrocities of the Fire Dancers. As if it wore on him, to see so much. Today in addition to the sash of gold, he wore a brocade robe, liberally threaded with gold and silver. Turquoise earrings and neck chains hung with ruby, topaz, and tourmaline were added to this.

Lin wore a dress of midnight silk belted with silver links, and her diamond earrings. Silver woven into her hair. Trailing from her shoulders, the six-colored cloak of the Court Poet. It was necessary, the day she presented herself in the Zahra, to appear so, just as her hosts had made themselves resplendent to welcome her to their city.

"Lady, that pall will be lifted only if you speak plainly." He sounded gentle. "I was wrong to think ill of you. A darkness wraps around you more surely than the six-colored cloak you wear, but now I see . . . it is not your choice. It is, perhaps, a grief."

She shrugged. "I don't owe you an explanation. Even some of those dearest to me don't know."

"If we are to work together in enchantments, I *must* know."

"Enchantments." She laughed. "*Gvir* Alcavar, I am only lately turned

Seer. Initiated into powers even the most learned Seers can only guess at. We know so little. I'm here because Valanir Ocune told me you need someone from outside your court to provide aid; but if it is magical aid you seek from me, you may be sorely disappointed. In this respect, I regret to say, Tarik Ibn-Mor may be right."

She had been steeling herself to make this admission, a dangerous one, since it revealed weakness.

Unexpectedly, he nodded. "My lady," he said, "I would be surprised if you fully grasped the nature of your abilities. The enchantments of Eivar—that which we dreamed of restoring, Valanir Ocune and I—lack the mechanical precision of our magic. It is not a system such as we have, ruled by the stars."

She stared at him a moment. Then all at once in a sweep of her skirts, she sat. The cushion sank beneath her. "Go on," she said.

He smiled, and sat across from her. He had very white teeth, slightly pointed. A sensuous mouth, to cover savage teeth. She redirected her attention to his words. "I am glad that despite all—despite whatever it is that torments you—you want to know," he said. "I take it as a good sign. Here is the point: your enchantments are not a system to be learned. Oh, there are laws, likely more than we have discovered yet . . . But laws are not the essence of it. It will manifest differently, in your hands, than it would for any other Seer. *Who you are* is at its core. Do you see?"

She shook her head. She did not understand how something taught in an Academy could not be learned. But knew it was Zahir Alcavar who had guided Valanir in crucial ways—his words could not be discounted. "What do you want of me," she said, "if you help me learn? I assume that is what you are offering."

"It is a part of it," he said. "And in return you will help me. What I told Valanir Ocune still holds—I am deeply uneasy in the Zahra. Something there evades me. But first I must earn your trust. So I propose an exchange. To begin anew."

Her eyebrows arched. "What sort of exchange?"

"A secret." He spoke low; she had to lean close to hear him. "For a secret." In the face of her silence, he went on. "If I don't understand the shadow that surrounds you, it will block any work we attempt together. But to cement our trust I will tell you . . . a thing no one knows about me. Not even Valanir Ocune, or Eldakar."

"And it will be something true," she said. "On your honor?"

"On mine and my family's honor, yes." His voice low, almost a growl, on the word *family*.

It was truth that she was hearing, Lin was almost sure. But there was another factor more decisive. It was due to Zahir Alcavar that Eivar had reacquired its enchantments at all. He was, in a real way, the reason she was here. Without his help she, Valanir, Darien—they would have been powerless to stop the thing that had possessed Nickon Gerrard.

"I will tell you," she said. And as the sky dimmed and stars emerged she told Zahir Alcavar what so far only the Seer who'd made her knew: about her dream, and the spell, and the wizard's words to her. The silver amulet on its chain. When she was done she discovered, with bewilderment, that Zahir held her hand. She was too surprised to pull away.

"This hurts to hear," he said. "Lady, a light shines from you. Even when you tell of this . . . thing that is happening to you. Do you know that?"

She shook her head. Disengaged her hand, finally, and crossed both in her lap. "Words," she said with narrowed eyes. "Words like that. Save them for the girls in night gardens." Not her words, her images. *Night gardens*. So much she knew of men from Edrien—how they thought, what they did—that was interesting, but also, in some ways, distressing to know. She shook her head again. "That was ill-spoken," she said. "You were being kind, and I . . ."

"I was not being kind," he said, in the low growling voice of before. Quickly he rose, as from an urgent need to stand. Going to a cabinet, he removed a jeweled and enameled box. From the box he drew a taper, which he lit, and with this kindled one of the brass lamps set in the wall. And then another, until all five were dancing. As he returned, Lin thought she saw a glistening in his eyes, and he turned from her a moment with a tightened jaw. When he looked at her again, however, he had mastered emotion. "Does Valanir know?"

"Only he," she said. "And now you."

"It is . . . unbearable," he said. Quietly, as if to himself. "How can Valanir bear it."

"Please," she said. "It does no good to talk about it. Let's proceed with our agreement. Your secret, now."

Zahir looked rueful. "It's not . . . has not the magnitude of yours," he said. "Though my life hangs on it. Here it is, then: it is true I am Rama-dian. But not from the capital, as people believe. Some know I was the son of a lute-carver and singer. It is true that my father made instruments for the court of Ramadus, and in girlhood my mother sang there. It is said . . . was said . . . that I have her eyes. But in later years they moved away, to a smaller city, where lands were available and a lute-carver might also have a garden, some horses. We lived . . . I am from Vesperia."

"Vesperia." She leaned forward. "The city that vanished?" She stared at him. "The tale has it that none survived."

"There was one," he said. Slowly, as if testing each word. She watched as he hesitated. A long hesitation before he spoke. *He is afraid,* she real-ized, and wondered if this secret was true, indeed. "There was one," he said again, and this time it was clear he had made the decision to tell her—or knew it was too late to do otherwise. "One boy, out in the hills that night. Fleeing punishment for disobedience . . . which I regret to say was not unusual." He was trying to smile, but it faded.

Lin felt her heart constrict. "Just now, you swore . . . on your family's honor."

He nodded. "They are gone."

"I am sorry," she said. Vesperia was a mystery from before she was born, but she recalled visitors from Kahishi speaking of it to her family. The destruction had all the appearances of an earthquake, but the Ramadus court Magicians judged magic as the cause. For years it was dangerous to be known as a Magician within the borders, or in any land allied with Ramadus. Some Magicians, on suspicion alone, had met ugly deaths. All this consigned by now to history. But a poisoned magic was said to linger in the ruins. The city was not rebuilt, and looters, if caught, were executed. Anything taken from the place was thought cursed. And of course, that would have included people, if any survivors had been found.

"How old were you?"

"I was eight," he said. "It's a miracle I wasn't killed or kidnapped in the hills. I ran. An old farm couple took me in, eventually. Somehow I knew even then not to reveal my origins. They were grateful for a strong boy to help with chores. I still think of them—they were kind to me. The woman, especially, was kind. Of course, they are long gone."

She bowed her head. They sat quietly. Seagulls called from the riverbank. Lin found she was sitting gripping her upper arms, as if for comfort. She had no words of comfort. *I am the last, too*, she wanted to say, but knew it was different. A different kind of sadness.

"My life is in your hands," said Zahir at last. His eyes were fringed with dark lashes, she saw now; a trace of the boy who had been. She recalled the melody he was singing the night they met. *From my childhood. Is it sad?*

"If anyone were to discover my history, I would be run out of the Zahra," he said. "In truth, I think Vesperia *did* affect me. My—affinity— for magic began after that. Through the years I hid where I was from. It became easier once I educated myself, made a name in the capital as a lutenist and then, later, a Magician. Once I became someone else. It became easier, with time, to tell no one."

"No one," she murmured. So long, to carry a secret like that. It felt unreal, to speak of cataclysm, and her own death, as they drifted on a royal barge in the silence of evening.

"No one," he said. "And now you."

WITH time until they were to disembark and with his orders in mind, Ned Alterra sought the queen. The barge rocked with his tread on the boards, reminding him he was not on firm ground. As if he needed re- minding. The Court Poet might be mad, their lives were at risk, and now he'd been assigned to discover more about a woman of whom the rumors were not encouraging. In the guard's tent when they were not making vulgar jokes about Rihab Bet-Sorr—coded, of course, and dared only over too many mugs of beer—they hinted at her lurid reputation. She was insatiable, they murmured, clearly regretting this quality did not extend to themselves. Ned was sober enough to realize such talk amounted to treason, could mean death to the queen if it was true. And if she was capable of such betrayal, he reflected, what else might she do? In which case Lin was right to set him to discover what he could.

The breeze wafting toward the barge brought the scent of orange trees. From the reeds along the shore, the guttural scream of a heron. Ned found his mind drifting back to his travels, and back. He remembered sadness. It was strange to look back on a distant self. Those feelings could still arise in him, though without the quicksand pull they'd once had.

He was shocked to find her alone, on a balcony below deck. The queen was usually surrounded by her women. But not now. Her back was to him as she gazed towards the mountain. Like her husband, she was attired in robes of state, thick and heavy and so beaded with gems he wondered how she could move. Her hair elaborately braided. In a cold voice and in his tongue she said, without turning, "What is it, Lord Alterra?"

The hairs on the back of his neck prickled, as before an attack.

"I hope my odor is not displeasing, your excellence," he said, trying for humor to cover his confusion. "I know not else how you guessed it was me."

She turned her head, chin high, her expression unmoved. Her lips stained the color of blood. "Do you customarily come upon women in this way?"

"Not customarily," he said. "I was looking for . . . quiet. There are a great many people above deck. Sometimes I find myself inclined to get away." As he said it, he realized it bore a ring of truth because in part, it was true. He *had* been looking for her. He also longed for solitude, away from the invisible, tensed strings that seemed to pull him in all directions above deck. The scrutiny, meaningful gestures, veiled manipulations among which, by contrast, Lin Amaristoth seemed to thrive. "May I join you?"

"I wish to be alone," she said. "But we might meet later, if you wish. Tonight." She was looking him full in the eye. Her eyes were an unusual color, so dark a blue they were almost black. Her neckline dipped low, what it revealed like dented cream. "You are so pale, Lord Alterra," she purred, with no trace of a smile. "I trust you are well?"

Ned felt heavy and light at the same time. *I can't do this.* But found himself saying, "Of course I will meet you. I await your instructions, my lady." *Good,* he imagined from Lin, her fevered eyes approving, and felt a returning surge of sadness. Anything he did to imperil his life with Rianna Gelvan could plunge him right back, he realized. That distant self was, it turned out, only as far as the next disaster.

A disaster that might be approaching now, with the ring the queen pressed into his hand. She did so without touching his skin. Ned stared at the inside of his palm. The ring was gold and set with pearls that took the shape of a swan, with a single amber eye. It seemed large for her small hand. "Show this at the seventh arch in the fifth corridor, three bells from moonrise," she said. "I think I might like you, Ned Alterra. Time and your performance will tell. Now go. I would be alone with my thoughts."

As Ned stumbled back the way he'd come, he felt as if he pushed through the mire of his own self-loathing. The ring clutched in his hand coated with sweat from his palm.

He had a choice. Who was to say what his desires were, his true motives? These were buried beyond consciousness, even for Ned who thought he knew his own darkness. *I have a duty,* Ned tried to tell Rianna Gelvan in his mind. But knew he would never tell her. The unsaid would consume him, perhaps forever. Yet to lose her would be worse.

As he surfaced above deck a wind swept over Ned and he tipped back his head to receive it, to be cleansed. But such ideas were illusory. They were nearly ashore now. The walls that soared in great curves around the mountain were painted crimson with the descending sun. The Tower of Glass like a bloodied sword. So Ned saw it when first they approached, and would afterward remember.

CHAPTER 6

THE servant kept refilling her cup; Lin didn't stop him. She even allowed his hand, muscled and smooth, to linger against her own. It was good wine. The servants appeared to have been selected for their beauty. Most servants and soldiers who served the Zahra had been captured, and traded, from lands far away. Among these lands was Sandinia, where a man could ride for weeks and see nothing but oceans of grass, overrun with wild horses. These men and women tended to be fair-skinned, strong. The servant who filled Lin's cup was one such, his hair drawn back with a jeweled clip, his jaw of impressive prominence. She registered serene approval, and drank some more.

An extensive ceremony had followed their arrival at the Zahra. Each courtier was presented, beginning with the Seven Magicians, in order of rank. The five beneath Zahir and Tarik, who had remained behind at the palace, were disconcertingly young; at least one seemed to regard Lin with a certain trepidation. That was the youngest, who looked to be no older than nineteen, with eyes like a doe. And then the rest of the court—hangers-on, mostly, in Lin's perfunctory estimation. People who gravitated to where the power was, made a trade of gifts and flattering words. She had seen enough of that herself, in Tamryllin.

The difference—or one of them—was that Eldakar commanded a significant army, swelled in ranks through the years by slaves. Added to this were the forces of the viziers in the provinces and the proud lords of the north, in Almyria. Tamryllin had nothing like such a force.

Eldakar himself presented Lin with a gift of welcome, a bracelet of gold links set with emeralds. "This belonged to my mother, Seiran Evrayad," he said. "Here bestowed as a token of our friendship with King Harald."

She allowed Garon Senn to fasten the heavy chain to her wrist. As he did, she kept her eyes on Eldakar, her countenance impassive. Not troubling to look at the extravagant thing as Garon fastened it. It would be beneath her, and the dignity of her office, to appear dazzled. Eivar had its pride. As the ceremony resumed, she saw Zahir Alcavar watching her and wondered if he guessed her thoughts; there was an understanding in his eyes, sharp, yet almost—was the word *tender*? She thought of Valanir Ocune, wistful as he watched her across the room from bed. Knowing she was changed, not yet knowing why.

She was what she needed to be. Wasn't that true?

The throne room was lit for evening with spheres that hung from gilded ropes. The chair itself was of gold and surrounded with a forest of pillars: these alternating onyx black, crystal white. The east wall opened out to a view of the gardens. Lin could imagine how sunlight, bent and concentrated by the crystal, would transform the room by day. She had heard the pillars were deliberately placed to bend sunlight towards the throne. Late afternoon, the radiance would be overwhelming.

The floor was a great mosaic of red and gold tile, the falcon again. Clustered around it the sigils of the houses that served under House Evrayad, those of the provinces and northern marches. A gazelle, a leopard, a wolf, a steed—east, west, north, south. And another, beneath these: a gryphon rampant. That one, she did not recognize.

Following these ceremonies came the banquet, where she was seated with the highest officials. By this time Lin felt strangely off-balance, as if she veered close to losing herself. It was not the wine. That was to make her forget. If she could forget, she could continue pretending, for the good of the court of Tamryllin.

Or that was the theory, Lin thought with a crooked smile, and drank. She didn't think she had mistaken the touch of the servant, though he would almost certainly have to be a castrate. What, then, was it—had he been sent to service her, spy on her? A thought that could have been depressing, but was not. *Can you vanish my dreams?* she thought idly as she smiled into the blue eyes of the young man. A smile with teeth.

Lin turned to Ned Alterra beside her after the servant had gone.

"They are extraordinarily considerate of our—needs, here, aren't they?" He looked distracted, said, "Sorry? What do you mean?" and she realized he was unaware of the little byplay going on with the discreet touches, the constant refilling of her cup. There was none more observant than Ned when it came to such details, and he was by now as finely attuned to her moods and behaviors as if they were lovers, so Lin was surprised by this.

"Ned," she said, tugging his sleeve.

He turned from his plate, which he'd barely touched. He was tearing a haunch of bread to pieces without eating it; he stopped, as if he hadn't known he was doing it until she said his name. "Yes? My lady."

"Is there something you ought to tell me?"

It was a long table and the clamor of conversation and tableware allowed them to speak without being overheard. Across from them, Tarik Ibn-Mor was eyeing them with more than passing interest. She wondered if, by some magic, he could hear what they said.

Ned stole a glance at the royal table where sat the king and queen. He looked miserable. "I will report my progress," he said flatly. "For now, all you need know is I am carrying out your instructions."

It took her a moment to put it together. Then she understood, and the blanketing comfort of wine was abruptly gone. "Ned, I said 'befriend,' not—"

He was cold as he cut her off. "I know what you said. So do you. I will have to live with what I do. Will you then disavow it—what I do for you?"

It wounded her, more than she would have expected. She knew they both had the same thought: *Rianna*. She closed her eyes. He was right. She had been trying to deny what she herself had bid him, make him shoulder the responsibility alone. He deserved better of her. "I will do no such thing," she said. "You know you are of great value to me, Ned." *There is little I would not do for you,* she thought, but did not say. It would have embarrassed him.

But perhaps he saw it in her face. He nodded, turned away. Seized a chunk of bread, dipped it in the fig sauce on his plate, took a bite. All the while looking as if he took poison.

She thought of Valanir and how angry she'd been with him years ago—for the strings he'd pulled, the decisions he'd made. *I understand,* she wanted to tell him now. *I think.*

The blue-eyed servant was back, this time presenting her with a rolled parchment. Its red wax seal was stamped with a gryphon: *Ah*, she thought, *so that is it*. After she read it she looked up, saw Zahir Alcavar was watching.

"THANK you," he said, "for agreeing to meet me at this hour." They stood in a courtyard at the foot of a winding stair.

Lin shrugged. The wine sang in her blood. "I don't sleep." She had passed several courtyards since arriving. The one near her bedchamber was lined with orange trees in bloom, overpowering in their scent, their dropped petals like a white satin carpet. This courtyard had a fountain at the center, around which coiled vines of white, starlike flowers that just hours earlier had been buds. They had since opened to the moon.

"These flowers, then, are like you," said Zahir as he guided her to the stair.

She said, "You must be popular in the night gardens, my lord," and he laughed.

Lin thought she could guess what lay at the top, as they climbed; she counted more than a hundred steps before the end. "Are you all right?" Zahir Alcavar said once, turning to her with an outstretched hand, as they passed through alternating lamplight and shadow.

She gave him a cool look. "No less than you, Magician."

At the top was a room wrapped in sky. She caught her breath, not just from the climb. What opened around them was vast. It was said Yusuf Evrayad had built the Tower of Glass to rival the famed Observatory in Ramadus. The artisans had employed magic in its construction, she'd heard, though this was disputed. She did think it should have been a much longer climb to go as high as they now were, and wondered if there was magic involved in this, too.

Rumors swirled about this tower. The center of the Zahra, as much as the throne. *More?*

The space was large enough to contain a small town. It was impossible, simply *not possible*, that it was in reality this large, she thought, imagining some kind of illusion wrought by Ramadian magic. Light came from everywhere and nowhere; there was not a torch to be seen, yet the room was flooded with soft illumination like moonlight. Lin's gaze was drawn up, to the walkways that ran alongside the walls in three levels, accessible by staircases of porphyry and gold. The walls that were entirely glass, clear as air, so that along the walkways burned countless stars.

All this overseen by an arched ceiling like a second sky, adorned with stars and spheres. Against a backdrop of black crystal, jewels made the constellations. Lin knew them: The Great Tree, the Warrior, the Witch, and many more. They glittered as if from within. Scattered among them the heavenly spheres, represented with enormous gems of various colors. In Eivar they used the Kahishian names for them: red Mahaz, for war and bloodshed; blue Maia, for the seas and navigation; diamond Vizia, for fertility; amber Sheohl, lord of the Underworld. Zahir said, quietly, "The dome shows the original order of the heavens. At the beginning."

"The beginning?"

"The creation of the world."

Not wanting to seem as if she gaped, Lin pulled her gaze downward to Zahir. He was looking up, however, as if in contemplation. The illumination from above softened his face. "There are seven heavens, you see," he said. "That which is above us—the one we *see*—is the lowest of these. Beyond are the upper reaches. The configurations of stars, the spheres—these are gateways, agents of higher powers. And prophecies—these are, if you think about it, like writing sent from above. Messages only the initiated can read."

"Upper reaches?" she said. "What—what is there, in the heavens we cannot see?"

He smiled. "There's little we know for sure. But it's where wisdom, and knowledge of what is to come, are infinite. That's why the god is with the Tower of Glass in all that we do. Our work is nothing but for the grace of Alfin." He beckoned to her. "Come."

The constellations were set into the floor in mosaic tile. They trod on a gold and green Great Tree, a silver Wheel. It took time just to pass over each one. In the deep quiet Lin could have sworn she heard, from far away, a snatch of music; this kept time with the spark of the stars.

At last they reached a stairway, this one more gilded than the rest, and slender, accommodating only one person at a time. It traversed the air in a spiral, unsupported as a curl of smoke, and seemed neverending; after a time, Lin found herself growing dizzy. Around her spun lights: from the candescent gems overhead; from the stars outside.

By the time they reached the top she was winded. Lin had a fear, as she caught her breath, her chest pounding, that her soul was about to fly out of her as the wizard had foretold. But as her breath slowed, she felt the blood return to her face. Zahir was watching her, not speaking. She could see he felt impelled to help her but held himself back, knowing she would dislike it. She didn't know how she could see that, from a glance. "I'm all right," she said. They stood on a platform of glass. It was cut in the shape of a square, fenced in with rails of gold. Lin looked down, through the glass, and saw they were at a vertiginous height.

Looking up, she saw the platform was encased in a glass dome. Lin guessed this must be the Tower's pinnacle—its observatory. Nearby stood a long brass tube on a tripod, that she guessed was a tool of observation; and a great gilded sphere inlaid with silver symbols and wrapped in gold and silver rings. That, she guessed, was an astrolabe.

Zahir Alcavar was waiting for her to speak. In her eyes he had altered, as someone who belonged to a place like this. The sourceless light seeming to emanate as much from him as their surroundings. His eyes less bright, softened, but harder to read.

Lin found her voice. "So from here you see it. The . . . shadow."

"That is a part of it," he said. He sounded deliberately casual, as if to set her at ease. "We can foretell catastrophes like drought, and war, and sickness. It is secret, because such things, if known, would drive the people to frenzy. And because such knowledge rightfully belongs to the king. It is him we serve, at the behest of the Thousand-Named God."

"But surely the people know *something* is happening," said Lin.

"They know of the battles in the north. Skirmishes. They don't know of magic. Though rumors will travel of the—the strangeness, if they haven't already. And soon more men will march north, fuel further rumors." He shook his head. "All this and more, we will have to deal with.

"Meantime, I wanted to show you our work here. It is not like the Academy, where mysteries prevail. The stars tell a tale." He swept a hand outward at the dome. "We have clear means to read it, worked out in calculations. These are the makings of prophecy." Here he indicated a desk pinned with a parchment, on which had been drawn a series of intersecting lines and symbols. Not the way Lin would have pictured a prophecy. "There are disputes of the finer points, of course. But the fundamentals are absolute. Along with our calculations, there are acts we can take—Seekings and—very occasionally—with portals. Like all magic, these pose a risk. Last time, in our Seeking north . . . we nearly lost a Magician. As it was, he was ill for a long time."

"It is that bad?"

He was sombre. "Lady, I would not have asked you here for less."

"I believe you asked me here," she said, "because you suspect one of your Magicians. Perhaps . . ." She watched his face, but he was impassive. "Perhaps one in particular."

"Yes," he said curtly. "But I don't have proof, and personal animosity might cloud my judgment. I cannot act, nor let on I suspect, until I am sure. That's where you come in, my lady. If you so agree."

"I agreed from the moment I set out," she said. She had gone to stand at the glass. Far below, curving with the riverbank were the walls of Majdara, made visible by the light of watchtowers. She saw the bridge that spanned the River Gadlan, lit so it resembled a jeweled strand. "That is not the question. The question is, rather, what you'd have me do."

"We'll talk about that," he said. "Not here. There is something else I want to speak of first." A change in his tone, but she did not turn. This was beauty, she thought, looking to the jeweled sky; and she did not know how long she had.

Zahir said, "Lady, the night we met, you accused me of being removed from danger. From life, perhaps."

"Did I?" She wondered if the pearl of light on the horizon to the east, more brilliant than any star, was Vizia.

His tone became more emphatic. "*What have you done,*" he said, in an accent eerily like hers, "*in your tower above the world?*"

She smiled, finally turned. "I suppose I did say that."

"In some ways, it's true," said Zahir. "What happened to you is more than most Magicians face in a lifetime. And there are other ways in which I keep myself—distant. You saw more than perhaps you knew, when you said that."

She inclined her head, studying him. "You never speak of a wife." Her thoughts went to Ned, who was possibly with the queen in that instant. *What I do for you,* he'd said so coldly.

"Magicians don't marry," said Zahir. "Some take concubines."

"And you?"

He was expressionless. "I am—careful with women. A child shouldn't carry on my blood, along with whatever happened in Vesperia." He held up a hand. "But I did not mean to speak, just now, of myself. You may be right that I am at a remove from life and its trials. And you have been so much in them. And what if that holds you back, now, from the thing you want most?"

"And what would that be?"

She issued it as a challenge, half-mocking, but he seemed not to notice—or else it didn't matter. On his face that same look she had glimpsed as Garon Senn fastened the emerald bracelet to her wrist—understanding, a trace of tenderness. "Valanir Ocune has told me, many times, that always it is about the music," he said. "And I believe . . . so it is with you."

She was about to reply, but later would not recall what she would have said. That was when she heard labored breathing, growing nearer. Someone mounting the stairs. Together they turned towards the sound.

"You brought her here." Tarik Ibn-Mor, his eyes like dark glass, standing at the top of the stairs. His silver cloak glistened.

"If she is to aid us, she should see how we work," said Zahir equably, as if he didn't notice that the other man, though expressionless, was seething. "You are here for your watch?"

"I am. Have you had word?" Tarik spoke as if Lin were not there, his gaze trained on the First Magician.

Zahir shook his head. "Tonight has been quiet," he said, and pressed his palms together at his chest. "Prayers be with the prince."

Clearly it was a ritual, for with the same gesture Tarik said, in flat tones, "Prayers be with the prince."

Later they were out in the courtyard, back on the ground after what seemed an interminable descent. The sky left behind. Lin keenly felt it, like a loss. Yet nothing was changed. Water splashed among the night flowers as before.

"So we part ways here," she said, stretching her arms above her head with a sigh. She thought of the chamber where she was to sleep, soft and perfumed and silent. Isolation rose in a wave. Not even a pretty servant-spy would dispel that, she knew. That, she had known all along—her thoughts of the evening meal a game of self-deceit. "I'll bid you a good night," she said.

"Not yet, if you will," said Zahir Alcavar. There was that cat's gleam in his eye. "The night isn't over."

THE route to her took him through the palace at night, a different sort of splendor than had been lit vividly at sunset. The king's boat had deposited them ashore just before dusk. In a procession they had ridden from shore up a road that wound with the curves of the mountain, past terraced fruit trees and walls ornamented with carvings delicate as a spider's weave. Ned had marveled at the entrance hall tiled with porphyry, at rooms gilded as the inside of a jewel box. Gardens interwove with rooms on every level of the palace, wild or tamed, with flowers like explosions of fire and trees in bloom. He knew what he saw was a fraction. The tales he'd heard were true, more than true.

With nightfall, the colors dimmed. Low-burning coals in the braziers cast a ring of light on the wall carvings, left the rest in darkness. On his way Ned came to a courtyard where pillars lithe as birch trees surrounded a still, square-cut pool that held the moon.

If he had been a poet, Ned thought, he might have lingered here. But someone like him had no business tarrying in a place like this. He was tasked to act: his thoughts about it didn't matter. He was no more than a concealed knife in the Court Poet's sleeve. Yet even after he'd left the courtyard behind, that image, of the moon doubled in water, lingered in his mind.

When he showed the pearl-encrusted ring to the door attendant, he was led inside without a word, down a hall hung with silk draperies, their embroidered designs vague in the half-light of braziers. The steps of the servant made no sound; in contrast, Ned thought his own boots rang a vulgar announcement on the tile. It would be painfully clear to anyone that he was not of this place. Nonetheless: he had bathed from the dust of the journey and changed into his best clothes, which included a jacket of blue jacquard of which Rianna was fond. Had shaved using the copper mirror and scented oils provided, taking care not to look himself in the eye.

What he had not done was apply the scent that had been presented to him in a handsome brass jar. Had resisted the urge to throw it back at the impassive servant who offered it. It might have been a gift for all honored guests. Scents were distilled and mixed in the Zahra itself, with some valued for medicinal properties. Some would have brought a fortune to Tamryllin merchants. He had learned something of trade in his travels—what seemed long ago.

The male attendant, garbed richly as a monarch, remained expressionless as he motioned Ned Alterra to enter. Without allowing himself to think—though a part of him still with the calm pool, its doubled moon—Ned parted the curtain that led to her.

She was seated at a table ringed with red candles that stood in tall brass sconces, each split at the base into four clawed feet. She had changed her dress from the opulent absurdity of earlier; her robe was simple and yellow, kirtled with gold thread. Peering from beneath the robe a slippered foot, all soft satin and gold beads. Her hair only partly braided, flowing soft around her face. "Come," she said. "Sit. Do you like wine?" A woman at her elbow held a pitcher and cups—porcelain glazed to look like gold. Ned remembered: there was a prohibition among those who worshipped Alfin against drinking from vessels made of metal.

With a murmured assent, he allowed himself to be seated at the table. And then saw the table for the first time. Ned felt his brows draw together. He looked from the table to the queen and back again.

"Wine," he agreed, and took the cup, drained it. When he was done, he saw the queen was watching him with a small smile.

In a way that gave him an opening. "You like to play games, I see."

"This is why I invited you here." She balanced her chin on her fingertips, looking mischievous. "Are you angry?"

"No." Ned could have laughed in that moment, but it would have come out wild, strange. He restrained himself. When at last he could speak, he managed a casual tone. "Though it does raise some questions. The first being: is this what you meant by my 'performance'?"

She laughed. But he thought, when her eyes turned to the table, figures of black and white lined up in rows on the squares, it was with a veiled look that was not amusement at all. "This is the game that interests me, Lord Alterra. And I so rarely have the opportunity for a fair match. No one wants to win against their queen, you see." Here her lip curled with scorn. "Or they imagine this is a whim for me, like a new face powder, and will not engage with all their wits. It is a bore, you know, to defeat someone not even in the fight."

"What game is it?" He narrowed his eyes in concentration as he took in the game board. A new, different sort of task. His knees were weak with relief; at the same time, he felt unprepared. And beneath that . . . he would not look too closely.

She was smiling as if they were already friends, as if his agreeing to play so delighted her. "Do you not know it? It is the Game of Kings."

"I have heard of it." He thought he had played it once or twice. A childhood memory.

But he would have remembered a gameboard like this. The alternating squares of black and white were marble, the white veined with red. Also carved from marble were the pieces, their faces dignity in miniature. Each side had its king and queen, the white with tiaras of diamond, the black with rubies. Alongside these he noticed the figures of bearded men in long robes who held staves, each topped with a jewel to match the royal crowns. "The Magicians," said Rihab Bet-Sorr, noting his glance. "I suppose in Tamryllin they would be Court Poets. Each side is a court, you see. The game . . . it's the only game that matters, isn't it?" She had taken up the king on her side, the side of black. Her slender fingers with their painted nails stroked it in a manner almost sensuous, or seemed so to Ned. But her gaze was far away. "Kings fight to keep ahold of the throne while the queen—their queens—must play the game. As you'll see, the king can do little on his own behalf, so hampered is he by tradition and ceremony. These weigh on him like the crown itself. The queen—she is more skillful at maneuvering. But surrounded by enemies. Much of the battle falls to her."

"When you say that," he said, "do you mean the queen is the more powerful piece?"

She nodded. "She can move this way, and that, and that, to capture a piece." She demonstrated with her own queen, using it to knock one of Ned's foot soldiers from his front line. "The Magicians have power, too, but they are at her command. Capture the queen," she said, staring at the board, "and more often than not, you've as good as won the game."

"It sounds . . . straightforward," Ned said, studying the positioning of the pieces. He wondered where on such a board he would be. He was no Magician. His eyes fell on the disposable soldiers on the front lines. They were not as finely carved as the rest, their faces crude copies of one another. But there were other pieces, too. There were horse heads as if inspired by a royal battle charger—not as disposable as the more numerous men-at-arms, perhaps. But loyal. In the end just as ready to die for their king, or queen.

Rihab was saying, "It may sound simple, but you will see it becomes complex. Sometimes power is its own price."

"What do you mean?"

She smiled, though it seemed forced, like a curtain coming down on a lamp. "That, I should keep to myself," she said, "if I want to win against you."

THEY followed a melody through trees. A lonely tune, picked out on a woodpipe. Or it sounded lonely to Lin. A harp was different: the strings keeping company with each other, a sound ethereal rather than plaintive. Melancholy, yes, but that was something else.

Perhaps Valanir Ocune would have disputed this point, she thought, keeping Zahir Alcavar in sight ahead of her, the gold of his sash. There were few absolute facts about their art, it was clear; her own thoughts were often at odds with the Academy. As if on her solitary path she had picked up other things, odd and random, like brambles caught in one's cloak on a walk through the wood.

She trailed him through the grey dark of moonlight into the deeper dark of tree shadows, scented with orange blossoms. A nightingale's song carried on the breeze. They were in the imperial gardens, those which could be seen from the throne room. Even at sunset Lin had noticed that there seemed no end to them. Upon entering now, Zahir had listened a moment, then said, "Ah!" when the woodpipe was heard. And smiled. Then motioned that she follow him, down the garden path before swerving from it, into an unmarked wilderness of trees. He didn't explain—not about the music, nor the garden, nor the reason for coming here.

It didn't matter. The alternative was the silence of her room and the dream. She would have agreed to almost anything.

At one point she did whisper, grabbing hold of his sleeve, "I feel as if . . . I've been here." The scent was overwhelming in what it recalled to her, despite the memories not being hers. As was the construction of this garden; the way the sight lines teased, made you think you were coming to one thing, only to see another in its stead. Every angle you stood, the prospect changed dramatically. There was a pattern to this, and an art, that was decipherable once you recognized it.

Zahir stopped then. He bowed his head as if she'd told him something disquieting. "Edrien Letrell played in the court of Ramadus," he said. "Was welcomed as a guest there. Yusuf Evrayad wanted his palace to resemble that court." The pipe had broken off a moment, but soon resumed.

"Do you think he succeeded?" Lin asked, recalling that Zahir had been in the court of Ramadus for a time.

He thought a moment. Then: "In some ways. But the Zahra—it is no copy of anything, in the end. Whatever Yusuf might have wanted. It is itself." The tune of the woodpipe soared, became wild. Neither happy nor sad—at a remove from both of these. For Zahir it seemed a signal. He held out a hand to her. "Come."

After a moment she took his hand. It was roughened, with a firm grip. So he was a fighting man. In bouts she wore gauntlets to keep the palms of her hands smooth, as befit a Court Poet and lady of Amaristoth. They walked together. The warmth of his hand, after days without contact, a reminder of isolation. This and the refrain of the pipe twisted within her as they trod the grass; she breathed deep of the garden scents to clear her thoughts. To forget everything but this moment, since nothing around it—before, or after—could be altered.

Soon they heard not only the nightingale and the woodpipe but the sound of falling water. She was not surprised when they stepped into a clearing and saw that the moon shone on a waterfall and beside it, a stream. She was more surprised that she recognized the man who played music at the water's edge. He sat cross-legged on a blanket in the grass. Willows dug their roots into the bank, their branches dipped to the water in curves, like a lady dropped in a curtsy.

As they approached, Lin disengaged from the First Magician. She bowed to the man by the stream. He stopped playing, looked bemused. "No need for that here," said Eldakar. "Sit with us."

"In this garden you—drop formalities?"

Eldakar's smile looked sweet to her, and sad. "Here, we become ourselves."

Zahir knelt in the grass, then stretched full length beside the king, the back of his head cupped in his hands. He let out a long sigh and closed his eyes, as if, at long last, he was at rest. Almost absently, the king reached over and squeezed the other man's shoulder. Zahir raised himself on an elbow. "A long day," he said, looking up at Eldakar's face. "How are you?"

"I am home," said Eldakar. "We—all of us—are home. For now that is enough." He looked to Lin. "Please make yourself comfortable, my lady," he said, indicating a spot on the blanket. "I swear to behave with every propriety, as will my friend."

She smiled. "A rash promise," she said, "if even half of what I've heard of this place is true. But I was listening to your playing. I did not know that you, too, are a musician."

"It is something my father despised," said Eldakar. "My love of music. Of poetry. Oh, these things he approved at his court—he wanted a name for sophistication. Kahishi was, before his arrival, too riven by feuds and dynastic battles for art, for music. So he took pride in these, as the fruits of peace. But not from me. Not from his son."

Now it was Zahir's turn to reach out, to lay a hand on his friend's knee. "There was no pleasing that man." A bitterness low in the throat. "You are worth ten of him."

"But I am no warrior," said Eldakar. "He was right about that. Mansur should have had the throne. I would give it to him if I could."

Lin curbed her shock—it helped, in this instance, that it was dark. A king did not say such things, her instincts told her; except just now, one had. She thought of Eldakar seated on the golden throne, alight with the sun. His mien impassive, stately. He knew as well as she did—better, even—what kings did and did not say.

But since he had, she could ask. "Why don't you give it to him?"

His response was a mirthless grin. "There is a belief in the country-side that if the heir—the eldest male issue—does not inherit, the land is cursed. The crops will fail, rains will not come. In the cities fewer believe this, but I cannot afford to induce panic—not at such a time. The same people who scorn my presence on the throne, who see me as a weakling king, would still see no one else there. Under only one circumstance will they accept Mansur as king." A silence, and there was no need for him to explain this last. A cricket chirped from the willows; another answered. Lin thought of a legend from her home, from northern Eivar, from a time before Eivar could have been said to exist at all. Of occasions when the lands were infertile, were said to cry out for blood in place of rain. A king's blood.

An image came to her of Eldakar with a black grin across his throat, his face waxen pale, and she shuddered.

The king said, "There is no real choice. If I were to abdicate . . ."

He trailed off. Zahir shook his head. His eyes were fixed on Eldakar's face, as if he could read it as he did the stars. A look that weighted his words. "These are dark thoughts. Why need you dwell there?"

A breeze wafted towards them. Roses, such as Lin had seen earlier. This intertwined with other scents she could not identify. In the gardens throughout the palace she had noticed lilies, irises, narcissus, and others she didn't know.

Eldakar smiled again, and Lin was sure now that it was with sadness. "Mansur is a fine brother," he said. "I know he cares for me. But if he became king . . . well, if he did not quietly have me killed, one of his supporters would do it. So we remain in this bind. So we dance. And I must try to save this place, which I love. Mansur's love is for war . . . he has little interest in the Zahra. While for me, this place is home. Anywhere else, I would be an exile."

On impulse, Lin knelt in the grass. "Eldakar," she said. "You honor me tonight with your trust."

He nodded. "Zahir has told me I can trust you," he said. "And to him I would entrust my soul."

A memory reared up: she was in the hills north of Tamryllin, in the company of two men. Before so many terrible things had happened. She felt Darien Aldemoor and Hassen Styr beside her. Not as ghosts, nor quite as memories. She simply felt them there. Almost she could imagine twining her hands in theirs, the comfort that brought—one that had evaporated so quickly.

Lin sank into a seated position in the grass. "How came the two of you to be friends?"

The two men looked at each other with identical wry expressions. Zahir laughed. "I assume you've heard the rumors."

"I . . ."

"Let her alone, Ramadian," said Eldakar, punching his shoulder.

"It's not my business," said Lin, and meant it.

"For some things there is a time, a season," said Zahir Alcavar. He had turned serious. "And after, one might go on in a different way. Now Eldakar belongs to Rihab Bet-Sorr. But some things are as before: we meet here, some nights, for music; by day, in the practice yard. And sometimes . . ."

"The city," said Eldakar. "Though that is . . . a greater risk than it used to be. To be recognized, as prince, was a game. As king . . . that is something else, again."

"What about the queen?" asked Lin. "Doesn't she want to see Majdara?"

"She would, most likely," said Eldakar with a smile. "But she knows the way of things. A queen is a treasure to be guarded. Otherwise her reputation is stained forever. I think she understands."

"Rihab?" Zahir shook his head. "She understands everything. More than we can imagine, probably." He must have seen Lin's quizzical look, for he added, "Perhaps you haven't heard how Rihab and Eldakar met. It was here."

"Here?" She gestured around them, at the waterfall, the willow trees. She remembered Ned's story of the king coming upon a singing slave girl, that he'd had from the guardsmen. It was hard to picture it now.

"Here." He turned to Eldakar, who was looking away, appearing embarrassed. "Our king—prince at the time—was in search of a rhyme, but quite in his cups. He couldn't think of a way to end his poem. And then suddenly from out the trees, one of the singing girls spoke up. The poem, as it stands now, has become a popular song at court."

Lin raised an eyebrow. "The singing girls."

"She had a way of distinguishing herself," said Eldakar.

"And still does, I am sure," said Zahir, and laughed when his friend winced. "Stop that," said Eldakar. "You ought not dare, considering what I know about you."

"True enough," said Zahir.

No longer did they make her think of Darien and Hassen. Nonetheless the presence of her lost friends was with her, as if they lounged here in the grass. They would have loved this place, and to make songs here.

As Zahir had said, Lin thought, one goes on. Even if not, not ever, as before. "I would hear more of the tune you were playing," she said, hugging her knees to her chest. "If you would be so kind."

They sat there a while. Eldakar took up his pipe, shut his eyes. The melody still sounded lonely to her; as if even loved as Eldakar was, a corner of his soul stayed apart. Some time passed, and then Zahir began to sing, wordless and melancholy. The two men leaned together. In their movements she read a story: of adventures in the city, a headlong passion, of plans that had faded like the roses would, once the demands of monarchy asserted themselves. And seeing this story, or even a piece, made her feel some of its sweet ache, and a desire to open her voice to it, release it that way. But she was silent. Somewhere the nightingale resumed its song, a counterpoint to music joined with a man's voice at the water's edge.

It was a moment, Lin thought, in which she would have liked to take root, stationary and content, as time and mortality slid around the three of them and away.

THE red candles burned low, and she had beaten him three times. Wine was replaced with steaming cups of *khave*, bitter and rich. Giving him a jolt of false alertness amid fatigue. Ned scowled at the board. Across from him Rihab Bet-Sorr sat with her legs crossed, one slippered foot over another. Her lips parted as she gazed toward the vistas of garden now more clear in the growing light. Every so often Ned would look up and see her in this same pose, unchanging, as if she'd forgotten their game. Yet this mattered not at all for his chances: at each turn she demolished him.

She did this without triumph, but also without seeming to think; her expression one of weary inevitability. By the time Ned Alterra realized that once again, her pieces were assembled to entrap his king, there seemed no way to reverse it. "How are you not tired?" he said at last, rubbing his eyes. They had spoken little in the course of the night. Ned was drawn into the contest despite himself. She, in turn, seemed to have no need of conversation.

She shrugged. "I see you are tired. There is no shame in losing, Ned Alterra. As time passes, you will improve."

"How long have you been . . . at this?"

"The game? Some months. Or weeks. I don't recall."

He swore softly. He had thought, perhaps, she was long-practiced at this. "Pardon me, lady," he added, remembering himself.

She smiled, though it was abstracted, as if her mind was elsewhere. "You are an intelligent man," she said. "Don't doubt yourself. It is a pleasure to see how fast you learn, compared to others I've played against. I promise you."

He did not know whether to be irritated or touched by this extensive reassurance. A salve for his male pride. Largely, he thought, it depended how tired he was.

The girl who served them *khave*—a new one, as he supposed the one with the wine had gone to sleep—approached the queen's elbow. In Kahishian said, "He's here, my queen."

Coming up behind her, in a silk robe and with shadows under his eyes, was Eldakar. He leaned over the back of her chair, hands on her shoulders, without sparing a glance for Ned. She tilted her head against his arm and closed her eyes. "Why are you still here, my heart," said Eldakar. A tone playful and weary, as if this had happened many times. "Come."

When she spoke, her eyes closed, it was a murmur. Both men leaned close to hear. "The game," she said. "It doesn't stop."

"It does when the king commands it," said Eldakar, teasingly, and kissed her behind the ear. She made a low, gratified sound in her throat. Ned rose hurriedly. "I shall . . . take my leave, majesties. Wishing you both a good night." *Or a good morning,* he thought sourly. How Rianna would laugh at him, if she could see where he'd gotten himself tonight. A thought like a sudden ache.

"Wait," said Rihab, rising too. She extended a hand. "Let us play again soon. Tomorrow?"

"As the queen commands," Ned said with a bow only slightly mocking, which seemed safe; Eldakar was distracting her with kisses again, this time on the nape of the neck. When at last Ned Alterra extricated himself from the room and found himself back in the long marble-tiled hall, he needed time to orient himself. Nothing seemed familiar. But there was an attendant, a new one, with movements like oil, to conduct him to the corridor entrance.

Ned's thoughts were a welter as he made his way back. He had arrived at the queen's chamber with a mix of dread and compelled desire; the latter was chilled, dampened, by hours engaged in a battle of wits. But Eldakar's arrival served as a reminder of what Ned had earlier been expecting to do; and he found himself disturbingly overheated as he recalled the sound Rihab Bet-Sorr made when kissed behind the ear. Yet he could not shake a memory that seemed important, despite the protesting distraction of his body. As he was leaving, Ned had met the queen's gaze once more. What he saw, in the moment before departing, was the same fatal inevitability as when she maneuvered her pieces on the board. Setting the trap.

CHAPTER
7

THE night of vigil ended with Dorn Arrin and the other singers bearing the body of Archmaster Myre in a procession to the water. Their singing pitched deep, wordless. Under fading stars they lay the dead man in a boat carved of blackthorn. Pallid as the robes he wore, the High Master looked more severe, even fearsome, than he had appeared in life. Hands folded on his chest, his ring towards the sky. A diamond, lightless in the grey dawn.

It was the Archmasters, the nine who remained, who bore torches to the bier and set the oil-soaked rags alight. As the ritual boat glided from shore in smoke, the Archmasters enjoined the procession to turn away—not look back. As a result of their night's work, the barrier to the Otherworld was thinned, dissipated. They released the High Master from this life through a portal of flame. The boat would catch quickly, a transient flare on the water. But to look into the dark realm was forbidden. Thus the men departed with the snap and hiss and scent of smoke at their backs, until even that was gone and they were once more in the wooded stillness of the Isle.

Dorn returned to his room, weary to his soul. Though all was quiet, the memory of music and of merged voices pursued him. In the next bed Etherell Lyr lay on his back, arm outstretched, lips gently parted. The impulse that overwhelmed Dorn in that moment was agony; he suppressed an unseemly keening that would have been from the heart. It was the night, of course, that had done this to him. Cut him open, the wound exposed to air. He hated it. His accustomed rage was painful, but still more easily borne than this.

He collapsed into bed and next he knew the room was too bright, every one of his limbs weighted to the bed. His mouth tasted of dust. It must have been past noon. The next bed was empty—and a mess, of course. Etherell saw the rules for students' tidiness as a suggestion, or a jest. Somehow he never got in trouble.

Dorn was ravenous. With an effort he dragged himself up and threw on his clothes as fast as he could. He did stop, however, to tidy both their beds. He didn't care much about rules, either, but from his father's workshop had learned to loathe a disordered surface. Or else there was refuge, a solace, in order. Either, or both.

He was in time for the noonday meal, as it happened. As Dorn sped down the spiral staircase to the main floor he heard voices in the dining hall. Had he been thinking more clearly, he would have realized it was past noon and should have been too late; but hungry as he was, and tired, he didn't think. So when he set foot in the dining hall Dorn was momentarily halted in his tracks. For while the other students were there, and the Archmasters, there was a man at the high table whom Dorn could not identify, who now addressed those gathered. Seated beside him was a smaller figure, cloaked and hooded in blue.

The man was tall, broad-shouldered, and very handsome. Instead of a robe he wore a simple tunic and trousers that showed a trim yet muscled frame. In short, he looked nothing like the Archmasters with whom he stood at the high table. As Dorn took his seat beside Etherell, the man was saying, "It will be my honor to take a place here, where I once studied the art like all of you. I have traveled much of the world, seen wonders most would not believe, but always I yearned to return to my home."

Dorn grabbed a roll and began to tear into it. Regardless of who this pompous blowhard was, Dorn thought he could eat the table itself by now, splinters and all.

Etherell leaned forward, murmured in Dorn's ear, "Arrived this morning. He's here to complete the ten."

"*He* is a Seer?" Dorn muttered back, and stared at the newcomer as he chewed. Then another thought, as he saw Valanir Ocune sitting across from them. Why hadn't *he* been chosen? Unless Valanir had been offered the position of Archmaster, and refused. It would be like him.

Etherell nodded. "He can't be as young as he looks—rumor is he was in Valanir Ocune's year," he said. "His name is Elissan Diar."

As he turned to look again, Dorn noticed Maric Antrell across the table. Dorn's companion in song the night before, Maric looked the worse for wear, haggard and of a sickly color. One hand restlessly juggled his cup. The same hand that had crunched Dorn's finger like a biscuit, leaving him unable to play the harp for weeks.

"I will say but one more thing, as I know all of you must be hungry," said the new Archmaster. "Come forward, my love." The hooded figure beside him rose. With a tentative movement the hood was lowered. The face revealed, that of a girl. Her hair like autumn, framing a delicate face. Her dress cut to her comely shape. Like a sunflower turning on its stem her head cast about, taking in the room. At last she lowered her lashes down to her clasped hands. To Dorn it seemed all around was a collective intake of breath. He glanced over his shoulder at Etherell Lyr, to see how he took this new development. His friend, whose every act was typically imbued with insouciance, had turned intent. His eyes heavy-lidded in a way Dorn had not seen. Perhaps there were girls on the mainland who had.

"My daughter, Sendara, has studied the art with me for years," said Archmaster Diar. "Now it's time for her to take her rightful place. She will be a Seer."

The taut silence of the room stretched. As if the air itself was suspended. Etherell gazed at the girl on the dais. His face was drawn in unfamiliar lines; he reminded Dorn, in that instant, of a wolf.

Needing to look elsewhere—anywhere else—Dorn found himself meeting the gaze of Valanir Ocune. The Seer was looking their way. As Dorn Arrin's gaze locked with his, the Seer's lip curled in a faint, private smile, as if there were but the three of them in the room.

THERE was a change to the Isle since last night. It was something to consider—to explore in the dark. It would be perilous, he knew, to seek such deep levels to the enchantments; but he had made a promise. How could he, Valanir Ocune, back down once he'd given his word? In the light of a new day and with the mourning rituals at an end, he felt renewed strength. More himself. The weight of grief that had marked his travels now seemed a fog, burned away with sunlight.

He would need that strength and all his wit in days to come. Events were moving fast. Elissan's arrival so soon after the death of Archmaster Myre was suspicious—there had hardly been time to summon him—but no one cared about that. That was how confident Archmaster Lian and the rest were, with the Court Poet away in Kahishi. And for other reasons, if he could discover them. If there was time. In a matter of days Marten Lian would be declared the new High Master. And Valanir had heard, through his own channels, that Vassilian would support his accession.

Lian, whom Valanir was convinced was a tool of Elissan Diar. Who was now returned after years abroad mired in the gods knew what sort of magic. Valanir at least had some idea, if the gods did not.

It was still daylight. He stood in an abandoned roof garden, overgrown with ferns and ivy. A toppled statue on the ground, seamed with cracks and by now so eroded as to be featureless. None could say what the unwieldy figure had once been—man or god.

Sometimes Valanir Ocune came to this rooftop to think; as far as he knew, only he had the key. Of course, he was not supposed to have it. But if Valanir Ocune had kept to laws, Nickon Gerrard would still be ruling in Tamryllin—or what would have been left of it if he'd had his way. That summer when everything turned, Valanir had sensed in Darien Aldemoor a spirit that was a mirror to his own, though young. So painfully young, he thought now.

Valanir had stolen the key to this garden years ago. He and Nickon Gerrard had planned it together. It was strange to recall clambering the hallways and staircases with his closest friend. With Nick. Even after their rites of blood in the wood, until the final severing between them. To walk these halls was, at times, to go arm in arm with ghosts. Or— in this case—to remonstrate with a ghost who leaned back against the wall with crossed arms, smirking, unrepentant. That was, had always been Nick. He was never sorry. But his wit kept Valanir entertained. Perhaps too entertained to see the truth, for too long.

So many opportunities Valanir had missed to fling Nickon Gerrard from this tower top. He himself would be damned, but perhaps had earned it.

Even the tangled wood was more navigable than the path Valanir Ocune had charted of his life—whether he'd chosen right or wrong.

From atop this tower he could see the lake, molten steel in the sun. The wall of mountain that opened to the sea, the wisp of green and black that was the mainland. A view he had seen in every season and time of day, the one he loved best. Despite where he'd been.

Archmaster Myre's mark was blackened, as if with fire.

Don't be confident, Ocune, Valanir admonished himself. The idea forming in the back of his mind would terrify him, if he looked at it. *The Seer's mark.*

He knew Elissan Diar, had known him since they were students together. Even Nick had feared him. That was worth remembering. He needed to keep an eye open wherever he went. When he slept, his door was locked in more than the tangible ways. None of this was foolproof. The only strategy he had was the long game, with the one card he had left to play. No doubt as Manaia drew near, the shadows that lurked in the corner of his eye would leap to the forefront; come out to dance.

THAT night when she went out to wander Julien could not have said why, only that she couldn't sleep and the day left her unsettled. The songs for Archmaster Myre had pierced her dreams the night before. She had awakened before daybreak with the sense of having grappled something: winded, blood in her wrists pounding. From the window she saw that the tops of the trees near the lake shimmered with smoke. She had rested her elbows on the sill and stared out, dry-eyed, knowing what this must be. The wind picked at her hair. She thought she heard singing far away, but might have imagined it.

Farewell. Julien wished she had words for the cold that tightened in her chest. The verses of poets from across centuries crowded her mind, mellifluous and assured, if she wanted them; but just now, she longed for her own. Some way to give shape to what seemed a crucial moment. What would the Academy be without Archmaster Myre?

That was the day's beginning. Later, there was the introduction of the new Archmaster and his daughter. She saw the response when Sendara Diar had revealed herself to the dining hall, bright as new copper.

This was not a girl who would be ignored. Beside her at table, Julien could feel rather than see the unhappiness of the other girls. They had fallen silent. Julien felt a tug of sadness on their behalf. For herself she expected little, but knew how it must be for Miri and Cyrilla to have this inescapable testimony to their insignificance.

Later when they were on the stairs to their rooms—the other two girls shared one—Cyrilla had said, hanging her head, "I want to go home," and Miri put an arm across her shoulders. "We should leave," she'd said. "This place is hateful."

A place that did not value what they were, nor give credence to what they could become. Perhaps they were right. Julien had not seen it before in that light. It seemed natural that she, herself, was invisible. But not Cyrilla Pyllene, with her elegant plaits and voice like a nightingale. Not Miri Caern, with her talent for drawing and mischievous eyes. Julien was ashamed that she had seen them as songbirds, harmless and unharmed, no more than future wives for someone. She had reduced them, too.

In her room that night, Julien thought it was not the response of the dining hall that had been difficult for her. It was something else: the way Sendara Diar's father—so handsome he seemed burnished, a second source of illumination beneath the rose window in the light of afternoon—looked at his daughter; said, *She will be a Seer,* with complacent pride.

Jealousy was a snake that ate inside your heart. In tales the heroine was a beauty, and beloved; her chief enemies were lonely, jealous women. Julien Imara clearly was not made to be a heroine. Was she, then, fated to linger on the margins of someone else's story? Surely it was too soon for that—for her whole life—to be decided.

In little more than a handful of years she would be finished with the Academy, sent out into the world. Everything would be decided here.

Julien was at that time pacing the length of her cell of a room, up and down. Past the harp beside her bed. It had come cheap, fashioned of wood and tin. Its tones innately flawed, because the instrument was.

Fair music cannot come from tin.

At that thought she stopped pacing. It was so clear. Now that it came to her. A truth to define her life. If the instrument was flawed, so too was its music. Irrevocably. *If the instrument is flawed . . .*

If she stayed in this tight room with this new, awful understanding she would choke. There was no breaking free of it. But she could at least be free of this room.

Julien stepped into the hall. It seemed absurd to worry about Maric Antrell; he had never noticed her before. She had certainly been watching him, noted the way he led the students of his year. In the dining hall today he had seemed unlike himself, appearing pale, drained of vitality. That was, until Sendara Diar was unveiled. Then he had revived like the rest, as if that hair were a beacon.

She had no candle to see by and the moon through the parting of the stones was faint, but Julien had grown accustomed to feeling her way. With light there was too great a risk she would be seen. She had a sudden image of herself lying at the bottom of the spiral stairs with a broken neck, and was more fascinated than afraid. But was still careful, careful, in her silent tread on the stair.

In the entrance hall was more light than in the stairwell, from three long apertures above the main doors. Pillars threw diagonal shadows across the floor. The intricate scrollwork of the ceiling was different, almost threatening, at night; a spiderweb fretted, here and there, with pools of black where light could not reach. Keeping to the shadows cast by the pillars, Julien crept past the arched entryway to the chapel and on to the next arch, this one graced by figures of the goddess to either side. She stopped a moment at these sculptures, each a representation of Kiara. One portrayed the aspect of the goddess called upon by poets—the patron of music. Between her hands she held a reed pipe to her lips, on her head a crown of lilies.

The sculpture opposite was opposed to it in all ways: the Kiara of judgment. Her face barely visible beneath a raised cowl, long hair streaming as if in wind. One long-fingered hand raised in the warding sign against evil—a sign she had invoked during creation. Against the advent of humanity. The other hand clasped a long, evil-looking knife.

That was for sinners. Julien thought of the sins of her heart, and hoped these were not counted.

With a slight shiver she passed through the archway, past the knife. She took care to step quietly, slippers soundless on stone. And here, at last, was light. She stood in the Hall of Harps. Like a piece of the moon set on a platform at the end of the hall, the Silver Branch. Its light eternal. Lining the room were pedestals which displayed the harps of Seers gone. Some of these bore engraved verses beneath the names.

Julien was not here for the harps tonight. She was not sure, in truth, why she had come; but she was continuously drawn to look at the carvings in the walls. She did think there was something forlorn about these harps, most of them golden, now all that remained of the men who had once teased music from them.

Though that was not true, she reminded herself. Seers left songs that would last. In his younger days Archmaster Myre had given the Academy work extraordinarily fine. Now his harp stood on a pedestal, the newest addition. There had not yet been time to engrave his name.

Near the pedestal for Archmaster Myre, which was nearest the entrance, were some of the wall carvings most familiar to Julien: the knight, the woman, the dancer. She stared, watched the shifting of light from the Silver Branch on the images, so that they nearly seemed alive.

Something moved in the corner of her eye.

Julien sprang behind one of the pedestals to crouch in its shadow.

"There's no reason to hide," said a voice. "You may as well come out." Not Maric Antrell—a girl. Since she was caught either way, Julien stood. Beside the Silver Branch, hair frosted in its glow, stood Sendara Diar.

Julien swallowed hard. "Will you tell your father?"

The other girl looked interested. "Why would I tell?"

They were speaking too loudly across the long hall; Julien moved closer. It was too dangerous, what they were doing. Dangerous for Julien, at any rate. She supposed the daughter of an Archmaster had little to fear of Academy discipline.

She couldn't think of a satisfactory answer. *I don't know you, for a start,* but that would not be courteous. With a helpless shrug she said, "Why does anyone do anything?" There was only the distance of a few feet between them now, and the cold light of the Branch.

"You don't trust me," said Sendara Diar. She sounded as if she didn't mind; her interest still piqued. Up close, Julien saw her cheeks were dimpled, that she wore earrings set with stones like beads of dried blood. Garnets. Her eyes deep set and blue like those of her father.

Julien stepped nearer. She felt fear, and hopelessness since she was caught, and something else. Later she would understand what she had felt most of all was yearning. She forced herself to meet Sendara Diar's eyes. Not knowing the source of her own impulse, Julien said, "*The hearts of men are dark, their secrets beyond count.*"

The other girl's eyes flickered, perhaps with surprise. She said, "But I shall rest my weary head where my heart leads, and then go on."

The melody of the lay hung between them.

"You like Lacarne," Sendara Diar said after a moment.

"Yes," said Julien, though *like* was the wrong word. That poet of centuries past had, throughout his life, written keenly of isolation. The life of a poet, ever wandering, had been the only one Caill Lacarne was suited for; yet it had brought him grief. That, as much as anything, had gone to the shaping of his art.

"I like him, too," said Sendara, casually as if she spoke of an acquaintance. "Though he falls short of perfection. The emotion is too raw."

"I suppose you must know everything." It came out sounding dull. "With a father who is a Seer."

"Not everything," said Sendara with a shrug. Looking around she said, "I didn't expect anyone else to be about. I wanted to see the Branch. I wanted . . . some time alone with it. I suppose that sounds silly."

"No," said Julien. Now was her turn to be surprised. "No, it doesn't. Sometimes when I am alone here I think—that I hear music."

"Is that why you came tonight?"

Julien was silent. She scarcely knew herself how to answer that question. And she had no reason to trust this girl.

Gliding past the silence, Sendara said, "Will you show me around the castle tomorrow? I don't know anyone else here."

You don't know me, Julien wanted to point out, but once again courtesy overrode instinct. "I will," she said. "If you truly want that—from me. Your father knows much more."

"No doubt, but he will be busy tomorrow, readying for his initiation as Archmaster," said Sendara Diar. A closed smile plumped her lips, a look epitomizing satisfaction. She reached out a hand. "Let's go back together. What is your name?"

Wordlessly Julien Imara took the other girl's hand. It was cool to the touch. Later she would scarcely remember what was said; what she would recall, mostly, was what she felt. A beginning, like the spring.

A feeling overlaid with surprise as they neared the archway when she turned one final time to look at the carvings and saw the dancer no longer held a torch in each hand.

Now in one hand, instead of a torch, was a long, curved sword.

"FIND this out for me."

Archmaster Hendin looked askance at Valanir Ocune from his chair at the hearth, his face ruddy in its glow. He was warming his hands. They were in Valanir's chamber, a simple room of scrolls and books, a harp that caught the firelight. It was past midnight. A light drizzle had begun outside. "It is closely guarded," said Hendin.

"I know. That's why I need you."

"You believe . . . he was murdered?"

Valanir shook his head. "The less you know, the safest," he said. "Just bring me what I ask."

Archmaster Hendin stared at him. "I've never known you to speak this way."

Valanir was silent. Outside, rain was gentle in the wood. "These are different times," he said. He laid a hand on Hendin's shoulder. His gawky friend, worn by years. His ring was lapis: *A loyal heart, life-giving as water.* Cai Hendin had given all he had to this place. It was true the Academy compensated with gifts of knowledge and power, but mostly it took . . . and took.

Hendin turned to watch the fire. "This place has been my home . . . because of Seravan Myre," he said. "I know he was hard on you. To me, he was different. I'd never have become Archmaster without his kindness. Never imagined myself worthy." His head bowed. "Now that he's gone, I have no place. I should have known something was coming. Stell Kerwin has been inserting little jibes into every exchange that he can. He is so proud of himself, to be allied with Marten Lian and Elissan Diar. The stature he imagines it gives him. It reminds me of how we used to leave him out of things, Valanir. You know we did."

"We left him out because he was a damned nuisance," said Valanir. "Surely you remember. He told when Nick and I were out that night. Myre gave us each ten lashes with the nettle-branch." He winced at the memory. The High Master at that time, Archmaster Sarne, had been a temperate man, inclined to forgive the boys their scrapes. Not so Seravan Myre, the grim Archmaster who oversaw discipline.

"Stell tattled because it gave him power over his superiors—namely, the two of you," said Hendin. "But I suppose . . . you're right. You're surely not to blame for how he turned out. Or I suppose I should say, what he's turned into. The ideas you've put in my head, Valanir . . . they horrify me."

"I may be wrong," said Valanir, though he knew it was unconvincing.

"You and Nick," said Hendin. He'd turned from contemplating the fire to look at Valanir. His eyes bright. "I can understand what motivated Stell, in a way. The two of you. I was envious, too. You were always kind to me . . . Nick was not, but you were. Nonetheless, I knew our friendship did not compare. That you were being kind."

Valanir's headshake was swift, vehement. "No," he said. "I'll admit . . . I undervalued you, Cai. I was a boy . . . I valued the wrong things. But you know, things with Nick were—like a forge that burns too hot. Often I was scorched . . . or found myself becoming someone I did not like. You were the nearest I had to—a refuge. To home. I believe, otherwise, I may have lost myself. As Nickon surely did."

The fire popped. The room had grown warmer, though drafts came in from the cracks and casements like they always did.

A long moment before Archmaster Hendin spoke again. "This favor you ask. It can be done—by breaking the rules." He shook his head, then, and almost smiled. "In that way, I guess it is like old times."

CHAPTER
8

THE screams began in the night. Dorn was caught in the pincers of a nightmare. Fires, closing in; he could smell the smoke. At first thought the screams were his own. But no, it was in the Academy: a shrill, anguished shriek without end.

He blinked awake. The room was dark. Etherell was already dressed and at the door. That shriek was carrying on from the floors below.

"Where . . . ?"

His friend turned. "I'm going to see what's happened. If someone needs help."

"Wait." Dorn flung his legs over the side of the bed. "I'm coming."

He half-expected a lull in the screaming, but it went on. The agonized sound raked his nerves. They ran. It seemed to be coming from the floor below. Doors were opening throughout the castle, students spilling into the halls. By the time Dorn and Etherell reached the source of the screams they were joined by other students, most in their sleeping clothes and appearing frightened, especially the younger ones. By this time the sounds had changed, become a kind of ragged choking that was, in its way, worse. They came from one of the students' rooms. Boys clustered around the doorway. They were waved away by Archmaster Lian, a grim sentinel blocking the threshold. Dorn realized it was the room Maric Antrell shared with his friend—some large fellow with a brutal grin who had helped pinion Dorn's arms the day Maric Antrell had broken his finger. What was his name?

"Gared Dexane," said Etherell. "I'd guess. It doesn't sound like Maric." The next moment they caught sight of Maric Antrell lounging beside Archmaster Lian, looking—of all things—sulky. His luxuriant curls, tousled, accentuated the impression of a pampered lordling. Dorn knew, of course, that he was beautiful; a patina that gave lustre to cruelty.

The other boys were falling back from the forbidding countenance of the Archmaster, eyes round with wonder and fear. Etherell strode forward. "What's happened here? Is he ill?"

Archmaster Lian's pale eyes were cold and fishlike as ever. Nonetheless he was forced to shout to be heard above Gared's cries. The indignity must have galled. "It is none of your concern, Etherell Lyr. Nor yours, Dorn Arrin. Be off to your rooms—and get the others to do the same. Go on, you're an example for them."

Seizing Maric's arm and pulling him inside the room, the Archmaster slammed shut the door. But not before Dorn had seen the bed where Gared Dexane writhed on the mattress, blankets thrown aside. His face was purple, except around his mouth, where it was dimpled white. Veins stood out in his neck and forehead with unnerving prominence, as if they would break. But worst were his eyes, Dorn thought, rolled up in his head until only the whites showed. Perhaps he was dying. *The bugger.*

But that was not even the strangest thing. Standing beside the bed, hands uplifted in a cupping gesture above it, was the new Archmaster: Elissan Diar.

"IT'S the enchantments, isn't it?" said Dorn the moment they were back in their room, the door shut behind them. The screaming seemed to have stopped. Whatever that meant for Gared Dexane. "Everyone knows what Diar gets up to with his 'chosen.'"

Etherell smiled. "You're jealous?"

Dorn shook his head, unable even to voice his disbelief at this suggestion. He pulled off his shoes and collapsed into bed fully dressed. With any luck there was still time for sleep. If he could sleep. He felt shaken—now almost as much by Etherell's indifference to enchantments and the dangers they posed. After tonight, none could deny it anymore. When Elissan Diar had formed his group of chosen students—the ones he would guide personally in the mysteries of the enchantments—Dorn was glad not to be among them. But also filled with dread, at the idea of what might be happening in those meetings that were always held at night. Rumors drifted the hallways like blown leaves: of lights in the wood at night, of strange sounds from a locked chamber or the Tower of the Winds. Such tales had begun since long before the arrival of Elissan Diar—that Maric Antrell and his companions met in secret to explore enchantments—but now that the activity was overseen by an Archmaster all was changed. As if the Academy were diverging into two worlds—the one Dorn and Etherell studied in, and some other, secret one.

Nothing good could come of these enchantments, Dorn was convinced. And there was something about the new Archmaster he had distrusted on sight, that very first day when Elissan Diar stood shining beneath the rose window in the dining hall. A predatory edge to those white teeth.

Turning to face the wall, Dorn had a new thought. He turned around again. Across their small space Etherell lay on his back, also dressed, contemplating the ceiling with a lazy faraway look that meant he was thinking something through. Dorn had come to recognize that when Etherell Lyr was deepest in thought was when he appeared his most serene and thoughtless. Though could not have said how he knew.

The night around them was quiet again. Sounds of wind and water all they heard. Dorn drew himself up on an elbow. "You want to join them. Don't you."

Etherell didn't cease his contemplation of the ceiling, which was bare, the whitewash cracked with age. "Have you considered the adventure?"

"Adventure?" Dorn stared. "It's dangerous magic. You saw what it did to Dexane." His friend didn't move or change expression. Dorn was nearly afraid to continue, that too much might come out in his voice. That his friend would think him a coward, which perhaps he was, since now he was afraid to speak. With difficulty he went on, "You've . . . never struck me as someone who wanted power. Not like these others." *Like Maric Antrell.* But even as he said the words, he wondered. For Etherell the art of poets had all along been a game, something to pass the time until he grew to manhood and his inheritance. Music didn't draw him as it did Dorn; he didn't, would never understand why Dorn so despised the enchantments that had—to his mind—distorted everything.

As if confirming Dorn's fears, Etherell still didn't look his way. His tone was cool. "In truth," he said, each word shaped with precision, "there is little I want. *Wanting* . . . is not something I do, Dorn Arrin."

With this baffling pronouncement he turned to face the wall, was in moments asleep. It was Dorn who was left whitely awake in the small hours, wondering when everything that mattered to him had been so upended.

In autumn he would have his ring. Would leave the Academy to its bizarre new regimen of night gatherings, whispers, boys going mad. Only the road and himself, until all he had cared for was folded into the mist of this Isle, into memory.

THE Academy was becoming strange around them, she knew; a thing she'd begun to see even before Gared Dexane awakened the castle with his screams. He had vanished the next day; the talk was Archmaster Diar had him ferried to the mainland, sent home. This in itself was shocking enough, though not without precedent by now: she had regretfully bidden farewell to Miri, and Cyrilla was leaving, too. And yet Julien Imara found it impossible to give much thought to these developments, which ought to have unsettled her. Even the departure of the two girls was only distantly felt. She was too happy.

"You'd be wise to do as we're doing," Cyrilla said bluntly, the day of her departure. They were in her room; Julien sat on the bed and watched as the other girl packed the last of her things in her trunk. Miri's bed was already stripped bare. "Really, Julien. This is no place for someone of your birth. There's little chance you'll become a poet if no one will teach you. Learning useful skills instead would secure you—a place."

A place. Julien could imagine, and it didn't bear thinking about. Sometime—was it recently?—that idea had crossed a line, from hazy to unbearable. But she couldn't say that to Cyrilla. She forced a laugh. "I'm not good for anything useful, you know that," she said. "Truly I wish you the best."

The other girl shrugged. She appeared older in her ermine-lined travel cloak, hair drawn tight beneath the hood. And elegant, as if already assimilating back into the world to which she returned. There would be the tasks of her family household, but also balls, and extended visits to other estates, to Tamryllin. All with the goal of introducing her to potential suitors, and the next phase of a woman's life—marriage, children. She looked nearly a woman already, in that moment. Her eyes were sharp, suddenly, and made Julien uncomfortable. "That Sendara Diar is what's no good," said Cyrilla. "I don't know why I think so. But I do."

Julien looked away. The other girls had immediately taken a dislike to the fast friendship between Julien and Sendara. The connection the two had had from the start, that night in the Hall of Harps. Even now Julien felt as if she performed a duty, seeing Cyrilla off; she didn't feel a true desire to be there. Nonetheless, with that same sense of duty—perhaps inculcated in every Imara—Julien stood on the lakeshore until Cyrilla Pyllene's boat had shrunk to a speck on the horizon. She felt a guilty relief as she turned to head back to the castle. The sun had just begun to rise, stroking in tender wisps through the trees.

She was in time for the morning meal, though by a hair. As usual she was overwhelmed when she entered the dining hall, faced with a roomful of boisterous boys. As usual they ignored her—in its way a blessing. She retreated towards the end of the table, where Sendara Diar was waving to her. A light kindled in Julien. She drifted the rest of the way to her seat as if in a cloud. Baskets of bread and pots of sloe berry preserves were the daily fare. Today there were apples as well, perhaps due to the recent flurry of activity between the Isle and mainland. But Julien was late, the breadbaskets empty.

"I saved one for you," said Sendara as she passed a roll wrapped in a napkin. Her hair was twined around her head in a braid coronet, exposing the length of her slender neck. "These boys destroy everything they see."

Julien bit into the hard roll and thought it was better than Academy bread often was. Lately everything, even the sloe berry jam, tasted better. "I saw Cyrilla off."

Sendara shrugged. "Those who stay are the true ones," she said. "That's what my father says."

The true ones. "You mean, like his chosen?"

Sendara smiled. "I mean, like you and me."

Julien dropped her eyes, suddenly shy. The joy rising from belly to throat seemed too large to contain.

Since the night in the Hall of Harps they were rarely apart. In lessons Julien now had a partner—one who tended to know most of the answers, and spoke up, compelling unprecedented attention to the girls at the back of the room. No longer did Julien struggle to keep up with the students a year ahead of her. Sendara helped fix her hands and fingers on the strings for greater ease of playing, and fewer cramps in her hands after. And outside of that, Julien Imara at last had found someone who shared her love of the songs; who would talk to her and had ideas about what she'd read. Julien was aware her own views were half-formed. She listened more than she spoke. She was not always willing to relinquish her views, such as her passion for the songs of Lacarne, but knew she needed above all to learn more. Sendara Diar offered not only companionship but a window to the world.

A window, if not a door. There was a space that was sacrosanct: when one of Elissan Diar's chosen would approach Sendara with a summons from the Archmaster. No matter what Sendara was doing or what they were talking about, she would hurry away to the tower chamber of Archmaster Diar. She helped with his work, she explained once to Julien; none else could be trusted with it.

Sendara showed confidence during lessons. That it was her right—in fact her birthright—to speak and be heard. Julien was accustomed to her place at the back, to listening quietly. Sendara changed all that.

During a history lesson with Archmaster Lian, soon after Sendara arrived, he was teaching about the kingdom of Ramadus. Julien knew scarcely anything of that empire far away. But now that the Court Poet was in Kahishi on official business, the Archmaster had decided they must know more of the east. Standing before their assembled desks, his nose lifted in the haughty way he had, Lian seemed to address the air.

"At one time," he said, "Kahishi was a land without magic. It was populated with men who worshiped the Three, as we do, and ruled by a council of lords in the great city of Almyria. But then worshipers of the god Alfin arrived, and conquered. The land divided into provinces that were constantly at war."

He was poised to continue speaking, but Sendara in that moment spoke up. Julien sensed rather than saw the shock of all present, that a student would speak without obtaining permission. Much less a girl.

She said, "House Evrayad schemed for the throne of Ramadus. They failed, and the king had the family killed. All but the youngest, Yusuf, who escaped. He came to Kahishi and united the provinces."

Lian cleared his throat, visibly attempting to regain control of his lesson. "So you know something of Ramadus," he said at last. To another student he might have administered a whipping—Lian was known for resorting to the birch rod for the slightest infraction.

But this was the daughter of an Archmaster.

"I have been there," said Sendara, lips curling upward. "Of all the courts I've seen, that of Ramadus is the most splendid. Magic permeates everything. In the gardens there are trees entirely of gold and silver, where jeweled birds sing."

The boys all sat perfectly still at their desks, not turning to look.

Another such moment occurred in a lesson about the poets of the Age of Praises—that period when in order to curry favor, the poets of Eivar had written abasingly and at length in praise of the monarchy. It was a time when the art could be said to have flourished—funded generously from the kings' coffers—but drew criticism for its cloying flattery. It was when the enchantments had long since departed, the power of the Academy drastically on the wane.

Archmaster Hendin taught this lesson. All that year he'd reviewed each of the Ages of poets. He had a self-effacing manner about him. His manner of walking more effortful, even stooped, since the death of Archmaster Myre. He paced as he talked. "There are questions, now, about the songs in the Age of Praises," he said. "If they rose to the heights of true art, while bent to the flattery of kings."

Sendara spoke, again without warning. "My father says not," she said. "He believes any poet who bends the knee is not a man. And only a true man may create at his full capacity."

It was like a challenge to all in that room.

Julien's feelings were complex on those occasions. She felt pride, that this girl who knew so much was her friend. Seething beneath this, she was aware, were other feelings. Later on, Sendara told Julien that upon her visit to Ramadus a prince, fascinated, had ordered her portrait painted. A painting of Sendara Diar now hung in a gilded gallery of the Ramadian court. Or perhaps even in the prince's own chambers.

On these occasions, Julien reminded herself that it was more important to *listen* than to give in to the feelings that had driven away Miri and Cyrilla. To listen and to learn. Interspersed with Sendara's stories of herself were insights she'd gained in her travels and studies, and these she shared with Julien freely. Julien knew she was lucky to have access to knowledge like this. To have been seen by this girl, and chosen.

The fulcrum of Sendara's world was her father. It seemed a prerequisite to friendship with Sendara Diar that one must acknowledge the superiority of Elissan Diar in all things. He was the most handsome, his voice the most tuneful and rich, and above all—he knew all. This was not a difficult proposition for Julien—she had no reason to doubt any of these things. She didn't see Archmaster Diar often in any case—he only taught the older students. Privately she thought Etherell Lyr was far handsomer than the Archmaster, than anyone, but would have died rather than admit it.

Certainly she could accept that Elissan Diar, who had traveled the world and seemed to know much of the enchantments, was as Sendara insisted—superior to the other Seers. Sendara more than implied, further, that it was the Academy that needed him, rather than the other way around. This was believable, too. Julien thought of the conversation she'd overheard between Archmaster Kerwin and Piet Abarda, that night that seemed a lifetime ago. If Sendara was right, Elissan Diar's influence, going forward, would be crucial. Though admittedly Julien didn't understand what that meant. The world of Archmasters and their politics was distant, incomprehensible.

She was surprised that for all his capabilities, Archmaster Diar had been unable to prevent what happened—whatever it was that had happened—to Gared Dexane.

That day, contemplative in the wake of Cyrilla's departure, Julien raised the subject for the first time. They were walking in the woods, as they often did when it was fine. The night before it had rained, raising the smell of moldering leaves. It was afternoon, bright even under the cover of trees. Sendara was picking wildflowers, on her lips that small, contented smile Julien had first seen when they met. Her mind clearly elsewhere. She and her father had been honored guests in courts throughout the world, had seen the mountains and seas of lands south and east. Her interior life was not confined to a room with a cracked mirror amid olive groves; certainly not to this tiny, rainy Isle.

When Julien mentioned Gared Dexane, however, Sendara's gaze sharpened to the present. She looked almost spiteful. "He was weak," she said, bending at the waist to pluck a snowdrop. The motion made a flurry of her skirts. "And a brute. My father was well rid of him."

"Then why was he chosen?" Julien was surprised by the response. Perhaps because Sendara was delicate, of gentle movements, yet spoke thus of someone who had suffered. Not that Julien doubted it was true— what she'd seen of Gared Dexane had been detestable, and she was glad he was gone.

Rising, snowdrop in hand, Sendara raised a careless shoulder. "My father never acts without reason. Perhaps Dexane was meant to be— temporarily useful."

A forcibly adult formulation, that. *Temporarily useful*. As if the presence of Elissan Diar, his brilliant smile, was here with them and the wildflowers.

"Do you know what the chosen do?" Julien said at last. In sunlight it seemed a harmless subject, of curiosity only.

Sendara was rearranging the stems of her flowers, which she managed even as she gracefully made her way over roots and stones. Her dress was imported lace, but she did not seem to worry about dirtying it. "It is secret."

"But do *you* know?" For some reason this seemed important.

Now Sendara looked irritated. "No. Like I said, it is secret. But"— and this with a flick of her head—"someday I will."

On their way back to the castle Sendara looked up suddenly from her work. "Look! Done." In her hands a chain of the flowers she'd strung together, white and yellow and pink. "Hold still a moment."

Julien did as she was bid. Sendara tied the chain at both ends to make it a circlet. Then she set it on Julien's head. "There, it's just right," said Sendara. Dappled in sunlight, her braided hair showed pinpoints of fire. Her gaze dispassionate, surveying her handiwork as if assessing an item for purchase. "You have pretty eyes," she said. "The crown brings them out." With a peremptory motion she reached for Julien's hair, efficiently loosed the ribbon that bound it, combed through the curls until they were tumbled out on Julien's shoulders. Sendara backed away with a satisfied nod. "Perfect."

Julien didn't know where to look. Smiling to herself, Sendara seemed not to see. "I have enough flowers to make another," she said. "We'll wear these home. Why not? We will be Seers someday. Seeresses. We *ought* to be crowned." It was hard to tell from her tone if she was serious. As she skipped lightly over roots and stones, her fingers were already at work on the next wreath.

"*Seeress*," Julien said, testing it out. She felt curiously light, herself. "No one says that."

"It's about time they did," said Sendara Diar. "Come. When we return everyone will be staring, but they won't dare say a word. You'll see."

So far that was the nearest she'd come to acknowledging her position among the other students. *They won't dare.* Sendara lifted her hands to her head, set her own completed crown of flowers atop her braids. Her eyes darting to Julien had a sudden mischief. *Like a wood spirit,* Julien thought, and wondered if this was the look that had entranced a Ramadian prince. "I've had an idea," said Sendara. "We should sing together. At Manaia."

Before Julien could ask what that meant, they had arrived back at the castle. They'd barely crossed the threshold of the entrance hall when one of the students ran up to them. Julien recognized him as one of the younger ones, a third-year, perhaps—near their own age. But also a lord's son . . . and one of the chosen. "Lady Diar, I've been looking for you," he panted. "Your father wants you."

"We have a lesson," Julien reminded her, and Sendara waved at her with clear annoyance. "This is more important. I left my harp in the schoolroom. Would you watch over it for me?"

Julien nodded dumbly, then realized a response might be called for. "Of course."

Sendara sped off. The boy who had brought the message trailing her like a neglected dog. For a moment Julien saw through his eyes, or imagined she did; saw how Sendara's red belt neatly cinched and drew attention to a slim waist above generous hips. And then Julien was alone in the entrance hall.

On her way to the schoolroom, she was forced to pass a group of older students in the hall. She scurried, secure in her perpetual invisibility; but this time in the corner of her eye saw one boy nudge another. Snickers arose from the group.

The blood drained from Julien's face as she remembered the flower crown. She snatched it off. That made them laugh harder. Behind her a voice she recognized said, "Laughing at a child? Try being a man." Spoken witheringly. She saw the tall, awkward form of Dorn Arrin, face contorted in a glare as he loomed over the other students.

I'm not a child. She felt on the verge of tears. He at least had meant to help. She hurried on to the schoolroom, head bowed so she would meet no one's eyes. The day had gone grey of a sudden. Most likely it was her own fault. She wanted, hoped for too much; it led to disappointment. Alisse could have told her that.

How she missed her sister in that moment, with her straightforward love and brown eyes like Julien's own.

She was first to arrive in the schoolroom. Sendara Diar's harp was sheltered beneath their desk, beside her own. Julien's instrument was tin. Sendara's was fashioned of willow-wood and gold by a world-renowned Tamryllin craftsman. The same craftsman who had made harps for some of the greatest Seers, including Valanir Ocune and, of course, Sendara's father.

Julien claimed her own harp, set it on her desk. Beside it she placed the flower crown. The petals were already beginning to curl and darken at the edges.

Jealousy is a snake.

Julien felt despairing, of herself most of all. She would lose everything if she could not keep away such corrosive thoughts. Would fail at this, perhaps the most important thing to happen to her. Sendara Diar had opened a window to her life that allowed in light, ideas—learning. Perhaps for the first time.

She could not fail at this.

Julien glanced down again at Sendara's harp and this time noticed something odd. A small folded parchment was wedged between the strings. It could have been accidental. Julien bent to touch the parchment and it fell to the floor. Fell open to words.

All the world's sun in your hair. All the moon's light in your eyes.

* * *

HE had the answer to two questions; one of death, one of life. Or in the latter case, potentially. He didn't know, but now that it was in his hands he had a responsibility. No, two.

Now Valanir Ocune thought he knew the method of the High Master's death.

Such had been his thoughts on the night—shortly after the ugliness with the boy Dexane—when Hendin had brought his answer. His thinned mouth and tensed shoulders telling their own story even before Valanir's door closed behind them. And after—after he'd confirmed what Valanir had suspected—Hendin had said, his face to the window, "I don't know if I should ask what you'll do with this. What it means to you."

As ever, Valanir Ocune was gentle with his friend. More and more he had begun to recall their times together as students. Now that they were coming to the end, the autumn of their years, he found himself looking back to the beginning. There had been a simplicity to Hendin even back then—in his loyalty, and kindness. Qualities that through all the years had lasted . . . were of inexpressible value to Valanir now. Trust was too rare, he thought, to be dismissed as simple. "It sounds to me as if you've guessed."

Hendin shook his head. "I don't know." But he sounded afraid.

"Cai, have you thought . . ." Valanir began. He gave a moment's thought to phrasing. It was important to consider a man's pride. "Have you considered that spring will be blossoming in the lands of your youth, this time of year? Who is there still—your brother? Would he not welcome you back for . . . a visit?"

Hendin stiffened, said coldly, "I will not be scared away." In a different voice, and while turning to leave, Archmaster Hendin said, "I hope the information I bring serves your purpose, whatever that may be. I go now to mourn my friend, this twelfthday of his passing."

With sadness and a measure of worry Valanir shut the door after his friend. He knew Hendin would descend to the chapel to perform rites of mourning, alone, for the High Master. *Ever the best of us. Certainly the best that is here.*

He had asked Hendin to seek in the archives that were locked and forbidden to all but the Archmasters. Specifically, those scrolls that recorded Seers newly made, alongside those who had given them their mark. Valanir Ocune was named in that register for making Lin Amaristoth a Seer. The one time he had performed the rite.

It was much to request of Hendin, a risk; he would have had to extend his search over several nights, late, to escape notice. The scrolls were thrown together haphazardly, which made the task arduous. When at last Hendin found the scroll detailing the Seers made by Archmaster Myre, the list was long. But he had known what to look for and returned to Valanir with the name that mattered: Elissan Diar.

Valanir found himself needing to walk—even at this hour; even if it was a risk. He left his room with a candle in hand, took a turn down the hall. Up one flight of stairs, then another. The castle was silent, not even a whisper of a meeting of the chosen, nor of poets writing through the night in the Tower of the Winds. As if the episode of Gared Dexane had suspended everything, at least for now.

A Seer's mark burned black.

Erisen, we are linked, Lin Amaristoth had said in his last visit to Tamryllin. The bond between Seer and maker, long unexplored, along with so much else that was lost.

Archmaster Myre's bond with a particular Seer had likely cost him his life.

Elissan had been made Seer at the accustomed time—what was usual was the age of thirty-five or upward. There was a series of tests, and the poet in question had to have produced work of distinction. Ultimately it was left to the Archmasters to decide. It made sense that Archmaster Myre, who had been High Master during Elissan's making, had been the one to perform the rite.

Valanir Ocune's thoughts circled to Elissan's chosen, to the boy with the broken mind who was sent away. Valanir's source had been unable to discover more than what everyone else knew—Elissan Diar safeguarded his secrets well, even as he flaunted them in the open. The clandestine meetings, the tensions developing in the past year, were one with a larger pattern. Elissan had schemed from a distance. Had used people like Marten Lian and Maric Antrell to achieve his ends . . . undoubtedly used them still. Especially now that Marten Lian was High Master, and Elissan entrenched within the Academy in proximity to his little coterie. His "chosen."

That was one piece of what Valanir Ocune had learned tonight. But there was yet another. The link between Seer and maker flowed both ways. If it could be used to kill . . . what else could it do?

I may yet repay you, he told the eyes of his memory, dark and weary in the pale morning. Death with life. If it could be done.

At the top of the last staircase Valanir unlocked the door to the tower roof. For safety he locked it behind him. The tangle of weeds, wet from rain, seeped through clothing to skin as he navigated the stone paths. The candle shivered at his movements and the breeze.

He remembered something else: the autumn day he had received an invitation from the Academy to return and be made a Seer. He'd been guesting in a castle in the south, enjoying the grape harvest. Awakened after sound sleep to see the note on the chest at the foot of his bed. No one knew how such invitations came. The timing was unusual: Valanir was not yet thirty. A very young age to be made Seer. He'd taken this in stride, though—as his due. He'd known no humility at that age, Valanir recognized with a wince. He'd arrived at Academy Isle, pleased with himself—to discover that Nickon Gerrard had been invited at that same time. Archmaster Sarne had decreed it was time for them both, young as they were.

It was a decision nearly unprecedented. And Valanir often thought about it since, and wondered. Rumors had perhaps reached the Isle— or even signals beyond rumor—that Nick was engaged in dark magic. Valanir had since wondered if this gesture was an attempt to bring Nick back to the fold. Before he was lost. In another time, another age, the Academy might have exerted its powers to punish him. Even have him executed. But in the age of an emasculated Academy, the best they could do was extend an offer of reconciliation. And they'd included Valanir because, in the end, the two were acknowledged equals.

It was the first time Valanir and Nick had seen each other in years, that dreary autumn they were called to the Isle. They kept to their own rooms, did not speak much. They were by then openly rivals, if not outright enemies.

When knowledge of the event reached Elissan Diar, it made him angry. Bruised his pride. That Valanir Ocune and Nickon Gerrard were to be made Seers before the age of thirty, and he was not. He sent messages to the Isle, letting his displeasure be known.

It was Archmaster Myre who put an end to that discussion. He had even sent a message back, cutting, to the effect that perhaps if Master Diar had cared to become a Seer, he should have spent more time in Eivar where Seers are made, engaged in the work of poets. Myre was unimpressed with Diar's extensive roaming in other lands, where he was better known for seducing foreign princesses than writing songs. They had stretched precedent far enough, to his view. When Elissan at last received the invitation, it was years later. But Valanir would have wagered that he never forgot the slight. That it rankled. Elissan Diar had kept a grudge against Archmaster Myre that he'd nursed, awaiting his chance.

It was windy that night on the tower top. The sky was clouded. Valanir thought of Lin Amaristoth in the Tower of Glass, engulfed in the night sky, its adornment of constellations. He imagined her perched on a broken crenel here—being small, she liked to perch on things—the old cloak from Leander Keyen wrapped around her, telling him her observations of the Kahishians. Their magic, their ways. He would have liked to hear.

Valanir could imagine other things, too—despite the hour and all he'd learned tonight—and shook his head in the dark. He pressed ahead through the weeds until he reached the hunched shape, a clot of blackness, that was the toppled statue at the heart of the garden. It loomed taller than he remembered.

That, he noticed right away.

The moon broke free of the clouds. It was on the wane, but he could still see the statue no longer lay on its side. For the first time in centuries it stood upright. *The key* . . . His first thought. Had someone else been here? Raising his candle to the statue's chest he saw more. With the aid of moon and flame Valanir saw detail etched in the stonework: a cloak draped across broad shoulders and pinned with a jeweled brooch; a sword buckled to one hip, the scabbard worked with interconnected leaves and lions rampant. No longer a weathered lump of rock was the face, carved in the proud visage of a prince.

The night was quiet. As the moon passed behind clouds again he combed through the weeds, a hand to his knife. Took every path that wound through what had once been a garden. Soon enough he was satisfied: he was alone on this tower top. Nonetheless Valanir Ocune thought there must be music here, and everywhere in the Academy, even if it did not reach the ear. Barriers were opened, in recent days, that would not be closed again.

CHAPTER

9

ELISSAN Diar's chamber was bright in the hour they came to him, as if in welcome. The windows seemed larger here than in other rooms of the castle and admitted a fresh breeze. Sendara crossed to her father, who had risen from his desk, smiling at her in greeting; his powerful body, lean and muscular as a mountain lion, was out of place in this room. The space seemed too small to contain him, as did the rickety desk.

Father and daughter stood together, their eyes turned to Julien Imara with unnerving synchronicity. Eyes that reinforced the feline comparison. He looked amused, detached, as if observing a small animal. "Who is your friend?"

"This is Julien Imara," said Sendara with a slight smile of her own, her gaze joined to his; as if a jest, privately shared, underlay this exchange.

"She likes to hover in doorways, I see," said Elissan Diar, and his daughter sighed as if he had pointed out the most exasperating thing. "You may enter, Mistress Imara," he went on. "Shut the door."

Julien did, but did not venture further inside. From here she could observe the tall bookshelf flanked by arched windows and lined with books, scrolls, and curiosities. Some volumes were bound in leather. On a higher shelf, a figurine of an impossibly slender, nude woman with long hair, done in white jade or ivory; a stoppered bottle that appeared to have been carved from a single block of amber; a gold penknife.

On the wall across from the desk hung a tapestry like nothing Julien had seen: she was accustomed to hunting scenes, depictions from myth or of the gods. This showed a pattern of colors and shapes that though inanimate, seemed to writhe, evaded her attempt to make sense of it. The art of lands far away, here at the edge of the world.

She wondered if, when Sendara and Elissan Diar viewed the tapestry, they saw something different. If these convulsions of color made a coherent whole to their eyes. After all they'd learned, and had seen. She wondered what it would be like to have eyes that could view such chaos and see in it some design.

It was sometimes hard to believe she and Sendara were so different; that the other girl stood so far ahead, as at a mountain's summit. At times like this, or in lessons, it was clear. At other times, friendship seemed to even the balance. Just the night before, they had sneaked out to the woods, suppressing laughter as they evaded the Masters who patrolled the hallways at bedtime. If they were caught? "You know they can't do anything," Sendara had said with blissful confidence. The moon was out, and besides, they knew the way. After a time they came to a hillock, bare of trees or knobby roots, where the moss was deep as a featherbed and softer. There they sat and shared cakes stolen from the kitchens, along with a flask of elderberry wine of mysterious provenance. Sendara would say only that such things were an Archmaster's prerogative.

The wine had warmed Julien against the chill of night. She felt possessed of such exhilaration that it was an effort to remain composed. But she was composed. It was essential not to show feeling.

The emotion is too raw, Sendara had said of Lacarne's verses.

After they had eaten and drunk their fill, the girls lay on their backs in the downy moss, side by side. Clouds made a tattered film across the moon. "That one," Julien had said, pointing, "looks like a lady." She saw a delicate profile, stars like ornaments caught in windblown hair.

Sendara agreed. "A goddess," she said. "Not Kiara or Estarre. One of the ancient goddesses. Vizia."

"Vizia," Julien repeated, the name strange and lovely on her tongue.

Later they returned to the castle. They moved with stealth, but the halls were quiet. Julien accompanied Sendara to her room, for the first time had a chance to see it. It was on another floor from hers, separate, in the wing where the Archmasters slept. Archmaster Diar had clearly wanted his daughter to have every luxury in her new home. The room was hung with lace and velvet draperies; lace swathed even the bed. All of it white. Her gold harp stood at the window. On a shelf were a few books, leatherbound and tooled with gold—treasures. Beside them a carved wood box, perhaps for jewelry. There were other things: A dancer carved of white stone, skirts captured in frenzied motion. A dagger with a jewel in the hilt. And more that Julien did not have a chance to take in, for it would be rude to stare.

"Stay," Sendara had said, when Julien turned to go. "That way we can talk until we fall asleep."

So Julien had undressed there, and got into the bed. It was wider than Julien had in her room, enough for two. Sendara wore a lace nightdress and lent Julien a shift that by some miracle fit, though it was long, and snug at the waist. They lay and talked for a time. Sendara was first to drift off, her lips going soft with sleep. When Julien realized, she felt as if, for the first time, she could think about how she felt, now that she was alone with her thoughts; but even still felt suspended in a dream beyond thought. Nothing felt real about that night. Or that was her fear, that it couldn't be real. So at last, after watching the clouds from Sendara's window for what may have been a long time, she, too, fell into sleep.

The morning brought a change in mood; Sendara was curt as she ran a brush through her hair, bid Julien dress and go to her own room before they were discovered. Julien had tried not to feel downcast, recalled to herself the confidences they had exchanged in the dark. And of course, later that day, she leaped at the chance to visit Archmaster Diar's rooms, the first time she had been invited. Various firsts were happening, it seemed to her—all at once.

Now as the Archmaster and his daughter stood together, Julien wondered if they had forgotten she was there. He addressed Sendara as if they were alone. "I wanted you to see this passage," he said. Though he spoke quietly, Julien thought she heard a repressed intensity. "It proves there was discussion of the idea much earlier than we supposed. See." He pointed to the scroll on the desk. The parchment wisped up at the ends, pinned in place with his finger. His ring, Julien saw, was a blue stone with an opaline explosion at its heart. A star sapphire. She could not recall what it meant, only that it was rare.

Still standing, Sendara bent to read, loose hair falling forward. She looked up at her father with a new awe. "Is this the original?"

"Of course not." He laughed. "Look at its condition—only a few hundred years old. It is a copy, though rare."

Sendara tossed her hair aside to look up at him. "The reign of Seers," she said. "Can it be?"

He was solemn, but it seemed put on with effort, a mask for rising elation. His fingers interlaced with hers. The window seemed to frame, contain the two of them in sun-filled radiance.

They shine. Julien thought of the note that had been stuck between Sendara's papers today. The girls had turned around a moment from their desk, talking, and when they looked back again it was there. The only sign Sendara gave that her composure was shaken was the hurried way she pushed back her hair as she opened the parchment. She turned it around so Julien could see. *For the gift of your light I would give my life.*

A bit clumsy—the rhyme within the phrase—and wholly unoriginal, Julien had thought; but Sendara had turned pink, her mouth pursed in her satisfied half-smile. She seemed unsurprised, even though she had no more idea of the identity of the note-writer than Julien had. That such an admirer would exist, she took for granted.

It was the fourth note in as many days. They were not improving in artistry, but seemed to be scaling up in their desperation. So Julien thought, knowing it was uncharitable. Now when she and Sendara walked together in the halls, passing groups of students, the girls would covertly glance about, but it was impossible to single out who the aspiring swain could be. Most of the students tended to avoid looking at Sendara Diar, much as one avoids looking at the sun. *They won't dare,* Sendara had said. Only Maric Antrell, leader of Elissan Diar's chosen, at times met her gaze with a heated, fearless look that made Sendara glance away with confusion. He was too pale, the skin on his cheekbones drawn tight; he had become painfully thin. It made his gaze appear ravenous. A thrill for her, but an uneasy one.

He might have written the notes, after all. Neither girl spoke of this possibility. Maric Antrell was handsome, and a lord's son, and moreover in obvious favor with Elissan Diar. But he made both girls uneasy.

Now Elissan said, disengaging his hand from that of his daughter, "So tell me." His tone turned playful. "What brings the two of you here?"

Sendara stood at attention as if to recite. Drawing a breath, she said,

"I've been thinking about Manaia. I think I should sing, and I'll need a partner."

"Manaia. Of course." Elissan Diar turned his gaze back on Julien a moment. "I hadn't given it thought, but you are right. You should sing, and of course Mistress Imara may join you."

At last Julien spoke. "So I may understand," she began, feeling their eyes on her, "what shall we be singing?"

Sendara looked askance. "How can you not know about Manaia? Well, every spring it is a festival held here on the Isle. The songs are for the competition."

"Competition." Julien swallowed. "With the other students?"

Sendara raised her eyebrows. "Who else? We must write and perform a song together. But Father," she said, "so far we've had no sessions in the Tower of the Winds. How are we to write?"

"The Tower is for advanced students only," said Elissan Diar, in a tone that settled the matter. He glanced at the window. "Is there something else? I hope to make more headway with this scroll before midday. And now with Valanir Ocune gone, I must meet with Archmaster Lian to decide which of his tasks will fall to me."

"Valanir Ocune, gone?" Julien squeaked. Her hand went to her mouth. "Sorry. Is he all right?"

Elissan Diar smiled—she thought, politely. "I expect so," he said. "He's left us with a fearsome load of work, and without warning. Sneaked off in the night, apparently. We'll need a new liaison with Tamryllin."

Something in Julien plummeted at the words. She recalled the exchange with Valanir Ocune after the death of Archmaster Myre. He had shown a trace of concern for her, albeit preoccupied with more important matters.

"He's untrustworthy," said Sendara.

"It was ever thus," said her father without rancor. "In any case. I must return to my work."

"Very well," said Sendara. "I'll see you later, Julien."

Julien found herself back in the quiet of the hallway, the door thudding behind her.

After the encompassing light of the room, the stairwell was dark. She felt she had shut the door on something of immense value. Each step down the dim stairway, a step nearer obscurity.

Julien reminded herself that she and Sendara Diar would be competing together at Manaia. She was a part of something; and as she learned more, this would become more true. Not forever would she hover in doorways.

These thoughts felt suspiciously like bluster, but she carried on down the stairs, trailing her fingertips along the cool stones. The noise of the main floor, of boys running and laughing in corridors, a ghost of a sound. It had been a long climb to the top. On the way up, that morning, they had spoken about mothers. She could not remember now how it had begun.

"I haven't seen mine since I was ten," Sendara had said. A chill threading the words. It was strange they had gotten on the subject at all, Julien thought now, considering how unwilling Sendara seemed to speak of it. She'd been ahead of Julien on the stairs, skirts an elegant sway to the movement of her hips. "It matters not. She doesn't understand . . . things. Father took me away to see the world, to learn all there is to know, and she couldn't stand it."

Julien felt kinship with Sendara, whose life was otherwise so different from her own. "I think I know what you mean," she said, and began to talk of her own mother, though in short, pained sentences. For some reason it was still painful.

Sendara cut her off. "It's not the same," she said, the chill in her voice intensified. "My mother is a Haveren of Deere. The most beautiful woman in Eivar, it is said. Noble and beautiful, both. The Deere estates are centuries old. Before my father won her, she had twenty suitors, each more noble than the last. Songs are dedicated to her name."

"All right," Julien had said, bewildered at this torrent. Her own mother was of noble blood as well, but it seemed clear that it was different to be a Haveren of Deere. Whatever that was. Sheltered amid olive groves she had been all her life. She knew nothing of power or politics.

It was true Julien's mother would not be considered beautiful. Neither of her parents was anything extraordinary. The Imaras were sturdy and enduring, it could perhaps be said. No songs had been written of them, nor would ever be.

When Julien arrived on the main floor the clatter of the students had abated—everyone was at their lesson. She was late for a history lesson with Archmaster Lian. It might be better, she considered, not to go in at all. She could instead go out to the wood and lose herself awhile. No one would remark upon it. In the distance, the sound of obedient singing; a class reviewing scales. A melody that lilted up, and up, before plunging all the way down to begin again.

She recalled the light at the top of the stairs, the abstruse art, the books. *The books.* Instinct had held her back from crossing the threshold of that room. Someone of her origin could hope, at most, for an occasional window to the greater world. Not a door.

"WHAT do you know about love?" This floated to Dorn Arrin when he was poring over a text on ancient lore in advance of their next lesson. His head made a quick shiver, like a dog swatting a gnat. "Nothing," he said. "Why?"

Etherell Lyr grinned. He should have been studying as Dorn was, but instead sat at the window in a shaft of morning light, whittling a bit of wood. His long, tapered fingers lent themselves to fine work. "No reason."

"I know you've been leaving notes for Diar's daughter," said Dorn. "I can only imagine the banality of the phrases."

"Yes, I should have asked your help with that," said Etherell, and laughed. "But I wouldn't want to set . . . expectations. She'll see I have other talents than poetry."

"You know enough about love for both of us, in that case." Dorn turned the page. With renewed resolve he tried to read the words of his text, but the letters melted out of focus. The silence between them seemed companionable from Etherell's side; he hummed as wood dropped in sinuous curls to the floor, like smoke in reverse.

Finally Dorn spoke again. "Are you hoping to become an Archmaster's son?"

His friend shrugged. "I haven't thought that far ahead. But Dorn, have you ever seen anything more lovely?"

"Any*thing*?"

"You know what I mean."

"What I know is she is barely sixteen," said Dorn.

"Where I come from that's of age to marry," said Etherell. "Don't be a stick, Dorn. It's tiresome."

"I'll try not to be tiresome." Dorn tilted his book upright to shield his face from view.

He heard the chair scrape the floor, just before the book was pulled back. Etherell had his hands on either side of its leaves. "I'm sorry," he said. He wasn't smiling anymore. "I didn't mean that. I rarely do."

"You say things you don't mean?" said Dorn, looking away, afraid not to look away. But he had seen his friend's stricken look and wanted to hold it in his memory, tight like a blanket on a winter's night.

He heard rather than saw the smile return as Etherell said, "All the time. It's integral to a gentleman's upbringing." He let go of Dorn's book and stood upright.

"Not surprising," said Dorn. He cleared his throat. "Well then. As a gentleman—what do you intend to do next?"

"What do I intend?" Etherell flung his arms wide like an actor declaiming. He jumped up to stand on the chair in the beam of sunlight. Captured there an instant in gold. "I intend, Master Arrin, to win the heart of a splendid beauty. To perform beside you at Manaia. And . . . I suppose earn my ring and graduate while I am at it."

"Quite a recitation. Shall I applaud?" Dorn said wryly. "You have impressive plans considering this place is tumbling about our ears. I'd be surprised if any of us graduate. What with Archmaster Myre suddenly dead, the chosen running things, and now Valanir Ocune gone—conveniently, if you ask me."

Etherell shook his head mock-sorrowfully. He dismounted the chair in an agile leap. "The cantankerousness of the bookbinder. I shall write a poem about it."

"A plague on golden lords," said Dorn. "Another poem for you."

"Set that plague against Maric Antrell—my rival for Sendara Diar's affections," said Etherell. "He looks to be starving to death, but it's not happening fast enough."

"That's certainly true . . . on both counts," said Dorn. But a heaviness had come over him. "Really, though, Etherell . . . don't you want to know what happened to Valanir Ocune? It seems unlike him to disappear without so much as a farewell . . . with not even a dull speech as seems the constant practice here."

"He's not an Archmaster," Etherell pointed out.

"Very well . . . with a not-dull speech. Or a song. *Something.*"

Etherell's eyes were intense on his. "What are you suggesting?"

"You must know," said Dorn. "I don't want to even say it. I like Valanir Ocune, as it happens. Most of my life I wanted to be him. Now, with everything that's happened . . . I wonder."

"So many worries." Etherell was shaking his head. "How *do* you sleep?"

"I lie to myself." His turn to say something he didn't mean. If he had succeeded in lying to himself, Dorn thought, he would probably sleep better.

But his tone was sufficiently convincing: his friend grinned and went back to carving. More wood curls trailed to the floor. Etherell's demeanor was entirely relaxed, as if the act took the place of thought. The shape that had begun to emerge from the wood was thin, elongated, but that was all Dorn could see so far.

Now when Dorn Arrin tried again to read, he instead found himself seeing the future, a vista in his mind's eye. He saw himself and his friend enter the dining hall that evening, and before everyone—student and Archmaster alike—Etherell advancing with purpose down the length of the table to the lovely thing at the end of it, and presenting to her the gift he'd made. And in that moment Sendara Diar would know who had written the little half-poems praising her beauty, and she would be enthralled. She'd have to be. Moments ago when Etherell Lyr had stood on the chair, arms outstretched, he could have been wrought in sunlight. Dorn knew himself for lost, but also knew—just as surely—he would not be the only one.

HE saw towers that rose from mist. That was the first thing. White they were, gilded in sunrise, with turrets like gold teeth. A whisper within him, a name, muffled as if by the mist. As he drew nearer, swooping from above like a bird, he saw the sweep of mountains beyond, a wall of green. Somewhere deep in there were the fires, he knew. He had seen them. Until the night they had reached him, and he'd burned. Shrieking, lost to agony.

Pain made him remember: the sword he had gripped in a ghostly hand. Slicing as if bones were butter. Too easy. Piles of limbs collapsing at his feet like dolls shattered in a child's rage. People seen as if through fog, their features indistinct, so they never seemed to him like people at all. Their blood a river that never stained him, left him clean.

It was all a game, until the fires.

A man's voice grated in his ears. That name again. Now he could hear it. *Almyria.*

And another voice, this one melodious and a part of him after countless long nights of joining with his. *"Be one with the earth. With peace."*

A blinding pain was last he knew. That and a dying murmur in his ear. *Almyria.* A final image—the towers, ringed in flame.

AT dawn the thing that had been Gared Dexane was entombed in a cove on the northern shore of the Isle—its most desolate, where no one went. There was not much left to inter. His flesh had rapidly liquefied from bone. Only the lidless eyes were intact, bewildered. Grey surf roared on the breakers as they worked, winds from the north a claw that struck again and again, as if spring had never come.

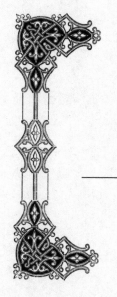

PART II

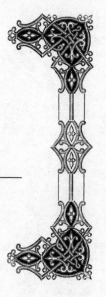

CHAPTER
10

IT had been years since Nameir Hazan had seen the mountains. The last campaign of Mansur Evrayad had taken them away from Kahishi, south to the Islands of Pyllankaria and a siege that had lasted three years. Yusuf had ordered his son to take the fortress there, that bestrode a profitable stretch of sea. Over years, rising in the ranks, Nameir had become accustomed to salt winds, relentless sun, the tedious privations of siege warfare.

What they faced here in the northern marches of Kahishi was different. In truth, Nameir didn't believe they were equipped to handle it. But even she, Mansur's second-in-command, couldn't tell him that. Besides, he knew as well as she how hopeless was their situation. They were faced with an enemy who could attack without warning, as if from nowhere; who evaded barriers as if they were air. Villagers told of awakening to find marauders within their walls with no sign of having scaled or tunneled under them. They set fire to homes, slaughtered and maimed, and by morning had vanished as swiftly as they'd appeared. Leaving no traces even for Mansur's most skilled trackers. Those who died on the field of battle remained; the rest vanished with the sun.

Another strangeness: the enemy dead disintegrated at unnatural speed—an added form of vanishing. The flesh melted from their bones within moments, a sickening spectacle even on the battlefield, where horrors were commonplace. Some of Mansur's men, overcome by the sight and smell, had been unable to stop themselves retching on the spot.

It was magic, and this forced them to rely on guidance from the Tower of Glass. The Magicians were often in Mansur's thoughts, warning of an attack on a village or town, so Mansur could mobilize his men to ride with all speed to the site. But this was a flawed strategy, and even the king's Magicians were not all-seeing. Only the god was that, and the One tended not to interfere in the battles of men, at least not as far as she could see.

Nameir still prayed to the One, the Unnamed, despite her years serving in battle with Kahishians. A secret she kept, along with that of her sex, from all in the battalion but Mansur.

She found him in the watchtower, alone. He liked it there, she knew, as if the vistas and steady wind lent him temporary reprieve. But this morning he had the look of a man who'd seen a djinn.

She climbed to sit beside him on the ledge. "Is there news?"

"Last night," he said. He blinked at her. Nameir thought she had never seen him so exhausted, his face drawn in rugged lines. Nonetheless she thought he was handsome as his smooth-faced brother. "I received a dispatch from Zahir Alcavar. My brother has ordered Vizier Miuwiyah to send his men here as reinforcements. Despite the political headache of that. Miuwiyah will demand the world in compensation. I'll have to give him joint command."

"What is happening?"

"They're done going after villages, it seems." Mansur's face was a mask of fatigue. "This time they want the prize."

She closed her eyes. Had been expecting this since the raids began. "Almyria." Proud city of the north. That unlike the provinces had never entirely surrendered to King Yusuf, but paid tribute in gold and men-at-arms. A city that long ago, before worshipers of the Thousand-Named God came to Kahishi, was the capital.

Nameir had seen it once. With its square towers and grey fortifications, Almyria was more austere than Majdara to the south. But within the castle, and the Temple that had once been dedicated to strange gods, were stores of wealth and art said to be without parallel. Even some treasures said to be enchanted, gifts to rulers of Almyria from their gods. Among the warriors of Nameir's acquaintance a particular favorite was the tale of a golden sword that could hew through rock. That seemed fanciful to her. As a girl she had journeyed to the Temple of Almyria and seen the altar where once animals had been ritually sacrificed for the glory of long-forgotten gods. In general, what people were willing to do—and kill—for their god was of interest to Nameir Hazan. It had, after all, determined the course of her life.

"I can only wonder what delayed them this long," said Mansur. "If walls mean nothing to them."

"The city poses a greater challenge," she pointed out. "So far the forces attacking the villages have been some hundred men-at-arms. Lord Ferran commands many more."

"You assume they will not send a greater force this time." He shook his head. "That's the worst of it—we don't know what they can do."

"Your grace, perhaps . . ." She swallowed.

"Tell me your thought, Hazan."

"Perhaps until now they've been—practicing."

The word was bile in her mouth. Too clear were the memories of ransacked homes and the scenes of an abattoir that greeted them—hacked limbs of entire families strewn in blood. It was senseless torture—no spoils were ever taken. Even the farm animals hacked to death. This, for practice? Nameir could see this thought pass through Mansur's mind before he said, "What a terrible idea. You may be right. Unless . . ." He gazed from the parapet of the crude wooden tower. It offered a view of mountains, green with the spring, distanced from them with a blanketing of wildflower fields. At this time of day the surface of Hariya, the tallest mountain, was as interlaced with shadow and light as cut crystal. There were tales of caves in the depths of that mountain. Rivers of gold, it was said, and crowns, and encrusted goblets of all kinds. Creatures that granted wishes to mortals foolish enough to hazard their destinies on magic. Such tales as were spun over so many years one never knew when or how they'd begun.

"I know little of the Fire Dancers, Hazan, yet . . . I wonder," said Mansur. "If something—something new—has happened that's made them more confident. Or stronger."

CLIMBING down from the watchtower, Nameir felt misgivings she could not have given a name to. That sort of articulation was better left to her commander. On some nights by the communal fires during the dragging years of the siege, Mansur would recite poetry of his own composition. Much of it about war; he might compare lovemaking to the frenzy of battle, a grove of cedars to lances, ripples in a stream to the rivets in armor. Other poems were tender, elegies for gardens that burst into flower as he lay siege on a bare rock in the sea, many leagues from home.

Those nights she would sit among the men as Mansur Evrayad spun words into intricate tapestries. And a fatalistic sensation would grip Nameir, as if she were armed with only a dagger, on foot, watching the swift advance of a horde of cavalrymen with spears.

So many things Nameir Hazan hid from the world, when she herself was not complex. At least, she didn't believe she was. She wanted only two things in life. One was impossible; the other could only be achieved through concealment. A woman in this army would not have been tolerated, and a Galician just barely. Years ago Mansur had guessed at the first, and she had revealed the second, with a defiant lift of her chin. And he'd laughed. In the early years, drunk on young triumph and the thrill of battle, he laughed often.

"Hazan, it's nothing to me if you are beardless or worship a false god," he'd said. "You have the fire that's needed, and a quick mind. You may not best a bull-chested mounted opponent wielding a two-sided axe, but . . . you just might, actually, by outwitting him. So never mind all this. You *must* stay at my side."

So she had done that, and over years risen to second-in-command. She had stood at the side of Prince Mansur on the day he was wed to a vizier's daughter, a pretty young girl named Alyoka. The vizier was of an unruly sort, with ideas about independence; Yusuf wanted him contained. An alliance of marriage would help there, and Eldakar was being saved for Ramadus. That had been several years ago. Alyoka lived with her parents. She had brought a daughter into the world, a princess, that Mansur had held in his arms only once. Sometimes at night he could be stirred to songs of the home hearth—of the tenderness of a wife, the sweetness of an infant child. These songs invariably seemed half-hearted to Nameir. She suspected they arose more from guilt than longing. Or perhaps a sentiment that arose at lonesome twilight, due to vanish with the dawn.

Mansur liked fighting too much.

Most of his time, and therefore Nameir's, was occupied with battle. As second-in-command to the prince, she was compensated handsomely. Lately she'd commissioned a sword and set of knives that would have been the perishing envy of her younger self. There had been some concern, when she was a girl, that as a woman she would fail to pass anymore. But the god in his mercy had made Nameir exceptionally tall and broad, and flat-chested. She claimed her father had been unable to grow a beard, endured jeers that in time faded to respect. She learned to ride and obtained a charger of her own. All that a warrior could want, other than a title and land, and these were undoubtedly forthcoming if she survived.

But in the course of things, the inevitable had happened. It was predictable, she knew. Mansur was everything a man should be. It was something to conceal for the rest of her life.

Nameir could do that. She had been orphaned very young in a raid and survived, fought her way to second-in-command. She could stand firm, even on nights when that horde of cavalry glowered across the horizon of her heart.

Thoughts along these lines were a litany she told herself, or a song, though one which would never possess the grace of Mansur's verses. One thing Nameir recalled from a childhood withered to ash was her father singing at an altar to the Unnamed God. The talisman that music and words, even forbidden words, could be.

MALLIN was watching Nameir when she climbed down from the watchtower. She smiled wryly; he must have found some excuse to be there. The pale-haired, square-jawed young recruit, formerly a child slave from the east, looked to Nameir more than most. She had made the training of him her particular project. He had the makings of a leader.

When he saw her, he shook his head. "So. A dispatch?"

She glanced around, but there was no one else nearby. "Almyria," she said.

He whistled. "At last."

"You're not surprised."

"What would those fuckers want with the villages? Of course this is where it was going." Mallin spat. "This is magic like nothing I have ever heard, Commander. Where I come from there are hexes, charms. There are dead that rise and drink the blood of maidens at sunset. But this? What *are* these Fire Dancers?"

"They are monsters," she said. "Perhaps they weren't always. Some foul magic has made them so."

THAT day Nameir oversaw preparations for the march on Almyria. They would depart at first light. Vizier Miuwiyah's forces would meet theirs at the crossing of the Iberra. As she inspected the ranks she noted how weary were Mansur's men from the past weeks. It was not only that they'd been called upon, repeatedly and without respite, to hasten to sites of attack. She thought even these men, not above pillage themselves, must be weary to the soul after what they'd seen. Not even hardened men like these wanted to see children lying split open in the thoroughfare. It was difficult for all but the most curdled among them. Especially when each time signified their failure. The mission was to defend the villages, and so far they'd had—at best—mixed results.

But Nameir knew that to show compassion for their weariness could lead to lapses in discipline, further failures. So she harangued the men to make ready their armor and weapons for the greatest fight they'd faced. They would have to draw upon all they knew of contending with a broken siege.

If Nameir allowed herself to think too long about the implications of an enemy such as this, she was gripped with an icy paralysis. How could they win? But what did it mean to lose? There had been no demands, no terms of surrender.

Too many gaps in all of this; it didn't make sense.

Unless it was simply that the Renegade, the self-styled King of the North, sought revenge on the sons of Yusuf Evrayad for the father's betrayal. The former king had promised the Renegade lands south of the mountains if they joined as allies. For a time, the Fire Dancers had fought at Yusuf's side in battles from Meroz as far east as Belgarve. But upon their return, something had gone wrong. The Renegade had taken his troops and returned to his mountain fortress. No lands were forthcoming for the Fire Dancers who for centuries had lived hardscrabble on the margins of Kahishi. Their dance still forbidden within the borders, punishable by death.

Now in possession of a new, dreadful magic, they sought vengeance.

IT was dusk when the man in white was sighted. Sunset faded towards twilight, and above Hariya there sparked the evening star. Nonetheless the men guarding the camp spotted the stranger. They saw he was alone. He walked with an odd gait, half-limping, for some hours in the distance. When horsemen from the camp rode to accost him, the man in white ceased his halting advance, and, standing with arms akimbo, watched them come.

So it was told to Mansur Evrayad and Nameir Hazan. The prince ordered the man brought before him.

His eyes would live in her dreams. That was the first thought Nameir had at the sight of the man in white. His garment was a robe, no armor or visible weapon. Nothing to indicate a threat. Only his eyes gave her pause. The pupils had dilated until the irises all but disappeared; black eyes, and mad. His cheeks sunken as if with hunger, rough from sun and wind. His face overgrown with greying hair.

Six men escorted the stranger to Mansur's tent. Twisting his arms behind him, they forced him to sit on a bench at the table. Torchlight made erratic shadows across the face of the man in white as he laughed. When he spoke she glimpsed broken teeth. "I come with the key to your lives," he said. "Or your deaths."

Mansur fingered his sword hilt. "You'd best not speak lightly of death."

The man in white laughed again. "The prince seeks a duel of tongues, since swords have failed him? If you would like to fail somewhat less, hear me out. I know the source of your enemy's power, prince. And how to stop it."

Nameir looked at Mansur; his eyes narrowed. "Do you? Why should I believe you?"

"You can choose whether or not to believe once you've heard the tale," said the man in white. "In exchange, I want a horse and a purse of gold. I weary of these lands, and the dance."

Mansur's fist came down on the table, hard. "You think to set bargains? I'll judge if this tale of yours is worth even that."

"It surely is." The man smiled toothily and wide. "It concerns the queen."

NAMEIR was uneasy that night. She paced back and forth in her tent. She didn't like that Mansur had ordered her and the guards to leave him alone with the man in white the moment the queen was named. It was not at all like him. It was a risk to his safety. Who knew what tricks this Fire Dancer might get up to? There was too little they knew of their ways—and their powers.

Her thoughts turned to Rihab Bet-Sorr, wed to Eldakar less than a year. Nameir tended to avoid thinking of her. During their last stay in the Zahra, she had seen Mansur's eyes when the queen was near. His transparency in those moments almost touching. It made Nameir Hazan sorrowful in ways she preferred to avoid.

Such feelings on his part were to be expected—Rihab had that effect. For her sake Eldakar had compromised his country's fragile peace with Ramadus.

It concerns the queen. With those words, Mansur had turned pale. When he ordered everyone from the tent it was with barely contained anger, but Nameir also noted the sudden terror in his eyes.

In that she had to have been mistaken—Mansur Evrayad feared nothing. A strength and a weakness, both, one she knew well. Nameir drew some deep breaths to soothe her nerves, a trick her commander had taught her. Whatever was happening, she would find out on the morrow. Her duty was to be rested for the long march at first light. She curled into her blankets for sleep.

DARK surrounded Nameir. Men's voices, braiding as one in wordless song. The dark began to clear, first with a glimmer of firelight. As the light strengthened it became flames. These leaped and merged until at last they were one, a whispering, hissing wall. The heat pressed on her cheeks.

The voices reached higher, as if with the flames. A man stood with his back to her, watching them. He turned and saw her. He was pale-skinned, with hair like a lion's mane. In his hands a gold, stringed instrument.

"In the stars," he said with a brilliant smile. "It is written."

And then he changed. A different man was before her, a different face against the flames: an elderly man, his beard entirely white. His mouth gaping wide, a silent scream. About his right eye fire made a complex symbol; his flesh began to melt. Now she heard him; his agonies stove through her skull.

Nameir woke with a start. It was still night. The only sound in the tent her breathing. Outside, the murmur of guards on their shifts, the metallic click of armor buckles as they paced. Nothing amiss.

Nonetheless she climbed from the blankets and began to pull on her clothes. She could not have said why. No time for armor, but the leather tunic, her swordbelt and dagger. With detachment she noticed she was shivering. Perhaps because of the night's chill on her bare legs as she drew on her trousers. Perhaps.

When Nameir exited her tent, the guards outside hailed her, but were noticeably surprised. "Just a walk," she said, and kept on. Her feet led the way before her mind had time to decide. But of course that was where she was going. Not why. But where.

Torches guided her in the dark. Men backed away as she passed, ceased their chatter. There were few guarding; most were asleep. It was—oddly, considering what they dealt with here—a peaceful night. The camp sheltered in a cluster of fir trees that fanned against the dark of the sky, lit at their base with torches. From the boughs crickets sang as if there were no such thing as pain, or war.

Nights could be deceptive, of course.

Men stood guard outside Mansur's tent, which was larger and grander than the rest. Without, the banner of his dynasty drooped toward the ground, gold on red. Nameir said, "I have orders. Let me pass." The men fell back.

Torches blazed in here, too, so the sight that greeted Nameir would forever be etched in her mind, incongruously, with a tint of gold. Mansur slumped at the table, chin in chest, eyes shut. As if asleep. But it was not a peaceful scene, if only for one reason: red, red, red everywhere.

She was shaking him, slapping his face. "My prince." She slapped him again. "My *prince*!"

He stirred. She had meanwhile had a chance to take in some things. Blood beaded his face, sprayed from cheekbone to forehead. Yet although the front of his tunic was soaked all the way down to the belt, there was no sign of a wound. "My prince." Her voice a whisper.

He looked as if she had aroused him from sleep. His drowsy brown eyes puzzled. "Hazan, what is it? Your battle . . . is not with me."

"Why are you covered in blood?"

His eyes widened. In those moments reminding her of a boy. "I don't know, Nameir." He stared down at his clothes. "I don't know what's happened."

She gripped his shoulder. "Mansur," she said. "You know you can tell me anything. Anything at all."

He nodded. Was looking down with a childlike fixation. "I know. I know." She waited, but he did not say more. He raised his hands to eye level, and stared. They were caked with red.

She kept her voice even. "Where is the prisoner?"

SHE was running. There was blood on her shirt now, as well as on her hands; men were staring. She sprinted to the tent where the prisoner was kept under guard. Except there were no guards at the entrance to the tent. A foul odor met her like a gut-punch instead. When Nameir raced past the threshold, there was none in the dark but her. Her and the corpse.

The man in white was sprawled facedown on the floor in a fast-spreading pool of blood. Kneeling, she gripped him by the scruff of the neck and lifted his head. The wound was to the throat, a slash so deep his head was barely still attached. His face already rotting from the skull, black and loose.

Gone to hell. She let fall the body and sat back on her heels. The stench of decay like an assault.

She recalled the last words she'd heard the man speak in this life. The center of the tale that would give them knowledge they sought desperately—a means to thwarting the Fire Dancers' magic.

The queen.

CHAPTER
11

VOICES raised in anger were not what Lin expected to hear outside her door in the morning. If it was, in fact, the morning. She hardly knew when it was that Zahir had escorted her back from the imperial gardens. But the light angling through the window beside her bed was wan, not the concentrated glare of a Kahishian noon. The raps at her door were frantic, and she clasped the knife from her bedside table as she rose and wrapped herself in a gown. She had enough time to think that this was unusual—a servant should have come to announce whoever this was. Whereupon she opened the door and saw her men standing before her, their breaths coming fast, and with reddened faces. Ned Alterra, looking furious. And Garon Senn, more composed but alert.

"You two." Lin drew back. "What is this?"

"We would have a word with you," said Ned.

Once the door had shut, Ned looked to Garon Senn as if he might spit him on iron. "Tell her."

Her master-of-arms grimaced. The gaze he turned towards Lin was one almost seductive, as if to solicit her confidence. What they'd shared had been intimacy of a sort—the dance of blades. She wondered if he thought it made her vulnerable. "You'd better tell me what this is about," said Lin, in a tone to end whatever such thoughts he might have. "I have rarely—no, never—seen Lord Alterra this furious."

"He is a boy."

"No," Lin said coldly. "He is my right hand. You'd do well to remember that, if you plan on continuing to serve me. Do you?"

"It is Ned who would have other plans for me," he said, spreading his hands.

"*Tell her*," said Ned.

Garon Senn shook his head. "It is no great thing. My lady, surely you knew that a man like myself—a fighting man—is no stranger to Kahishi. It is how I gained the skill and experience to serve you."

"He served under Yusuf Evrayad, years ago," said Ned. "They know him here. The guards. They recognize him. That's why you avoided them on the journey," he added to Garon Senn. "You were hiding."

Lin stared. "Is this true?"

"I hide nothing," snarled her man-at-arms. "I avoided men who might, if they recognized me, cause trouble for my lady. Yes, I served King Yusuf for a time. I helped him conquer this land for himself. Laid siege, with him, to the fortress of the Fire Dancers. Later, I served lords who offered greater bounty. There are, then, some grudges. I attribute it to jealousy." His fierce grin a gleam of teeth. Lin found it appealing, and it also made her shudder inwardly. *What have I brought into my camp?* What appealed in him was what lay at the root of her, from which the likes of Rayen and their mother had sprung. She had not understood it before. She felt cold all over. Power lay, so much, with knowing whom one could trust.

Ned's rage flared. "*Jealousy*." He turned to Lin. "In the guardroom they have a name for him. *Zevek*. Do you know what it means?"

Her gaze was on Garon Senn as she spoke. His eyes were emotionless as ever. "Tell me, Ned."

"The Jackal." Ned drew a breath, attempted to speak calmly. "This man has a reputation for savagery beyond even what is usual for—a fighting man. Or let's be honest and call him what he is: a mercenary. So monstrous were his acts in the field that even the lords who hired him were forced to distance themselves. That was when he returned to Eivar where the pay was less, but jobs still to be had. That is how, in the end, he came to you."

"And now my name is to be associated with—with this." She turned from both of them, aware of what lay at her back. Her knife still in hand. She stretched out on a divan. Without looking up, she studied the play of light on the blade. Tested the edge with a fingertip.

"My lady," said Garon Senn, "these were events of years ago. I was a different man. In the heat of battle—"

"Be silent." She was most angry at herself. All the signs had been there. She had not wanted to see them. "I can have you killed," she said. "Though it sounds like if I don't take measures to protect you, the guardsmen here will do it for me."

His grin had turned feral. "You would kill me?"

What she saw in his eyes would have shocked her, had she been some-one different. She saw her brother's eyes. "If I were to say yes to that," she said, "you would rape and kill me right here, wouldn't you? Or you imag-ine you could. Two against one, though, Garon Senn. And you'd become a fugitive. Not that that is a new experience for you, but . . ." She sneered. "It seems to me you've had a good life as my creature. Up to the moment your luck ran out. A good life in the palace of Tamryllin, and here."

Garon Senn emitted a hiss. Ned had caught hold of his sword arm. At the same time Lin had risen to stand before her man-at-arms, her knife balanced in hand. He had a grip on his sword hilt, but did not try to draw. If he did, it would be the end, and he had to know that. She knew he was pragmatic enough to wait, and hear her out a moment more.

Lin said, "You may yet be of use to me. Now is your moment to prove yourself, Garon Senn. I have need of information. If you aid me, I will let you live. More than that—I will reward you. Lands and a title are what I offer you, if you deliver what I need. Such as you've always desired."

Garon Senn inclined his head rather than bow, since he was other-wise held fast by Ned. "I will continue to serve my lady with utmost loyalty. As ever."

"Lin," said Ned. He sounded anguished. "The stories they tell . . ."

She shook her head. "Ned, I know—"

"Of *children*." His eyes were agony.

The words were a blow to her heart. She knew they thought of the same thing: a tiny girl in Tamryllin with Rianna's eyes. But: "Ned, let him go," she said gently. To Garon Senn she issued a curt order to leave, to await her in his chambers and speak to no one. She would request Eldakar's help protecting him from vengeance-seekers.

When she was alone with Ned, standing before him and now aware of the inadequacy of her robe in concealing herself, in asserting her rank, she felt acutely tired. "My dear," she said. "I'm so sorry."

If ever he had looked near tears, it was now. But his voice was flat. "I will spare you the specifics of what I heard about him," he said. "I suppose you need never know. For the good of the kingdom, which I assume you serve."

Lin could have wept, too. She would be utterly alone without Ned, and felt him whirling away from her now as if in a current. "Justice would be sweet," she said. "But it wouldn't return anyone's life. I can't explain why I think this is necessary, but . . . the instinct is strong. I must trust it, Ned."

He stared without speaking. Lin noted that he was disheveled, his clothes not hanging right, in a manner similar to when she'd first known him as the awkward suitor of Rianna Gelvan. His hair popped from his forehead, a lank mess that needed cutting. But from his gaze he was hardly awkward and not the boy Garon Senn had called him. He had been up late, she recalled, on assignment for her. And then early that morning, again for her sake. All this she thought before he spoke.

"An instinct, you call it," said Ned Alterra. "But I am not sure what to believe. When I see you I am sometimes not sure it *is* you, Lin. As if something else has taken you over."

"I have to be hard sometimes," she said. "Surely I need not tell you that."

He narrowed his eyes. "Hard, yes," he said. "That, you have always had, even if you didn't know it. But there is something more."

"I'm sorry," she said again. Hearkening back to a prior incarnation of herself, when she had been wont to apologize too frequently; but now it was to sidestep what she would not say. The truth would cause distress to him, and otherwise change nothing.

Ned shrugged, tight-lipped. Looked towards the window. He didn't want to deal with her now, she knew, but also knew he had to.

Lin sat back on the divan, and motioned him to do the same. It was red silk, luxurious like everything else in this room. It was improper to receive visitors in here, she realized belatedly, with the bed adjacent and still tumbled from her sleep. A Court Poet was not meant to receive people thus. But he had come here in a rage, not thinking to do the proper thing. She understood, of course.

"Are you ready to make your report?" she said. "What happened last night?"

"Last night . . ." Ned was staring straight ahead. His lip curled wryly. "She wanted . . ."

"Yes?"

He shook his head. "To play chess with me."

"To play chess with you," she repeated. "That isn't . . . some sort of euphemism."

"No," he said. "We played chess. I lost every game, if you must know. We played for hours. Until Eldakar came, some time near first light, to seduce her."

"I see." Though she didn't at first. "Oh," she said then, imagining the scene. "Oh dear."

"Exactly." He met her eyes. They both froze that way, in search of words. At last they gave up, gave in to impulse. First he, and then they both began to laugh.

THIS time during the game she spoke with him. It was day and they drank tea as if Ned Alterra were paying a social visit, though he did not in truth know what this was.

"You have a wife," she said this time, after they were several moves into the game. She had captured two of his men. Her eyes lifted from the board to study him. "You'd have betrayed her with me. Knowing what is said of me, you went along with my little game on the boat."

If she thought to shock him, it was effective. But by now Ned was becoming inured to shocks in this room. And in daylight he found her less disconcerting; not so much a creature of voluptuous shadow and scent as a girl who liked to test him. Though damnably clever—there was that. He had learned enough of the game by now to know the strategies she deployed against him were baroque, eluding his grasp each time. Only at the end, when she had captured his king, could he look back and understand the path she'd wrought getting there. During, he was a fish caught in her net, struggling uselessly until it was over.

He took his time with an answer. It seemed to him he existed here for her entertainment. Nonetheless he could not afford a misstep. He said, "Betrayals are measured differently between Rianna and me."

"How *interesting* for the two of you," she said with raised eyebrows. He wondered, with a quicker pulsebeat, if she now thought to call his bluff. But she lowered her eyes again and said, "Oh, look," with delight. She raised one of his Magician pieces in the air, a victory. The diamond on its staff winked in sunlight that streamed from the windows with a breeze.

"Splendid." He wished for something stronger than bergamot tea. It was his move now—but in more ways than one. She had opened the door to questioning. Ned brought to mind the parties he had attended in the Tamryllin palace gardens, the flirtations that took place—whether from boredom, or some other motive. He had a habit of observing more than participating . . . but in his duties to the Court Poet, had observed quite a bit. "So perhaps you'll tell me why you find playing *this* game preferable to . . . the other?" said Ned, taking a tone of genteel mockery. "Careful, though—you may wound me."

For a moment he thought he glimpsed—was it surprise?—before her eyelashes fluttered, a move in that other game. "I enjoy this," she said. "Does that surprise you?"

"I admit it does." He watched her closely. "Not that you enjoy it," he said. "But to stay awake into the night, doing this, long after everyone else is abed, and awake to do the same . . . you must admit it's not usual. Your husband doesn't seem to think so, certainly."

"That's not all, you know," she said. No trace now of flirtation or a smile. "The library has a surprising number of books on the game. Some very old. I can spend hours with them, Ned. Sometimes days."

"An obsession," he offered. He made his move, knowing it was feeble. His knight was now in easy trouncing reach of her queen.

She was staring at the board. When he moved, she made a sound of annoyance, and he wasn't sure if it was at the stupidity of what he'd done, or the comment that had preceded it. Then: "There you go, giving me your knight—but Ned, if you gave thought to a plan, it could have been for your gain. There is a strategem just like that—the Knight's Sacrifice. Often, in this game, one intent nests another." As he watched, her expression changed. When she spoke again it was in response to his earlier remark. It wasn't the first time she'd done that, casting back to an earlier comment or question when she was ready, as if everything he said was stored in her mind for later. He would have been flattered, if he did not suspect she employed it with everyone.

"You might call it an obsession," she said. And Ned thought he had been wrong, or at least a little bit wrong, about the effects of daylight on her; there were still enough shadows to beguile him, around the eyes and in the hollow of her throat. "Or . . . perhaps I seek a way to reshape this game. A way out of these fixed patterns. The calculations, the costs." With sudden violence, she seized his knight and flung it down on the table. "It doesn't work. Despite all I've read, all the strategies I implement." When she looked at him he thought for the first time she revealed herself fully, open and pained. "There's no way out of it, Ned. The game never changes."

MORNING mist drifted in the valley as Lin made her way down the mountain. Sunlight filled it, transformed it to smoke infused with gold. Majdara was a checkering of red slate roofs and white domes that now and then peered from that smoke. The river wrapped around it was a silver diadem that morning. Lin had taken a side gate out into the gardens and from there to the stairway that connected the terraces. There were three levels to the palace and gardens, that increased in grandeur as they progressed upward. Hundreds of stone stairs separated each of these, leading down, and down some more, to the main road. They cut a path through manicured hedges and trees. Lin passed between fragrant walls of roses, a heartbreak of red; beneath an arch that dripped lilacs; through legions of cypress trees standing at attention and trimmed, in the course of her descent. It took most of the morning.

Zahir Alcavar had remembered her mention, in passing, of a desire to go into the city alone. He had not asked why. But that morning Lin had found a message from the First Magician outside her door on a jeweled tray. It was a map that showed the way to a concealed door, along with the key that opened it, iron and gilding woven in a pattern of leaves. She could tell—based on what she'd seen of the prophecies in the Tower of Glass—that he had drawn the map himself, as it was with the same firm, ornate strokes. The door turned out to be hidden behind a velvet drapery in an unlit, abandoned hall, and led out to the kitchen gardens. She had walked through rows of cabbages and carrots to reach the main path.

Lin expected the effects of the night in the garden with Zahir and

Eldakar to be transient, as such exchanges often were; waking up to that carefully drawn map made her smile. And she appreciated that he had asked nothing, understanding her need for privacy.

As she descended the mountain through the gardens of the Zahra, Lin thought about the talk she'd had with Garon Senn. She'd come to him already dressed for her excursion to the city, in a man's shirt and trousers. Her hair was braided close to her head and concealed with a cap. Anyone who looked closely would know her sex, but most would not look closely. In contrast, a woman alone, unescorted on the streets of Majdara, would attract the wrong sort of attention.

He received her in his rooms, without the animosity she had anticipated. So it turned out he was a political creature above all else. Perhaps he had spoken the truth about being a different man. Now, he'd never indulge in violence without cause. Palace comforts had perhaps grown more than agreeable as age took its toll on his bones. Though the man could still wield a sword.

Assessing him across the expanse of the polished marble table, Lin thought of Ned playing games of chess with the queen and it occurred to her that this, perhaps, was not so different.

"I'll want you to tell me everything you know," she said. "Everything of this place, these people, that might be useful. But let's begin with the Second Magician."

"Tarik," he said.

"Do you know him?"

A brief nod. "We fought alongside each other. He has been . . . discreet, in saying nothing to expose me."

"Why do you think that is?"

Garon gave one of his fierce smiles. "We were comrades in arms. I saved his life more than once. He saved mine, too. Together we led battles in two of the provinces."

Lin leaned back in her chair, considering. Suppressing irritation that he'd concealed this from her.

"Tarik was in line to become First Magician when the previous one died. Kashak Saban was old—everyone expected Tarik would succeed him. It seemed expedient to cultivate a friendship with Tarik, so I did."

"Well, Garon," she said, exhaling her breath. "This is excellent news.

As you must surely know. Tarik Ibn-Mor has shown nothing but enmity towards me. He seems to want us gone. What are your thoughts?"

He shrugged. "It's obvious, isn't it? He's angry this younger upstart, Zahir Alcavar, was made First instead of him. It is Zahir who urges action against the Fire Dancers, so Tarik must push back. To what end, I am not sure."

"Ned thinks Tarik might be in league with Ramadus."

Garon remained expressionless at the mention of Ned. "It makes sense. He may be biding his time until Eldakar is sufficiently weakened by the northern attacks."

"I want you to find out." Lin made sure he met her eyes. "Rekindle your friendship with Tarik Ibn-Mor. Naturally, your being my man will present a difficulty. You may want to tell him you are . . . seeking an alternative partnership." She grinned. "I imagine the feelings of antipathy you express with regard to me will be genuine. Don't hesitate to be honest. That is, if you're capable of it."

"An alternative partnership," said Garon, surveying Lin as if she were a balance scale he was weighing.

"Remember this, Garon Senn," she said. "Whatever he offers you, I will exceed. Come to me with the amount he promises, and I will more than match it. Ultimately he has less use for your knowledge than I do, for what can he want with me? I am only the Court Poet of Eivar, a place he despises." She rose. "But if you do betray me, know I will come after you with all the forces I can muster. Magical and otherwise."

"I understand," he said. He appeared unmoved by this. There was little else she could do, she supposed, other than have Ned arrange for him to be watched. Garon was far too useful to be killed out of hand.

If the conversation had ended there, Lin Amaristoth would have been pleased with a morning's work, before the day could even be said to have begun. It was a dangerous game—she could not trust Garon Senn. But perhaps she could trust his greed.

The conversation did not end there, however.

IT was late morning by the time Lin reached the city walls. Majdara was a city of seven gates; this one, that faced out towards the palace, was the Gate of Falcons. Statues of those birds, wings uplifted, flanked the gate to either side. They were twice the size of a man, and gilded. The effect could have been garish, but the detail on the figures—the way each feather was finely delineated—made it breathtaking instead. Passing between the falcons she emerged into a plaza, and had to pause in her tracks. There was nothing quite of this magnitude even in Tamryllin.

Two fountains graced this plaza. One, she recalled, had been designed by Tarik Ibn-Mor himself. Around these, a market was in progress. It comprised what seemed to her a maze of hundreds of tents; to explore it thoroughly would take days. Lin drew herself up, laid a hand to the knife at her hip, and plunged into one of the many pathways through the market. She was hungry. Spices assailed her nostrils: cinnamon, cardamom, coriander, pepper. These were sufficiently alluring to overcome feelings of intimidation.

Later, as she emerged from the tents with a bowl of lamb grilled in honey and spiced with turmeric, Lin approached the fountain of Tarik Ibn-Mor. In this part of the world where water was more scarce, the interplay of art and water was considered on par with magic. It was undoubtedly this skill of Tarik that helped elevate him in the ranks—in addition to skills in battle and diplomacy.

This fountain took the shape of a mountain, studded with rocks and trees. Forming a circle around its peak, the beasts of the provinces. Each gazed with noble mien over the plaza as if they could see beyond. Each was level—the wolf, gazelle, steed, and leopard forming a circle as they faced outward. The message was clear—the provinces were equal. Rearing above them on an upper level, wings outspread and beak gaping in a cry, the gryphon: symbol of the Tower of Glass.

The message in this was clear, too.

Surrounding the carved marble beasts, water soared in arcs and jets to the height of a tree, into a basin that could have contained Lin's chamber back at the palace. Sun knifed off the water.

People lounged here, on the rim of the fountain. They wore garments more loosely fitted than at home, of lighter fabrics, layered against the sun. Some, like her, were eating what they'd bought at the market. She did that for a time, spearing morsels of lamb with wooden sticks, watching the water course its triumphant arc overhead.

She thought, as she chewed and savored the sweet and sharp elements of the dish, that Tarik Ibn-Mor would be a stimulating opponent.

As in the imperial gardens that had been modeled close to those in Ramadus, Lin felt a sensation of familiarity stir in her, as she sat by the fountain. She rose, surveyed the scene. Beyond it—the market tents, the wares set out on carpets, the smells of sweat and spices, the cries— were archways, shadowed black, that led into the depths of the city.

The address Valanir had given her was secured in her purse. But it was with Edrien's help, his memories, that she knew how to get there. Majdara had changed hands, conquerors, in the intervening years between the age of Edrien Letrell and this one; but its street plan was the same.

Likely even this market had been held here, in this same plaza, for all the years.

It took a great deal of time to cross the plaza; after the descent from the palace, and now this, her legs were tired. Sellers called to Lin; so did beggars. To one she gave her bowl, now picked clean. But once she reached the arch that led into a dark, cool tunnel, the noise of the plaza began to fade. A street sign declared it the Way of Water. The street was slender and winding as a stream. Shaded, too, with several tunnels. She would emerge from these, look up to see windows where laundry of all colors waved in the breeze. And then she was back in a tunnel again, where water dripped and the smell of urine was at times overpowering.

She came to a small courtyard with the statue of a man, a mounted warrior, at its center. This, too, was enfolded in piled windows strung with laundry. There were trees, boughs set to murmuring in a warm wind. On its current Lin thought she caught a new scent, of rotting fish. She was close.

The Way of Water led, ultimately, to the harbor.

Lin arrived at a back street near the waterfront, elevated and thus allowing for a view of the River Gadlan and the fishing boats upon it. From here, stairs carved in the cliffside led to the water. Seagulls perched on a nearby wall or circled, crying, overhead. Here, out in front of what looked to be residences, a pair of old men, white beards nearly to their knees, played a game involving a board and dice. Nearby sprawled a large dog, head sunk in its paws. The men didn't look her way and the dog was motionless, lazy in its puddle of sun. Lin had a sense that some form of this scene could have been found here, on this street above the harbor, in all the years the city stood. The game the men were engaged in, *tabla*, had roots in games much older from lands far to the south and across the sea, where once had ruled an empire.

That empire was dust now, blown on winds around silent tombs. In a time before, when it was near desolation but still a glory, Edrien Letrell had traveled there. If Lin allowed her thoughts to drift that way, she recalled a temple complex with clear pools set in marble, a slender boat on a lake before bronze gates. A princess reclining on a gold couch—a girl who had loved music. And poets, or at least one. For a time. Always with Edrien it was for a transient, murmurous time.

Lin's business was not at the waterfront. She turned up another street, setting her back to the harbor. This one ran steeply uphill. She smiled a little at the sight that greeted her. Now the sun rode high, and the call of seagulls mingled with those of vendors.

Before the shopfronts, books and scrolls were piled on barrows or displayed on shelves—works more precious or rare would be sheltered inside. The Way of Booksellers was one of the city's longest, running the distance from the Plaza of Justice to the harbor. At the top, nearest the plaza, were well-appointed shops frequented by wealthy clients or their servants. These sold some of the world's finest manuscripts and books, in all languages. As the street wound down to the river there was a change. The shops became increasingly musty, dark, with ragtag offerings. Here nearly any work written might be obtained—for a price. Some were rare, drawing travelers from other parts of the world.

And some, Lin knew, were forbidden texts. That was another side to the Way of Booksellers, in shops nearer the river where laws were lax. It was not her purpose today.

As she ascended the street Lin thought about the last part of her exchange with Garon Senn. Now in the warmth of a noonday sun on a city street the memory was less unsettling, though not by much.

Leaning across the table she'd said, "Tell me about Yusuf Evrayad."

Garon's lips stretched into a thin smile. "He was meant to die. The Ramadians killed his entire family after a failed bid for accession and civil war. It seemed the end of House Evrayad. Yusuf was the youngest son, ever known as the weak one. But somehow he escaped Ramadus, made his way here."

"How about more recently," she said. "Eldakar seems to think the Fire Dancers hold a grudge because of Yusuf. What did he do?"

"That is simple enough," said Garon Senn. "Following a truce, Yusuf invited the Renegade to join battle alongside him, in exchange for lands. He did not keep his promise."

"You knew Yusuf well, didn't you?" Lin asked. "You began under his command soon after he arrived from Ramadus with his men."

At this Garon looked away from her. For the first time, he betrayed feeling; but she could not tell what it was. "I did," he said. "I led battalions of his men, and grew to know them well. Enough to know this." But here he tightened his lips, fell silent.

Lin leaned forward when he did not speak. "To know . . . what?"

Unexpectedly, Garon spat. *They were not men.*"

"You mean . . ."

"It was magic," he said. "I don't know what they were. I didn't ask. I took my payment, led his troops to conquer the provinces. It was enough."

Even now as she recalled this, Lin's heart beat faster. She wished Valanir Ocune was not so far away. He had known Yusuf—they'd been friends. Perhaps he could have made sense of this.

Finally Lin arrived at the place she sought. There were books outside the shop door, on neat shelves. The door was painted red, and shut. The shop window was likewise shuttered, also red. Lin had a moment of dread, that she'd come all this way for nothing. But the door latch turned easily, the scent of mouldering paper greeting her like a friend. At the back of the shop, standing at one of the shelves, was a slender woman in a red cloak. She looked up when Lin entered, alerted by the bell. The place seemed otherwise empty.

"Hallo," said Lin. She was startled; she had not expected the merchant to be so . . . attractive. But of course, she thought with an inward grin—a friend of Valanir Ocune. Her appearance was otherwise notable for being almost colorless: hair so pale it was almost white, with skin to match. Her eyes very odd—the color of amber, like those of a raven. "Good day," she said, not smiling. "Do you seek a book?"

Lin stepped farther in, let the door close behind her. The smell of paper was comforting, and she felt real regret she could not linger here, or elsewhere on this street. Perhaps later. If someone such as herself could be said to possess a *later*.

"Not as such," she said, and watched the merchant's face. "The Seer Valanir Ocune sent me."

The woman narrowed her yellow eyes, made stranger by pale lashes. "Really."

"It concerns the Fire Dancers."

An unmistakable edge. "What about them?"

Lin took another step forward. "Valanir thought you could help me. It's about the attacks in the north."

The woman bit her lip. Then: "Bolt the door." She indicated a curtain that led to an adjoining room. "Come. We can't be heard to speak of this."

CHAPTER
12

THE room behind the bookshop was small and dimly lit, but there was a fire for the teakettle and deep cushions for sitting. The effect was cozy. Lin saw why the merchant retreated here for privacy—the one window was a slit near the ceiling, allowing in a sliver of sunlight and sounds from the street. Children's laughter filtered in, faint, as if from underwater. Lin could imagine retreating here to read by lamplight until dark. Being at once a part of the city tumult and detached in her own world.

Of course that was a fantasy. No doubt this bookshop owner was as entangled with the chaos of ordinary life as anyone.

Just now she was watching Lin. "Who are you?"

"Have you heard from Valanir Ocune?"

The other woman looked away. "I have—followed events in Eivar. So you are the Court Poet."

"Good guess." Lin sprawled onto one of the cushions. It was a welcome respite for her aching feet. "And who are you?"

"My name is Aleira," said the merchant. "Aleira Suzehn."

"Suzehn." Lin watched as the woman got out two small, delicate white cups. "The name—it sounds Galician."

The woman shrugged. "If you take issue with that, you see the door."

Lin was surprised into a grin. "I would deserve that if I did. Of course."

"Very well," said the merchant. "You may call me Aleira, in that case. Since you are a friend of Valanir Ocune. How is he?"

"Well enough, I hope," said Lin, quelling a fear that had been lately been stirring in her. "These are not good times."

"They never are," said the woman, and handed Lin a steaming cup. It had a dark, heady smell, tempered with mint. As Aleira took a seat on the second cushion, Lin was able to get a better look at her. Lines marked her forehead and the corners of her eyes—a face etched with experience, refined by it. Grey in the pale hair gave it a complex shine, gold and silver blended. Lin could imagine what had passed between this woman and the Seer. Valanir had mentioned this being someone he had known when he was thirty. Some two decades in the past.

As if she read Lin's thoughts, Aleira Suzehn said, "Did Valanir Ocune tell you anything about me?"

"Nothing. I had only a name. And—that it was long ago."

"Yes." The woman sipped her tea. "I thought I'd heard the last of him. That tends to be the way of it with poets." She smiled faintly at this. "It is of no matter—he did me a good turn."

"Why would he send me to you?"

"So he really told you nothing." Aleira pursed her lips. "Valanir saved my life." Something must have shown in Lin's face, because Aleira looked amused. "You're surprised? I have a sense that he does not reveal much, for whatever reason. Yes, when I was much younger and . . . fleeing . . . I blundered into the camp of the Fire Dancers. At the time, I didn't value my life. When I heard they kill trespassers with a knife to the throat, then mount the head on their ramparts as a message . . . I can't say I cared."

"So what happened?"

The other woman's eyes were far away. There was satisfaction in her recounting of the tale; Lin guessed it had been a long time since she'd last shared it. "At that time, Valanir was a guest of King Sicaro."

"The Renegade."

Aleira lifted a delicate shoulder. "So they name him here. Either he owed the Seer a favor, or Valanir simply managed to persuade Sicaro . . . I'm still not sure. I had lost a lot of blood. In my mind, was as good as dead. But Valanir stopped them. They let me stay. In exchange for household chores in the fortress, I lived there for some years. It was the home I'd never expected to find. For a time."

Lin was silent. She divined that horrors ran between the other woman's words. No longer did she feel inclined to smile indulgently at whatever Aleira and Valanir had once shared. She only hoped that as a young woman Aleira had, at least for a time, found a measure of peace.

It was a silence Lin allowed to grow, for the other to fill as she chose. From the window came the sound of a beggar intoning a plea: one word, foreign to her, again and again. A barked conversation between two men, joined by a third. A child's incessant whine that grew piercing, then faded away. The life of a city. Lin said, "So. The attacks in the north."

The transformation was immediate: Aleira's calm demeanor became clenched. "It's a lie."

"What is?"

"About the Dance. It is not used that way." Agitation drove the bookseller to her feet. She began to pace. "I'm not saying the Jitana are above acts of violence. Who is? Yusuf eroded what land they had in the north, piece by piece—whatever was not already taken by the Lords of Almyria. The Jitana were there before all of them. Of course they would reclaim it all if they could."

"The Renegade is said to be fierce in battle."

Standing in the meager light of the window, Aleira smiled. "There's a reason none dare attack his fortress. And why Yusuf Evrayad tried to ally with him."

"You are devoted to them," said Lin. "It is understandable. But isn't it possible that their magic has—changed? Valanir sent me to you because he believed you could help. That begins with the truth."

"The truth." Aleira shook her head. She looked sad. "Do you know the tale of the Jitana?"

"I know nothing of them."

"Long ago when the Empire of Mizrayam still reigned in the south, two princes went to war for the throne. The younger, Prince Cambias, had a dream that revealed the goddess of the moon had chosen him, but only if he departed their lands forever. She guided him and his followers north and across the sea. They came to Kahishi when it was a wasteland of Ellenican homesteads and cattle herds." Aleira's tone dripped scorn. She stood tall in the slant of light. "The Dance—that is one of the mysteries the goddess gave to Cambias. Its purpose is worship. It is done only at certain times of the year. Certain nights."

Lin was watching the other woman narrowly. "You have done this. Haven't you?"

Aleira's chin raised. "They invited me once. Only once. Whatever effect the Dance has, Lady Amaristoth, it is only on the dancer. It has no other . . . power . . . as people understand it." Her lashes veiled her eyes. "That one time . . . is always with me."

"I know what it is to be changed by magic," said Lin, gently from where she sat. Everything about this meeting, so far, had surprised her. "I want to believe you. But a prophecy indicates there is a shadow emerging from the north, from the Jitana."

"Show me this prophecy." Aleira stood before Lin with her hands on her hips. "Oh, I know it is forbidden. The lore of Magicians—none of the common folk may study it. A man might be jailed, or worse, if an almanac is found in his possession. None but the king and his Seven may know what is in the stars. But here on the Way of Booksellers . . . one might chance to find anything." She stood near Lin now, speaking near a whisper. "You understand me. I've made magic a field of study all my life. I know how to read these prophecies."

"You think I've been lied to." It was a disquieting thought. More than that. Lin thought of the night in the Tower and realized that in all that happened, that night had been serving for her as an anchor.

Could Zahir be lying?

"I will bring you the prophecy." Spoken heavily. Why was it that trust could only come hard . . . so hard?

"Thank you," said Aleira Suzehn. She crossed her hands at her hip, a formal gesture. "I swear to act in good faith."

Lin rose slowly, a new weight in her heart. "My thanks to you."

"Don't go yet." Aleira's voice had grown husky, as if she struggled with some emotion. "You should see something." Lin waited, expecting the woman to go retrieve something from the shop, or perhaps from the pile of manuscripts heaped on her desk in the corner. But instead, Aleira turned her back to Lin, then unfastened her red cloak. It made a sanguine puddle around her.

Silence. Lin waited. Aleira was working at the front of her dress, out of Lin's view. The beggar outside had ceased his cries. A deeper quiet had settled on the street. It was the heat of the day, when many took their rest. The gulls could be heard more starkly now, and once, the aggrieved screech of a hawk.

Aleira shrugged her arm out of her dress. Drew aside the curtain of her hair. "Look."

Lin stepped nearer, but not too near. She felt caught in the strangeness of the moment—this unexpected intimacy with a woman she didn't know. Something caught the light on Aleira's skin above the shoulder blade. A gleam of gold. Lin squinted, saw its shape. A bird, its beak like a hook.

"The ibis." Aleira reached back into her dress, was soon closing it again.

"A mark of the Fire Dancers?"

Aleira tossed back her hair so once more it concealed her shoulders. "The Dance leaves you marked." She turned to face Lin again. "This— the ibis—is the mark one sees."

NEAR the end of the day, she wanted to show him something. By then he had lost count of their games, of his inevitable losses. Had come to feel that he was barely a presence here—could have been machinery that fulfilled this need of hers, and it would have been sufficient. She seemed to have no curiosity about him at all, not since that morning when she had asked about his wife.

Dusk was stealing into the corners of the room and casting its veil over the gardens when she put an end to that, led him to an adjoining room. Ned was by then so tired that his legs were like jelly when he stood. He had hardly slept the night before, and had been roused early, and from there it had been—*this,* all day. They had not even taken the noon meal. Just one cup after another of *khave,* the effects making themselves felt in his gut. He felt a failure, on top of that . . . with no new information for Lin. When he tried to ask questions of Rihab about herself, the palace, she looked annoyed. The game was the thing, for her. That moment when she had seemed to reveal herself had gone, so that he wondered now if it had happened.

Ned grimaced. "What did you want me to see?" They stood at the threshold of a room like any other in this palace—delicately furnished, scented with fresh-cut roses. All he cared about was the deep velvet couch, where he could imagine curling up right now, without even bothering to take his boots off.

"This," said Rihab. There was something tall in the corner, the height of a man, concealed in yellow silk. When she whisked the cover away, he saw a dress hanging on a garment tree.

He was so tired. "A dress." Why she would want him to see this, he had no idea. And wasn't sure he cared anymore.

Rihab seemed unaware of his exhaustion. "You've shown interest in our customs," she said. "In two weeks is the Feast of Nitzan. That is, I believe, how we say it in your tongue."

"Nitzan?"

"The celebration of spring." She spun around with sudden gaiety, her loose hair an accompanying shadow. "See? This is the queen's attire. So it has been—well, forever, really. The queen wears this dress, see, and this mask. And takes her place at the side of the king. So it has always been in Ramadus, and Yusuf Evrayad brought the traditions here."

Ned saw what his fatigue had overlooked: the dress was so vast and magnificent as to be somehow monstrous; several of Rihab's slender shape could have fit inside that belled skirt. It was made of heavy brocade worked in thread-of-gold and pearls. The underskirt was red and covered with rubies; this pattern was echoed on the bodice, too: a belt of rubies led the way to more, up the center of the bodice and across the chest. And draped over all this, a cape, its outside gold brocade and pearls, the underside jeweled crimson.

"It is quite something," said Ned, finally.

Rihab snatched up a mask of gold, pearl-studded. "And this for the face," she said. "At the Feast of Nitzan, the king plays the role of the god, the queen is the land. Really it is the goddess she is playing, the ancient goddess Vizia, but you can be killed for saying that." Uncharacteristically, she giggled. "Now it is a solemn festival to Alfin, of course. The ceremonies are not . . . what they were."

"What were they?"

Her eyes were limpid with amusement, and something else. "There was a time," she said, "when it would have been Eldakar's task to make love to me before all the city. To take me when I'm in this dress. Standing, perhaps, with my back to him. Or . . . perhaps any way I prefer. Who knows?" Her smile was one he had not yet seen, of satisfied power. "And of course, my pleasure—that would be immensely important. As the goddess's pleasure must be."

Ned found his response nearly unbearable. And also felt anger. For surely she knew . . . she *knew* what she was doing to him. If nothing else, Rihab Bet-Sorr was extremely clever.

He affected indifference. "Interesting," he said with raised eyebrows. "I take it that's not what's done these days."

Her smile changed, to one of appreciation. *You are learning the game,* said her eyes—or was it just his desire to read it there? "Nowadays it is all quite sedate," she agreed. "The queen and king are alone together in a tent after the ceremony. I'm told they do nothing more exciting than sit for a meal. But the ceremony, and the symbolism of their confinement together—that is a rite of fertility. The first such rite Majdara shall see in some years."

"Well," he said, "I am, of course, delighted to learn your customs. Your grace is too kind." He kept sarcasm from his tone as best he could.

Now her smile changed again; became guileless as a child's. "Ned, it's the one day the queen is allowed out of the palace," she said. "All the rest of the year, I may wander the gardens, most of the rooms, but I can never leave. But soon that will change. Maybe, for some moments, I will feel as if—*almost* as if—I am free."

"I NEED your help," Lin had said, and Ned Alterra had looked as near to long-suffering as she'd ever seen him. But he had not said, "Of course you do." He'd said, "I'm at your service." Too late, she recalled he'd been up all night and early that morning. But there was no time to waste.

She would, when this was over, find some way to adequately reward him, and Rianna, too. Money would have been meaningless; they had plenty of it. They didn't care about extravagance, lands, titles. But some gift would be necessary. After all this.

Her instructions were simple enough—he would keep Zahir Alcavar occupied at dinner, watch his movements. Keep an eye on all the Magicians, in case one of them decided to leave the dining table for the Tower. Lin would be absent from dinner, claiming a headache. It seemed the best plan: dinner was the only time everyone gathered in one place. But if anything went wrong, she needed Ned to keep watch for her. To try and stall the Magician, if need be.

The idea that Zahir was someone to scheme against was like a layer of frosted rime on her bones. She could not believe it. But knew she could not afford to believe only what she wished.

It was too soon to think through the possible implications. Whether it meant he was lying to Eldakar, too, or if the king was involved in the deception as to where the attacks were coming from. Though what would be the purpose? She could see no end to such a plot that would benefit the First Magician, let alone Eldakar. But that only meant, possibly, she did not yet have all the necessary information.

With Aleira's help, she would soon know more.

All was quiet in the courtyard, but for the fountain; the flowers began to show pale blades as night fell.

The stairs, winding round and round, seemed endless now that she was in a hurry. She had forgotten, too, how dizzying they were. But Lin thought, as she arrived gasping at the summit, that the presence of the First Magician must have made a difference the first time. It was his place; magic like his had gone into its fashioning.

And perhaps, in his absence, there was some—resistance. She was not supposed to be here.

As Lin emerged in the open, her eyes were immediately drawn to the starry heavens of that ceiling. So massive and quiet was this place, yet with an undercurrent of music. Jeweled constellations shone in light that came from everywhere and nowhere. It caught her breath. It felt a sacrilege to set foot here without a guide. Without permission.

She thought of Alfin and Kiara and murmured, in her heart, a small prayer to any that might listen.

The diamond stars sparked coldly on.

Lin stepped farther into the Tower, tried to compel herself to think of a strategy. She needed to find the staircase to the Observatory—where was that? She recalled it was a long walk, and this part in particular she dreaded: when she'd be trudging, fully exposed, across the vast floor. Like a deer in a treeless glade. But there was no alternative. She recalled Zahir Alcavar, his finger on the parchment that was the prophecy clipped to the desk. She could only hope it was still there.

She saw in the distance, branching out from this space, a row of arched doorways. There were more on the high levels, along the walkways. Doors and doors and doors, such as in the place she had dreamed after Darien died. Faint illumination came from each, but not enough to see what was inside. Despite everything, curiosity got the better of her. She crossed to one of the doorways and leaned along the lintel to look inside. She saw an octagonal room walled entirely in silver mirrors—anyone who stood within would see themselves repeated, eight times and forever. At the center a wide, flat marble bowl on a pedestal, dancing with bright silver that slithered around endlessly. Was that mercury?

She moved on. Stole a glance in another doorway, feeling as she did so like a bit of a fool, or a child, to be so inquisitive. That room was full to the brim with potted trees. She squinted, saw what she had first thought was not an illusion—the leaves of the trees were gold. Red gems the size of a fist hung from the branches of one; bunches of amethysts like grapes from another. Lin wondered at the extravagance, considered that there were hundreds of rooms in this Tower. What could the purpose of such things be?

There was order to their magic, Zahir had told her. Every room here, then, had a purpose.

A sound, like a song, but with a mechanical lilt. She looked again. Clinging to the branch of a tree was a copper bird, beak split in song. And then another. They were clearly not real, but were more alive than a mechanical bird ought to be; it was unnerving. Lin hurried away, resolving not to look into any more of the rooms.

After a time, the stairs to the Observatory came into sight, a floating spiral. It took considerably more time to reach them. When at last she reached the first stair, something changed. All at once she was not alone.

Zahir stood at the foot of the stairs, barring the way.

"So I'm in time," he said. He looked grim.

"How did you get here?"

He shook his head. "You know I am a Magician, what do you think—dear, what do you think that is? But this was a terribly foolish thing, my lady. Anyone who climbs these stairs without invitation . . . they die instantly."

Lin took a step back. "Ned—"

"Had an intense eye on me all evening. I suppose now I know why."
His hands shook; he looked down at them as if surprised. Let them fall
to his sides. "*Why* did you do this? I thought we could speak freely."

"I had a conversation in the city today," she said. Inserted a confidence
in her tone that she did not feel. "I need—I need the prophecy.
For this person to see."

"Of course," he said at once. "Only keep it secret. The law forbids
that anyone else see it. But you—you may have whatever you ask. Don't
you *know* that?"

She was accustomed to Zahir as a wit, with sparkle in his eye; this
man whose hands shook and whose color had fled was unfamiliar. "This
place," she said slowly. "It is strange to me. I can't be sure of anything."
Or anyone, she added silently. By his stricken look, he must have heard
it anyway.

"I see I have yet to prove myself to you," he said. "Take this." He
handed her a leather-covered cylinder plated with gold at each end. "It is
a copy. If you wish to check it against the one upstairs, then by all means.
Now that you have been invited to ascend, it holds no further danger."

"Why go to the trouble?" she said as she took the cylinder. "Of proving
yourself." Her voice lost in the enormity of this space, under stars. "What
does it matter? What I think." Her hands gestured, an attempt to articulate
something for which she could not find words. "There is so little
time, anyway."

Zahir gripped her hand. There was fierceness in it, but she didn't
wince. She felt suspended from sensation, or thought. Or rather, observed
the sensation, and herself, from a distance. He said, "There is
never enough time."

Lin felt rooted to the spot. The Magician released her hand. He
rubbed his forehead with his fingertips as if an ache there was starting.
"You gave me quite the scare, Seer." He forced a smile. "If nothing else,
Valanir would have killed me."

"I will take up no more of your time, *G'vir* Alcavar," she said, with a
stiff nod.

"What? No!" He seemed fully at ease now, as if they were back in the
garden. "Lin . . . I understand why you couldn't trust me. Someone in
your position—you can't blindly trust anyone, particularly not someone

you've just met. Before we go on, I want you to check the prophecy in the Observatory against the one you hold in your hands."

"Before . . . we go on?"

He grinned. "It happens that by coming here, you've saved me a trip. I was trying to tell you last night, before Tarik came by, that I have something for you. Now I may show it to you without interference."

THEY were crossing the great tiled floor. Their steps were silent, their shadows faint on the great balance scales depicted in a mosaic of blue and gold. He was making for one of the stairways to the next level. "More stairs," he said apologetically over his shoulder, and she snorted. "I'm dying, not old, Magician."

Zahir Alcavar's laugh was harsh, clipped. "Oh, *miryan*."

"What?"

He paused on the stair. "*Miryan*. The name for the flowers in the courtyard below."

"Because I don't sleep?"

Zahir did not smile. "People pass them by, until their time comes."

"And then?"

"The dark brings out their beauty." He turned away and proceeded up the stairs hurriedly, head bowed, as if suddenly shy.

They were on the second level. From the balustrade, if Lin looked down, the Tower floor was an ocean of mosaic, stretching an impossible distance. And all this enfolded in a sky that had just begun to darken.

As on the first level there were many doorways, most emitting a faint light. These they passed. Lin trailed her hand on the rail, her eyes alternately on the ceiling above, the floor below, and the sky that ran alongside them. At last Zahir halted at a closed door. This was different from what Lin had grown used to seeing in the Zahra, though it took her a moment to understand why. Everything in this palace was new and polished to a high sheen, often gilded; this door was of oak pitted with age, reinforced with iron. And then she saw the symbol carved in it. A labyrinthine knot, such as was etched around Lin's eye, that might be seen only in moonlight.

Her voice was weak. "Zahir, what *is* this?"

He opened the door with a bow. A candle had materialized in his hand where before there was none. Its holder plain brass. Again nothing like the furnishings of the palace. He handed it to her. "I will not venture inside," he said. "This place—it is yours. For as long as you desire it."

Uncomprehending, Lin began to circle the room, candle in hand. It was a tower room. Its walls were stone. Drafty, with a scent—she sniffed. *The sea?*

As her eyes adjusted, she saw a large space. The walls cut with many windows. Beside each, a cubicle of carved stone, rough as if hewn from the heart of a mountain.

She had been here before. Once.

Lin went to a window. Dusk outside, hazed with clouds. She saw water breaking over rocks far below. Outlined against the sky, the great shoulder of a mountain. There was a smell she recognized, too, of wet leaves and pine and unnameable, moldering things. From a time that had passed quick as a sunbeam yet remained lodged in her as an ache. She remembered: warmth of a narrow bed, scents of loam and rain, a harp and golden voice singing her to sleep.

Lin's breath stuck in her throat. "Impossible."

"You have questions," said Zahir. He was on the threshold, between worlds. "Of course. But you need not know how this is done. This is the Tower of the Winds. Not a duplicate."

"Shouldn't there be . . . other people here, then?" She looked wildly around. "Might someone come in?"

"The place is captured in a moment in time. Neither past, nor future. There is only the present. And what better way for you to write, Lin? Your past . . . it weighs so heavily. Likewise the future. *This* moment must be what matters. And this, the place that was denied you. The music you could have made . . . It need not be lost."

She had her hands to her mouth. She, who took pride in the aloof manner she'd cultivated until it had become second nature. Lowered her arms to her sides. "It is too much," she said. "Too great a gift."

He was avoiding her eyes, as if to allow her the privacy of emotion. "Your mark," he said, brushing the edge of his eye socket with a fingertip, "it grew bright as we entered." He reached into his belt, extended to her a simple iron key the size of his hand. Simple, but for the mark of the Seer engraved in the handle. "When you return to your room tonight," said Zahir, "you'll see a door in the wall beside your bed that was not there before. None but you may open it, with this key. It leads here. None may enter this place until I remove the enchantment. Not Magicians. Not even me."

Lin closed her eyes. "How . . . did you know? What I wanted more than anything?"

Moonlight from Academy Isle cast Zahir's features as if in marble. "I felt it the moment I saw you," he said. "Your need . . . was a thing that burned me. These two things you carry, lady: a shadow, and a flame."

CHAPTER
13

HE was alone that day in the room, as he now was most days. Dorn tried to make light of it, told himself he no longer had to share the small space with another as he tried to work. That the presence of Etherell Lyr no longer distracted him. But the quiet was consuming. Dorn had never minded—at least, not unduly—when he'd known his friend was on the mainland seducing some tavern maid. Perhaps the difference was that this time it was more than a trivial seduction. Sendara Diar, daughter of Archmaster Elissan Diar, was no tavern maid.

It did distract him if he recalled the time he had been in the hallway on the way to their room, was just about to open the door, when he'd heard Sendara's voice within. In their room, Dorn's only sanctuary. He had felt anger, his hand frozen on the door handle. Wondering if he should knock. Heard her say, with a little laugh, "I . . . don't like to be touched."

And then Etherell, in silken tones. "Are you sure?"

A silence. Dorn stood trembling. He knew he should move from the door but yearned, horribly, to hear more of that voice, which he'd never heard from Etherell before. Even if it drove him to despair, he wanted it. But Etherell didn't speak again right away. What Dorn began to hear were soft, shocked gasps, decidedly feminine.

"That's right," Etherell said, his voice a caress. "Bite me if you need to, darling. That's right."

Dorn knew then with cruel clarity that he had stayed too long. He ran.

That was a bad day. Dorn had wandered the hallways without pur-pose, feeling himself an exile. And now something new to taunt him: *That's right*.

Etherell had arrived to the next lesson late, disheveled. Dorn ignored him all that day and in the evening when they prepared for sleep. It seemed to him a scent clogged the room that should not have been there, some-where between lilac and musk. He felt cold.

At last Etherell had said, "It won't happen again."

"What?"

"Will you look at me?"

Reluctantly Dorn looked up from the fingernails he was trimming. Etherell sat on his own bed across from him. "I can only think of one reason you'd be angry with me," he said. "We will go . . . elsewhere, in the future. The room was convenient, but . . . it was unfair to you."

"Doesn't she have a room?"

Etherell shook his head. "It's too near the Archmasters—we might have been seen. Soon I will make a formal offer to her father. But he must come to know me, first. See that I am an asset."

He sounded, Dorn thought, more like the young lord than in all their years together. *Formal offer. An asset.* "So that's why you want to join his chosen. To prove you're an asset."

Etherell shrugged. "You understand now."

No more was said. But his friend had kept his word, and from then was rarely in their room at all. Dorn grew to know that small dusty space better within those weeks than he had in all of six years. It was his now. Though Etherell Lyr was yet a student in the Academy, in the ways that mattered he was as good as gone. He had ceased to make even a pretense of attending to his studies. All his energies were now focused on wooing Sendara Diar and proving himself worthy to her father.

So it wasn't a surprise when his friend stopped coming to their room at night. That had been the only time, aside from meals, when Dorn could expect to see him; but one night he simply wasn't there. He was not there in the morning the next day. Dorn didn't worry; it was known by now that Archmaster Diar and his chosen did their work at night. And there Etherell Lyr was at breakfast, looking tired but pleased, with heightened color and tousled hair. His attention to the modest meal of porridge and bread was ferocious, like a dog attacking scraps. But that wasn't what gave Dorn Arrin pause as he approached the table—why he hung back.

Between ravening bites, Etherell Lyr was deep in conversation with Maric Antrell. Elissan Diar's favorite sat beside Etherell, in Dorn's accustomed seat. When at last Dorn found himself another seat across the table, his friend didn't look up. The two leaned close, gold and auburn locks nearly mingling, oblivious to all else in the dining hall. Down at the end of the table, Dorn saw the girls, the small, curly-haired one attending to her porridge half-heartedly, pushing the oats around with her spoon, while Sendara Diar kept glancing down the table in their direction. She would do so furtively, looking away if she caught sight of anyone watching. But even from here Dorn could see in her eyes what he did not want to see: hunger for anything Etherell Lyr might send her way, any amount of attention.

Dorn saw there an unsettling mirror and was glad to look away.

What has happened to me? he wondered once as he traversed what now seemed the endless distances from his room to lessons to meals. The hallways that seemed silent and vast even when they were crowded with students. All he'd wanted was to devote himself to being a poet; his life to that sacred road. Instead he was losing sight of that—of his purpose—day by day. The petty politics of this place and his own weakness worked against him at every turn.

He hadn't lost hope of recovering that road. He had only to last out the remaining months. He couldn't even grieve yet. Later, at a distance from this place, he would do that, too. He was paradoxically alone all the time yet never alone enough.

Sometimes he encountered Etherell Lyr in their room at odd hours. He might awaken in the night and see him there, standing motionless at the center of the room. "Go back to sleep," Etherell had murmured to him one time, in a tone so commanding that Dorn did, even though he wanted to ask where his friend had been. Another time Etherell startled him by coming in one afternoon, while Dorn was practicing a new song. He still intended to play at Manaia, whether Etherell joined him or not.

That time, in the unforgiving sunlight, Dorn had seen some of the changes wrought on Etherell Lyr in the past weeks. His friend had grown haggard, with days-old stubble on his cheeks. His eyes shadowed purple beneath. "You look as bad as Maric," Dorn had observed. "Might it be possible to carry this *chosen* business too far?"

"I must prove myself," his friend snapped. He went to the basin, blade in hand. Slapping oil on his face, he began to shave. Soon he would appear the perfect lordling again, Dorn thought with annoyance. All it took was a shave and a trim.

Still Dorn pressed him. "What does Sendara Diar think of all this?"

Etherell managed his signature shrug as he scraped the blade across his jaw, tautening the muscles as he went. "She knows I do it for her father. She is pleased I have joined with him. If I can demonstrate as much skill as Maric Antrell, Archmaster Diar will readily agree to my suit."

"Skill—in what, exactly?"

Etherell had begun to wash his face in the basin. It was some moments before he lifted his head, darkened strands clinging to his forehead. His eyes larger and brighter than usual. "Everything you oppose, Dorn Arrin. But you knew before you asked."

IT was during this time that another of the chosen departed the Isle, though not in the manner of Gared Dexane. There were no screams in the night. There was simply a vacancy at the table one morning. A whisper went about that Syme Oleir had broken in a meeting of the chosen, was sent away to recover at home. Dorn was startled. What did Elissan Diar have to gain by losing followers in this way? Or . . . and this thought disturbed him more . . . what sort of work was he engaged in that made such losses acceptable?

He thought then of the Order of the Red Knife and his heart quickened. Not something he'd put past the cold-eyed, ambitious Elissan Diar. But Etherell would not involve himself in blood divination . . . surely not. Something else must be at work. Not for the first time, Dorn regretted he couldn't speak with Valanir Ocune. Not that the Seer had been particularly available even when he was around, but since his departure the Archmasters clearly felt they had free rein to do as they pleased. The eye of the Crown, as embodied in the Seer Ocune, was no longer upon them.

Perhaps the disappearance of Syme Oleir—a lively fellow, more popular by far than Gared Dexane—would have garnered more scrutiny if events even stranger had not immediately followed. One morning three students, second-years of fourteen, were sent to gather kindling in the forest. This was customary—it was a chore considered beneath the more advanced students. But they didn't come back. None were known for disobedience, yet as day waned to evening still they did not return. For two days the castle was in a state of panic, as the Archmasters organized search parties and some, like Archmaster Lian, were in a rage. Apparently two of the boys were of noble blood. Any harm that came to them would need to be accounted for.

Noon on the third day the boys staggered through the castle gates. They trembled with exhaustion, their garments in tatters as if they'd been flung through a hedge of thorns. But their story, which was meant to stay confined to the Archmasters but swiftly circulated throughout the Academy, far eclipsed their appearance in strangeness. Dorn heard a full retelling at dinner that day, by a solemn fourth-year who believed it his duty to keep all informed.

The tale ran that on their way back to the castle the boys had taken a common shortcut, marked by an oak that was one of the largest on the Isle. As they passed the tree they had begun to grow tired. Next they knew they were waking from sleep on a mountain, bare and stony, with no sign of the season's green, torn by a wind that had the bite of winter.

After a long, desperate climb, they came at evening to a cave where a woman sat at a tall fire. Here the tone of the tale-teller became reverent. "And they say she was lovelier than a hawthorn in spring," said the thin boy, rubbing his nose wistfully.

"I'm sure," said Dorn. Though he had to admit that if they were lying, the invention was impressive.

The woman was clad in diaphanous gold, they said; the outlines of her body near-visible even while hidden from view. Her hair black and shining like onyx, a mass of braids bound in gold thread down one shoulder, falling past her waist. Her eyes . . . here he stopped. These were indescribable, it seemed.

"I can imagine what happens next," Dorn had said.

The boy had shaken his head, equal parts negation and reproach. "It wasn't like that," he said. His tone hushed with that same reverence. First she had waved a hand and a table spread with a great feast appeared

before the boys. Neatly folded on each chair was a change of clothes, soft
and woven of bright, costly colors. Later, after luxurious baths in hot
springs beneath the cavern, the boys would discover the clothes suited
them as if they'd been tailored to fit. New boots they had as well, and
fur-lined cloaks against the chill. They then attended to the food: soft
loaves of bread still fragrant from baking; meat so rare it was bloody;
colorful, sweet fruits they'd never seen. Their gold chalices that brimmed
with wine remained full no matter how much they drank.

The woman did not eat or drink. At first she stood watching them at
their feast. When they were done, having eaten the last of the fruits and
meat and bread, a harp appeared in her hands, and she sang for them.
And with her voice she possessed their hearts.

She declared she would give herself to the one who succeeded at
three tasks, each of which sounded more impossible than the last. They
were first to build a ship of their own hands from whatever timber they
could find on the mountain, sail west seven days, until they would come
to a land where lived a giant; their mission, of course, that he should
be slain. Following this second task, they were to recover a necklace the
giant had stolen from her, an amulet of engraved gold that belonged to
her kin. So they had set off, bound by their common purpose yet in
competition with one another; only one could be winner. And the desire
that drove them was like none other they'd had. For her they would die
or kill many times over.

Here the boy trailed off. He looked around at the expectant listeners,
of whom most were younger than he. Shifted from one foot to the other.
The meal had long since ended; chairs had been pushed back, food long
since devoured. In the dining hall there grew, despite the number of
boys there, an unbearable silence. At last one of the students urged,
"What happened?"

The boy swallowed. "They say . . . they say they wandered years in
pursuit of the lady's tasks. One thinks it was eight years, another ten,
another fifteen. They would not say more, only that . . . that at the end
they failed, all three, and were sent home."

They had returned in the clothes they had worn on departing. Nor
did they show signs of age. No trace upon them of another world.

Years? Dorn wanted to laugh and found he could not. The memory
came to him of a night of lament before the corpse of the High Master,

when it seemed the doors of the world were opened. He said, almost accusingly, "That is truly all they say?"

The boy glanced at Dorn with alarm. "That is all. And . . . and that they are done with music. That they will never know joy again, now that they've lost the lady."

"Such words," one of the other students scoffed, and cuffed the tale-teller's arm. "Now they have material for nights in the Tower for years to come." A ripple of laughter went around at this; all students had suffered nights in the Tower of the Winds when they would sit for hours, stare at the caperings of their candle or out to sea, and struggle to find words.

So it became a jest at the end. But later that same night one of the boys who had been lost was discovered hanging by his neck from a beam in the kitchen storage room. He had used his own belt. It was only by randomest good fortune that the cook had needed something from the storage room at just that time. The boy was cut down, and lived. The Archmasters sent him away.

In later days the two who remained kept to themselves, vouchsafing not a shred of interest in their peers, only grudgingly heeding the Archmasters. On the few occasions when Dorn met their gaze he was shocked by the emptiness he saw there. Soon they, too, departed, and were not heard from again.

Whether or not the tale was true, *something* had occurred in the woods, at the site of the great oak tree.

JULIEN thought she would always remember the evening it began. She had guessed what was happening even before Sendara did. When she saw Etherell Lyr advancing towards them, eyes respectfully downcast, she had known all that would happen. Perhaps fear was foresight of a kind.

When Etherell was near Sendara Diar had noticed him, had an uncertain smile. With a flourish and in full view of the dining hall he had presented her with a wood carving: slender, elegant, utterly strange. Julien Imara had never seen its like, with its noble, equine head and serpent's body. Sendara had turned it over in her hands. "A seahorse," she said. Her breath unsteady despite herself. "It is fine work."

"It is like you." Etherell's eyes, the color of water, were solemn. "A rare, graceful beauty in a place of darkness."

"Oh," said Sendara. Blood rose in her cheeks.

They strolled from the dining hall together, after. Sendara with her eyelashes cast down, still with a high color. She wore the white lace dress, cinched with the red belt. The neckline dipped to show white, tender skin and the hollow of her breasts. Etherell was not seen to look there, however; his gaze, gentlemanlike, was trained on her face. He spoke with an appearance of care, Julien thought, as if in his hands he held a delicate, untamed bird.

Not that he held her then. Not yet.

Julien Imara wandered that night. The last time she'd done so had been weeks earlier, the night she'd encountered Sendara Diar in the Hall of Harps. Since that time she hadn't felt the need. All the nights she had slept soundly, soothed as if the calm breezes of her childhood were returned to her, instead of winds that wailed across the Isle from the mountains to the sea. Mornings she would spring from bed with anticipation of the day. Each conversation, each new walk in the woods was a moment of potential; a seed which any moment might flower into some new understanding, a revelation. The chamber of Elissan Diar, bathed in light and lined with books and art from distant places, seemed a beacon in the distance: an embodiment of all that someday might be. Someday she would walk beside Sendara Diar and they would be equal, or just about; they would share knowledge, power, a bond. Not a bond like she had with Alisse— something edged and intense, answering a deep-rooted need.

Maybe it was better not to have hopes, she thought now, as the shadow of the corridor swallowed hers. Not to get above herself, as she clearly had. When she had seen them together she'd understood. His beauty and her beauty. Both with a light to draw the eye. She had been a fool—pitifully stupid, really—to think she could approach that, touch it in any way.

On the ground level now. All was silent. Faces leered from the walls. Or rather the Mocker did, as if with a sneer intended for her. The Mourner's tears too close to bear. And the others—the Poet, the King— more distant than ever. The idea that she would ever be a poet was ludicrous.

Julien ducked into the Hall of Harps before she had a chance to think. Hardly noticing the outstretched knife of Kiara that jutted in her path. No one was about tonight, though she kept alert for sounds of the chosen. They were not usually in the Hall, so far as she knew. At times she would awaken from fitful dreams to hear a chorus of voices, faint, ghostly on the wind. And she would know it was Elissan Diar and his handpicked boys out in the forest, and from there pass into dreams stranger still.

It had nagged at her since that night in the Hall, when she had first met Sendara—her certainty that the carving of the dancer had changed. Later in daylight Julien had visited it again, confirmed that it was indeed a sword the dancer now held in one hand, while in the other still a torch. A sword with a wicked curve. But by then Julien had begun to doubt her own memory. Who was to say it had not been thus all along?

Silver light from the Branch guided Julien down the length of the Hall of Harps. Her eye searched for carvings she recognized. And there was one: the knight, riding to what seemed his certain demise in the teeth of a monster. Julien blinked. It was not a monster's teeth she saw anymore, rising around about the knight. Nor was he riding. And the image shifted as if before her eyes; the horse was gone. A lone man on foot, a harp at his side—a poet. What arose around him were flames.

Her breath caught in her mouth, Julien searched for another carving she knew. Instead she spotted one she had not seen before: Three men stood in a row, a sword lain across their necks. Their faces blank with sorrow. In the upper right corner of this tile a symbol—a circle threaded with a loop, as if to represent some charm. In the upper left corner, a harp.

What means all this?

"And yet." A voice behind her. Julien spun around. Valanir Ocune was not looking at her. His eyes were fixed on the carvings past her head. "You haven't noted the one that concerns me most."

"*Valanir,*" she whispered. Then hastened to correct herself. "Seer Ocune."

He lay a finger to his lips. Though his mouth turned upward, he looked sad. "Look here," he said in his low, magnificent voice, and pointed. This was the carving of the woman who, Julien recalled, ran her sword through a harp. Her movements ferocious as if channeling a great anger, apparent even in the simple lines of the carving. But now it seemed even as Julien watched the picture changed, shifted in the play of pale light. The harp had lengthened, changed its shape. Become another woman, a sword through her heart.

Julien noticed something else. The strokes that made each of the women were identical. The same woman, twice. One running the other through with a sword.

"What do you think it means?" Julien dared ask. There was far more she wanted to ask, but it seemed trivial. Valanir Ocune was here. He had not vanished. But wanted the Academy to believe he had.

He wasn't looking at her now. He said, "I sent her into danger, and didn't tell her everything. And now I begin to wonder . . . if I even *knew* what I should have. What there was to tell."

"Lady Amaristoth."

He didn't answer. Julien waited. Valanir Ocune continued to study the carving.

"Is it for her you've made yourself vanish?" she said. "Or . . ." She thought of Elissan Diar at his desk as he calmly recounted Valanir's absence. "Are you in danger?"

"I'm waiting," he said. "Readying things, and waiting. I will have only one opportunity, you see. And yes, some here would have had—other plans for me."

The quiet unnerved her. If someone should come . . . yet he seemed unworried. "What do you wait for, Valanir Ocune?" And then stifled a gasp, for something wholly unlikely was happening: the Seer Valanir Ocune had got down on one knee before her. His eyes, now nearer her own, were like green glass.

"I have a favor to ask, Julien Imara," he said. "But I fear putting you in harm's way."

"Is it—is it for the Court Poet?"

He nodded. "I will have only one chance. You've seen here tonight— and in other ways—gates on this Isle are opening. Since Darien Aldemoor restored the enchantments it began, and now with each thing we do . . . it is a wondrous but terrible thing, and I don't know . . . I don't know what the ends will be. If we can survive it. The barriers between this world, and others, are melting away. And so much of the knowledge we had is gone. I don't know how Seers dealt with it in the past. We are all in danger here, Julien Imara—more so each day. If I were the man I'd like to be, I'd send you home."

"I'd rather die than go home."

He laughed softly. "That can't be true. There is so little here for you.

No one teaches you as they should. And your friend . . . well, that is another story."

She looked down at his hands: the callused fingers, long clean nails. His ring, the moon opal ring, had a glow all its own. She didn't know what to say to him. *I have no home.* It seemed more true than ever. Then it sank in that he had spoken, if obliquely, of Sendara Diar. "Another story—how?"

He shook his head. For the first time he seemed aware they might be discovered, his glance darting towards the door. His brow dark with anger. "They return from their vigil. It was outside this time . . . near the lake. They prepared for this one, this night, for a long time. And . . ." His voice changed. "Another. They've lost another. Syme Oleir this time." Valanir covered his eyes with both hands. "He would have been a good man. He *was* one."

"Lost." Julien stared at him. "But I thought . . ." She stopped. Gared Dexane had been sent home, it was said. It was said. Julien planted her feet, as if in advance of combat. Spoke the words with which her life's course, already diverted by her arrival to the Isle, would be changed yet again. "Tell me how I might help."

HE left her alone in the Tower of the Winds that first night. The door to the Tower of Glass closed behind him and then, as Lin watched, the planks of the door wavered strangely, as if masked by water. Moments later there was no door, only the stones of the wall. The only way out now was through the second door, the one that led to her rooms.

Before Zahir Alcavar left her in the Tower to herself, he had some departing words for her. "Do not be grateful to me, Lady Amaristoth," he'd said. "We still are who we are. You are the Court Poet of Eivar, and I, First Magician of Majdara. I give this to you with a purpose. You never had a chance to discover your enchantments. Now you will."

"And then perhaps I may help you," she said. They were standing close, perhaps more than necessary. She remained very still.

He bent his head. "There is a chance. Valanir Ocune believes you possess the potential for great skill—he told me as much. I see no reason to doubt it."

"I don't even know what I'm looking for."

"I know. I'll help however I can. But for now—just allow yourself to be here. You are taking what should have been yours. Through this, discoveries will come. And something tells me—you may find something I've missed, here in the Zahra. The missing piece to our shadow."

So she sat within a cubicle of stone—one of many in this Tower. The candle at her elbow lit the paper before her, nothing else. Waves crashed outside. Spring on the Isle, at night. She had been there only once before, in autumn.

That was, unless she counted the time Valanir had brought her here and made her Seer. But like the gift of Zahir Alcavar, that memory seemed to exist outside any time or place.

The blank paper mocked her like an insurmountable mountain. This itself was a subject of poems, of course—the taunting of the virgin page. A fear well-founded in fact: so little differentiated between songs great, good, or mediocre, yet that minute element—that which accounted for greatness—was impossible to produce on command. As with a mountain, she could attempt it, and most likely fail in the attempt. But to turn back would be to wonder for the rest of her days what she might have done.

It was late now, it had to be. On the Isle, too. How was it that the moon had risen, if the place was fixed in a moment in time? Something to ask Zahir. But if she did, he would pull out his charts and pictograms to explain it to her, and she realized she preferred not to know how it worked. It didn't matter. Here she was, with the music of wind and sea; the reality of ink and paper. Where she might, at least for the space of this night, find words.

ALEIRA Suzehn frowned as she studied the prophecy Zahir had drawn in his elegant hand. She sat at her desk in the back room of the shop, her hair today pinned up, exposing long earrings of red and blue beads that clinked when she turned her head. Lin could not bring herself to sit, so anxious did she feel now that the moment had come; she shifted her feet, paced the room, as the merchant bent to her task. She had taken care to check this copy of the prophecy against the original in the observatory. It all seemed in order.

It was morning and Lin had hardly slept. She had stumbled down the dark passage from the Tower of the Winds when it was nearly dawn, to be awakened soon after by the temple gong. She'd retained a burning awareness, even in sleep, of the pages she had left on her desk in the Tower. As if she had left behind a piece of herself. Nothing had happened in the course of her night there, no signs of an arising enchantment; only a fever of words as if she had been waiting all this time for them to come.

She had written some nights in Tamryllin, to avoid her dreaming. That had been different, though. Always she'd been weighted with the awareness of what her true duties were—in the council chamber at the side of the king, or in meetings with political figures to settle disputes. There was that sense, too, of having been denied something important that even the lowest of the poets got: the chance to compose in the Tower of the Winds itself. If enchantments would ever come to her through art, it would be here.

He wants me to help him, she reminded herself. She could not allow herself to feel indebted to Zahir. Such an imbalance between them would be inappropriate. He himself had understood as much.

Aleira made a sound of irritation.

"What is it?"

The merchant shook her head. She looked unhappy. "It is as you said," she said. "As the Magicians are saying. The threat comes from the north." She slumped, balanced her jaw on both hands. "It doesn't make sense."

Lin felt a flood of relief, but knew Aleira would not want to see that. She ironed the expression from her face. "I am sure there is an explanation. Perhaps the Jitana have discovered a new power."

The other woman looked up, eyes like amber chips. "There is an explanation . . . yes. What it *is* remains to be seen. The north is vast, Lady Amaristoth. The Jitana are surely not the only people there who might pose a threat." She was again perusing the prophecy. "I want to study this more carefully. Will you leave it with me?"

"Of course." Lin knew she said it too quickly, glad to be done with that worry. With a sigh she settled into one of the cushions. "Tell me," she said, "why do you call them Jitana? I haven't heard anyone else use that name."

Aleira sat upright, set down the prophecy on her crowded desk. She inhaled a breath and let it out in a long sigh. "Who is it," she said, finally, "that gives people their names? The Jitana have always been called thus. But those who banished them to the land's edge call them Fire Dancers, based on tales brought back by travelers. It is the same way, you know, with Galicians."

"I didn't know."

"Few do," said Aleira Suzehn. "Once there was a city in the east—

long ago, before Ramadus was the power it is. That was the great city Galicia, and most of my people took refuge there. You know how we came to be there, don't you?"

Lin dropped her eyes, feeling for the first time complicit in something. "I heard . . . it was . . . a curse."

"Our home was an island. One day in the middle of autumn the oceans took it away. Most of the people were killed. Those few who escaped on ships . . . well, Ellenicans and Alfinians alike had long despised worshipers of the Unnamed God. And now here, at last, was *proof* that they were cursed—the ocean itself had opened to swallow them.

"So it was declared, then, and for always. That we were to be called Galicians after a city not our own—though soon exiled from Galicia for some imagined offense. And that our doom was to wander forever without a home—a reminder that the Three are just, or that the Thousand-Named God rules all. There is no place we are not outcast and our home is gone."

"It is a great wrong," said Lin. "I would make it right if I could. What, then, is the name of your people?"

Aleira shook her head. "It was lost. The waters swallowed everything, all the writings. And it was very long ago."

Lin noted the anger that animated the other woman through this conversation. It seemed of note that she had never mentioned a family. No one who would have grieved if the Jitana had slit her throat. Lin knew that there were massacres of Galicians, going on all the time and especially during the wars between provinces. She was ashamed not to know more. "I am glad to know what you have told me," she said. "Even though it does no good. Still I would know."

"You are a woman highly placed," said Aleira. Her face had softened. "It matters that you know what happens in the world. Someday a life may depend on it."

Lin felt embarrassed by this, though could not have said why. It seemed repellent, that someone should ever be at the mercy of either her ignorance or knowledge.

"I have one more question for you," she said. "I recently spoke with someone who claims . . . well, this is strange. He claims the troops who helped Yusuf Evrayad in his conquest of Kahishi were . . ." She stopped, thought about how it sounded. But Aleira waited patiently, so Lin went on. "His words were, '*They were not men.*' He could not tell me more . . . but you know something of magic. More than I do, I am sure."

"They were not men." Aleira tilted her head as if something called to her. It made her seem birdlike. "Those were his words? But they must have seemed like men, correct? . . . Otherwise the accounts would have mentioned something. So he is saying these soldiers had the *appearance* of men, and yet were not." Color rose in Aleira's face. "A drastic revision of history, were it true. I know scholars who would give their eyes for proof."

"What do you mean?"

"Well, what do you think?" The merchant's cheeks glowed. "It could mean Yusuf Evrayad, the great conqueror, unifier of the Kahishian provinces, was a black Magician—or employed one."

AS she strolled the Way of Booksellers back towards the river, Lin let herself linger at a display of books on shelves outside. Most were not in her language or even in Kahishian, but the sight still stirred excitement. And regret—there was so much to learn, even for the most abundant lifetime. In a way it made no sense for her to keep returning to books as she did, to new knowledge. But she could not imagine stopping.

On the way she noticed workers stringing up colored lanterns. When she reached the harbor she saw more of these—a massive undertaking was underway to line the riverfront in festive lights. It recalled to her a night of the Midsummer Masque in Tamryllin—one of the great turnings of her life.

Once she saw men putting together latticed boards, intricately crafted and worked with gold. So far what they had built was nearly the size of a small barge, but could not be meant for water. That was when she remembered something Zahir Alcavar had mentioned in passing. The Feast of Nitzan.

Lin turned up the Way of Water in the direction of the plaza at the Gate of Falcons. It was a long walk and it might have been wise to bring a sedan chair or other conveyance, but she took pleasure in her independence. Besides, she wanted to make sure Aleira's identity remained secret. The politics of court were a danger that must not touch the merchant, who was innocent.

Innocent might not have been the right word, perhaps; the flush in Aleira Suzehn's face as she contemplated exposing a royal scandal had bordered on lust. She hated Yusuf Evrayad on behalf of the Jitana. Perhaps on her own behalf as well? Lin didn't know what precisely had happened to make Aleira end up an orphan in the Renegade king's fortress. She didn't plan to ever ask.

One's shadow is private, she thought. Then wondered—as she often did—if the thought was her own.

One's shadow. Rayen flinging her down stairs to the music of their mother's laugh. His fist springing to take her in the jaw. The time he'd carved the blade of his hunting knife, slowly, in the palm of her hand. And that last day she'd seen him, when he'd tied her down and sketched on her chest a sign in blood meant for magic.

It was not a darkness to share with the world. Sharing would not serve to illuminate it. It was hers.

"There is a story," Aleira had said, in a low, throaty murmur, rooting through a pile of books. "Yes," she said, drawing out a volume of battered brown leather and finding the page. Lin glanced down, but it was not in a language she knew. When she refocused her gaze on the merchant it was with new admiration. Kahishian was the only other language Lin could read. "A Samarrian tale," said Aleira, eyes on the text. "A man once sought revenge against the king for the death of his son. The boy had been unjustly put to death. This man, this Salman, he knew the only way to move against a king was with an army. Of course he had no means of assembling one, as a common craftsman. But there was a spell . . . this is where it becomes unclear." Aleira pursed her lips. "There are no details as to how Salman called upon his army. I must do further research."

"I appreciate it."

"Not at all." Aleira shut the book with a snap. "If Yusuf conquered that way, I want to know."

THE Tower drew her to return later that evening. It felt that way—that she answered a call. As dusk lowered on the Isle outside the window Lin dipped her pen in ink and with a melody striking its first chords in her, she wrote.

It had been a day of duties. After her sojourn in the city she had met with Garon Senn, who reported news to her of singular interest. It seemed that that afternoon, for a light repast of figs, dates, and olive bread, Tarik Ibn-Mor had met behind closed doors with the ambassador of Ramadus. Lin had noticed the man during the court introductions—slim, with a thin, clever face, going by the name Bakhor Bar Giora. Pale hair—a Galician, perhaps. Galicians were said to fill prominent offices in Ramadus.

"So?" she said to Garon. "What was said?"

They were in Garon's chambers again, this time with tapers lit as evening crept at the window. They'd just sat in an interminable council with Eldakar, the Magicians, and various courtiers who represented the viziers; there was no news yet from Almyria, but an attack was expected at any time. Mansur Evrayad expected reinforcements from Vizier Miuwiyah to arrive any day. But Zahir had spoken passionately about the inadequacy of this number, based on seekings of the Tower of Glass. This attack of the Fire Dancers would make previous ones look like skirmishes. Eldakar had conceded that more men must mass in Almyria's defense. Though Tarik did not raise the issue of Ramadus again this time, the pall of Eldakar's fateful error was tangible in the confines of the chamber. Without a marital alliance, only shameful capitulation could gain the support of Ramadus. And Majdara had its pride.

So Lin had left the council feeling as if Kahishian affairs weighed upon her. This was nothing like the comparatively minor matters she dealt with in Eivar, complicated as those might become. These events evoked the tension of an indrawn breath.

And now, according to Garon, a meeting was held in secret between Tarik and the Ramadian ambassador.

"How am I to know what was said?" He was annoyed. "But the fact of the meeting is itself significant. I found out only because I was keeping close watch on his rooms—it was not announced. And Bar Giora entered through the side door. It was clearly meant, as much as possible, to be kept private."

"All right," said Lin. "Well done. But I must know what they are saying to each other."

"The Ramadian's rooms are heavily guarded at all times," said Garon. "But a look at Tarik's papers would tell me much, I suspect. They can't often meet. There must be correspondence of a sort."

"And you're telling me *his* rooms aren't guarded?"

"They are locked," said Garon. "Guarded? Only when the man himself is there. It is the Magician's person that's of value to the throne, not his possessions. And the Feast of Nitzan is soon."

"So?"

"It is a time when the Magicians will be out in the city, participating in the rites," Garon explained with an obnoxious air of patience. "A good time for me to make a move. To see what I can find. I'll befriend Tarik now . . . see if I can get an idea where such correspondence is kept." His smile here reminded her what he was. "Locks don't hinder me, my lady."

"That's no surprise," she said. Sardonic, to cover the revulsion she felt. "Very well. So that is our plan. You'll search his rooms during Nitzan."

AT her desk in the Tower these concerns—of war in Almyria, of intrigues with Garon Senn—receded. If she were honest, she did not care about them at all. Not in ways that mattered. With each passing day she neared the abyss, and knew it; what else could truly matter to her? By day she did her duty as best she could. Her nights . . . these nights had become everything.

She had moved beyond the favorite topics of poets. She had begun with pretty verses about the gardens of the Zahra, but had not felt satisfied with these; had moved on, from there, to a time-honored refrain—that of the poet on the road recalling home. But this didn't draw her, either, perhaps because the idea of a home had never taken root for her. Where, after all, was *home* for the last Amaristoth, and a female poet, and a woman on the threshold of the final portal? Vassilian was a cold castle without her soul. Tamryllin, a place she loved, but where she was compelled to armor and mask herself. *Home,* to her, was a night singing at the fire with Darien and Hassen when they'd still had hopes; or when Valanir sang to her in the chamber overlooking the harbor, and she had let herself forget—for a moment—that they would be parted soon and besides, he had loved so many women. Moments like flame that danced to ash were all she knew of home.

And what underlay these moments? What was the thread, the throughline, that drove it all?

What belonged to her, not to the Seer who crouched in her soul?

When she pressed the pen to paper again, Lin was thinking of the song that drew her, that must draw her now that it was soon to end. The one she owned in a way Edrien Letrell could not touch. The arc of her life.

Lin Amaristoth wasn't sure when it happened that night—the first time the world dropped away. She was at her desk, crafting a verse with painstaking care, crossing out lines, inserting new ones, starting over again. The next moment she stood in a corridor. One she recognized too well. Doors marched into the distance, as if multiplied by the reflections of a mirror: they were endless. The details of the place changed continuously, the eye couldn't hold it. She saw gilding and marble, then whitewash and cobwebs, then carpeting and plush shadows, and on. This was not one place, she knew, but several, all at once.

Kiara guard me here, she thought, but with a bitter edge; the goddess had done little yet to guard her that she could see.

The only way out was through. Lin opened the door nearest her. She saw a room in the Academy; she knew this right away. It was lit only by a fire and smelled of rain-soaked leaves; the windows moonlit. Seated at the fire were two men, one with his back to her, hooded against a draft. Facing her, the mark at his eye a shimmer when he turned his head towards the window, was a face she knew well.

"The girl will act as a concealment for me," said Valanir Ocune to the man seated across from him. "An elementary task, without much in the way of danger. She is stronger than she knows. I want you to keep watch over her if—whatever happens."

The other man leaned forward. His voice was young, mellifluous. "It sounds as if you expect danger."

Valanir shifted in his chair. "I don't expect it. But it makes sense to be prepared. That's why I need you there. I know you have your duties. You must find an excuse to get away."

The other man stretched. Even from behind, his movements were graceful, confident, qualities that also informed his voice. "Of course. As you know, I have my ways. But I'm interested to know what you'll be doing that night."

"I'm sure you are," said Valanir in acid tones. "But there's a reason we're meeting in this abandoned tower—which is awfully drafty, by the way, even with the firewood you brought. I must keep what I do secret."

"Even from me?" The man sounded half-teasing.

Valanir shook his head. "It is not my secret to share," he said. "What I can tell you is . . . It will be one of the most perilous acts I've attempted. Manaia is when the portals are thinned, more than they are already. The only time I might have a chance."

"So you do it for another."

Valanir smiled. "Someday you'll know what that means, boy. Even if you don't think so now." His smile faded, and he looked bemused. "You could say what I intend to do the night of Manaia . . . I do for love. Gods help me."

"Love!" said the younger man. "You'll need the gods' help, indeed."

They both laughed. And then a darkness came over Lin's eyes, as if someone had flung a bag over her head. A sickening jolt, and the room was gone. Lin found herself back in the corridor. When she tried the door again, it was locked.

Dread tugged at her. Valanir going into danger. *For love.* She had been telling herself that she was the one in danger; that Valanir was safe. But had all along known better.

The quiet in the hallway was oppressive. Lin knew there was no way out until the Path had had its way with her. It was still with that dread that she grasped the doorjamb of the next door, and pushed.

The scene that greeted her, bright-lit and warm, brought to mind one of the paintings that sold to the newly rich, sneered at by the aristocracy. Such subject matter was seen as too cloying, too unashamed in its simple joy. It was the front room of a house, where a woman rocked her baby, a man at her side.

The house was one like Lin had seen in paintings but never in life: small, cozily furnished, lit with a warm glow. Humble, yet rich with comforts. The home of an artisan, perhaps, or a moderately successful merchant early in his career. There was a fire in the hearth, and a carpet and couches. It was a place to take one's ease, away from the cares of market streets.

It took her several moments to recognize the man. He was in the far corner, after all, and blond hair half-hid his face as he bent over the woman's shoulder to gaze at the child she held. The moment Lin knew him was when he began, softly, to sing. His hand came down to the woman; she grasped it. And then he turned his head so Lin could better see his face, just as his voice had made her know him.

The glow of the home was within him, too. As Alyndell Renn sang, Lin saw, the melody was carried by a light from within. That light, of course, was love.

The first, perhaps the only man she'd loved with her whole heart. Who had deserted her, pregnant with their child, when the offer of her hand came stripped of gold and titles.

It had helped to think him incapable of love, Lin thought, as she closed her eyes. It had helped.

She opened her eyes. The two of them played with the baby, each with a finger clasped in its fist. She saw the woman, lovely and curly-haired, with features soft and sweet.

She saw Alyn bend towards the woman, kiss her hair. Closing his eyes a moment as if drinking it all in, the wealth of her and the gift of new life she had given him.

Lin found herself at her desk in the Tower of the Winds. The air swam before her though she was dry-eyed yet. *Maybe it will be all right to die,* she thought, and hated herself for it.

She looked down at the desk. The pen still gripped in her hand. Before her now, on the desk, a page of verses. They were unmistakably in her hand. But not written as her earlier attempts had been, in careful strokes, with words and phrases crossed out, rewritten. This had flowed swiftly and without corrections. Lin took up the page.

> *I came to a place awash in light*
> *It stabbed me to the heart.*
> *Sweet and strong the contained hearthfire*
> *Sweet the voice that once*
> *Breathed through my hair, called me by name.*
> *Those days are done.*

Here, then, was the throughline, the arc of her life, as some part of her had known from the start: it was loss. The lies that had assuaged her heart were turned like a knife in the hand; from defense to a truth that eviscerated. Lin's head slipped into her hands. She remained that way as night fell on Academy Isle and a wind rose off the water, carrying the promise of rain and the old, much older scents of the sea.

SHE found them in the gardens, though not in the way she expected: Rihab Bet-Sorr was there, too, standing with Eldakar by the waterfall. Lin was not sure how she recognized the queen in the dark—perhaps it was her proud carriage, her willowy body like the trees along the bank. And Zahir was there, but stood apart as if to allow the couple their space. It was he that Lin had been seeking.

As she approached she saw that Eldakar and the queen did not quite stand together. "You don't listen," said Rihab.

Eldakar reached across the space to touch her cheek. "Every word you speak is precious to me," he said. "It grieves me to see you unhappy—more than you know. But this is my home, Rihab. My duties are here. What would you have me do?"

"I don't say to leave forever," she said. "Just . . . for a time. Until the tensions of the city have eased."

"This city is my responsibility," said Eldakar.

The queen shook her head. "It has cost me so much to love you." She turned abruptly, vanished into the trees.

"Go to her," said Zahir.

"No." Eldakar was like a sorrowful statue beside the water. "Nothing I say can assure her. Nothing I do. She is going to her game, most likely. The only thing that can distract her mind. That mind," he said, sounding tired, "that is always, always at work, even when we make love."

"That need not be altogether a bad thing," Zahir said gently, and his friend laughed, but even as he did so covered his eyes with both hands. "I can't make her happy," said Eldakar.

Lin stepped forward, though with a pang of guilt for disturbing them. Both men looked up. "Lin," said Zahir, in the same gentle tone he had used with his friend.

"I must speak with you."

"Of course, *Miryan*." He held out a hand. "Tell me why you look so sad."

* * *

A SERVANT had escorted Ned to the spot where they were to meet, making it oddly official. For what seemed a long time they had wended the paths of the imperial gardens in the dark, with only the servant's lamp to light their way. He expected it would be the site of another chess game. But when they arrived at the pavilion—dainty, carved of pale wood, surrounded by rose hedges—Ned saw there was no gameboard on the table. There was a pitcher of wine, and two cups, and the queen presiding over these with an expression he could not read in the lamplight.

"Leave us," she commanded the servant, who bowed low, lower than perhaps he need have; it occurred to Ned that this particular servant, a burly, grim-faced man who did not speak—who might have been mute—was more loyal to the queen than most. It would make sense, as her meeting Ned out here, away from the eyes of her maids and the other servants, was not the custom. For all he knew it was a breach of their laws, one that could pose a danger to him as much as it did to her.

She indicated a seat beside her on the cushioned bench. A bench that seemed uncommonly long, wide, accommodating to anything they might do. Ned swallowed hard. "I believe I'll sit here," he said, and took the chair across from her instead. Making a decision as he did so. There was only so much he would do for Lin. And another thought—if he let this woman beguile him, if he made love to her, Ned knew it would not be out of loyalty to his lady and Tamryllin. It would not be for any purpose beyond himself. That made the act out of bounds for him.

"You are an unpredictable man, Ned Alterra," said the queen in a voice that made him need to draw breath, slowly, as he sat down.

"Not if you knew me," he said. "Some very straightforward principles guide me, as it happens." He poured himself some of the wine, without waiting for her to offer. Formalities had sometime, along the way, collapsed between them.

"It's a shame," she said. "I had him leave the lamp here because I thought—better to see you."

Ned swallowed some of the wine. He allowed himself a moment, feeling the warmth stream the length of him. Potentially a dangerous warmth and yet . . . for now it composed him. "My lady," he said, "if I may, I'll be honest. I believe I know you to some degree after these few days." When she did not speak, but only watched him with that unfathomable gaze, he went on. "It's not me you want. You are in dread of something, and hopeless, and for whatever reason you can't tell Eldakar. You are using me. Want to use me. As a distraction." His breath quivered but he steadied it, as one did the prow of a ship in a high wind. "If it please you, my lady," he said, courteously, "I will not be part of your game."

A long silence. He didn't look away from her, would not betray how she affected him. Her eyes were pools of darkness.

At last she said, "I love Eldakar. Do you believe that?" Like a child she propped her elbows on the table and her chin on her hands. "Ned, I'm so tired."

"I know," he said. "*The game never changes,* you said. Care to elaborate?"

"I love him but I can't protect him," she said, her voice dull now instead of smooth. "I try, but even I can't decipher where the danger is coming from. And worst of all . . . *I* am being used against him, Ned. A web is spun to trap us both. I can see it. Eldakar—he sees only what he wants to see."

"But what do you mean—a web?"

She leaned across the table. "Think about it. I am the slave girl he married. Instead of making the political alliance that might have saved him. Saved us all. It is used against him at every turn."

He nodded. He could not argue with that.

Her gaze was fixed somewhere beyond him, now, into the night and the garden. A cricket sang. Her face relaxed into wistfulness. "More and more," she said, "I have begun to think of home. Of my father, whose prize I was. He prized me for my mind. Now I am trapped in this palace—an ornament, and worse, a weapon against the man I love. It all went wrong. I've looked for a way to fix it and . . . now I believe there isn't one. It can't be fixed." There were tears on her face, Ned saw, and he looked away. Knowing himself well enough. If he was not careful, her pain could succeed at luring him where more obvious lures had failed.

"I have a plan for Nitzan," she said, and Ned looked up. There was a new purpose to the way she spoke, a sharp enunciation of the words. Like a field commander. "Ned, I can do it nearly alone, but need help with one small thing. Will you do that for me?"

And just like that he was on the cliff again, looking down and being asked to take a leap. Just when he'd thought he had control of the situation. Had thought, in fact, that he was steering it in the direction he chose, as he once had a merchant ship. Fool that he was.

He asked, "How small?" And in doing so set in motion events beyond that sweet-scented night, the crickets' song, the stars.

LATER Lin couldn't sleep. In truth, she didn't try. Using the key Zahir Alcavar had given her, she returned to the Tower of the Winds. By then it was so late that it was not night at all, but already morning. The sky outside the window was featureless, in that space when the stars were gone, before the emergence of the sun. It seemed fitted to her mood.

She sat at the cubicle she had chosen, where her papers were piled on the desk. Lin could not even look at the words she'd written the last time, to recall what had led to them. With a violent motion she seized that paper and buried it at the bottom of the pile. Taking out a fresh sheet, she dipped the quill pen and set its nib to the paper before she could think.

Thought didn't seem to have much to do with how it worked, not in this place. The pen seemed to move of its own accord, though she knew she guided it with the violence of what she felt. Not just violence—a desperation. There was in her tonight a longing to escape herself.

When she found herself in the hall of doors, she felt no surprise. *Again.* As ever, the Path between the doors, the endless hall, was silent. This was a space between worlds. Nothing happened here.

So she thought. But this time something strange was happening in the corridor. There was, fluttering in the air ahead of her, what looked like a spark. It was a yellow-green and kept sputtering in and out, bobbed and weaved in circles, as if it played a game with itself. Or with her. Lin stepped towards it. The odd light darted forward, as if galvanized by her movement, and kept moving as she did. When she halted, so did the light. Unsettled now—though she didn't know why she'd expect anything *but* strangeness here—Lin resumed walking. Again, the spark flew ahead.

For the first time since she had entered the Tower she heard a muttering from Edrien Letrell. A foreboding. Something here was familiar to him, and made him wary.

The light halted suddenly. So did Lin. As she watched, it moved to a door handle, began to circle around it. One spark broke into several:

numerous tiny lights made a procession around the door handle. The invitation was clear. Again it had the feel of a game. *I suppose that means I go in.* She ignored Edrien.

The room she entered was lavish, and instantly recognizable. With its silk hangings, the carpet depicting scenes of the hunt, it resembled her bedchamber in the Zahra. So she was in the palace.

The playful sparks had gone. She stood on the threshold of this room and no longer knew why. But she had already opened the door. Lin crossed the threshold.

On the bed lay a man. No. It was a woman, arrayed in splendid dress and a gold headdress set with gems. And again: a man, his face rigid as if with pain. His clothing rich, and yet: his wrists were manacled and chained together. The chains were gold, but Lin had a sense—she was not sure how—that they were strong as iron.

And a stranger thing: rising from the chains, when she looked closely, were curls of smoke.

The muttering of Edrien had become a hiss.

A smell assailed Lin's nostrils, harsh after the accustomed scents of perfume that pervaded the Zahra: this was the smell of burning and rotted eggs. Sulphur. Nausea rose in her throat.

The man's eyes opened. His face changed again; when he smiled— even though his body remained as it was—it was the woman's smile. "Free me," he said. It was a voice of many voices, as if a legion of people, men and women, spoke at once through that mouth. "Free me, and be rewarded."

The hiss from Edrien had become vicious, like a wildcat on the verge of pouncing. She turned her attention inwardly: he was reciting. *Creature of hell, begone. Creature of hell, I rule thee. I banish thee.*

The face of the man in the bed became frantic. Again he changed into the woman with the jeweled headdress. The chorus of voices at a fever pitch. *"Free me."*

Edrien spoke to her now. *You think you are in hell. You're wrong. That thing would put you there.*

Frozen, she stared. For an instant she saw, instead of a woman on the bed, a flare like green fire in human shape. Heard a tortured howl. But only in the barest instant: and now it was a man again, panting on the bed with smoking manacles on his wrists.

Lin backed from the room and shut the door. It was with a quick step that she made her way down the hall. Soon she found herself back in the Tower. But even as she told herself she was safe, Lin recalled the familiar trappings of that room. The window overlooked a courtyard she knew, with yellow-blooming jacaranda trees. Its fountain clearly visible, warm-lit in the first light of morning.

Everywhere else she'd been, in her forays from the Tower of the Winds, had been elsewhere in the world. But this was right here—in her time and place. Somewhere nearby was that figure of fire with its howl of the damned. Held prisoner.

Who in the palace would have such a prisoner?

You may find something I've missed, Zahir had said when he'd given the key to her.

Lin slept little for what remained of the morning, and fitfully.

CHAPTER
15

THE need-fires of Manaia began as branches piled to the sky. For days students hauled firewood to the courtyard, assembling two mountainous piles with a space like a corridor between. Sendara Diar and Julien Imara made a slow circuit of the piles, inspecting them. The night of the festival, they would blaze as pillars of flame. It was hard to picture on a drab afternoon after rain, mist stealing through the courtyard like a ghost's fingers. But Julien had heard from Sendara a little of what would happen on that night. The festival was to be held in two days; as it neared, Julien felt as if tension was squeezing her around the middle, that it would break her in half. The secret she carried—Julien Imara, a girl of no consequence who until now had had nothing but the pitiful fact of her own loneliness to hide.

They'd kill Valanir Ocune if they found him. He hadn't said as much, but something in his manner told her that. And that had shocked Julien—more than finding him had, more than being selected for his plan to help the Court Poet. That such things could happen in the Academy.

After their meeting in the Hall of Harps that first night, he had taken her to an abandoned tower, where she huddled in her cloak against drafts. They'd sat at a small fire and he'd explained what he needed of her. "There is no danger in the work," he said. "Not for you. But if you are found with me . . ."

"I'll take that risk," she said, when she saw he found it difficult to go on. It pained him to risk her safety, that was clear to her. It was the reason she trusted him—that, and the fact of who he was.

"My associate will be there to guard us," said Valanir. "After all this is over, you must never let on to anyone that you know him, or people will wonder. His name must not be linked with mine. For his protection." He paused. Firelight outlined his face, the mark on his eye. "It will be a dark night. No candles are permitted in the castle while the need-fires burn. The dark may serve us well."

Now strolling in the courtyard alongside Sendara, she thought that they each, in truth, walked alone—if Sendara could be said to be alone, with the devotion of her father and Etherell Lyr at her beck. But certainly they were cut off from one another.

Julien would have thought to feel a degree of pridefulness from harboring a secret. To take comfort from the new importance it gave her. When she and Sendara walked together in the courtyard to inspect the piles, the other girl walked with her head bowed and her cheeks a rose tint as if her thoughts were far away. It was not hard to guess where they were. She'd once said, in response to something innocuous, "There's so much you don't know, Julien."

Julien had not had a response to that. It was true enough.

In that moment she had reached for the knowledge she carried, of her meetings with Valanir Ocune and the vital work she was to do. It had the substance of cobwebs. Nothing remarkable about Julien had made Valanir Ocune choose her; nothing but that she was overlooked, certain to escape notice. What made her slip so easily through the corridors of the Academy was of essence to the Seer. She wanted to help him, to be of aid to the Court Poet; beyond that the secret did nothing for her but weigh in the pit of her stomach.

She would have liked to confide in Sendara, as it happened. It was strange in a way that they walked together, when the other girl seemed to hold her in contempt. Once on a recent walk in the woods Sendara had said, with an edge of derision, "Have you *even* ever been kissed?" And Julien had wondered when the girl with whom she'd stolen away in the night to drink wine on a bed of moss . . . a girl with whom she'd shared the confidences of her heart . . . had become cruel.

"No one wants me and you know it," said Julien that time, with force, jarring the silence of the wood. She had sat down on a rock. "Why don't you go ahead," she'd said, though dusk was falling.

"Don't be such a child." Sendara's lip was curled in that way she had—an air of weary impatience, disdain. For a moment prolonged by disbelief Julien stared at that face. Searching for any sign of warmth, any opening. Any evidence of what they'd shared. The memory of their night under the stars surfaced, seemed a trick. Sendara's eyes were ice.

Deliberately, Julien folded her arms and shifted to stare straight ahead, at a random spot in the trees. Hoping she wouldn't cry. Drawing from whatever strength she could find in herself to remain impassive.

"It's clear you're jealous," said Sendara. Out of the corner of Julien's eye she saw her shrug. "I'm going back. You'd be a fool to stay out here."

She had turned and walked away. Julien had waited for what seemed a long time, seated on that rock, until she was sure the other girl had gone. But she couldn't let herself cry then, either—someone might come by, or they'd notice her red eyes at dinner, as they'd noticed the flower crown. She swallowed hard. Sadness lodged like a pebble in her throat. After a time she rose and trudged back to the castle, to arrive just before dark. Archmaster Kerwin reprimanded her in the entrance hall, in his unctuous way, for being late to dinner. Sendara Diar did not seem to notice when Julien arrived; she was watching Etherell Lyr across the table, equal parts excitement and an odd anxiety. He glanced her way only occasionally, being—Julien imagined—reserved in public. Somehow Sendara's adoration made him appear to shine even more than before; this despite the new thinness, the weariness, that marked him as among the chosen. Their pallor was a thing Etherell Lyr wore better than the rest; Maric Antrell, though equally handsome, was a flame-haired skull beside him. Under Sendara's worshipful gaze Etherell seemed to laugh more often, tell more jokes that Julien at her end of the table could just barely catch. His friend, the tall and often silent Dorn Arrin, seemed more silent than usual. Withdrawn into himself, somewhere deep. Sometimes when she caught his eye, she wondered what his thoughts were. She thought there was something in the way of torment about him even though he did not speak.

She kept thinking it was over between her and Elissan Diar's daughter, after each incident like this. But most days they fell back in step beside each other. Julien couldn't guess the reason. Perhaps it was because, in their lessons, there was no one else for Sendara to talk to barring the younger boys; outside lessons, Etherell Lyr was often busy with the other chosen, with whatever it was they did. Now that Valanir Ocune had hinted they engaged in something profane and wrong, it pained Julien to think of Etherell involved, along with other students whom she had thought decent enough, before Elissan Diar had come to the Isle.

That was when she thought of something else Valanir Ocune had said to her. Amid the clamor of the students at dinner, the laughter from the chosen as Etherell purveyed another witticism, Julien cast her mind back to that night in the drafty tower room.

"Manaia will be different this year." The Seer said this with his eyes fixed on her, near the end of their talk, as if he wanted to make sure she heard. "Now that the enchantments are back. I don't want you there. Not anywhere near those fires."

"I am to sing with Sendara," Julien said listlessly. That was another thing still binding the girls to one another; the song they had ostensibly written in collaboration. In the end, Sendara had marked it up beyond recognition, made it hers. Julien could hardly gainsay her, since she still had much to learn. She knew what she wrote was, most likely, embarrassing. Once in a while they met to practice, Sendara's voice a liquid counterpoint to Julien's softer one. Sendara's voice was, she asserted, another legacy of the mother who was a Haveren of Deere; one which had bewitched lords and kings along with her beauty. "I am in the competition," Julien said now to Valanir, though it sounded in her ears like a lie.

"I advise against it." The Seer leaned forward. "Listen, Julien Imara. Once, the festival was just some songs at the fire, the lottery no more than a joke. We knew it all hung upon ancient rites of spring, some stories, so the proceedings took a certain gravity from this—nothing more. This time will be different."

"In what way, different?"

He settled back into wings of shadow cast by the high-backed chair. His eyes in shadow, too. "Look around you—you see for yourself what's been happening," he said. "The tales made real."

DORN Arrin paced in his room. That morning he had confronted his friend—if Etherell was still his friend.

"Syme Oleir?" Dorn had said to Etherell's back. His friend was seated at their desk, writing something. Whether it was verse for Sendara Diar or a letter home, Dorn neither knew nor cared. "It was one thing when it was Gared Dexane," he went on. "Syme was . . . well, not at all like that. Doesn't it bother you?"

Etherell kept writing. "Why should it? He'll recover."

Dorn swore. "If you are stupid enough to think that, you're not the man I know. And I don't believe that."

Now, at last, Etherell turned his head. "What *do* you believe, Dorn Arrin?" His tone half-mocking.

"I think he's dead," said Dorn. Letting the words fall like so many logs to the ground. The room seemed to become very quiet. Dorn found himself speaking nearly in undertone. "I think Gared's dead, too. I spoke to the cook. She was wondering when the boys were transported back to the mainland—she never saw boats, either time. She is awake and about before anyone and would have done. I think they're gone. Their bodies burned or buried somewhere."

Etherell whistled, and turned back to his desk. "Dramatic. You'll make a fine poet, at any rate."

"*Stop.*" Dorn tried not to sound pleading. "What's happened to you? You can't think men like Elissan Diar . . . like Maric . . . are worth following?"

A moment. He thought he saw one of Etherell's hands clench on the desk. "I follow no one, Dorn Arrin." So coldly Dorn felt it in his spine. "Mind yourself. Stay out of the woods at night." Folding the paper he'd been working at, Etherell stood. His expression a match to his voice. "I can't protect you anymore."

Thinking back, Dorn could no longer recall what he had said to that; it had filled him with anger, along with a chilled sense of abandonment.

Now sitting on his bed, looking out at the lake, he felt curiously empty. As if he'd been prepared for this moment already, in various ways. Perhaps he had been preparing for it since the day Etherell had carved the seahorse. Standing illumined in sunlight. Dorn watched the trees along the bank stir to the wind's invisible hand like the strings of a harp. Their tune reached him even here.

Have you considered the adventure? his friend had said lazily about the prospect of joining the chosen. But then, soon afterward: *Wanting . . . is not something I do.*

Dorn thought of the hollows in his friend's cheeks that even a week previously had not been there. Of the feverish light in his eyes, so similar now to those of Maric Antrell. This from enchantments that Dorn felt sure were killing off the chosen, one by one.

I can't protect you anymore. Such a thing to say to a man. Even to a mere bookmaker's son. One could not help but be stung by it, made to feel small.

Was this what being welcomed in the highest circles had done to Etherell Lyr—made him scornful of Dorn's friendship? Or was it something else?

What if he knows? Dorn thought. *What if he wants to protect me?*

In which case, Etherell walked knowingly into danger for reasons of his own.

You want that to be true, Dorn told himself. He reminded himself of other unassailable facts, too, about his friend, about himself. He could not let the reality he wished to see obscure the truth. That was for people who lived within the confines of a story. Dorn made stories or sang them; he did not inhabit one himself. His thoughts must remain as crystalline as he could make them, unclouded by self-deception. That, he believed, was the essence of what it meant to be a poet. Not to work magic. Rather it was to see, and weave verse from, life's manifold truths. Even if they hurt.

They nearly always did.

I follow no one, Dorn Arrin, Etherell had said. A violence Dorn had never seen in him. Brought out, perhaps, by whatever force was burning away his flesh.

It was a strange thing to say if Etherell was to be an eager disciple of Archmaster Diar. As if his friend could not help but chafe at that authority despite himself. Despite the show he made of obedience.

There is something here. Dorn found that he was strumming his harp, a song that arose from habit. It was an old lay about glory in battle, among the first students learned. Dorn held the instrument close in his arms. He felt more himself, this way.

His own truth was bared to him. Regardless of what Etherell Lyr felt for him, Dorn could not let him die. He didn't know what he could do to stop it, but nothing was of greater consequence—not for him, not in this life. And so as he played a song about bloodshed and victory he tried to summon his strength, though being himself, still, he could not help but undercut it with irony. He might lose his life if the danger was as he thought. That would be his song in the world. It was a grim world, anyway, now that his home was disintegrating, and along with it his art, and the man he loved.

Dorn shut his eyes and hummed to himself the words, too low to be overheard.

> That crimson day, side by side they fell
> with hauberks blooded.
> Yet arose again, stronger still
> It was not then their time.

"IT will be different this year."

"What do you mean?"

They were standing before the mirror in Sendara's room. It was large enough to capture the two of them from the waist up. The frame was alabaster carved with woodland and garden scenes. Julien stared at the frame, at the shapes of fantastical flowers and birds, of fountains and trees, rather than at her own reflection. Balanced atop the mirror frame was the gift from Etherell, the lithe, bizarre creature called a seahorse.

Sendara was combing out her hair before dinner. It fell in flame-threaded waves to her waist. She quirked the corners of her lips in a way that brought out her dimples without showing teeth. Observed its effect in the mirror. "The lottery," she said at last. The smile became a smirk. "You may want to stay away that night."

"What lottery?" Julien hated to ask these questions, especially now that Sendara was smirking, but thought it was better to look ignorant than to remain so.

Sendara Diar put down her hairbrush and sighed. "I keep forgetting how little you know. Each Manaia a sacrifice is chosen at random. A very old rite. For centuries it was without meaning. But now . . ."

"The enchantments are back."

Sendara's eyes veiled as if with surprise, or suspicion. "So you've been paying attention."

"I have," said Julien. When next she spoke, it was more boldly. "I've noticed that your father's chosen keep falling sick, for one thing."

But if she'd hoped for a reaction, it was denied her. Sendara only shrugged. Picking up her brush again, she resumed running it through her hair. Gripping its strands midway, she applied herself, with increasingly violent strokes, to the ends. Her brow creased from the effort. "Not all are man enough to handle the demands of power."

"What about us?" Julien said. "We'll never be *man* enough for anything."

"It's a figure of speech. Obviously."

It sounds like something your father would say. It would be unnecessarily provocative to say that. Still she could not resist asking, "Do you think Etherell is—man enough? You're not worried about him?"

"I could tell you the ways in which he *is* man enough, and more," said Sendara. "But you don't seem to like hearing about it."

"Why would you tell me stay away from Manaia?" It was important to stay focused on the topic at hand, Julien reminded herself. Her need for Sendara's knowledge, to understand what was happening, was stronger than hurt. Though it seemed now, with Sendara warning her away from the festival, that the other girl had already decided they were not to sing together after all.

"Did I say that?" Sendara turned from the mirror to face Julien. Her expression unreadable. "Perhaps you should come, after all. A long time ago, it used to be a fattened lamb they sacrificed. Or a calf." Sendara looked pointedly at Julien's midsection. "You'd be ideal for that."

Julien stood, transfixed. Whatever she had expected—despite the recent, subtle hostility the other girl had shown her—it was not this. It felt as unreal as the night under the stars had, albeit in an entirely different way. Julien ventured, "Is this because of what I said . . . about the chosen?"

"No, Julien." Sendara pursed her lips. She held herself upright as a queen passing judgment. "Perhaps I'm starting to realize that I require . . . more educated company. Your ignorance, and neediness . . . it's begun to grate. I'm at a critical time in my education. I can't afford to be held back. You make me feel like I have to hold back, because you can't stand my success. You *watch* it all . . . like some kind of shadow."

Julien stumbled back a step, then another. She had been wrong about Sendara Diar—but also about herself. She'd imagined she could approach the question of Manaia, the darkness surrounding the chosen, as if it were a puzzle. With detachment. But as it turned out, she was not detached. Had put herself in the way, instead, of what felt like a cold, thin knife in the ribs.

Your neediness. All her efforts to be composed, not to show feeling. Somehow it had bled out anyway. It had been folly to try to hide what was blindingly clear: she was, in herself, not enough.

Some kind of shadow.

As Julien reached for the door handle, she wished she could think of something to say. Something that would lend her at least the appearance of pride, or worthiness. Nothing came. Her heart was a broken-winged bird that staggered in circles. Outside, the windowless hallway seemed to beckon to her, its bleak recesses the only place she belonged.

She turned one last time at the door. Sendara was watching with a wary expression, as if Julien might bite. Yet still retained an upright posture, a haughty tilt to her chin, as if she did not care either way.

At last Julien said, with a tremor she despised, "I won't come back." And shut the door.

"I WANT to go home," she said that night in Valanir Ocune's drafty tower room. She had brought a blanket for her shoulders but still shivered in all her limbs. "When this is over. I can't stay here."

"Julien, sit." He sounded tender in a way that almost made her cry. No, wait, she *was* crying, Julien realized to her horror; a tear had slid down her cheek. The chair was hard beneath her. She huddled within the blanket for a warmth she couldn't find.

"This place has been cruel to you," said Valanir Ocune. The compassion in his words, so unexpected, was like a twist of the knife still lodged in her ribs. More tears sprang into her eyes. She covered her face, deeply embarrassed. *The emotion is too raw.* Here she was, being raw all over the place. Her unsuitability to be a great, rather than a merely passable poet, in evidence even here.

"I wish I had words of comfort," the Seer said. "I know you want what this place offers. I don't know how to give it to you."

"Couldn't you teach me?" She looked up from her hands. Temporarily forgetting her streaming eyes.

"Julien, I—" Uncertainty blurred his features, unless it was her tears. "There's something I haven't told you. I . . . You must promise not to be frightened."

"No one can promise that."

He laughed. "True. But please try." His eyes were merry as flames of green. But beneath that Julien thought she glimpsed a heaviness. "The enchantment I try tomorrow . . . I don't know if it's been done. It's been used to *kill* . . . this I know. An exploitation of the link between a Seer and the one who made him. I intend, tomorrow night, to use that same link . . . but differently." He paused. The small fire in the hearth popped, shot up a spray like lit rubies. It should have been a cheerful sound, yet Julien felt a chill that went deeper than before.

"Differently," she murmured. "You mean . . ." And this with a wild leap, "To give life instead?"

He laughed a little. "To think you could have been my student."

"But . . . to give life . . ."

"Yes," he said. "A more complex undertaking than killing. I'm not sure what I may need to . . . give. Please understand, I go to it willingly. Our lady has paid enough. Largely because of me." He smiled faintly. "I haven't told my associate . . . I can't predict how he'll react. I've made sure he knows to keep you safe. But it means . . . if things go that way, I won't be here to teach you, Julien. It would be wisest, then, to go home. When the Court Poet returns from abroad, seek an audience with her in Tamryllin. She is . . . though she may not always seem so, she is kind."

"How can this be?" said Julien, finally. She felt a fist clenched in her chest. *I'm not sure what I may need to . . . give.* "How is it that you are so . . . calm?"

He shrugged. "There's a chance it won't happen," he said. "Perhaps such a cost won't be asked of me. Or perhaps . . . I will fail, and fail her. But I hope not. You must understand, Julien . . . I am taking responsibility for my own actions. That's all."

"No." She reached for his hand before she could think, surprising herself. He was warm, though the band of the moon opal ring was cool. "It's more than that. And all Eivar shall have cause to grieve."

"You're too young for that," he said. It was unclear what he meant. He withdrew his hand gently and brought it to rest on his knee. The moon opal caught the firelight, its depths aflame with every imaginable color. "Don't be old before your time, Julien Imara. There's so much yet for you. Go home when this is over, and live. It is the right thing—I promise."

16

FLOWERING rowan branches were strewn everywhere in drifts like snow. They lay across mantelpieces, wreathed the statues of Kiara in the Hall of Harps, were twined fancifully around pillars. The first-year students, whose task it was to decorate, had been thorough. The dining hall at breakfast brimmed with flowers and filled the room with scent; several times Julien thought she would sneeze. At the morning meal were special oat cakes with honey, a custom of Manaia.

She sat beside Sendara Diar at their assigned end of the table. The girls ignored one another. She wondered if Sendara meant to sing in the competition that night, alone. It was Sendara's song anyway, Julien had to admit. Julien's contributions had been pared away until there was almost nothing left.

Some of Elissan Diar's chosen wore garlands of rowan flowers on their heads as a joke; Etherell was naturally one of these. He and Maric Antrell, garlanded and roaring like drunken princes, had their arms around each other's shoulders. They hoisted pewter cups of well water as if it were wine, making toasts to one another's health with raucous gaiety. Once they'd exhausted this line of mockery, they went on to toast other students, with attention paid to the foibles of each. After various of these, Etherell declared, raising his cup, "To Dorn Arrin, whose scowl could freeze a crow midair." And he drank.

Dorn was watching with a detached air as if the spectacle was what he'd come to expect, his long legs stretched out before him. Julien thought he had an air of waiting.

"Oh, indeed," said Maric. "To Lord Bookmaker, whose love is not, methinks, for the ladies."

Dorn roused himself as if from dreaming. His eyebrow raised. "Are you ready to admit your desire for me, Lord Antrell?" he said. His voice, though soft, carried over the table. Caused many of the boys to look up. "Or do you feel . . . inadequate?"

The boys appeared to shudder where they sat, with delight and fear, for no one could predict what Maric might do. Maric, in turn, broke from Etherell's arm to sway forward until he was inches away from Dorn. The fire-haired lordling, a hand to his belt knife, loomed over the bookmaker's son. "Tonight it happens," he hissed. "I'll make you beg. Don't doubt it. You'll beg for love before we're through with you."

"Tonight," said Dorn, eyebrow still raised. "Do tell."

"He's an idiot," said Etherell, appearing now behind Maric and grabbing at the lordling's shoulder. "Come away, idiot."

Maric Antrell laughed. "You're a soft touch, aren't you, Lyr," he said. "You don't want that getting back to our lord."

"No, indeed," said Etherell, grinning widely. "And it will not." His eyes glittered beneath the wreath of flowers, that suddenly did not look ridiculous at all. He all but pushed the other man back into his seat. Maric was still laughing. Etherell's expression flattened, became genial. "Another toast now," he said with a bow, "to our illustrious Archmasters." He flourished his cup in the direction of the high table where the Archmasters, clad for the festival in silver-belted black instead of their grey cloaks, sat conferring among themselves. All but High Master Lian, who was dressed for the occasion in white.

Julien wondered if Etherell saw any but one of these men: a man who, though of the same age as Valanir Ocune, appeared young; who wore the black and silver as would a lord. Elissan Diar appeared touched by sunlight, even on a day the Isle was swallowed in mist. He would be there tonight, Julien thought. Though it was not he with a mantle of white like the rowan branch, not he who would lead the ceremonies of Manaia, still Archmaster Diar was the one to watch.

* * *

ALL their names went into the basket. At the end of the morning meal
the High Master called the name of each student in turn, dictating to a
second-year student whose task it was to write it on a scrap of paper. The
student would then give the paper to the High Master, who dropped it
into the basket that sat upon the high table. A ceremony Dorn had witnessed often, every year in the spring. After the students' names were
called, Archmaster Lian went on to call the Archmasters. Elissan Diar
grinned when his own name rang in the dining hall.

It was a custom. Later that night, after the song competition of
Manaia, the High Master would draw a name. The one called, if a student, was subjected to predictable raillery, though it always ended the same
way: he was made to stand almost between the fires, just near enough to
singe his hair. In elder days, it was said, the "winner" had been run between the fires, perhaps even burned to death. An animal sacrifice, was
one theory—perhaps an optimistic one; an attempt to keep at bay a deeper
darkness that might attach to the rite.

Now it was a drunken game, a gesture made towards Eivar's past,
when there had been no cities nor even walled towns; when instead,
tribes and their kings roamed the hills with cattle.

Tonight, Maric Antrell had said. And Dorn had soon recalled
Etherell's earlier words. *I can't protect you.*

Dorn eyed the pair of them: Maric whispered in his companion's ear
as the latter gazed straight ahead. Dorn thought Maric had the appearance of a courtier playing advisor to his lord; certainly the way Etherell
Lyr appeared in his crown of rowan flowers was regal, his only reaction
to the whispering an occasional brusque tilt of his chin.

Dorn wanted to warn him. A man like Maric Antrell would not
consent to a servile position, not for long. If Etherell did not make some
concession to Maric's status, the man and his posse would turn on him.
And that was if the enchantments that were decimating the chosen did
not reach him first. Dorn saw his friend walking heedlessly between
twin dangers that loomed to either side like the need-fires of Manaia.

Now rippling through the dining hall there came applause; Archmaster Lian bowed before them—his name, the last one, had gone into
the basket on the table. His first time conducting this ceremony, which
for so many years had been the task of Myre.

Tonight. Dorn studied the floor. He had only one possible plan.

* * *

THEY stood before the Silver Branch. Rowan flowers were piled around it on its dais. It was evening and outside the songs of Manaia were beginning. The singing reached the Hall of Harps as if blown on the wind, lonely against the night. More voices called in answer, their timbre falling, falling until they and the winds combined. It was all one, thought Julien Imara. The song, the winds, the Isle. Dark would be enclosing around towers of flame that licked the sky.

She tried to stand relaxed with her arms at her sides, found she was trembling all the same. Ever since he had told her what he meant to do, she felt complicit in something terrible. He had donned formal attire, the silver-belted black of a Seer. Julien thought of Archmaster Myre, arrayed in robes for his final rest.

It is to save the Court Poet, she reminded herself for the hundredth time since he'd told her. *His choice.*

At dusk they had glided through dark corridors to the Hall of Harps; all fires in the castle were doused, and even a candle would have raised outrage. Knowing the way in darkness as well as she did, Julien had not had trouble with this, and Valanir Ocune, too, seemed familiar with the corridors at night. They had slid between the twin stone gaze of the statues of Kiara, crowned in their white flowers. And lastly they had heaved shut the great doors to the Hall of Harps.

His familiarity with the hallways even in darkness reminded Julien that Valanir undoubtedly had stories of his time at the Academy. Now it was too late to ask.

Across from her Valanir was waiting, listening for something. At last they heard a bird call, resounding too loudly in the Hall to be outside. It seemed to come from beside the door.

Valanir appeared to relax. "My guard is here. Now, with luck, no one will disturb us."

He stepped nearer to Julien and reached out his hands. She took them. Earlier at another meeting he had linked with her through enchantments. So he'd told her, though she had felt nothing; and now he could draw upon her strength to conceal what he intended to work tonight. Otherwise the enchantments would be detected by one such as Elissan Diar and they'd be discovered, stopped before he could complete what he meant to do. But he did not call upon Julien to work enchantments herself. He would not put her at risk.

It weighed on him, she knew, the lives that had been lost or maimed through his maneuverings. Even as he believed he'd been in the right.

"I had to write of her, for this to work," said Valanir Ocune. By light of the Branch his face was softened. A hint of laughter in his eyes. "Don't tell her, Julien. I don't believe in flattery."

His song began quietly. Julien tried to still her shaking knees. The Seer Valanir Ocune was singing, a song none else had heard or would ever hear. It would be something to tell for a lifetime, or would have been, if it had been only a song. But this song was to bring an enchantment, and possibly the Seer's death; how then could she ever tell of it?

His voice, unaided by a harp, filled the Hall nonetheless, transfigured for Julien the abiding silence of that place. He began, as songs often did, with a story. In her mind's eye Julien saw the shining city of Tamryllin, a place she'd never been. It was the time of the Midsummer Fair. In his song, the Seer assembled the people: each with their Midsummer masks, each with a song of their own. In time, masks would fall away and songs would change, irrevocably. And in the midst of this, a woman who desired music against the loss of all hope. Julien realized she had forgotten to breathe.

The tale unfolded. Julien opened her eyes to look at the Seer. His eyes were distant, and she could not read his face.

It was a story everyone knew, in Eivar and beyond; but this was seeing it at a slant, in a way Julien had not heard it told before. This song was not about Darien Aldemoor's sacrifice, nor the martyrdom of Hassen Styr. Nor was it about the treachery of Marlen Humbreleigh. The fox, the hound, the snake—that was a tale everyone knew.

This, rather, was about a different sacrifice—an intimate one, of which the songs were silent. Heart's blood in a forest glade; gilded rooms where the art of a Seer was bent, distorted, in service to a foolish king. And then . . . very soon, death. Julien recalled the carving of a woman putting a sword through the heart of another woman; the *same* woman—herself. The notes of melancholy were gathering like storm clouds, sharpening in intensity until at last, fury; the Seer's eyes were fire. Fury coarsened his voice, turned it deep. The sacrifices were too much;

he raged against them like those men of myth who defied the gods. Until like the break of light after rain, Valanir's face began to clear. He looked to be remembering something.

> *The fire has made of you*
> *A bright steel blade, a golden chain*
> *A light that blinds.*

For the first time Valanir Ocune looked at Julien, smiled a little. The Branch lit half his face; the rest left dark. Gentleness had returned in full, to which he gave the final words.

> *I would have you walk in light,*
> *Not become it.*

Outside the song of Manaia had climbed, risen higher, as if it might break through to the heavens; and Julien saw in Valanir's face a look of recognition, a realization dawning. "That is not of Manaia," he said. "They work towards something else now, for some end I can't see. But that will have to wait. I must find Lin."

She watched the Seer's eyes become abruptly absent, like the windows of an abandoned house; he had gone to another place and she was alone now even with her hands joined to his; with the sound of that unnerving song growing fuller, louder, tearing through the night as surely as those towers of fire; reshaping it towards an end even a great Seer didn't know.

NIGHT cloaked the battlements, and Nameir Hazan kept watch. Almyria was built on a mountain, its fortress the spiked crown at its peak. From this height, looking down, the streets unspooled in a tangle like noodles. Nameir had earlier that day walked those streets, felt her calf muscles strain from steep inclines that followed the shape of the mountainside. It was hard to tell where the mountain ended and the streets began. Not for nothing was Almyria regarded as impregnable. Its Five Lords retained their relative independence from the Zahra at the cost of this austere hardiness, this isolation. Ferran, first of these lords, looked himself to be cut from stone. His trim beard was silvered black, his aspect one of grim authority. He was not pleased to shelter within his walls an army from the south. Distrust was a miasma in the ancient gold-pillared hall where the Five Lords and Mansur Evrayad held council.

Nameir approved of this distrust, thought it eminently sensible. In fact so far she had been impressed with the steely authority of Lord Ferran even as it had inconvenienced them; he was a man she could imagine following in battle. History had often demonstrated the fatal error of allowing an outside force through one's gates, even one that offered aid. This one was swelled greater than ever, with a detachment sent by Vizier Miuwiyah. It had taken hours to negotiate terms with Ferran as they had stood outside the gates in the punishing sun. When at last Mansur's men were permitted to march through the gates, the streets were desolate. The city's inhabitants had taken refuge indoors, watched from upper windows.

Once inside, negotiations had continued in the fortress. Mansur still led the troops alone, assisted by Nameir; against all expectation, Vizier Miuwiyah had not accompanied his own men. Though she did not say it, this seemed an ominous sign to Nameir—that the vizier had forgone the prestige of command. He claimed to be in the midst of orchestrating the marriage of his eldest son with a foreign princess; was thus unable to get away. Nameir thought, given the protracted nature of such affairs, that this was unlikely. She could tell Mansur thought the same, though his comment was, "We're better off. Miuwiyah would complain if his pristine new battle cloak got a tear."

She'd wondered if Mansur comforted himself with the words, if it was true. For there was a deeper truth she knew. A man might die with his sword in hand and thank the god, with his last breath, for a chance at glory. But there was scant glory in these night raids, with their taint of obscene magic, of hopelessness.

Tonight the streets were lit, every one. That was Nameir's idea. It carried risks, but she thought it far riskier to be surprised by Fire Dancers in the dark. Lord Ferran and Mansur had acquiesced. There was no precedent for the fighting they were about to experience; no one could be sure what was a wise course of action.

Before she had departed for her watch, Lord Ferran had approached Nameir. It was the first time she saw him up close, saw he was no taller than she, even as his presence commanded one's attention. "We are unlikely to survive this," he said. "I would rather die here, in the place of my ancestors, than flee like a rat to its bolthole. Leaving my people to their fate. Is that a thing that makes sense to you, Nameir Hazan?"

She was able to meet his gaze with clear eyes and conscience. "It is how I've lived my life, Lord Ferran."

"I had thought as much." His dark eyes were direct. "I've heard much about you, Nameir Hazan. Enough to know Prince Evrayad has been fortunate—perhaps more so than he deserves. If we survive this, I am offering you a chance to work for me. Until these troubles began, I had my eye on lands to the east of here. I'll need talented command to aid in taking them. You could name your price."

"What is said of me?" Nameir could not help asking. Her world was garrisons and fields of battle; surely she could leave sophistication, intrigue, to others. She wanted to know.

The directness of his gaze did not change. "That you are, in fact, a woman. And, perhaps, a child of the sea. Oh yes, that is how we call them, in the north. Once we had many children of the sea here in Almyria and they were massacred, their temples burned. A black day. Perhaps one for which we now pay the price."

She let out her breath; it had caught at *woman*. "Yet you'd put me in command of your men."

Lord Ferran waved his hand in a gesture of annoyance, as if a dish had been served to him too cold, or cooked to toughness. "Who cares for that sort of thing nowadays?"

Almost she could have laughed; and later, recalling it again as she awaited imminent attack, allowed herself an inward smile. Only a man such as Lord Ferran, glorious, imperious, could imagine that petty hatreds had outlived their time. She liked him for it.

It was a temperate night, with just a slight breath of wind from the mountains. The streets of Almyria were this time of year adorned with curtains of lilac; the scent carried up to her even here. Nameir allowed herself a moment to imagine a different life: one in which this was her place of service—even, perhaps, her home.

"There you are."

She stood immediately at attention. "Yes, my lord Evrayad?"

"Nameir."

"I must keep watch." She felt suddenly tired. It was easier not to look at the prince, to keep her eyes ahead, downward, on the goldenly lit city streets. No moon; it was young yet, and shrouded in clouds tonight.

"I've been wanting to speak with you," he said. "I can't seem to find you alone."

"Whatever is between you and Rihab Bet-Sorr isn't my business," she said. "As long as it doesn't get us killed." She had an awareness of her spine lengthening, impervious with a strength she willed herself to feel. "It may get *you* killed, which matters to me . . . but that's not my business, either."

"Do you think I would betray my brother?" He sounded more anguished than outraged. "There is nothing between Rihab and me, Hazan. I swear I told you true. That man said nothing to me of the queen after we were left alone. I don't recall anything he said. My only memory is of you, finding me. The blood on my hands."

It sounded too plausible, given how he'd acted when she found him. "I may believe you," she said. "But I was not the only one privy to that conversation. Men will talk—have talked. And it will get back to your brother. By then, it won't matter what you've done or haven't done, my lord. People will suspect the worst—of her, of you. The crime, of course, mostly hers."

"You think the Fire Dancers plot against the queen?" It was not quite a question; he had the sound of one who had made a discovery.

She was startled by how logical it sounded, once he uttered it aloud. "It may be." He was about to speak again, but at that moment she raised a hand. "Wait." In the street she had seen . . . a flicker. Something dark pass by. It could have been a bird, but . . .

"What is it?"

"I don't know." For the first time she realized the night was very, very quiet. A curfew had all the city residents in their homes; in that silence, other sounds of night ought to have surfaced—birds, insects. There was nothing.

"Something's wrong," she told Mansur, and as her eyes scanned the streets, she began to walk briskly towards the ladder that would take them down into the keep. "They may already be . . ."

He understood. *"Inside."*

It was dark in the courtyard where she descended the ladder. It shouldn't have been. It had been lit before, she was almost certain. So she was not entirely surprised when on the ground at the foot of the ladder, face-down, Mallin lay. Gore made a sticky mass around his head. The years of training, of her hopes for him, passed before her eyes in that instant.

There had been more men assigned here. As Nameir squinted into the dark she thought she could make out even darker shapes sprawled here and there on the ground. At least five of their men. It must have happened quickly, silently.

Mansur dropped down beside her from the ladder. She couldn't tell, in the dark, if emotion showed on his face when he saw Mallin, and made out the other shapes in the courtyard. In the next moments they would raise the alarm, run with swords bared into the keep to defend what they could. It was the last coherent thought Nameir would have for a long time, as the enemy came for them that night in a way that made all the other times seem a game—cat and mouse, bait and bull; a mockery of death that at last gave way to this, a cold awakening.

By morning the story of Almyria would be on every tongue. That story would spread south, down the River Gadlan and, at last, to the capital. Of the red, clotted rivers the streets became; of the heads of the Five Lords arrayed on pikes above the fortress battlements, bodies cruelly mangled and flung to the streets below. Chief among them Lord Ferran, who was said to appear stern above the battlements even after vultures had picked out his eyes. The deaths that day numbered in the thousands. It was said, in centuries to come, that the city would never be scrubbed clean of its blood, or ghosts.

Deep in the night Nameir would find herself slipping on flagstones coated in blood, in her arms carrying a wounded man who wept tears of blood. She would be screaming as she cut her way through warriors that were faceless. Only once at the brief emergence of the moon she saw, within a Fire Dancer's cowl, the thin, scared face of a boy. Eyes wide, almost innocent, as if stunned by the carnage around them. But he'd then towered above her again, features fell back to concealment within the cowl and his sword upraised; became again an appendage to a horde that showed neither mercy nor fear.

None of these events were known yet to Nameir Hazan when she first descended from the battlements to find her men lying dead. She ran into the dark of the keep. The young prince followed after.

* * *

HE'D feared to come here, though had not said so to Julien. Not because he might give his life for Lin Amaristoth. A man might go to his grave secure in the knowledge of his worth and place in the world—such as could be reckoned a good death. His last time in the Otherworld, Valanir Ocune had faced the reverse of this: an image of himself that he did not believe, could not credit, yet knew was the truth.

This rite of sacrifice he had claimed to do for love, but likely it was also to counter that image that had risen before him: of the Seer he had not wanted, yet in that moment known himself, to be.

Who are you, Lady Amaristoth? He'd wanted to know, wondering at her difference, at the alternating flame and chill of her; but he'd wanted also to compel her to think of the answer, really think it through to the end. Not discover that answer late, as he had done.

He was in a hall that went on forever, where he'd been once before. He had sung himself here. This time he had an idea where it would lead, since he had engineered his journey deliberately: through one of these doors, he would find Lin, the Seer he had made years ago. He wasn't sure she would be aware of his presence, how it would work. But Valanir Ocune thought, if the enchantments had indeed returned and a Seer could bring death to his maker this way, surely he could offer his life. For every enchantment there was that doubling—the light, and the shadow it cast.

In this case, it was light he brought. This time.

For my sins, perhaps, some recompense.

There it was.

The mark around his eye was burning in all its strands; it shone with its own light, not the reflected light of the moon.

He felt pulled forward, summoned by echoes of a song he had himself created. The melody, the elegy for Lin's life as he saw it, which was likely to be different from the way the Court Poet herself might see it. He heard strains of his own music and knew they bore him forward, so when at last he chose one of the doors, he expected she would be there on the other side.

What met Valanir Ocune instead was a sensation like an ice wind, and silence, an abrupt cutting off of that song. The shock that lanced through him in that moment was a sacrifice for nothing; it was nothing he'd planned. It crushed his voice from him, his art, his words, until nothing existed in the world but a howling center of pain.

It was someone else, not Lin, who was waiting.

SHE saw the change in his eyes; the way the pupils began to distend, like an inkblot spreading on paper, until the green had all but disappeared. His face drained to the color of lime, terrifying her. Julien shouted into his face.

His jaw hung slack; the sound that emitted from the cavern of his mouth was terrible. It was the sound of a tree branch cracking, but going on, and on, like nothing that should have come from a human mouth. The black of his eyes still swelled; now the green of them was gone; now the white. His eyes were holes. And that cracking sound went on.

She was whispering, whispering his name. Her terror was complete; she had a sense, though she kept her eyes on his face, that the carvings on the walls had come to life at every side: the dragons and women and poets and knights, all alive, lips cracking open to mock the horror that had come to that room. The harps still in their places, improbably serene.

Yet it was worse when he did respond. When in that horrible rasp he said her name in turn. Forced from seamed lips, "I'm done. I failed. Will you try and do . . . what I could not?"

"Valanir . . . how?"

"You accept it?"

"What—"

"Do you accept it?"

She stared into his obliterated eyes, caught her breath. Said, "Yes."

With his right hand, the Seer grabbed hold of the Silver Branch beside him, gasped as if it pierced him with its light. Silver bathed his face, gentled for a moment its dreadful color. His left hand, he reached out to Julien. She tried to seize his hand; he evaded her grasp and kept reaching forward, lurching as if he might topple off balance. But he didn't. He set his hand on her forehead. Its texture like a gnarled tree. Yet it was nearly in his true voice that Valanir Ocune made his last utterance in life. The mark on his eye gathered the light of the Branch to itself, flared like a star. *"All that I am . . . to you."* He sagged, buckled at the knees. "Gods. Forgive me."

The light surrounding his eye had died. Was gone. Julien stared: Valanir's mark of the Seer was gone.

At first, registering this, she felt numb. The world around her seemed to freeze. She saw Valanir Ocune, grey-faced, in the act of pitching forward, still suspended midair. She felt the dry dead hand on her forehead. It was only in the next moment that time resumed, and the change began; and then it was as if she had been strolling alongside a cliff, suddenly tripped, and could not stop falling.

CHAPTER 17

HE'D followed Etherell all that day, but it hadn't gone as expected. When the singing began outside, Dorn had thought surely now Etherell would leave his position outside the Hall of Harps, go take his place beside Elissan Diar at the need-fires for the gods knew what purpose. Dorn's plan had been to do whatever he could to save his friend from the effects of enchantments, even if it meant pummeling him where he stood. But instead Etherell Lyr had set himself outside the door—why was it now closed?—to the Hall of Harps, and commenced to look casual. From his hiding place on an overhead balcony Dorn saw the transformation. While there were no fires that night, the entrance hall with its many windows was open to moonlight. Dorn saw as his friend glanced about, a studied coldness; and then suddenly, after a pause, relaxed his stance. Took on an appearance of boredom.

Dorn knew the other man well enough to recognize when he put on artificial mannerisms. What he didn't know, yet, was the reason.

Some time passed. His friend paced below. It seemed to go on for quite a while, and Dorn found himself beginning to doze where he crouched. He awoke with a start to an irritated voice from below. "For heaven's sake, Dorn, you may as well come out."

For a moment he hesitated. But Etherell was looking directly at the spot where he had imagined himself hidden. Dorn leaned over the rail of the balcony. "I could tell you why I'm here, but so could you," he said, "and that is a child's game."

"I know why you're here," said Etherell, idly wiping at a spot on his sleeve. From this height, Dorn could see the top of his head, the smooth fall of his hair. "You're following me. Why, I am not sure. But if I had a guess—I'd say it's because you want to save me from myself. Which is touching. Never mind that I don't need saving."

"All right," said Dorn. "So you know why I'm here. You have the advantage. As usual." He grabbed hold of the rail, flipped himself down to the landing at the midpoint of the stairs; grabbed hold of the rail there, flipped again, and he was level with his friend at the door to the Hall of Harps. He had performed that little trick many times through the years, though not recently; this castle, with its corners and crannies and jutting surfaces, had offered the delight of discovery, those early years. Now was different, perhaps because he was older; though he had engaged in an act that made light of the place, still he felt within him its solemnity.

Etherell looked on, expressionless. "I never meant to lead you on."

It was like being punched. "Shut up," Dorn said. "It's not like that. I'm—I wanted to make sure nothing happens to you. These people—they're not what they say they are."

"I know what they are."

"Then why—" He was cut off. In that moment they both heard it: a long, drawn-out scream from the Hall of Harps.

Etherell crashed through the door. He had drawn his knife.

The scene that greeted them was one Dorn would remember vividly all his life. A horror at odds with the lambent Hall.

Before the Silver Branch, the Seer Valanir Ocune lay crumpled on the floor, his lips drawn back from the teeth, face bloodless; it was so clearly death in the room with them that Dorn cried out. Sprawled beside the Seer in a sitting position, her back supported by the stone dais, was the girl Julien Imara. She lay lifeless, stared open-mouthed at nothing.

The moonlight that poured in showed it clear: the mark of the Seer etched around her eye.

Etherell was snarling imprecations. His face had gone purple. "Fucking Seer." He knelt by Julien, passed his hand before her eyes. Seized her wrist and felt for a pulse. "She's alive. He's done something to her . . ."

Dorn's heart was hammering. "She is a Seer." There was no mistaking the mark and its meaning.

Etherell had moved on to Valanir's body. Was shaking the Seer by the shoulders. When at last he turned, it was with a rage so intense that Dorn fell back. "He *knew*," Etherell spat. "Knew he would die. I see it now. Of course he didn't tell me. Now it is too late."

"Too late?"

"To repay my debt to him." Etherell's teeth clenched. "I cannot *stand* to be in debt." Regaining control, he motioned to Julien. "Help me with her. We'll take her to our room. No one must see her this way—there would be questions."

"*You* work for Valanir Ocune?"

But Etherell wasn't looking at Dorn anymore. His eyes were trained off to the side, over Dorn's shoulder. His lips curled in his whimsical smile, though Dorn thought he could see the effort it cost him. "Just the man I wanted to see," he said. Dorn spun around.

Maric stood framed in the doorway. With a single bound he was in the room and had wrapped one arm smoothly, almost tenderly around Dorn's neck. The pressure at his windpipe was knowing, strategic; any move on Dorn's part would seal off his air.

"I was wondering if you'd be here," said Maric. "But won't the Master find *this* interesting."

Etherell stepped forward. "I expect he will. Unless," this said with earnestness, "I can persuade you to keep it between us?"

Maric laughed. "And why would I do that?"

"No reason." Etherell's wrist darted; Maric gasped. Dorn felt the grip around his neck loosen and broke free; turned to stare as a gout of red erupted from Maric's throat. Dorn backed away, hardly aware of what he did, how he moved. The young lordling fell to his knees. Face taut with shock. He tried to scream again; it came out, instead, as a gurgling. Maric fell to his side, clutching at his throat with skittering fingers.

Etherell surveyed the knife in his hand. "More nuisance," he said with a curled lip. "Perhaps it can be salvaged." He turned his back on Maric, who still bubbled and spluttered on the floor, and knelt by the corpse of Valanir Ocune. He closed the dead Seer's hand around the knife handle. "There. So that's done. They killed each other." He rose and went to Julien, drew her haltingly to her feet. She was unresponsive still. The knotted lines that made the mark around her eye were red, etched as if with a blade. The skin around the lines ruddy, too, angry. With a nod, Etherell signaled for Dorn to help carry her. "Let's go."

Once upstairs, they laid her out on Etherell's bed and covered her. Etherell lit a candle and placed it on a table beside her head. She had begun to mutter and grasp at the air. Eyes sightless, as if in a fever. "Hush, dear," said Etherell with what sounded like a forced gentleness. "Quiet now." After a time, her eyelids drooped shut—or mostly; an unnerving sliver of white still showed. Her limbs gradually ceased their frantic movements, at last lay still.

"An herb mixture in that candle does the trick," said Etherell. "I never asked him what was in it. I suppose now I'll never know."

Dorn had dropped to sit on his own bed. Staring at the man who bent over the unconscious girl . . . the man who moments before had swiftly, carelessly killed. Blood splashed the front of his shirt, left a mark like a slash on his cheek. Dorn said, "Who are you?"

Etherell's smile was too wide again, as if he was out of patience. He swept a bow, exaggeratedly, almost to the floor. "Etherell, heir to the estates of Lyr, if it please you."

"No."

"What is it you want to know?"

"You will force me to ask?"

Etherell drew himself up, ran a hand through his hair. It seemed like a gesture of acquiescence. "All right." He went to the window. All this time they could hear the strange singing that arose from the courtyard. Against the violet sky he saw an orange tint of flame. The songs were wrong, he knew.

Everything about this night, this spring, was wrong.

Looking down at whatever he could see in the dark Etherell began to speak. "I was ten when Valanir found me. At the time I was being kept by a lord of the north. Not Amaristoth—their neighbor, farther west. It is said."

Dorn waited, but the other was silent. "Being kept?" Dorn ventured. Still no response from the man at the window. Dorn felt himself go cold. "Oh no."

"Since I was six, I believe. I don't remember when I was taken from home, or where home was. I'm not certain, to be honest, how old I am." His profile was soft in the moonlight. Outside, the singing had entered a lull; they heard the lick and chatter of the fires. "As a boy I was—well. People saw me, and wanted me. And so. The lord kept me as his favorite, and there were parties." He turned to Dorn with what seemed a genial smile. "I learned a lot in those years. About people, and what they want, and what they will tell themselves to get it."

Tears were tracking down Dorn's cheeks. "I am . . . so sorry."

"It hurts, then?" Etherell's smile had gone; he looked across to Dorn with what seemed polite interest. "I suppose it would." He strode from the window, as if from a need to move about the room; began to stride back and forth near the bed where Julien lay, though he did not seem aware of her. "Valanir Ocune was at one of those parties—the entertainment, bought for an evening. Entertainers were paid in great sums to forget what they'd seen. Yet Valanir didn't do that. When he saw me, I remember, a change came over him. I looked in his eyes and I could tell right away, somehow, that he *saw* me. He knew what I hid in my heart. That I was crafting a plot of revenge, for when I was sufficiently grown . . . and that I would be good at it. At the plan, its concealment . . . and execution. Strange as I know it sounds, I think he saw all that. We entered into a partnership, he and I, in that glance across the firelit hall as my lord drooled in his fourth cup of wine.

"Later that night, plying him with more wine, Valanir challenged my lord to a wager . . . and won." A note of outrage in Etherell's voice. "He *bought* me. Spirited me away before anyone was sober enough to know what had happened. Of course, I thought I knew what he wanted. But no. Valanir Ocune wanted something else of me. He knew I would be quick at learning. He would train me in the ways of a lordling—letters, history, music. Swordplay. And send me to the Academy to be his spy. And I? I would, upon the completion of my time here, have fulfilled my debt to him. No one could ever again claim to own me."

"Where . . . where did you plan to go? After?" It was with effort that Dorn made himself speak.

Etherell grinned. "I thought to pay a visit to a certain castle in the north. With my knives. And take my time. I don't want him to die slowly. Justice is important, don't you agree?"

Dorn was shivering, though the room wasn't cold. He held himself coiled inward, tight. He would not reach to give comfort where it was not desired. He would not say *my love*. He said at last, "What happened to you . . ."

"Forget it. Forget what happened to me." Etherell's face had taken on that stone cast Dorn always dreaded. "You want to help, don't you? It's commendable. You want—other things, too. I know that."

He moved quickly, as he had with Maric and the knife. He drew Dorn to his feet and was gripping him by the shoulders and walking him backward, back, until Dorn was tripping but couldn't stop marching backward, held upright by that painful grip. It happened too fast for him to react; back, back, Etherell's face close to his now; breath warm on lips, eyes level with his. The wall pressed at his back. Etherell pinned him there, leaned close. In that silken voice such as he'd used with Sendara Diar he murmured in Dorn's ear; it warmed and made him shiver all the way down. "I know what people want. I could make you explode in ways you'd not forget." Breath turned to hiss. "But I would feel *nothing.*"

Etherell flung himself back and away, did not look down at what would have been Dorn's shame where he stood pressed to the wall. The tears had not ceased, to his humiliation. Profound humiliation was what Dorn felt, joined to grief, and what seemed a hundred other things he could not have put into words. Yet he said, "That's not . . . what I want," with unexpected clarity. Kiara had returned to him his voice, at the least; that last shred of himself. He shut his eyes, head tipped back against the wall, his traitor heartbeat racing on.

It had begun to slow, somewhat, when he opened his eyes. Etherell was moving swiftly about the room, in the midst of changing clothes. He'd untied his shirt and slid out of it like a lizard, let it fall. Then went on to the basin, bent over it, began to rinse the blood from his face.

When the bodies of Maric and Valanir Ocune were discovered, suspicion would fall on anyone who had not been at the fires.

With that glimmer of rationality, a return of his ability to string together actions and their consequences, Dorn found he had regained his ability to move. He crept to the door. Opened it.

"Where are you going?" Etherell, sounding irritated. Dorn let the door swing behind him. A harsh report as it shut. Then silence. He kept on, stumbling even though these were *his* hallways, had been for nearly half his life. As if he'd been pitched from the room, like a cast-off stone, and could not regain his balance. The dark enough to swallow him whole. He fell into that dark. Let himself fall. It opened to him, that and a silence, complete. Not even music, anymore. One sound: his heart.

Then another, coming from elsewhere, or from within him—he didn't know.

Dorn Arrin.

His own name, breathed in the dark. As if uttered by a lover, or perhaps the opposite—if he could be said to know the difference.

Arising ahead, the slightest change; a pillar of stone now visible, with its medley of carved faces: mocking, mourning, frozen in icy hauteur. Its scrollwork fluid as the ripple of water. Some moonlight must be filtering in, then, from the foot of the stairs.

Dorn Arrin.

It came from downstairs. Dorn grasped the rail, began to descend with care. It seemed important to take care, though he did not know why. If he fell it would not matter to anyone, surely; it would not matter even to him.

One step, another. The stone bannister cold to his hand. Dorn recalled himself, an earlier self, curled on a rug in his father's workshop with a book he'd pilfered for the night. A vivid memory, for his father had set the book aside to show to wealthy clients, having acquired it from a rare book dealer passing through their town one market day. Illuminated with capering, splendid figures, it told of the deeds of heroes. Men armed and clever, confident and brave, engaged in the only aim that mattered: to make a lasting mark on the world. Death came for all; but some shone beyond it for all the days, enshrined in a firmament of legend.

In their blue and red cloaks adorned with gold leaf, swords gripped in their hands, the men of epics shone from the page. There were battles, but that wasn't all; there were journeys to the Otherworld as casual as stepping across a creek, of grappling with hounds of hell and the King who led them—all with dreadful red eyes. The King wore a horned helmet of black. He could be tricked, his evil contained for a time. Never killed.

Dorn stood on the landing of the entrance hall: from here could see the way moonlight had settled on that place of pillars and stairs, carvings and doorways, like an encasement of glass.

Dorn Arrin.

Beings of the Otherworld could neither be conquered nor destroyed, not decisively. It was not the place of mortals to attempt it. The most they could hope to do was turn them back for a time. Deeds could not last. But stories did, and the names they illumined; though stories might go through quicksilver changes with the years. Some core of them—that core that made you recall that helmet and its dull absorption of all light, the hills of impossible green beyond the border of what was real— that was lasting.

It was that which he had taken with him from hours of reading in his father's workshop. What he'd hoped to discover within himself in the Tower of the Winds, when released at night to solitude; showered with the extravagant gifts of time, a supply of candles, paper, and an emptiness into which words might come. The only things a poet could be said to need.

But in the end there had always been himself in the way, his self like a hostile stranger that obstructed his path. The luxuries of time and solitude compelled Dorn to grapple his rage. His songs went to that rage, emerged from it, too, as in a wheel that would not cease to turn. He was a spiral of smoke, a cyclone trapped on water. There could be value in what he made; at times, it was good work.

It did not take him to a place beyond. Would not be set into legend.

Dorn Arrin.

He had turned the handles of the great doors and walked out. Now was light; the fires, rearing up to make the sky bleed. Arrayed on benches were all the Academy—Archmasters and students alike. Firelight splashed them with color, yet also made them look flat as manuscript illuminations. Skin shone gold and white. Copper hair of the Diar pair, father and daughter; she in a dress of red and gold trim that he could see even from here, bared at the arms. A crown of rowan flowers in her hair. Beside her, Elissan Diar also crowned, with a circlet of silver.

Music came from them, from everyone present, mingled with the roar of flame; they were singing. Of course—he'd been hearing them. All along.

Dorn Arrin.

It was they who called to him, in a layered, harmonied chorus; solemn with an undertow of excitement, a frenzy yet contained. They summoned him now, to step into the sphere of light. To be exposed.

Dorn Arrin.

And he was so tired, and the light that beckoned was, perhaps, the thing for which he'd been searching all the years; a thing incandescent, consuming. A thunderous wall that stood for more than it in itself was. The enchantments were back, after all, and if Dorn could not escape them, perhaps the only alternative was this. To surrender.

He saw that Archmaster Lian, white robes gold in the firelight, held something upraised like a battle standard. A slip of paper.

No need for Dorn to read what it said. He knew.

Dorn dragged forward another step, and then there was no longer a need: they'd seen him. Their eyes lit in a way that would have scared him at any other time. He stood and watched them come. Students came running, swarmed him like locusts; and then they had grabbed his arms and legs, he was being borne aloft by many hands, and they ran with him, faster and faster. They carried him as if he were weightless, a feather, or as if their strength had increased tenfold. His name their song, their cry, their eyes bright and blank as mirrors. The heat an annihilating blow. Smoke stung and blurred his eyes.

Once at the fires they halted. There was a hush. For an instant it all stood still. It seemed no one breathed. And then he was hurtling into the flames. Dorn Arrin's name, as they sang it one final time, the last thing he heard.

"WHY did you let him go?" She had turned onto her side. Etherell lay on his back in the next bed, hands beneath his head, looking thoughtful. When she spoke, he did not react at once, but rather with a deliberate motion raised himself on an elbow. He looked amused. "So you heard that, did you?"

"I asked you first." Julien felt shaky, but the room did not seem to be spinning around her anymore.

He laughed. "True. Well. I think he needs to be away from me. Probably he's gone to the library—his favorite spot. The old songs will give comfort to him."

"I . . . don't think so." With effort, she'd begun to raise herself up.

He seemed to consider it. "Perhaps not. Unfortunately I must stay here. As far as anyone knows, I have a fever—that's what kept me away from the ceremonies. Not much of an alibi for when they find the bodies down there . . . but I have a feeling Elissan Diar won't ask a lot of questions."

"Why not?"

"He's begun to see I can be useful, whereas Maric . . . he was volatile. Was likely becoming a problem."

The bodies down there. A nightmare·returning. Valanir's eyes pooling black. *I've failed,* he'd said.

To distract herself, Julien looked about the room. Her thoughts were confused. Wherever she looked, she saw a double layer of meaning. There was all that she had known, what she took in as Julien Imara. But then, overlying that, was an added dimension that wasn't hers. It was especially disorienting when she looked at Etherell Lyr. His beauty was bright, piercing, as an icicle; she felt that subterranean longing she always felt, seeing him. But another layer revealed things to her, images, playing about him like dust motes. A boy with gold curls and too-large blue eyes, practicing the sword with a determined expression. Another . . . but this she recoiled from. He was older, but not by much, and covered in blood. His lips stretched in a grin.

"Valanir let you kill." Her voice barely above a breath.

"Once in a while it was needed," said Etherell Lyr, stretching himself out on the bed. "Never anyone you would have liked, my dear. I take it you've obtained this along with . . . whatever Valanir Ocune has done to you."

She nodded. She was beginning to feel vertiginous again, as if all the double seeing she was doing would split her head in two. "You can't help me, can you?"

"Sorry. I know little of magic. I was trying to find out what Elissan Diar is up to, but I've only touched the edge of it. So far."

Julien drew her knees up to her chest. Her hair fell forward to conceal her face, her eye which ached. "What am I going to do?"

"That's a good question. I am not sure. If anyone sees you . . . especially given the mess below . . . there'll be trouble." He spoke as one would to a child, or to someone who was ill, reassuring and cheerful. "We might have to spirit you home. At least until all this dies down."

All this. Julien covered her face with her hands. It was becoming harder to forget how Valanir Ocune had looked, and sounded. The ruin of his eyes. The intensity of his grief, at having failed. He had left it to her to find some way. Had given her . . . what? The Archmasters might have known, but she couldn't possibly ask. All she knew was that he'd made her a Seer, the youngest there had ever been. No one would like that. She would have expected to feel something, anything other than what she felt—excitement, or triumph. Not this fear, and a sense of being unmoored, alone, on dangerous waters.

He would have wanted her to speak with the Court Poet, she thought. To tell her what had happened. That was surely what he'd have her do.

Those were her thoughts. The next moment all thoughts were eliminated. Julien felt a jolt to her body, deep inside. In her eyes she saw nothing, then a burst of blinding light.

When she came to she was on the floor. Etherell was bending over her.

"The fire," she murmured. "Let me up. *Let me up.*"

They were sitting on the floor, staring across at each other. She'd never forget: Etherell Lyr, usually cool and debonair, looking in that moment as disconcerted as she. "What is it?" he demanded.

"Dorn didn't go to the library," she heard herself say. Grasping with effort for words. "He is—"

"*What?*"

"The sacrifice."

His face didn't change. In a single motion he bounded upright, sprang to the door, and was gone.

Julien shook her head. In the time it would take, even running, to reach the courtyard from here . . . She felt another shuddering jolt to her frame. Tried not to let it undo her. She tried to focus her attention on it instead—an idea that came to her suddenly, as if someone behind her had placed a steadying hand on her shoulder. It was the night of Manaia, when portals were thinned. And she had done this before. Or rather Valanir Ocune, whose lived experience nested somewhere within her, had done something like this. Years ago, he had brought Lin Amaristoth from the palace of Tamryllin to the Tower of the Winds and back again, all in one night.

She thought of fires and the face of Dorn Arrin. She remembered how he had interceded for her, shielded her from the jeering of the other students. Someone good, that this place with its new-awakened powers and rivalries had consumed.

She heard, this time more loudly, the lift of voices. Chanting the one name.

A breeze tugged at her hair. Julien opened her eyes. She was in the courtyard. Before the fires, a crowd of boys had gathered. The man they carried a black outline against the glare, featureless. She began to run. Past benches where the Archmasters were, where they stood in a solemn row. She glimpsed Sendara Diar beside her father, stately in her red gown.

Everything happened too fast from there. Julien was running toward the boys who held Dorn aloft. When she was close, she cried out, screamed with all the force of her voice: *Stop! Stop!* Heat made a molten mask of her face; the roar of flames swallowed her shouts. No one glanced her way. Up close, their eyes were glazed, empty. Neither thought there, nor feeling. Horror stopped up her throat.

She elbowed savagely at the students in her path, flung herself at the part of Dorn nearest to her, his lower leg. Closed her hands tight around it, pulled as hard as she could, digging her heels into the ground. And then was flung, when he was, into the tunnel between the pillars of flame. Julien tumbled with him, clawed for purchase at his leg. And afterward saw nothing, felt nothing, as if they plummeted—both of them—through a gap in the world without end.

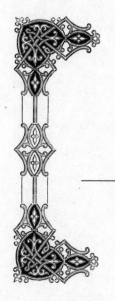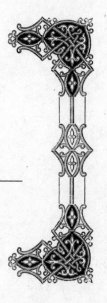

PART III

CHAPTER 18

PIPES and flutes sounded, along with a continuous roar like the sea. That roar was of people, thousands that had erupted from their homes, the streets, into the Plaza of Falcons. The crowds packed so tight it was a wonder people had space to walk, let alone dance. But dance they did, for earlier that day Tarik Ibn-Mor had unveiled his contribution to the Festival of Nitzan: the fountain he had designed now flowed, rather than with water, a succulent red. Wine spewed from the jets, made rivulets down the sculptures. From the height of a balcony above the plaza, at the peak of noon, the crimson was like an erupting wound. Lin was disturbed by it.

Guards were stationed at the fountain to prevent a riot, but people were free to bring cups and goblets. No jars—the only sign that the supply might have some limit. Wine streamed from the summit of the sculpted, forested mountain, down the back and wings of the gryphon, pooled in the basin beneath before spilling downward again, onto the backs of the creatures assembled in their circle. The Tower of Glass, provinces—all Kahishi thus consecrated.

So despite cramped conditions, the people of Majdara—enlivened by wine—found the means to rejoice. The market tents were up, selling sweet pastries of honey, almond paste, and poppy seed for the festival. A selection of these, and wines, were served to the nobility who watched from the balcony. The king and his queen were fasting since the morning, in observance of the laws of Nitzan.

Though Lin watched the proceedings below, it was not with her full

attention. Aleira Suzehn, at their last meeting, had said enough to oc-
cupy her mind.

"Are you certain of this?" Aleira had demanded after Lin had recounted
to her of the figure of green fire on the bed: its fluctuating shape, the
chains. The stench of sulphur. "How do you know it is a creature of
hell?"

"I . . . don't know for certain," said Lin, recalling that she'd had that
from Edrien. No reason for Aleira to know about that. "It begged to be
freed."

"Someone is keeping one of these in the Zahra—like a *pet?*" Aleira
shook her head. She placed her teacup, barely touched, on the table beside.
As if to herself she added, in a lowered voice, "Perhaps the rumors of
that place are true after all."

"Why? What was it?"

Aleira seemed to hesitate. At last she said, "When armies of Alfin
conquered here, now a century ago, they brought their god. But that
isn't all. At that time, Kahishi was not a place known for magic. Eivar
to the west had its enchantments and poets—what was left of the enchantments, at any rate. The lands to the east had their own magic,
centered on the stars. And alongside this there were . . . beings . . . from
other parts of reality."

"The seven heavens," Lin supplied. "The seven earths."

"Yes, these," said Aleira, looking surprised. "So you know some of
it. Boundaries between this reality and others were made porous by magic.
This has long been true of Ramadus—the place teems with these . . .
well, they are everywhere. People wear charms and amulets to avert the
creatures, though I'm not convinced of their efficacy. They leave offerings in doorways, of barley meal and wine. Paint their doors and window shutters the color of heaven in a bid to protect their homes. And so
on. When the armies of the east came, they brought that here. Now we
have djinn here, too. Haunting bathhouses and underground wells,
homes that haven't been consecrated—that sort of thing."

"Or imprisoned in the palace?" Lin felt as if she were missing something.

"No! That—what you saw is an abomination. To enslave a djinn is forbidden by laws most binding. The cost—most would not consider it worth
their while." She shook her head, with bewilderment or repulsion. "The

more powerful the creature, the greater its toll on the Magician," said Aleira. "I suspect what you saw, from the description, was an Ifreet. These are not only powerful. They are utterly amoral, evil. They seek to bring harm to humanity any way they can. To hold one in thrall . . . that takes a degree of magic only a rare few might wield."

"Such as . . . a Magician of the Tower of Glass," Lin said grimly. "But—you say there's a cost to keeping it prisoner. What is it?"

Aleira had taken up her cup again, was gazing thoughtfully through the steam somewhere beyond the furnishings of the room. "Life," she said. "No one who did such a thing would live to grow old. The effects are like a wasting disease. Each day, each year spent with the Ifreet in one's grasp will wear years away." She set down her cup, avoiding Lin's eyes. "There are terrible stories, of what happens to Magicians who try to bind an Ifreet. Worse than death . . . torments everlasting. That anyone would *choose* that fate . . . they'd have to be mad."

The words returned to Lin here, on the balcony. Seemed at odds with the clangor below.

Aleira had promised to continue investigating the prophecy, though Lin had not asked her to do so. It seemed an innocuous concern, beside the facts Aleira had told her today. The idea that someone in the Zahra was willing to give their life to achieve a goal. Risking not only death but an eternity of torment.

It wasn't how she saw Tarik, Lin thought. He did not seem like the sacrificing kind. He had his ambitions, clearly, but these were much of the material world. That left one of the other Magicians.

How many could be so powerful as to hold an Ifreet prisoner?

What have you done in your tower above the world? Lin had said to Zahir Alcavar, mocking.

Yet he did not seem mad to her. She was missing something, something important. As Zahir himself had intimated, subtly. It occurred to her: he'd given her the key to the Tower. As if he knew what she'd find. As if he *wanted* her to.

A HANDFUL of days after her talk with Aleira, Nitzan was upon them. In that time, Lin had avoided the Tower of the Winds. The key sat in the pouch she wore at her belt. A presence like a burning coal. She allowed herself to be caught up in the intricacies of Kahishian council meetings, the serenity of nights in the imperial garden. Throughout that time, preparations for Nitzan were underway. The kitchens were in a clamor to concoct the festive meals that would be served in the Zahra for seven days. There were ceremonial dishes required at each of these, made from recipes handed down for generations.

Throughout the palace had been placed candles in great sconces, striped with many colors, their size like saplings. These would burn, unstinting, for the full seven days of the feast, filling the corridors with scents of ambergris, musk, lavender. There would be dance troupes from around the world, singing girls, poets. Delicacies, wine, and unending entertainments would mark the feast as they had every year of Yusuf Evrayad's long reign. Here was Eldakar's opportunity to demonstrate, in extravagant terms, that the reign of his father continued, unbroken, through him.

The nights in the garden had changed to a degree: sometimes Rihab Bet-Sorr joined them at the water's edge. She would recline beside Eldakar as he played his pipe, a soft smile on her lips; and between them there seemed to have fallen, for the first time, a kind of peace. Sometimes she would lay her head in his lap as he played. In those moments, Zahir would meet Lin's eyes in the dark, his smile indulgent, as if the king and his wife were children in his care. Then he would lift his voice in song, and Lin thought there were times his singing took him away from them, from the place where they were. It was not a song of this place.

Once Zahir came to the gardens very late. He was wild-eyed. "Sorry," he'd said as he collapsed to the ground. "I was detained." Then he laughed.

Eldakar had been instantly alert. "What happened?"

"I went to pay Vizier Miuwiyah a visit," said Zahir. "There is . . . there is a site near his castle that allows me to travel there. The grave of a powerful Magician. No matter. I went to see if he could be persuaded to send more aid to Mansur. The number of troops he has sent so far is pitiful—a disgrace. I went to make him see that." His face darkened. "We must see to justice, when this is over," said Zahir. "Miuwiyah must be made to show respect for House Evrayad."

Eldakar leaned forward. "Did he try to kill you?"

"He wouldn't dare. But I was accosted outside the walls by masked men. I can't say if it was Miuwiyah who sent them, or if they were brigands. Or who knows—Fire Dancers! Nonetheless. It was near the gravesite; its magic aided me. I escaped with barely a bruise."

"Your arm—"

"It's nothing," said Zahir. He shifted so his sleeve fell to cover his forearm, which showed several welts. Lin guessed he'd used his arm to shield against a blow. "When this is over, we must make him pay," he said. "Miuwiyah fancies himself quite the lord these days."

Lin had listened silently, absorbing this. The unity of Kahishi, the loyalty of the provinces, were things she'd once taken for granted.

Another night, Lin found herself alone with Eldakar. By then troubles in the north were especially pressing, or so she'd heard; Zahir and the other six Magicians were at work in the Tower.

"I feel useless here," Eldakar had said to Lin, with disarming frankness. She still was not used to a ruler who spoke as he did. "I see how this conflict wears away at my friend and can do nothing to help. I sent more men north, to be sure—but what else? I could march there myself, but . . ." He stopped, and Lin thought she knew what stopped him. If there was a traitor at court, Eldakar couldn't risk leaving the place unattended. Kings throughout history had fallen that way—when they marched to battle with a naked blade trained at their backs. But it was a shameful admission—of weakness.

She looked around. There seemed to be no one else about. It was dark, the trees pooling shadows on the grass. No way to be sure they were not overheard.

Lin lowered her voice. "Eldakar—may I ask you something?" She leaned nearer to him. He seemed interested, if a bit dreamy, as though half his thoughts were elsewhere. Perhaps in the north with his brother, or with Rihab, who it seemed was always in his thoughts. Lin tried to catch his eye. "Have you ever noticed Zahir . . . the First Magician . . ." she stammered, trying to figure out what formulation would be appropriate here. The king watched her compassionately, waiting.

She gave up trying to be appropriate. "Have you ever noticed him behaving strangely? Forgive me," she added quickly. It already seemed like a bad idea, knowing how close the two men were. But there was no one else she could ask.

She could not read his eyes. "You've been engaging in your enchantments, haven't you?" he said. He sounded calm. "You go where I cannot."

Lin was silent.

Eldakar went on, "And perhaps you're learning more about my friend, that way, than I ever could. Despite the years. I had a feeling it would be so. The first time I saw you. I saw that the two of you might end up sharing something he and I cannot." He smiled. "I was a little jealous."

"I don't understand."

His smile faded. "I'm sorry. You asked a question . . . it deserves an answer." A pause. The song of the crickets made a chorus tonight. He said, "There were times when it seemed to me that two people could not be closer, more like to a single man, than Zahir and me. Other times . . ."

She thought of a creature of green fire. Its screams. "Yes?" she prodded him.

It took him some time to speak, as if he considered. Then, "He holds himself at a distance," said Eldakar. "I don't know the reason. But if I had to guess, I think . . . it's to protect me."

THE day of Nitzan, Lin had donned a green brocade gown trimmed with gold that was bestowed on her, with ceremony, by Rihab Bet-Sorr. When the queen saw her in it she applauded. "It is your color," she said silkily, and Lin had forced an answering smile. She did not think so.

But it was her diplomatic obligation to wear the finery they gave her, to ride in a palanquin down the mountain and be waited on in a palace that overlooked the Plaza of Falcons. From here they would observe the festivities as they unfolded. Much of this, it seemed, involved waiting, feasting, making conversation—Lin would rather have been conferring about politics and war in the king's council chamber. Daytime was her weakness, when her vulnerability to dark thoughts was at its peak. If those hours lay vacant, a black wave might override the barriers: each moment falling leaden and with more import than a moment should have, like grains of sand in an hourglass. The nights in the imperial garden were a tonic on which she'd come to depend.

That day she was unaccompanied by her right-hand man. Ned had sent word, earlier that morning, that he was unwell. Something that had not agreed with him at dinner, he guessed, in his missive urging her not to worry. How well he knew her—that she would worry for him. But it was too busy a morning to pay a visit, and besides, the doctors in the Zahra were among the world's best. He would keep until evening, at least, when she might steal away to check on him. She could not miss the day's ceremonies.

On the balcony, Zahir Alcavar had brought her refreshments; she had tried to enjoy them. Afterward they watched as Tarik Ibn-Mor's miracle, his inadvertently gruesome gesture of celebration, bloomed in the plaza below.

Soon she would know if the Second Magician was conspiring against the king. In this moment, Garon Senn was in the Magician's rooms—if all went according to plan. He'd reported on overtures of friendship towards Tarik which the Magician had reciprocated, albeit with caution. It was doubtful that Tarik entirely trusted him, but like Lin, saw ways in which he might be useful.

The king's entourage and courtiers intermingled in polite conversation, refreshments in hand. There were equally polite murmurs of astonishment when the fountain burst forth wine. Among the courtiers, Lin noticed the grave countenance of Bakhor Bar Giora, ambassador for the king of Ramadus. For a moment she even thought he would speak to her, and welcomed the opportunity for what it might reveal about Ramadus's intentions. But he moved away, and kept to himself for the remainder of the time—though being skilled in his vocation, he did not repel conversation so much as remain subtly adjacent to it. He was, perhaps, learning a great deal as wine vanished in goblets and was replenished by discreet servers. Lin made sure to limit herself to small sips, guarding her own cup from those soliciting, generous pours. Rarely did she trust what she might say—or worse, what Edrien Letrell might say through her—if her floodgates came undone.

Below whirled the revelers. Women seemed to have been granted a reprieve from the restrictions of modesty, skirts swelling on the air like petals. Music, circular in structure and faintly plaintive, carried to the balcony in the clear heat of the morning.

"I wait for the night, too." Zahir Alcavar was at her side. When she didn't answer, he went on, "I find days such as this—arduous, though many enjoy such things. There will be a parade all the day that will be— well, there's a reason people journey here to see it. And then the ritual at sunset that marks the high point of the day. But tonight—that is when we have songs, poets reciting, before the king. You may recognize a few from Tamryllin. Some of the best come out—though alas, not Valanir Ocune this time. The first year he will not grace us for the Feast in quite some time."

"The Academy occupies him," said Lin, and allowed herself a sip of wine.

"So I gather. Last we spoke, he hinted it was a complex situation there, though I know nothing more. So we shall not have the greatest Seer of the age. Perhaps the Court Poet of Eivar shall grace us instead?"

He did not sound as if he were teasing. "Perhaps, if I've drunk enough," she said. "And what will you be doing?"

"The First Magician must stand ready to assist in the rituals which Eldakar will perform," he said. "But tonight, mostly, I will have a chance to join in the celebration myself. I wondered if—if you might, at some point tonight, join me."

Her stomach cartwheeled a little. "I've joined you every night, to my recollection."

"Yes," he said. "I'm asking more of you. If you decline, we will go on as before—with nothing changed, I promise you. As friends."

She did feel giddy, and did not think it was the height of the balcony. Her eyes stayed on the glass chalice she held: eggshell blue, with a slender stem and bell-like cup.

"I mean what I said." He sounded calm. "I think you know—you must know what I think of you. I will take whatever you offer, Lin Amaristoth. Even if that is simply nights of music beside the water."

"You are not taking the obvious approach," she said, with a hard smile. "You're not telling me I should make good on the time I have. With a man sufficiently skilled as to make it worthwhile."

"That's right," he said. "In truth, none of us know how much time we have. But if I were to presume yours is best spent with me—that would be truly abhorrent." He stepped nearer. When he spoke again, it was low, yet she heard him as if there were nothing else around, no noise; as if they were alone. "The Tower caused you pain—what you saw there," he said. "The last thing I wanted was to give you more pain, and I did. When all I want, really, is to be alone with you for a night and give you all that I can, all that is in me to give, until you forget everything. I admit, I am selfish—I want to forget with you. To be entangled with you until I forget my own name."

She reached for words. Said, finally, "But afterward we must return, and remember."

His fingertips grazed the inside of her palm, stroked the lines of it as if he knew them. And she felt, with a catch of breath, that he did.

He said, "If you decide in my favor, Lady Amaristoth, meet me in the courtyard of the *miryan* flowers, two gong soundings from midnight. I will be there. If not, we will go on as before. Now I must go in and attend my liege. You will be in my thoughts, as you must know by now you often are."

I didn't know, she thought, then wondered if it was true. The sensation of being outside herself, watching events from a distance, still was strong. When he was gone she felt it as an absence. She was alone on the balcony with a crowd of strangers—courtiers and functionaries whose colorful attire blended in the corner of her eye like tinctures on a canvas—when the festivities began.

A platform draped in gold and crimson had arrived in the plaza, drawing up under the balcony. It was huge, for standing upon it were two dozen trumpeters, their instruments flashing back the sun. Behind these were lutenists, and at last whirling in green and gold, singing girls. Gold scarves flashed in the air. But what caught Lin's attention in particular was that the wheels of the platform seemed to turn of their own accord. No machinery she knew of could do this.

None in Majdara were surprised, however. Whether magic or machinery, it must have been tradition. She saw the figure of Zahir below, clad in porphyry and the sash of gold. He sketched a bow towards someone she couldn't see. Then she saw them: Eldakar, robed in gold trimmed with crimson, stepped forward, Rihab Bet-Sorr on his arm.

The noise of the crowd stopped suddenly, as if cut off by a slammed door. When Rihab came into sight, Lin saw why. The queen's dress was of a grandeur unparalleled. Its circumference compelled Eldakar to keep his distance, as if he was the sphere to her star. Even so, their hands were joined, their faces turned towards each other. Together they mounted the platform to stand at the front, as the music swelled a triumphal note. Throughout the plaza, the people of Majdara had prostrated themselves on the ground. With clasped hands the king and queen surveyed their subjects, and the sun that made them shine seemed also to emanate from them.

And then, with the sluggishness of a mammoth bestirring itself, the platform began to move again. It carried them—king, queen, musicians, and dancers—down the length of the plaza. Marching alongside in gleaming formations, the palace guard, bearing shields with the falcon sigil. Lin guessed these were for more than ceremonial purposes, for it would have taken just a single arrow to change the course of fate. The great platform, borne aloft on a sea of metal, headed for the arch that opened to a main thoroughfare. It was to make the rounds of the city.

She expected once the platform had vanished down the street, there would be a lull. No one had told her that following after the royal platform would be others, each bearing a new, dazzling display. Never in one place had she seen so many dancers and singers at once. From the world over they had come, but in particular from lands nearby—Eivar, the Islands of Pyllankaria, and the lands to the south. Lin was charmed to see one platform bearing a collection of Academy poets, cradling their harps. From the Islands were tumblers who, even as the platform shifted beneath them, intertwined and spun and tossed each other in elegant harmony. They seemed to fly. So laden with gold chains that each movement—each wrist turn and leap—flashed like a treasure gone lost.

"No dancers from the north. Not this year." Bakhor Bar Giora had materialized beside her.

"Indeed," said Lin, without betraying her startlement. "This year, it seems, the Jitana do another dance. But what is your opinion?"

"I think," the ambassador said, his eyes fixed on the crowds below, "this is a great city. I grieve, truly, for what now seems inevitable."

Below was a platform of dancers, their music an unfamiliar lilt, their appearance striking: they were all in white that fluttered like bits of cloud, their skin like black velvet. As they danced, castanets on their wrists and ankles made a rhythmic *tap tap tap*.

Lin edged nearer the ambassador, her heart beating fast. "Is your king so vengeful then?" she murmured. "Does he begrudge Eldakar the one error—to such a degree?" *One error*. Incongruous phrase for the radiant woman who had mounted the platform at Eldakar's side, hands joined to his.

A pause. She looked at the ambassador, a man of olive complexion and pale eyes. Melancholy eyes, it seemed to her. "Not at all," he said. "My king has his conditions—such as would be expected of one who rules an empire. He cannot send troops to this corner of the world— however lovely it is—without the expectation of certain . . . adjustments to the relationship. And in this, Eldakar has been reluctant."

"You'd make Kahishi a tributary. Majdara, a satellite city."

He remained patient. "Sometimes, to survive, we must entertain the unthinkable. Sometimes it turns out to not be as terrible a fate as we imagined. Not if it means we preserve what we love."

"You'd know something of survival, perhaps," she said, thinking of Aleira's anger.

"Such is my birthright," he said. He appeared calm. "And yet, I still know pride."

The *tap tap tap* was fading. A new spectacle greeted them: twelve women, each in a different color dress, brandishing fans of dyed feathers that they waved in time to their dance. The fans were encrusted with gems, and matched the headdresses. The dancers had the appearance of preening, fantastical birds.

"I expect we will meet again, Lady Amaristoth," said the ambassador. "My hope, in times of peace. If you'll excuse me." He bowed and slid into the crowd of courtiers.

The subsequent hours passed quickly. The day was a series of visions of places she'd never seen, would almost certainly never visit. A glimpse of other possibilities, other worlds, if this one had not granted her a destiny so definitive. So Lin thought as she watched performers from around the world, with music strange and lovely, pass beneath the balcony.

Yet she was seeing Majdara at the Feast of Nitzan. Had seen the Tower of Glass in its immensity and strangeness, and of course, there were the gardens of the Zahra. These were gifts, albeit small ones against the scope of what unfurled here. Most, even the long-lived, couldn't hope for more.

After a time the courtiers retreated to a hall within, where an elaborate meal had been prepared. The king and queen had returned from their rounds of the city, visibly tired but with the exuberant glow of the morning. They sat together at the table's head and it was as if they'd just been married; they fed each other morsels from one another's plates, laughed into each other's eyes. After their fast all that morning, it was a meal of ritual importance, but that didn't seem on their minds as much as the simple fact of one another. Some might look on in distaste, Lin knew—given the queen's reputation, and the regrettable error of diplomacy she signified. But Rihab Bet-Sorr in jewels was like a sun to eclipse such mutterings. Which made no sense, was not *rational*, no doubt in the same way the king's decision to marry her had not been rational.

And yet, Lin thought, she of all people could understand the irrational. She had spent hours in a drafty tower, searched the bleakness within herself. Even when it hurt. There was little that made sense about art. So it was, she supposed, with love.

When the meal had ended, the queen and king retired, each to separate chambers as was mandated by law. The ritual to follow was, Lin was given to understand, the climax of the day. What had once been an explicit rite of fertility was now tamed, sanctified before the God of a Thousand Names. In conducting it for the first time in decades—since his mother's death—Eldakar Evrayad solidified a pact. That he and his queen were wedded not only to one another but to Kahishi and its mountains, fields, and rivers.

At day's end the plaza lay under a yellow haze. The vista of roofs, domes, and towers visible from the balcony was black, foregrounded against a sky like fire. No longer did sunlight glance like a bloodied spearpoint from Tarik's fountain. The mild light at day's end was absorbed into that great redness, turned it dark and rich. And as the day subsided, so had the mood of the crowd. They were quieter, their energies spent. That, or they sensed the gravity of the final ritual to take place, and what it meant to the king before Alfin.

The queen emerged first. She lay upon a litter, hands folded at her chest. The litter borne by six armored men. No women in attendance. She looked fragile lying there, gown dripping copious folds to skim the carpeted ground. Covering her face from forehead to chin, a pearl-encrusted mask. To Lin it was an unsettling image—the mask eradicated what made Rihab herself. She was a symbol, lying passive. It reminded Lin of a wedding she'd attended years ago, where it was known the bride was terrified and unwilling. She had been small, that bride, her jaw clenched against tears. Her bridegroom had seemed to loom over her, menacing, the lords and male attendants crowding around for the ceremony like a net to bind her fast. Lin had left that wedding intensely shaken; it was in her mind years later when she made the decision to flee Vassilian. Better to die a free, starved deer than live a trapped one.

Lin reminded herself: it was wrong to impose her experience of the world on another person. *One's shadow is private.* Rihab was no sacrifice on the altar of a forced marriage. Quite the opposite. And although she fulfilled a duty, the ritual would not compromise her dignity. In years past the king would have taken her before all the people, but not anymore. That was now considered barbaric. He would set aside the mask, raise his wife to her feet. The couple would share a cup of wine as a prayer was recited. A metaphor for intimacy, genteel ritual, had replaced its raw actuality.

A velvet couch strewn with flowers was waiting to receive the queen: the guards laid her upon it. The hush of the plaza deepened, as if the populace, as one, held its breath. Sunset bathed the scene, the gold of the queen's finery, in red.

When Eldakar Evrayad came forward, it was with slow steps. A carpet charted the path for him. He proceeded to the rhythm of a single, steady drumbeat. No music. Though he was some distance away, Lin thought he looked solemn. At least from the stiff way he held himself, the deliberate pace. Time seemed to have slowed. It took an unnervingly long time for him to reach the couch where the queen lay draped in jewels and gold, and masked. Behind him, following at a respectful distance was a priest in black robes, the wide sleeves embroidered with gold stars and silver crescent moons. He held the wine, a chalice of glass.

When Eldakar reached the couch, he knelt. The drum went on; Lin was breathing in time to that sound, caught in it.

From a kneeling position, Eldakar bent over his queen. He grasped the edges of the mask in both hands, lifted it. It came away easily. There was a pause. Frozen in position, Eldakar let the mask fall. Its clatter as it hit the cobblestones was startling in the silence. And still he didn't move.

Zahir ran to Eldakar's side. They both began to shake the shoulders of the woman on the couch. She remained prostrate. Finally Eldakar fell back, still on his knees. From the crowd a noise had begun to arise, similar to the roar of the morning. But this time was different. This was not revelry. Its dissonance bespoke confusion, worry. Anger.

Stricken, Lin grasped the balcony rail and leaned forward in an attempt to see. Her heart thudding. *Is she dead?*

Until word reached the balcony, passed from below, from courtier to courtier in shocked murmurs with, perhaps, an undercurrent of pleasure. Rarely had any bit of gossip, any event at court, been this delicious.

Lin heard, "*It's not the queen.*" Then with an uptick of shock, "*She's gone.*"

HE'D begun to have conversations in his head: with his father. With Rianna. In the days before the Feast of Nitzan, Ned was freed from most duties. He was still accompanying Lin Amaristoth at meals, delegating tasks to those in his employ, but otherwise allowed to drift. Lin had noticed his haggard appearance, he could only assume, and imagined he would—what? He knew there were attendants waiting, if he but requested it, with massage oils, hot baths, tweezers to manicure his hands. There were perfumes to put him in a stupor of sensual contentment—he supposed; Ned was vaguely suspicious of scents.

There were other ways he could productively spend his time. The Zahra housed a library famous—or notorious—for its profusion of texts in all languages. Yusuf Evrayad had sought to build the greatest library in all the west, and had not always used the most exemplary means to achieve his end. Ships and merchant caravans, upon arriving in Kahishi, were ransacked for books and manuscripts. These were duly dispatched to the king's copyists. Eventually, the texts' owners would receive copies— most of the time. The originals stayed in the Zahra.

He knew this from Aleira Suzehn, the bookshop owner with the gold ibis mark on her shoulder blade. He had not seen the mark for himself, but Lin had told him of that, and all the rest. Lin wanted him to find out if Aleira had news of the prophecy, which she was studying. The woman struck Ned as lovely and oddly ruthless for a bookshop owner. She was short with him, until he told her the name of his wife. The name Gelvan, which long ago had been Gelvana and thus more obviously eastern, and Galician, was like a signal to the fierce-eyed merchant; her manner had visibly relaxed. Eventually she'd told him of the lush and ill-gotten library of Yusuf Evrayad. Envying Ned's access to that hoard, despite her contempt for the man who had acquired it.

That particular assignment had given him much time with his thoughts. There was the long trek down the mountain through the gardens at daybreak, where breezes kept petals and leaves in a constant state of motion. He had felt borne on the warmth of that breeze. Later, the upward climb as the sun sank behind the mountain made his calf muscles burn, his heart fill with amazement at the prospect of that rising tower that ignited with the sunset.

The dialogues in his head might have started that day, in the long walk down the mountain, through the city gates, and onward to the Way of Booksellers. And the long way back. They had certainly been happening by then, interpersed with long internal silences, when his consciousness seemed merged with the rhythms of leaves and petals on the breeze. Rhythms, sensations of warmth ruffling his hair, no words. Ned thought he'd never been so entirely alone. Not even years ago when he'd thought Rianna lost to him, was himself lost to sea.

There were reasons for this. He avoided holding these to the light. Nonetheless, he knew that what isolated him, more than anything else, was culpability.

I have a plan for Nitzan.

Even now, he had only an intuition what this could mean. Had been given only a snippet, his miniscule part to play. In the life of Rihab Bet-Sorr, Ned's role was that of the servant who existed for a single purpose—he knew this. Saw their games, their exchanges in a new light: she'd been guiding them, every step, from the beginning. Even when he'd thought he had the upper hand. But even if he didn't know her plan, Ned could well recall her glowing exaltation as she'd revealed her dress for Nitzan; and a contrast, her eyes like shadowed pools that night in the pavilion. These contrasts, these contradictory moods, were joined—two sides of a coin. *Almost as if . . . I am free.*

He recalled too much, was *too* aware of the shades of mood that molded Rihab's features and lit the dark of her eyes. He was an idiot, and there would be consequences. He knew this, but awareness was buried under the pure sensations of a breeze, the fragrant garden; beneath conversations in which Ned reached out in his heart, if not in fact, to the people nearest him in life.

The dialogue with his father was predictable enough. It concerned disappointment. In lighter moments Ned Alterra told himself it was the fate of sons to disappoint their fathers one way or another, so he had at least taken an efficient route. But even this wasn't true: he had not always disappointed his father. In the past year he had risen at court, in the service of the most powerful figure in Tamryllin—in fact, if not in name. It was Ned who had spearheaded the search for the poet Lin had wanted imprisoned three nights; he acted not only as her eyes and ears, but as her sword arm. It was a role that gave him pride—he was helping her build something; a court which had before been founded on ignominy, murder, corruption, now took orders from a Court Poet who led with honor. For the first time, Ned's father saw that his son did not always have to be inept. Much of Ned's awkwardness had become deliberate—people spoke freely before a fool. With time, as he learned to use his awkwardness, Ned paradoxically felt himself attain a quality of grace.

Perhaps, Ned had thought as he took a path that cut through a hedge of white, fresh-smelling roses, this had been his undoing. This new, ill-founded confidence.

Birds called raucously in the trees, welcoming the sunset, as Ned reached the third and highest level of the imperial gardens. There were orange trees, an overpowering sweetness. Such scents had a way of wrenching at Ned's emotions, made him acutely aware of where he was and the beauty he was, moment by moment, failing to appreciate. He already could imagine that in later years, the scent of orange blossoms would return him to this time . . . this strange between-time in his life. And he would grieve as if the wounds—for he foresaw wounds already— were fresh.

It *was* a between-time, that seemed beyond doubt.

His conversation with Rianna was, in truth, a monologue. It had not occurred to him, before, that much between them was unsaid. In some ways their bond was stronger for that. It was with actions that Ned had proven himself to her. Until now, that had been enough. But since the night in the pavilion, familiar ground had vanished. In this new state of affairs, he would have liked to clarify some things to Rianna. Such as, for instance, that she was the beacon fire he relied upon, the reason he had resisted the temptations of a queen's shadowed eyes. Years ago she'd saved him from being dashed on the rocks of his own self-loathing; each day, continued to save him.

It was the queen's agony rather than her allure that he couldn't resist; it bent him double inside. Her grief at being trapped, at causing harm to Eldakar with no more than the fact of their marriage. Ned didn't know the particulars of her plan for Nitzan, but he was sure of one thing. Her little digression about missing her father had surely not been a coincidence. She wished to return to her people. To vanish from public life. Almost any other woman he would have cautioned against such a course of action. The streets of Majdara were no place for a woman on the run, let alone an unpopular queen.

He was not concerned about Rihab Bet-Sorr's ability to fend for herself . . . not at all.

He could still change his mind. In Ned's pocket was a small vial, green glass, that he had obtained from the Zahra's pharmacy. The old man who mixed ointments, medicines, and scents had eyed Ned with suspicion. "I've been sleeping poorly," Ned had said. As he had been instructed to say. It was all too plausible, given how little sleep he'd had of late. Exhaustion had become routine, between late-night chess and Kahishi's politics. No doubt it had served Rihab's purposes well, to pry at his defenses when he was tired.

The man had made Ned a mixture, of pennyroyal, poppy, valerian . . . who knew what else. Ned didn't plan on touching a drop.

It was his nature, Rianna would have said, to allow himself no quarter, no succor. She would have mocked his aversion to scents and massages. "You need not be constantly punished," once she had said to him. And then, with a grin, "Not unless *I* do it."

None other knew him as profoundly, yet still, somehow, she loved him. That had amazed Ned from the first and still did.

Since he was genuinely wracked with exhaustion what he'd said to the herbalist was not, in the strictest sense, a lie. There was always the possibility, unlikely but still extant, that Ned would succumb to temptation and use the potion to help himself sleep. That he'd perhaps quietly ignore the queen's plan, let Nitzan pass without taking action.

Strictly speaking, it was the dawn of Nitzan when Ned told his first lie. He sent word to Lin that illness would prevent his joining their party.

His first time lying to her, and doing so had made him feel sick in truth. But he had committed to his course. There was no other way. Ned needed the freedom to roam the palace that morning, something he couldn't do if he was bundling himself into formal clothes for a journey into the city.

The queen was closely watched, her possessions scoured by female attendants constantly. So much so that even a small glass vial would have been discovered among her things if Ned had given it to her too soon before time.

It was forbidden for the queen to indulge in such substances, when all hopes were pinned on an heir. As it was, the delay of her pregnancy was as much a danger to Eldakar as the fact of their unfortunate marriage.

Ned told himself he was aiding Eldakar, rescuing him from his fatal mistake. Another lie? He was not even sure.

He thought—in fact assumed—that the delay of the queen's pregnancy was no accident. There was little she left to chance, he was convinced.

The halls of the palace were clamorous with preparations. The servants made ready for the night's festivities. There was a bustle of cleaning, the waft of tempting smells from the kitchens. Even the path through the courtyard of the pool, usually quiet, was rife with activity: gardeners trimmed hedges with the chink of shears, servants busily polished the marble sculptures. Ned felt as if his walk to the queen's chambers, once a solitary ritual, had been spoilt somehow. And by evening she'd be gone.

For a change it was she, not one of her attendants, who opened the door to his knock. She was laughing at something one of the women had said, seemed hardly to know him at first. Then her face smoothed and her smile altered, became less open. Her face was painted a waxen white, cheekbones rouged, lips a dark shade of red. Eyebrows penciled to arches above thick-lashed eyes. For the one day of the year Rihab would be allowed out in the city, she had been made to look like someone else.

She was wearing the ritual dress, all gold and gems and massive skirts. Gold around her neck, at her ears. Too much that glittered, it seemed to him; unnecessary ostentation. Rihab Bet-Sorr needed no adornments at all. The dress was cut low; he kept his gaze averted. When he gave her the vial, she tucked it into her skirts with a quick darting gesture no one saw.

"It was kind of you to visit," she said in a prim register, as if to caution against impropriety. He supposed that for a man to visit her now, as she dressed, appeared improper. Yet she contradicted her own manner with the next request. "Ned," she said. "Will you tie my sash? It's come undone."

It was a wide length of brocade, clasped at the front with rubies set in the shape of a flower. With a rustle of skirts she had her back to him. Her hair gathered, just then, over one shoulder. The dress dipped to reveal her shoulder blades. Ned reached forward, as in a daze, to tie the sash. Trying not to look, but nonetheless: his eyes grazed her exposed back. Caught a glimpse of gold. A shimmer, subdued, that was not jewelry.

A mark, engraved in the skin.

She turned to face him again. "I wanted you to know. I don't know why."

Ned opened his mouth. Couldn't seem to form words.

She looked unspeakably tender, regretful. Rose on tiptoe to kiss his forehead. Her lips cool and dry. "Farewell," she murmured. "My Knight." And he was out in the hall, the door closed behind him. With no idea how he'd gotten there. She hadn't exactly shoved him, but deftly she'd separated herself from him and he'd ended up outside with the door shut. Just as Ned scrambled to think what he might do, guards emerged to escort him away from the queen's chambers, back to the courtyard of the square-cut pool.

The place was abandoned. Gardeners and servants had gone. There was no one to see as Ned Alterra approached the edge of the pool and looked down. His own reflection, crisp and pale, stared back.

THE fountain of wine had stopped. At first, milling with courtiers in a suddenly tense atmosphere, Lin hardly had a chance to notice. All was chaos; in the streets, in the palatial rooms where the court had gathered. Eldakar had retreated to privacy with his Magicians. Last she'd seen him, he had looked as if he were borne upright on Zahir's arm, boneless and, suddenly, much older. The lady-in-waiting who had impersonated Rihab in the ceremony was still unconscious; the king's physician judged it a sleeping drought of extreme potency, administered in wine. Once hearing that, Lin had ceased to think it could be a plot against the royal couple. Rihab must be at the heart of it. Everything Ned had said comprised a portrait of a woman who was brilliant, strategic, profoundly discontented.

And, too, there was the exchange Lin had witnessed in the imperial gardens. Those strange, accusing words. *"It has cost me."*

Rihab had pleaded with Eldakar to leave the Zahra. He'd refused, so she had gone on herself. A betrayal of breathtaking scope, and yet. It made sense now.

The only thing Lin could not be sure of was motive. She felt a vague annoyance with Ned. Surely he could have foreseen this—else what had been the point of all those games? Could he not have found out what Rihab had meant by those inexplicable words to the king? What had their love cost her—other than the demeaning life of a slave?

Of course Ned was probably a little bit in love with the queen—any man would be—but loyalty to his duty, first and foremost, had always been something Lin thought she could count on. Some days, the only thing.

This arising disquiet kept her from noticing, at first, a new flutter of raised voices finding its way around the room. Lin's gaze darted about as she tried to find someone, anyone, she recognized. She felt relief when she spotted Garon Senn in the crowd. He was cutting a path through to her side. His smile triumphant. "I've been looking for you," he said. "The morning's distractions were useful. It's done."

"What's done?"

He edged closer, lowered his voice. "I saw Tarik's correspondence. He's been exchanging letters with the king of Ramadus himself."

She bent towards him. "And?"

"It's as we thought. Tarik solicits the Ramadian king's support against Eldakar. Promises that the Zahra is weak and—once attacks in the north intensify—close to undefended. There is only one thing he says might impede their plans."

Lin waited. "Well?"

Garon's eyes made a calculating circuit of the room again. At last he said, "Tarik believes magic is at the root of all this. Dark magic. Not just from the north. Here. Possibly even . . ." He glanced around again. "Well, he speaks of the king being blinded by love."

"The queen?"

"It sounds that way."

"And now she's vanished. Humiliating Eldakar, who was already thought weak." Lin shook her head. "But Rihab? Magic? She was— before she was queen, she was no one."

"True," said Garon. "Almost—*too* true, you might say. Nothing is known of her. Not even the land where she was captured. She refused to speak of it. Of course, Eldakar made sure she had her way."

Just then they were made aware of what the new wave of murmuring was about. Garon's eyes widened momentarily. He helped himself to another sip of wine. "You hear that?"

"The fountain stopped. So . . . ?"

His eyes, meeting hers, dark with bright pinpoints at their centers from the lamps lit for evening. "That fountain was Tarik's enchantment."

"You don't think—"

That crafty, unwholesome glitter in his eyes became more pronounced. "If Tarik was trying to weaken the court from within, what better way than aid the queen in her escape? My guess is, we won't see him again."

HE was right: Tarik Ibn-Mor could not be found. As evening unfolded into night word began to go around that the Second Magician had aided the queen's escape—that they'd run away together. That all along his dislike had been feigned, a concealment. He'd used his powers for the most unimaginable treason.

And why? Well, that did not even need to be said. Anyone who had met Rihab Bet-Sorr would know why. He was bewitched.

Lin thought of what Garon had told her. It was her duty as a friend— if not as Court Poet of Eivar—to relay the information to Eldakar. That his Second Magician worked against him with Ramadus. She had the proof. But tonight didn't seem like the time.

What was to have been a festive dinner was perfunctory, small. It was not the meal of various imaginative courses, replete with music and poetry, such as had been long prepared. The king and his Magicians were not there. Nor, for that matter, was the Ramadian ambassador. Lin could hardly pay attention to the food, though the aromas of rosemary and saffron would have been appealing at any other time. She was too busy trying to listen to the chatter around her. Despite the practice she'd had in recent weeks, she needed to concentrate to understand the murmurs in Kahishian that were not directed at her. More than ever Lin was aware that she was a stranger here. In a time of crisis like this, she did not belong.

Search parties had been sent out for Rihab. The idea made Lin shudder. If the queen were caught . . . Lin didn't know what the punishment for such a thing might be. She did know it was something Eldakar was unlikely to want to administer, even if he was angry. He'd have no choice, now that she had insulted the throne.

She was thinking of this, remembering the melancholy pipe-player she'd come to know in the palace gardens, when a shock of cold ran through Lin. She suppressed a gasp. Then came another, worse than the first, as if a wall of ice water rammed into her. Her brow was clammy. She rose, slowly, as she felt another wave approaching; with a forced smile she excused herself, tried not to run.

Lin thought it was the hardest thing she'd ever done, compelling her arm to move slowly, with apparent nonchalance, as she reached for the door handle. She grasped it, and another shock hit. She nearly fell to her knees.

I'm dying, she thought. *It's finally happening.*

She was in the antechamber to the dining hall where servants bore trays of food. They did not seem to notice as she shakily planted one foot in front of the other to reach the hall. It would have helped to have Ned here. Even if there was nothing he could do.

Well, he could have provided his arm, at least. An acid thought. She swayed, nearly collapsed into a pillar. *Could have let me die with some support.*

It almost made her laugh, that thought. As if it mattered, in death, whether she was clutching at the arm of her man or sprawled on the mosaic tile.

I didn't get to say goodbye, she thought, as a new, even more frigid wave cut off the air from her chest. But that was inane, really. This she thought as she took slow, labored breaths. She knew herself, didn't she? She hated saying goodbye.

She also hated the idea of being found crumpled in a sad heap on the mosaic tile, in a dress she didn't like, in a palace far from home. She'd brought it on herself. Valanir had urged her not to come. Had foreseen this sort of thing, probably.

It was when Lin was gripping a pillar for support, wrapping herself around its glassy solidity, that she began to notice a new sensation. A burning around her eye. It went from strange to agonizing in a matter of moments. The Seer's mark was like flame, hotter and hotter, even as chill waves ran through her. She bit her lip, hard, until she tasted blood.

She stayed there. Lin stayed draped around the pillar for what seemed a long time, limp as a fish, before she realized that no new waves had come. The burning around her eye had subsided. Her breath still came in gasps but this might have been the aftereffects; she wasn't sure. She was afraid to let go of the pillar and be knocked to her knees.

More time passed. In the distance she heard the sounds of the meal down the hall: the hum of conversation, the clatter of the kitchens. A door opened, and the smell of saffron and rosemary along with the noise of the banquet table drifted, briefly, out into the hall. The door closed again. It was all returning to her awareness, drawing nearer, when before it had seemed to fall away. She heard people talking. The clinking of tableware. A patter of footsteps, probably a servant. In time her breathing slowed. She put a hand to her chest; the frantic pounding was less. When at last Lin disengaged herself from the pillar and stood, unsupported, the attack—whatever it was—seemed to have ended.

She smoothed the folds of the green dress with hands that still spasmed, as if she was chilled. She could think of only one reason for what had happened. A penumbra of the fate she'd glimpsed in dreams.

Even so, a voice within muttered uneasy dissent. *The Seer's mark . . . like fire.* What had the mark to do with Darien's spell . . . or for that matter, with Edrien?

Without having necessarily made a decision Lin found herself making her way to the courtyard of the night-blooming flowers. She met no one on the way. She was still shaking, subtly, like a branch stirred in a breeze. *The mark of the Seer.* Given her by Valanir Ocune. They were linked, weren't they? She had known the day he'd arrived in Tamryllin.

The First Magician was already in the courtyard, as if she'd summoned him. All life drained from his face. There was a world of meaning in that face.

"No." She was dizzy again. Of a different kind.

"Valanir Ocune, and Almyria," he said. "In one night." He held his head in his hands, as if the entirety of it hurt. "It can't be coincidence. Can it?"

To Lin his voice had grown distant. There was a roaring in her ears. She dropped to her knees in the courtyard.

* * *

EARLIER that morning as the Feast of Nitzan was underway, Ned Alterra walked down the mountain and into Majdara. At first having in mind one intent: to find the queen, and stop her.

The gardens were deserted. Most palace residents had departed already for the city. In the journey down, Ned had an opportunity to think, but found he could not grasp a thought for more than an instant. Everything was falling away faster than he'd even imagined it would. From the moment he had set events in motion, it had all moved very fast. Now he saw it. The herbalist would talk. And Rihab . . . was that even her name?

In her way, she had warned him. With subtleties, as she did everything. You could even say it was fair warning. She'd given him clues when she taught him the game. But Ned hadn't seen it, had imagined she was only referring to her own life. Nothing to do with him.

There was a good chance he was exactly like the people he most disdained—those who saw what they wanted to see.

By the time Ned reached the city he encountered crowds, was immediately enveloped. It was useless to try to stop Rihab from doing whatever she planned to do. The only way to expose her would be to confess what he'd done. And much as he believed in justice, Ned didn't for a moment invite the prospect of being executed—in whatever manner was customary—in the Plaza of Justice in Majdara. He valued his life in a way he hadn't years ago . . . and more, the lives tied to his.

Ned let the crowds carry him like driftwood in a tide. Pretended he was another faceless visitor to the city, here to enjoy Nitzan for the day.

Instinct took him away from the Plaza of Falcons, where the court ceremonies would take place. He headed to the Way of Water, letting crowds guide him to a cleared space on the pier. Smells of grilled meat and tabak fumes were strong here. There was a game underway, Ned saw—boat racing. The winner would take home silver pieces, the name of champion. The onlookers were mostly men, the rough types one associated with the waterfront. At one time, such men had been Ned's companions—not a few of them Kahishian. He could fall back into their dialect if need be, he thought, without much effort. Interspersed with these were men more finely clad—at a guess, people who had placed bets on the contest results. The mixed crowd cheered and jeered as their favorites reached the markers ahead of the rest, or didn't. Ned stayed and watched for a time. It was something to do while he thought, or didn't think.

Later, the onset of dusk saw an end to the games. The air grew brisk and cool. Flasks of wine and beer were tossed about, in celebration or defeat. The crowds began to thin as some—perhaps the more pious—departed to watch the final ceremonies in the Plaza of Falcons. It was rumored that the queen's dress was a sight to behold, that she outshone any queen Majdara had seen before. The last time anyone in the city might have glimpsed her, from a distance, was at her coronation. Curiosity, especially of the salacious sort, was a feature of the exchanges Ned overheard. Rumors that combed the Zahra of the treacherous, sensual queen had not remained within its walls, nor stayed perched on the mountain, but trickled down into the streets.

As the sun sank and paper lanterns of many colors bloomed on the harbor, Ned sensed disquiet amid the crowds. Something had gone wrong in the rite. Ned listened, but could not discern any details. At last he asked a man nearby, with a prosperous belly and trimmed beard, "What's the news?"

"They're saying the queen is dead," said the man. Then he laughed, a well-fed sound, accompanied with a wobbling extra chin. "I don't believe it. That witch has the lives of a cat."

"Then what happened?"

He shrugged. "That fool of a king put us in a fix, that's what I know. Marrying that whore."

Ned stayed by the riverfront. He bought grilled lamb wrapped in warm bread from a vendor. The mood of the crowds had changed, become increasingly uneasy. The chill of evening more pronounced. Further news arrived from the Plaza of Falcons: the queen wasn't dead. She was missing. And not kidnapped, either. She had engineered her own departure, though none knew how.

"The witch had her way with Eldakar, then left him," Ned heard one old woman say. "On the eve of Nitzan! A heresy."

The witch.

Ned wished he could blame witchcraft for his idiocy. Despite that she was a Fire Dancer, Rihab's skill—at least, what she'd used with him—wasn't magic. She'd manipulated weaknesses he already possessed. Any attempt to place blame on her would just rebound to him, like those clever curved blades that, when thrown, spun back at you.

The knight's sacrifice. For it to succeed, the knight had to act of his own will. And he had. He could not ever deny that he had.

It grew dark on the pier. In the warmth of lantern light Ned saw that the crowds had not abated. He soon found out the reason: now, as people continued to eat festive foods under a blanketing of stars, fireworks were released from great barges that crept on the river. Against the night they were brilliant torrents.

The drinking continued. Now there was music, spaces cleared for dancing. Women joined the scene at the riverfront to flourish their voluminous skirts in mimicry of dancers they had seen that day. Holiday finery—rings on fingers, ears, toes—winked in time with their dancing. Men clapped and cheered.

Ned was coming to realize that without quite thinking about it, he had made a decision—if it could in fact be called that. He could decide to be killed, or not. Decide to serve Lin Amaristoth, still, or vanish.

It was unbearable that the people he loved would hate him. More unbearable, Ned thought, that they'd be right.

He stayed by the water, arms draped on the rail of the pier. He was still there when news came that halted all music and dancing on the streets of Majdara even on a night of Nitzan. Yet this turned out to be only a pause—a temporary lapse. Days to come would bring more revelry than before, on every street, amid intoxicating scents of the spring. When people knew their end was in sight, some retreated from the world; others, in heartbreak or defiance, kept dancing.

SHE went to the Tower in the hours before dawn. Followed the hall again, the sparks to guide her way. Again it led her to that door. This time, before she turned the handle, she looked more closely at the door. Noted that its handle and fittings were gilded. Hanging at eye level was a metal plaque in the shape of a face, mouth strained in a scream. It was like a human, though also in some way not. It had red jewels for eyes.

She opened the door.

The room was lit with red candles in brass sconces. A muted, warming light.

Zahir was there this time. She didn't see the Ifreet—the bed was empty. But the First Magician was bared to the waist, his flesh irradiated with green fire. His eyes were shut. He looked to be in pain. There were markings on his arms, long and sinuous as snakes. As his fists clenched, the snakes seemed to writhe on his skin. She stared. They *were* moving, crawling, up and down his arms, as if with a life of their own. They were black, edged with a gold that flashed against the green.

Lin was rooted to the spot. She remembered the hiss of Edrien Letrell, years ago, when Darien summoned him from death. *First, you must lose everything.*

Zahir's eyes opened. He saw her. She stayed in place, still.

He said, "You found me." He looked tired. The green glow faded from him. So did the snakes, which changed from black to gold and finally, to the dark copper of his skin. His eyes seemed more green now than blue, reminiscent of that fire that was gone. He said, "Now we can talk."

CHAPTER
19

LIN had allowed Zahir Alcavar to seat her on a couch that overlooked the courtyard of jacarandas. Its fountain audible from here, a whisper. Otherwise it was still, and dark. She sat staring out.

There was a hollowness in her that she had not felt even when Darien died. Perhaps that was the nature of the Seer's mark. Her maker was gone, a loss carved out of her. It meant that she could hardly bring herself to care about what she'd learned, and witnessed, here in this room. It seemed of so little consequence.

That first night Valanir had lifted her carefully and with ease, as if she were a bird. A memory that had nothing to do with the Seer's mark.

"I am tired," she said aloud. Outside, a breeze swayed the boughs of the jacaranda trees.

You must first lose everything, Edrien had said. She was, surely, the most adept pupil he'd ever had.

Zahir sat on a couch across from her. He'd donned a robe. She'd noted, before he did so, that his arms and shoulders were corded with muscle. Not what one might expect of a Magician. Between that detail, and the particular calluses on his hands, it was likely that he had seen battle. He was strange to her now; but this fact of his hardened body and trained reflexes was a thing they had in common.

"You want to die young," she said. "I suppose you'll tell me why?"

"I want no such thing, Lin," he said, and she startled a little; he rarely called her by name. "I love this life." He sounded hard, even cold.

"But sometimes we are called upon to put ourselves aside. And so I have been. On the night on that hillside when I was the only one to survive the destruction of my city . . . I was chosen for this."

She curled in on herself, repelled by his coldness. The night had been hard enough. She wished she were away, back in her room, to mourn Valanir alone.

His tone softened. "I'm sorry," he said. "He was . . . he was my friend, too. And don't forget—you've had a loss, but here—what happened to Almyria is unspeakable. We will be forced into war now, against some horror we don't know. The kind that can obliterate cities."

"Again," she said softly.

He shook his head. "You're right, it does feel that way, but . . . it's not the same at all. When I told you of Vesperia, I left something out. I had to. There are rules that govern the binding of an Ifreet, if the bond is to hold; one is that I can't speak of it unless asked. I wasn't sure if giving you the key to the Tower of the Winds would lead you here. I admit, I hoped it would. And I hope you'll forgive me for that. It's been hard, through the years, never talking to someone." He was silent for some moments. The fountain and breeze made soft music below. "Here is what happened. The night Vesperia was destroyed, I returned to the ruins." He swallowed as if a lump had come into his throat. Went on. "For days I searched the stones. Risked getting crushed by falling masonry, but I didn't care at the time if I died. Well, I did care a little. But mostly I was focused on finding my parents. I don't remember how long it was that I was there, searching the rubble of our house. It was exceedingly important. If a body is exposed to the elements, the soul . . . the soul is subject to torture. The texts speak of a demon the color of black tar, with a whip made of nettles and thorns. It arrives at sundown to administer lashes to whatever wretched soul is left unprotected. It's because of this that Alfinian funerals are held within hours of a death. I *had* to find them, or their souls would never find peace. I kept thinking of . . . the whips."

Zahir rose and strode to the window, then away again. "I will spare you the details of that night. And the days. I scarely remember them now myself. I can tell you this, though. And it was later confirmed by others who searched the ruins, before the king banned all contact with the ruins of Vesperia, on pain of death." He halted before her. "There were no bodies in the ruin of Vesperia."

Lin sat upright. "No bodies."

"Not then, not later. No trace of its people ever found. All the people of my city . . . vanished. From that time, my life was decided." He stood limned in candlelight. There was a young cast to his face, whether because the light was kind, or because as he reached back to his early years they somehow returned to him. "Until then, you know, I'd dreamed of becoming a singer. You may well laugh, but . . . I had a voice that could bring the people of our street to gather around, in evenings. I stood on a box and sang the ballads that were popular, and some that were not." For the first time, he smiled. "My parents were hardly overjoyed, but they didn't stop me. They knew it was hopeless—I was my mother's son. They knew when I came of age I would leave for the capital and try my luck there, in the wineshops and *khave* houses. It was not exactly a respectable ambition, but it was clear I was born to it. And after all, they loved me." He cleared his throat, glanced at the floor. "So. That was the plan. It never would have occurred to me to study magic. That was for old men, I'd have thought, if I'd bothered to think of it at all. But after Vesperia—Lin, what could I do? What is more important than family?"

Lin had no answer for this, not right away. He didn't know what she came from. She had never shared that. She recalled, as she had in the garden, the presence of Darien and Hassen and their hands in hers, that brief time in the hills above Tamryllin. "Nothing," she said. "So you became a Magician."

"It was not that difficult." He sat down on the couch across from her, heavily. "I won't go into how I got myself accepted to the University of Magical Arts in Ramadus . . . it is a tale. I was young and would let nothing stop me. And no one. I was not always good. I did things that were questionable . . . reprehensible, even. I . . . got into a relationship with an aristocrat in the city, a handsome fellow with a kind heart. I was not forthright with him. He thought I loved him, and I didn't. Or rather, I *thought* I did for a time. Later I would realize it was one of those instances when we delude ourselves, so as not to despise ourselves. I still have regrets about it. Telling myself it was love, I used him to advance my standing in the University. For a penniless orphan to achieve status, there was only one way—connections. I was invited to parties. I learned to beguile those around me with wit and verse. And in time, I began to delve in that which was off-limits. Forbidden."

She sighed out a pent-up breath. "The Ifreet."

The candle threw shadows across his face, but his eyes were bright. "I captured the djinn. It almost destroyed me to do it, and I knew . . . even then I knew the cost. I'll never live to be old, Lin. Well. If I can free the souls of a city, what is my life?

"What I didn't know was how tortuous was the path ahead. Time moves differently for Ifreet—they are eternal. To them, a year passes with a cough. I have spent years using my djinn to pierce the cloud around Vesperia. And I am still not at my goal, though I can see it ahead. I *can* see it." He shrugged. "At any rate, when I was younger I didn't know any of that. I was confident and moved among the ruling class of Ramadus. I thought I could do anything."

"But you came here."

He nodded. "I came here. I was twenty-three. The court of Yusuf Evrayad posed an opportunity for an upstart like me. His dynasty was young, his First Magician an old man. There was much that could be done here by someone who grasped the reins. It was not like Ramadus, where the old order of Magicians is entrenched, an institution hundreds of years old. The Tower of Glass was new. There was need of new blood."

"But you had another reason, too," said Lin with sudden sharpness. She was worn, and in grief, but it hadn't entirely dulled her wits. "You are involved in forbidden magic. You came to a place where fewer would notice. Isn't that true as well?"

His expression was strange—as if he might at any moment start to laugh. "I don't deny it."

"And then you won the favor of Yusuf Evrayad, and he made you First Magician," she went on. "Which angered Tarik Ibn-Mor."

"It was a mistake," he said. "Tarik's road to treachery began there, I'd guess, when Yusuf passed him over. And I would have been content to be Second. But I confess, I knew how to charm Yusuf. I knew the right things to say. I was ambitious, Lin, though even now I can't tell you why. It made no difference to my plans whether I was First or Second. But the decision was out of my hands. Probably what clinched it was my performance on the battlefield. You must understand this about Yusuf Evrayad—what angered him most about Eldakar is that he saw too much of himself in his son. As a boy Yusuf was known as the sensitive one of his family, given to poetry, not to war. Dismissed as useless. After the Evrayad family was murdered, he made it his life's project to defeat these tendencies in himself. It's how he raised an army to invade Kahishi, and conquered here. I believe that in his mind, conquest of *himself* mattered most. To find that his eldest son and heir was like himself as he'd been . . . it was a bitter blow.

"And then I came to his court. I did not remain in the Tower, not in those early years. There was constant unrest on the borders, north and south. There were rebellions to quell in the provinces. I went into battle with Yusuf's men. Soon I was leading a battalion. Yusuf liked that. Tarik Ibn-Mor was a good fighter in his prime, but I was the better commander. On the battlefield our rivalry came to a head. It had nothing to do with magic. It had to do with who Yusuf was, what he dreamed of for himself, for his legacy. A kingdom united that would endure. I helped give that to him—he never forgot. Not even later, when he saw that Eldakar and I loved each other."

"It didn't bother you, that Eldakar took a queen?"

Zahir looked surprised. "Bother me! The contrary. I would have harmed his standing at court. The king must be married. And, too . . . Eldakar needs more than is in my power to give. And deserves it. In him I found a reason to be good, for the first time—but also found I wasn't worthy. You know him, so perhaps you know I mean." Anger darkened his face. "He did not deserve what happened today. I never believed the rumors about Rihab Bet-Sorr . . . Now I don't know what to believe. If she was united in treachery with Tarik, or working her own game. I gave Eldakar a potion to help him sleep. But soon I'll have to wake him. Inform him, in my official capacity, that we are about to be at war." As he spoke of present-day concerns, the traces of boyhood that lingered around his eyes fell away. He looked drained, prematurely aged by events and—now she knew—by other things.

"I understand, I think, why you felt you had to detach from him," she said. "To spare him." She watched his face. "When you proposed a night with me. What exactly were you thinking?"

He didn't hesitate. "I was selfish," he said. "I shouldn't have approached you, any more than I should have allowed myself to become close to Eldakar. Not with the dark that clings to me. But Lin." He almost smiled. "I am still glad you know the truth. If someone had to know. I'm glad it's you."

* * *

Two letters, given to Lin Amaristoth the next day. The first delivered by a boy, commissioned on the riverfront for a silver penny. The second she would find later, in Majdara, beside a corpse.

The first was written in a clear, painstaking hand she recognized.

> Lin,
>
> *By now you know how she escaped. If I return to you I am dead. I may deserve it, but would sooner make amends. I will find her for you. Please tell Rianna that I am sorry.*
>
> *She has the ibis. Had I known, I'd never have helped her. I swear to that, for what it's worth. I can only guess what it means—what she is up to. I will do my best to find out more.*
>
> *If there is any way to make it up to you—all of you—I mean to try.*
>
> *—N.*

The second letter was in the bookshop of Aleira Suzehn. News of the sack of Almyria by a magical force, and impending war, had caused a panic in the streets of the capital. What often happened at such times happened then: a massacre in the Galician quarter—and Galician-owned businesses as well.

When Lin arrived, Aleira's bookshop was in disarray. Books and papers made cascades on the floor where they'd been thrown. In the back room where the women had met in secret was a corpse flung over a chair: a man with a dagger pressed so deep in his chest it might have been an ornamental pin. The blood around it was dried black.

In a compartment of the merchant's desk Lin found a sealed letter with *Seer* scrawled on it. It had stains on it, dark brown. She tore it open.

> *I had to kill a man of precious Alfinian blood, so must go to ground. Once more the city bestirs itself against Galicians.*
>
> *I've examined the prophecy. What I've found is too grave to tell by letter, but I'm left no alternative.*
>
> *The shadow comes from the north . . . yes. But look to your*

own, Seer. It comes from the north and west. Your land. You'd best warn Valanir Ocune. Whoever these people are, they are not his friends.

I wish you luck and health, Court Poet.

Aleira.

CHAPTER
20

"He's dead?"

A voice out of darkness. Winds were keening outside the tower; within, the air was damp and smelled of rain.

A smile in torchlight. A man, pacing out of the shadows, his broad shoulders appearing first. Hair like a torch as well, an unstable brightness as he slid in and out of shadow. "My contact handled it. It is unfortunate, of course. But Valanir would never have ceased to be a threat."

"Who is this contact?" The figure doing the asking came into focus, though was somehow indistinct. Compared to the other man, he gave the impression of being weedy, of little consequence. This was true despite that he wore the robes of High Master.

Elissan Diar shook his head. "What matters is this: with Almyria in ruins, Eldakar's forces diverted north, and his court weak from within, our goal is near."

"Elissan," said the High Master. Sounding desperate to uphold authority. "I understand why you assert our power. That the sacrifice of Manaia—regrettable as it was—perhaps gives us strength. But this talk of *Kahishi*, of all places . . . no one has ever tried to extend our influence so far. The court of Majdara is an ally." He licked his lips. "What do you play at here?"

The light that fell on Archmaster Diar's face sharpened his cheekbones to knifepoints. He flashed a grin. Over his shoulder called, "Etherell Lyr. Will you come out, please?"

A new voice now. This one light, hinting at music. "At your service, my lord Diar."

Though not so broad as Elissan Diar, Etherell similarly gleamed in the half-light as he came forward. A bit of a swagger in his step. Elissan clapped his shoulder. "Boy," he said. "I have a mind to appoint you my second-in-command. Maric Antrell was, alas, not quite so dependable as I'd hoped. Whereas you . . ." He tilted his head. A piercing look into Etherell's eyes, which were serenely unwavering. "My sense is you possess talents for discretion. And perhaps . . . others, as well."

Etherell returned the Archmaster's grin. As if they two shared a secret. He bowed. "It would be an honor, my lord Archmaster," he said. "What is our mission?"

Elissan Diar turned back again to the High Master. Still with that smile. "Marten Lian, my old friend," he said. "How would you like to rule in Tamryllin?"

IN a shaft of sunlight they leaned together: bright hair and eyes a match. Their eyes only for one another. A scroll spread on the desk before them. Her hair fell across the page. She said, wonderingly, "The reign of Seers. Can it be?"

He laced his fingers through those of his daughter. Together they did a dance, elegant and brief, before he let go her hand. "You know you were born to rule. It won't be long now, love."

Words that sounded again, an echo, after the chamber had faded and left blackness behind.

It won't be long.

BLACKNESS became his eyes, windows on the world's end. Just to look into them, the nothingness they contained, made her terrified. His hands gripping hers. *"Do you accept it?"*

Fear stoppered her throat; this time, she knew what would come. This time, when she fell, she knew there would be an end, eventually, to the terror; but no end, at least not as yet, to the falling.

* * *

JULIEN gasped. Air was scarce. She flailed as if drowning. But when she opened her eyes she saw a night sky and superimposed over that, a face; dark eyes that looked searchingly into hers.

She lay gasping, filling her lungs. Doing so again. And again. After a time, the act became less desperate; gradually, with more time, it steadied her. So did looking into eyes she knew, which above all showed concern.

"Give me a sign, if you're awake and can see me," said Dorn. "Gods know, I'm tired of being alone here."

THEY were in a place where winds swept over bent grasses. Lumpen rocks tumbled across a landscape similarly tumbled, the earth fixed in waves like a storm-tossed sea. From their perch on an outcropping they could see patches of fir trees, or a stunted birch in the shape of a crone, wrought by wind. There were few trees. A glister, here and there, of quick streams threading the stones. Coming from below, a distant thundering. Julien guessed that farther down the slope ran a waterfall.

They went without a fire. Dorn, having grown up in a town, was unacquainted with such skills. Julien showed him how to create a spark from sticks, and to gather what mushrooms and berries they could scrounge. She knew which were safe, and which poison. It was a branch of knowledge that had interested her even when there had been no need. She'd had illuminated books of botany, taken long walks in the fields and along the downs about her home. That experience came now to their aid. They would be hungry, she thought; but though she'd glimpsed, farther afield, the occasional scurrying animal, neither of them was a hunter, nor even equipped. At least they would have cold, clean water.

She avoided thinking of what would happen if they were here for long. Forever? Dorn seemed to avoid this thought as well. She supposed they would strike out and see if they could find habitation. If there were people at all in this place.

The first night, chilled under the stars, they sat back-to-back for warmth. He said, "I think you saved me. My memory is . . . I was headed for blackness. A pit that had opened for me. I don't know if it was death. My sense was . . . it might have been *like* death, but worse. You pulled me from the brink. I felt as if I were suspended, then brought somewhere else. Brought here."

She tried to laugh. "I hope it was a kindness."

He shrugged, or at least it felt to her as if he did. That, or a shiver. "Well," he said. "I'm not dead."

Soon Julien would tell what she had seen and heard before she'd joined him here. Not immediately. She was finding it difficult to speak. Pieces of her life lay around her as if in tatters; to speak would be to assemble them into something, or to try. Julien Imara didn't yet know what these tatters would make. She did not even know—especially when the scorching around her eye reasserted itself—who or what she was.

Morning found them dew-soaked and tired. Julien had slept only a little. The prospect of not changing clothes did not sit well with her, either. She thought longingly of the dry, soft contents of the chest by her bed at the Academy. Dresses and underthings sewn by her sister.

Dorn gave voice to her thoughts. "Magic is all I feared it was," he said as he wolfed his share of gooseberries. "A gods-damned inconvenience."

Whether or not she'd ever see her sister again was a question she hardly allowed herself to acknowledge; it lay deeper than thought. But at the moment she could divert herself with other concerns. Or at least, with a purpose.

"I think . . . we head for the waterfall," she said. "If I'm quiet . . . I mean, quiet *inside* . . . almost I can hear the mark. Telling me to do things."

"Excellent," he said. "So it's good for something."

They were clambering down the slope, boots sliding in the dew-wet grass. Grey brambles crept where trees failed to grow, interspersed with piles of heather. Julien tried to keep to the flatter rocks, which were not as slippery as the grass. "Don't you want to be a Seer?" she asked. "I thought that's what everyone wants, in the Academy."

"Yes, well," he said. "I always had trouble wanting what I am meant to. No . . . my plan was to go away. Become a wanderer, like Lacarne. Not bother with the Seer business, or any enchantments."

"I also like Lacarne," she said. Haltingly, as if in confession. "I . . . I hadn't thought much about becoming a Seer. I didn't really think it was possible. For me. Though there is the Court Poet . . ."

"Yes," he said. He'd stopped, and was looking out into the distance. Julien followed his eyes. Beyond the sea of grasses and rocks was nothing but sky. The sun blazed pale behind dusky clouds of windswept shape. A wind tumbled to them, damp and smelling of grasses. Dorn said, "I saw her once. Before she was Court Poet, when she came to the Academy with Darien Aldemoor. Only a glimpse, but I never forgot. There was something about her that drew the eye. Or mine."

Julien came up beside him. He appeared lost in thought—but perhaps, she thought, he was still in shock from all that had happened. She imagined she probably was, too. "Dorn," she said. "Before I came here, I went through . . . I saw some things. Things you should know."

His smile was wry. Arms waved wide, as if in surrender. "Go on."

First she gave him a summary—what Elissan Diar had done and would do. But when she saw his face, realized she must explain. She described the scene in the tower, which she recalled in detail as if it were painted before her eyes. When she reached the part about Etherell Lyr becoming Elissan's second-in-command, she looked away from Dorn as if to give him space. But he said, "He told me he was a spy . . . this could be part of it. Couldn't it?"

"I . . . don't know." In her mind's eye she saw Etherell's careless grin. More: she remembered him with blood on his face and hands. "He was spying for Valanir Ocune. Who is . . ."

"Dead, yes. And you're saying this, too, was the work of Elissan."

"Someone working with him in Kahishi. Elissan seeks to undermine their court, as if that way the Academy masters might rule in Tamryllin. I don't understand it . . ."

Dorn shook his head; the hair blew back from his face. "I think I might. Kahishi is our closest ally. If they crumble, Tamryllin is left open. Defenseless, practically." He sighed. "Do you see? This is what it comes to, when poets have power. It ought never to have happened."

She hung her head. The tale of Darien and Lin Amaristoth and the Otherworld . . . it shone for her, much as the Silver Branch shone in the Hall of Harps. Something to which Valanir Ocune had dedicated his life, and now she bore his mark.

Dorn was looking at her. She was reminded, in that moment, of the first time she'd noticed him: tall, projecting dignity, as he rose to sing a lament for Archmaster Myre. His song following her into dreams. "I forgot I was speaking to someone with ideals," he said. "I wouldn't have you lose that, Julien. Not on my account."

Julien didn't know what to say to that. She had never thought of herself that way. She wasn't even sure what it meant. *I'm only fifteen*, she wanted to say. *This is all new, for me. I shouldn't be a Seer.*

That last she knew was true. If Sendara Diar could see her now, she would be contemptuous. She would point out, rightly, that Julien had done nothing to earn the mark above her eye. And knew nothing of what it meant or could do.

There was so much she needed to know. She knew now that she'd hoped, above all, that Valanir would guide her. Instead he'd given her something that she carried like a weight of stone around her neck. Though it was the only thing, now, to give her purpose.

For the rest of the day she guided Dorn, and he followed, as they headed down to the waterfall. Its thunder a backdrop to their climb. Once a flock of terns arced overhead, shadows fleeting on the grass. It made her wonder what manner of river or sea might be nearby. "Where do you think we are?"

He smiled with half his mouth. "Where do you think those boys went . . . the ones who vanished by the oak tree?"

She asked no more questions.

They felt the waterfall before they saw it: mist bathed their faces and tongues and made their clothes damp. The smell carried to them by the wind was fresh and green, like moss. When they came to it, finally, they saw the falls were like a wall of glass plunging into foam and green. The rocks here were slick, treacherous; Julien fitted her feet with care amid their ridges and small plateaus. There was a sound she thought she could hear through the roar of the falls, an undercurrent. She stopped in place, and listened. Watched as afternoon sunlight braided gold in the streams of the waterfall.

"What is it?" Dorn said.

She turned, felt herself smile. Reached out her hand. "Come."

DRAMATIC irony was something you thought about at times, if you were a poet. It was one of the instruments in storytelling that poets of the current age enjoyed, now that an age of heroes was long past. Some blamed Darien Aldemoor and Marlen Humbreleigh for this; influential even in the short time they'd had, and so young. They'd made people want to see stories twisted in sardonic ways.

It was not a tool that Dorn was accustomed to employ. He thought its popularity came of a simple truth: it was easier to mock a hero than to act as one. Yet he struggled with writing about straightforward heroes, for despite himself he had an unmerciful eye for the flaws and foibles even in those he admired; but neither could he so gleefully undercut their virtue as had become the fashion. In the Academy he'd felt sheltered from fashions and trends, in truth; the remoteness of the Isle, and within it, of the Tower, had that effect. It was one of the things he'd valued most about his time there, even as it also chafed, hemmed him in.

Dorn knew he was confronting some form of irony now. He despised enchantments . . . all forms of magic that had distorted his art and its practice in the world. He was in the Otherworld, and his arrival here might have been what saved him the night of Manaia. Enchantments had saved his life. Then again, enchantments had imperiled his life in the first place.

He had awakened in the night, sweating, after a dream of that abyss. As at Manaia, it seemed to call out for him. Dorn Arrin wasn't sure how much he feared death, but nothingness . . . that was something else again.

So here he was. In a place across the boundary between worlds.

Would Etherell Lyr have laughed at this turn of things? He enjoyed dramatic ironies rather more than Dorn did. On the other hand, Dorn couldn't know at this point how much of the Etherell he knew was a disguise. When he allowed his mind to linger too close to this thought, he felt equal parts pain and shame.

There was no shame in being lied to, surely. Why, then, was he ashamed? He could berate himself for gullibility, but really, Etherell had had all of them fooled. If Elissan Diar had made him his second-in-command, he must surely still believe Etherell was what he claimed, the son of an aristocratic family.

Dorn had a great deal of time to think as he and Julien Imara made their way down the slope for the better part of a day. He was glad to stay behind her—the mark of the Seer on her rounded young face unnerved him more than he wanted to let on. The poor girl, after all. He had

thoughts about what Valanir Ocune had done, not all of them compli-
mentary. And now with what she'd delivered to him—what she'd seen—
that was more responsibility than anyone of her age ought to have. Or
perhaps, anyone at all. "We need to get out of here and tell the Court
Poet," she'd said, after he'd explicated the politics of the matter as he
saw them. He had been touched by the dawning horror in her eyes as she
absorbed the implications. The downfall of an ally, the ascendance of
someone like Elissan Diar.

A clear danger to the Court Poet.

There was beauty to the unevenness of the slope, Dorn thought early
in the day, when the sun made dimpled shadows beside each arc in the
grass. Bright, emerald green and its twin shadow, repeated unceasingly
into the gold bar of the horizon.

He would have liked to share that—the view, and the metaphor—
with Etherell Lyr. A mindset from which he must extricate himself,
and quickly. It was, at the very least, embarrassing.

Bending his head to the winds, Dorn thought he could understand
the source of his shame (which was not the same as embarrassment).
People saw me, and wanted me, his friend had said, his profile turned to
moonlight. Dorn could still see it.

People saw their desires in Etherell Lyr. Not who he was.

And what if Dorn was no better, in his heart, than the lord's guests
who had seen and taken what they wanted? Telling themselves that
acquiescence meant desire, that skill meant sensuality. He felt ill, to see
himself that way. But to confront the truth . . . he had committed himself to that. You couldn't choose where it took you.

I would feel nothing.

Many confused thoughts, but they all led to shame, and a hurt that
seemed to creep up on him unawares, and constantly.

He was lost battling these thoughts by the time they reached the falls.
Dimly he was aware that Julien was stalking on the wet stones like a
lynx after prey, not an image he'd have hitherto associated with the tim-
orous girl. The mark made a tracery of silver around her eye. He wondered
if she was aware of it.

"Come," she said at last, reaching out with a smile that he thought
jarringly confident, as if she wore someone else's face. She was indicating a fissure in the rock beside the falls. Dorn looked closer, realized

it was not merely a fissure. It widened and extended deep into the wall.

"A cave," he said. "Why . . ."

"I don't know. Come on."

DEEP in the cave, someone was singing. There were words, but in a language she didn't know. The voice sad and lost. Julien moved nearer to Dorn as they stepped into the dark. She wished they had a candle or torch. Sun from outside fell on walls which looked creased, like folded cloth.

To him she murmured, "This must be why we're here." He said nothing, only appeared thoughtful. She kept up the pace as best she could on the uneven footing. Her mind went to the boys who had vanished: they had found themselves in a cave with a luminous, unearthly woman. A woman who had sent them on quests. But if that was why they had come to this place, Julien thought, best get on with it. At least she was not in danger of falling into a tragic passion for the woman; and neither, as best she could gauge, was Dorn Arrin.

Water had collected at the bottom of the cave. There was no way to walk through it without soaking their shoes. Submerged in the water were sharp rocks that threatened to tear their soles. Julien nearly slipped and fell on the first of these, which taught her the imperative to slow her pace, to step with extreme care. Dorn seemed to have little trouble; possibly he had a talent for balance.

An odd thought for her to have, as if she assessed his qualities. As if she expected to make use of him, take advantage of his skills for some purpose. Something Valanir Ocune might have done. (Had he made use of her? She didn't want to think of that. It seemed disloyal—both to him and to herself. For different reasons.)

The singing drew her on. It was music utterly strange, its chaotic form not like anything she had studied. It would have been nearly impossible to mold it to the requirements of a harp. Yet what she found herself thinking of now was home, and her sister, and the grove of olive trees that sheltered the lower windows. Leaves like silver, murmuring at the touch of the wind. That faint song had been the bedrock of her life. She'd thought it would never end; that even when she went away, she could always someday return to it.

She'd treated her childhood like a doll that could be put on a shelf and taken down again, at will. Instead of what it was: a leaf already browning when she'd set it down.

"Feel that." Dorn was beside her. Something wistful in his face. "That wind."

A bit of wind stirred both their hair. "So?" It came out shorter than she liked. She didn't know how to disengage from this melancholy. The song conveyed a loss that was alien, yet still her own.

"Don't you see?" he said. "There's no one here. No one singing."

"You scorn enchantments . . ."

"It's true," he said. "But I'm not entirely a fool. I can accept that we are in an enchanted place. But it seems to me we are alone in this cave. I think you'll see."

They were in a place like a narrow hall; the light that knifed from the entrance flared out to the sides, edged the creased walls in ochre shades. As they advanced deeper, the light died away. In time, the hall expanded: they had reached what looked like an antechamber. Now the light grew again, turning the water beneath them green. She saw a narrow aperture near the ceiling of the cave, spilling sunlight. Hanging beside it a spiderweb that trembled in the wind.

The wind. The spiderweb moved in time to the melody, back, forth, thrilling like the wings of a hummingbird.

He was right. No one was singing—there was no one here. She'd taken them on a wrong turn. A dead end.

"I'm sorry," she said. Her shoulders drooped. "You were right. I was . . . headstrong."

"Don't be silly." He gripped her shoulder a moment, as if she were one of his comrades. "You are guided by something. I'm sure of that. Just because there's no one here . . ."

She wiped at her eyes covertly—she hoped, before he could see it. It had been a long night, she supposed, and an endless time after. "You are kind," she said. Her voice pitched low, as if in reverence of the song that continued on the wind. Though she knew now what it was, still it affected her. "You always were. I had a thought about you, earlier . . ."

"Oh?"

She was beginning to gather strength again. Perhaps her mistake had not been so egregious. There was music here, after all. "You called me someone with ideals, in contrast to you," she said. "But that's not right. You want to devote your life to music . . . without enchantments. With no reward but the work itself. Dorn Arrin." She met his eye. It was a pity, really, that she liked him. It was more pointless even than usual. "You may be in possession of some ideals, yourself."

He laughed. "I was afraid you'd notice that." He bent his head; there were tricky stones ahead. Casually he said, "Not many have noticed what *you* are, have they, Julien Imara? Your intelligence . . . and your courage. I thought I might at least do that. Since you saved my life." He smiled again, a more genuine, open smile than she'd ever seen from him. She thought it was like the light that broke through the aperture. *How silly you are,* she told herself.

"We should go back, I guess," he said. "See if that mark of yours does more than lead us into a hole in the earth. You're sure it doesn't want us dead, by any chance?"

She laughed, too. But only a moment, for that was when she saw, over his shoulder, the glitter of eyes. *"Dorn."*

He spun, somehow without losing his footing on the stones. The figure that emerged into the light was slight. A face etched with sorrow. A woman.

It may have been Julien's imagination but she could have sworn that in that moment the music changed. Something in it now made her think not of sunlight on the olive groves of home, but of other things. Dreams she'd had that she forgot by morning, yet remained still in her bones.

The woman spoke. "I am to be your guide." A voice with a rich undercurrent. Like a singer. She was long and lithe. When she moved, seemed to glide above the water and jagged rocks.

That gliding movement, more than anything, struck Julien as unnatural. She shivered. *"Guides of the Path . . . are not of the living,"* she murmured. It was not quite a question.

The woman simply looked at her with eyes like turquoise stones.

CHAPTER
21

"I THINK . . . I have to go home," she said.

Lin had told Eldakar everything. He knew about Tarik's ties to Ramadus; about the mark on Rihab's shoulder blade. He knew about Ned. A brutal search was on for all three; she would be powerless to protect Ned if he was found. Eldakar did not want to kill him, but there was honor to consider. A king's honor, in particular, could not be compromised.

None of the queen's servants had held up to questioning—whatever that meant; Lin did not want to think about it. There were ways in the Tower of Glass to obtain information, perhaps painlessly? She hoped so. The drugged servant girl with whom Rihab had changed places knew least of all. When she awoke and was told what had happened, so intense was her terror, her flailing panic, that she'd had to be drugged again. She had most likely been chosen for her size, a superficial resemblance.

Lin's prayer to Kiara, all through that day, was that Ned was well on his way to where he could vanish. She recoiled from the thought—what would she tell Rianna? But it was the best outcome she could imagine.

She had not had time to absorb what he had done. She was angry, but she blamed herself. At the same time, his actions shocked her. She'd imagined his loyalty to her was absolute. But even Ned had his underside of weakness. Rihab Bet-Sorr, already a deceiver of kings, had found it.

In daylight, Eldakar's rooms should have shone with all the splendor of which the Zahra was capable. But today they were dark. Gold-embroidered brocade shut out the sun. Lin understood. Though he could not afford time to grieve, the king was in mourning. Would possibly want to avoid a view of the gardens. She and Eldakar sat on cushions on the floor. Every so often she would run her hand through the soft carpeting that was close, as if for comfort.

The eyes he turned to her were devoid of ill feeling or guile, as if it was not her own man who'd betrayed him. That was the kind of man he was, she knew, and was humbled by it. Upon first learning of Ned's actions, and confessing them to Eldakar, she'd fallen to her knees. She knew it was her place to offer whatever restitution she could. He asked that she send some of her own guards to join the search party; a modest request, for appearances only. It gave her the appearance of making things right. Even now, he thought of what was best for her.

No wonder Yusuf Evrayad had despaired of his eldest son.

"Have you news of your brother?" Lin asked.

"Nothing," he said. "He may be dead. The Magicians are trying to find out more. Meanwhile . . . what I most dreaded is coming to pass. We mass what is left of our men to advance north. It will leave us exposed here, but I don't see another way."

"There *is* another way. For both of you."

It was Zahir, standing over them as if he'd always been there. Lin startled, but Eldakar did not react. Either surprise was not an emotion he could currently muster, or he was used to his First Magician making unexpected appearances. Both seemed equally likely.

Zahir sat on a cushion across from them. He turned to Eldakar. "What we've learned from Lin's friend is valuable. We now know—or have reason to believe—that the Fire Dancers are not our attackers. That means whoever is attacking us may also pose a danger to the Fire Dancers."

Lin came to it quickly, and saw Eldakar did as well. "Allies," he said, musing. "If such a thing can be imagined."

"Rihab was most likely their spy," said Zahir. He touched his friend's shoulder. "I am sorry. I believe she cared for you. I suspect that at the end . . . it was hard for her, too."

"We'll never know," said Eldakar, in a tone that discouraged discussion. "So you're suggesting we ally ourselves with the Fire Dancers against this—shadow from the west. If we can get that close to them. So far no one has been able to penetrate their camp and live to tell of it."

Lin, meanwhile, was thinking hard. "I can't go home," she realized. "Not without help. This magic most likely comes from the Academy, given its location. From Seers. I'd be walking into an ambush." *Damn Valanir.* He had known something was happening in the Academy; had thought to protect her. The consequence was the opposite—now she faced something utterly unknown.

But in thinking of him she could feel only sadness rather than anger. It was touching that he'd acted for her protection. Wrongheaded as it had been.

Eldakar smiled, a mirthless twist of the mouth. "I see where this is going," he said. "You both propose to leave me."

"Keep massing your troops . . . slowly," said Lin. "That is my opinion. Give the *appearance* of readying for war. Meantime I will go north in secret. I'll have words with this Renegade."

He looked stern, as if she were a wayward cousin or sister. "You think to succeed where no one else has?"

Lin felt her lips curl in a grin. A touch of Edrien in it, though that was known only to her. "I am generally good at convincing people not to kill me," she said. "If still they do . . . you'll have lost nothing."

"That is untrue in all sorts of ways," said Eldakar. "In any case, I doubt Zahir will let you go alone."

"Someone must represent your interests," Zahir said to Eldakar. "Someone acquainted with magic, who has a chance of surviving theirs. And . . . two of us increases our chance of success."

"In case one of you dies," said the king.

"Come here." Zahir had stood, reached down. Eldakar allowed himself to be drawn to his feet. They held each other a long time. Eldakar was inert at first, as if he were asleep. But at the last his arms tightened around his friend's shoulders, hands closed into fists against his back. Eyes shut, for a moment, in a manner that made Lin look away.

When they drew apart, Zahir spoke again. His voice was hoarse. "You know why I have to go."

"I know." Eldakar glanced around them. "These walls, the height of this mountain . . . they appear to protect us, but I know they do not. My father's legacy . . . it can all be destroyed in an instant."

Lin bowed her head. There was no gainsaying the truth of it.

"I do my utmost to serve you," said Zahir. He knelt in the carpet before the other man, as if for a blessing.

The king traced his friend's face with his fingers. "Come back to me." He turned to Lin. "Both of you."

THE landscape had changed too quickly, as if they'd stepped into a painting. It wasn't possible, Julien thought, for that lush green to give way, without transition, to sands like folded gold and no green at all. A sky the color of amber and bare of clouds. Before, in the lands above the waterfall, sunlight had been a pale thing, nearly blue. White was what it became now, savage as an attacker.

The woman glided over the sands, her legs barely moving. She seemed not to feel the heat. Loose brown draped her, a simple dress, belted with blue linen. Cliffs of gold and red stone arose on every side. At their lightest, they matched the sky. They were jagged, dimpled with shadows made sharp and black by the sun.

Dorn said, "Wait." He seemed to hesitate. They still did not have a name for the woman. He was shielding his eyes.

She turned. Waited for him to speak.

"We won't survive this," he said. "Maybe *you* don't require water or shade. We do. We don't have enough water, or protective clothes. We'll die out here."

Julien felt her eyes become round. She hadn't thought of any of that.

But the woman shrugged. "We do not travel in the conventional way. You *can* die here, if we are set upon by bandits or djinn. But not from dehydration or hunger—I am forbidden from allowing that."

Julien's fears were hardly abated by these words. Dorn looked annoyed. "So we have to be on the lookout for these—threats—without any sort of weapon to defend ourselves. That's splendid." He sounded cutting, as if speaking to one of his schoolmates. "Perhaps you'll at least tell us *where* we're going?"

The woman was unmoved. When addressing them she never seemed fully engaged, as if they were as unreal to her as she was to them. "I have my instructions. I will try avoid threats." Her eyes looked past his shoulder, past them both. "We'll soon be at the city."

* * *

I⊤ was time to feed him. Though Nameir had to crawl through the grass to his tent, dragging her injured leg behind her, she never let anyone else do it—though few were left who could have, anyway. Of the thousands who had marched north, less than a hundred fighting men remained. Most wounded. Across the hills they made agonizingly slow progress, dependent on the goodwill of villagers for food and water. People came out to them with what supplies they could spare, their faces drawn. They knew what the armies had gone north to do. Knew what failure could mean.

In the north, smoke was still rising. Nameir had helped build the pyres along with those few able-bodied enough for the task. It went against the will of Alfin, but rules were relaxed in times like this. There was no way to bury so many.

No additional attacks had followed the sack of Almyria. Not yet. Nameir did not know what this meant—if it meant anything—and only knew it was imperative that she and the prince reach a place where he could submit to the care of a medical practitioner. In other words, his home.

Meanwhile news from the Zahra had come. The queen had fled the palace, along with the Second Magician. Rumors and speculation flew thick and fast even in the villages. *A demon woman . . . a witch . . . a Ramadian spy.*

That last gave Nameir pause. Not that she had any reason to think Rihab Bet-Sorr was Ramadian, but the idea that she might be spying . . .

It concerns the queen, the Fire Dancer had said.

She and Mansur had initially thought, perhaps, the Fire Dancers were in collusion against the queen. Perhaps they were, and the queen, afraid, had fled.

Or perhaps she was a spy, and Tarik abetted her somehow.

Either theory left a good deal unexplained. They were missing pieces.

Summer was arriving early in the hills, blown from the desert. It was clean air, at least, sweeping away the smoke from the north. Still the stench remained.

Nameir's throat was dry as she dragged herself on hands and knees into the tent. "My lord," she said, though it came out in a hoarse wheeze.

He was lying still on his blankets. A fly buzzed on the wound on his forehead. Another circled. Nameir swallowed her fear. "My lord," she said again, more loudly. He gave the faintest of groans, enough to confirm he'd lived another day.

When she reached his side, she did as she had every day since they'd fled Almyria. Though those first days had been spent in a desperate fight to stanch his bleeding skull. She'd known enough to sew it shut, with the needle run through flame to rid it of contaminants and disease. A Galician doctor had shown her that trick, years before. Mansur's cries had nearly undone her; she'd needed more heart to force the needle through his flesh than she did on the battlefield.

By now he had stopped bleeding. It remained to be seen whether the damage had reached his brain. She hoped the Zahra with its staff of Galician and Ramadian doctors would have reassuring answers. She tried not to think of the reverse possibility—if the news was bad, they'd be the ones to know.

Painfully—it was hard while balanced on one leg—she raised him partly upright. Then, when he was balanced against the wall, used both hands to prise open his jaws. First came water, dribbles of it, distributed slowly. Too quickly and he would fail to absorb it, would dry out again as swiftly as did the yellowing grasses of the hills. She did this several times each day.

The other thing she did, after, was feed him. This was a liquid, rennet and curds in a flask, that she poured down his throat in dribbles as she had the water. She worked his jaws around it, was glad to see that he swallowed.

He had neither opened his eyes nor said a word since Almyria. The worst fight they'd ever seen. She had been engaged in one combat after another—the enemy kept coming—her throat torn with shouts. She was certain that night that she would die and meant to take as many Fire Dancers with her as she could. Through a haze saw Mansur from behind, surrounded by three men. She began to run towards him, cutting her way. Not fast enough. She did not see the blow that shattered his helmet; only later recalled how it lay on the ground in shards like bloodied seashells. Borne on rage she arrived at that spot, too late, to confront the Fire Dancer who landed the blow. From that time, her memory blurred; she had been more intent on defending the body at her feet than on anything else she'd ever done.

By then it was close to dawn. That was her good fortune, as it happened—the only reason she and the few who remained had survived. At daybreak the living Fire Dancers vanished, leaving behind the bodies of their slain. As always these rotted within moments, leaving behind a boiling stench and the remains of white cloaks.

Nameir's memory of the lost battle was drowned in a red mist. She'd been aware at the time of what was happening: that they'd been swarmed, taken by surprise despite precautions, by a force larger than they could ever have planned for. But she'd been too preoccupied, from the moment it began, to absorb it as an experience.

The same could not be said for what came after. When she and the stragglers who remained paced through the bones of that golden city. The red and black and sickening green of what should never have seen daylight spattered on the cobbles, roiling in gutters.

When she'd seen the heads atop the battlements, she almost turned to flee. But then recalled the dignity of Lord Ferran. That knowing what she was, he'd wanted her in command of his men.

In the end, she'd climbed the battlements and cut him down herself, as well as the other lords. It had taken days to recover his body and she had done that, too. While at the same time making sure to tend Mansur and his ghastly wound, day after day and every night when he woke screaming.

She had served under the prince for five years, six before that under various viziers and warlords after lying about her age at twelve. Yet nothing aside from childhood memories that with the years had faded like dried blood could compare. These were the darkest days of her life.

Later her torn hamstring had given out, as it was going to, and all the harder for the neglect she'd shown it when initial shock had numbed the pain. She'd directed one of the surviving men in the task of binding her leg. All the horses were slain; she'd requisitioned a mule at one of the villages and rode that, dragging a cart bearing the prince behind her. It was the stuff of dirges and elegies, what they had come to.

She recalled Mansur singing beside the fire and thought about how even when you knew a particular moment mattered more than all others, it was impossible to feel as if you'd contained it. She had always known those moments in her life would matter, for whatever length of time she was given. But the knowing was not enough.

It was, at any rate, Mansur who had introduced her to dirges and elegies. For the losses that had made her what she was, Nameir had neither music nor words. At first because she was too preoccupied, as an orphan adrift, with staying whole; after, because the business of war precluded such things. Until she joined the prince, saw how his passion for battle ran alongside other passions until they intertwined.

With the few words of her childhood that she remembered, Nameir Hazan prayed in the night. The sky was choked with smog, a fervid red without stars since Almyria. She hoped her prayers could nonetheless reach the god. Sometimes she even prayed to Alfin—though she loathed to do so—if only for expediency's sake. For how could the Alfinian god *not* adore a warrior like Mansur Evrayad? And why would the Unnamed God save a descendant of people who had murdered so many of his? So she dodged the memory of her father's face, the candles at his forbidden shrine, and sent a prayer to the tyrant god.

The smell of death trailed them on the wind, day by day. She'd hoped to shake it off eventually, but they never did. On the bright afternoon they reached the River Gadlan and saw minarets of the capital nested in the valley, the death smell was still there. It had followed them all the way home.

PART IV

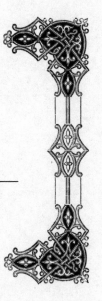

PART IV

CHAPTER
22

SMOKE the color of saffron clouded Lin's eyes, made her blink as she played. She half-reclined on a floor cushion, a lute cradled loose in her arms. The song was one Zahir had taught her earlier that day. She was sprawled at his feet in a languid pose, as if she'd been drugged. He stood, hands gesticulating as he sang.

Her head was tilted back in a semblance of drowsiness: she peered through the smoke and about the room from under her eyelids. The master of the house was rubbing his hands together, eyes fixed on Zahir Alcavar. Nearby sat his son, looking polite and attentive—if a bit expressionless, Lin thought. Perhaps he didn't care much for music. He was thin and unassuming as his father was powerfully built.

For her part, Lin was fast gaining an insight into the people of Vesperia who had come out in crowds to hear Zahir sing. The friendship between him and Valanir Ocune took on a new dimension—had the apprenticeship run both ways? She wondered if Valanir had given the Magician some pointers.

Khadar Zuhalan and his son Zweir were some of the most powerful operatives in Majdara. But that wasn't exactly why she and Zahir were here. Lin stole another covert glance at Khadar, the father. A fleshy man, though muscular: he kept himself fit, likely knew how to wield the cudgel that rested in a corner of the room. He traveled often on business, which had mostly to do with investments. And travel necessitated an acquaintance with the art of defense. Or at least its brute fundamentals.

Just now his defenses were down: the yellow smoke rose from a long pipe he periodically drew from, his features relaxed. From time to time he passed the pipe to his son. But he otherwise kept his full attention on the song.

Zahir gave himself to the rapture of his performance. His silk shirt, bloused at the wrists, was finely tailored; a cluster of sapphires caught in a net of silver hung from his left ear. Khadar kept his eyes fixed on the First Magician as if at a delicacy he would have liked to eat.

So far it went according to plan.

It was a plan Lin despised. Deception, skulking, were not acts of which she approved. She didn't know what Zahir's feelings were. How he felt about deceiving this man. But she thought of Eldakar, and what was happening in the Academy, and of course of Valanir, which caused her to bow over her instrument and tighten her lips as she played. She was wearing a silk gown, bare at the shoulders, lavender and infused with cheap scent. Her hair was curled at the top of her head and crowned with gold chains that flowed to her shoulders, were cold on her cheeks. Her sandals, hastily borrowed, were too large and slid on her feet. A vain getup—she disliked that part as well. It recalled too clearly what it had been like when she had been a possession of Rayen's, to buy and sell. But tonight, that was how it had to be. She was a singing girl, prized only in part for musical abilities. Bought for a night by a wealthy man to perform alongside a celebrated singer. Tonight, that was who she was.

Shantar Nir had made it clear that she was not the focus of the evening. That all would be well if she stood aside for Zahir. And Zahir himself—well, that was another surprise. The man currently singing for a bewitched aristocrat was taller than the First Magician, with broad cheekbones and dark, soulful eyes.

She had watched him transform. He had suggested she watch, so there would be no doubt in her heart who he was. With so many enemies around and about, with people like the queen and Second Magician having turned out to be other than they presented themselves—even Ned, even Ned—it made sense.

So at first light before they went into the city she followed Zahir Alcavar into the Tower of Glass. The Tower at that time of the day was all a greyness, neither dark nor light. He led her to the chamber of infinite mirrors, where she saw too many copies of herself, hollow-eyed and gaunt, from every unforgiving angle. From the back, her head looked bowed, spine curved, as if she had begun to curl inward like a decaying leaf. Since the news of Valanir she hadn't eaten. A lump in her stomach had settled there, filled her like a sickening kind of meal. Now she saw what a week had wrought and vowed to do better. She was indulging in grief by letting herself weaken.

The mirrors were kinder to Zahir. She wondered if fatigue and long hours of close conversation with Eldakar had made her begin to see the First Magician through his eyes. Not that she ever could. Lin did not think she could view anyone with a gaze so unselfconscious, so uncritical. There was too much Amaristoth in her.

Zahir stood in the center of the mirrored room and spread his arms wide. He began to chant an invocation that might have been Ramadian; it was strange to her. His head thrown back. In his tone, an unmistakable ring of command.

It was only when the green glow engulfed him that she realized it was not the magic of the Tower of Glass Zahir was drawing upon to make his transformation. When the light had dissipated and Lin found herself looking at a different man, taller, with dark eyes, she shook her head. "You used . . . that thing . . . for this."

He smiled with teeth that were larger, and more white. "Scratch a djinn, get a long history of shape-shifting. It's what they do best. Turning into unearthly beautiful women or men to lure their prey, or to have a jape at a mortal's expense. I've been doing this for a long time. How else could I go about the city unnoticed? Various of the aristocracy know my face."

"And you are sure there is some . . . hideout of Fire Dancers in the city?"

Zahir had proposed that instead of proceeding directly north, that they try to procure information that might be to their advantage in the city. A secret lair of Fire Dancers would be one such place—if they could find it. If it existed.

"I can't be sure," he said. "It may be a legend. But my thought is . . . the Renegade considers himself a king, like any other. And a king must have spies."

"How will we find it? This . . . lair?"

Zahir turned to her with his strange new face, bared those strange white teeth in a grin. "I know a man." The cut of his clothing looked different on this new body, somehow careless. The mirrors reflected his new form from all angles, thousands of them. "There's one catch. He'll want a favor."

On their way down the mountain as the mists of early morning lifted, he told her of the sort of man they were to see, the sort of favor he'd want. They had departed the Zahra by the same concealed door Lin had used on her trips to the city. She wore a scarf of blue silk wrapped around her head and neck—concealment as well as protection from the sun—carrying only whatever she could on her person. The simplest of clothes. Her knives. She left behind her guardsmen from Tamryllin, under the command of Garon Senn; and she'd sworn their service to Eldakar for as long as he might require them. Garon was not happy, she knew—he didn't like being outside her sphere of confidence, that he did not know where she was going. She didn't care. He would serve faithfully and ingratiate himself with Eldakar, the better to secure his self-interest.

She left behind the songs she had written, in that Tower of the Winds only she could access. Had been tempted to burn them, but couldn't. They'd emerged from pain she didn't know she had, and for that she hated them, but she could not destroy them. *One's shadow.*

Zahir traveled similarly, without burdens. A simple shirt and trousers replaced the brocade and jewels of office, though he did wear an embroidered vest. He looked prosperous, carefree. The lute strapped to his back looked well-oiled, with strings that gleamed, but with a worn finish. She suspected it predated his arrival in Kahishi—a long time indeed.

Once in the city, he led her through back streets. These were darkened even in the morning, so narrow and hemmed in were they by rows of black-eyed dwellings that left only a sliver of sky. The gutters that ran down the center of the streets, down steps, were not as clean as elsewhere she had seen. This was one of those parts of the city such as she knew well from her time as a destitute poet in Tamryllin; a part that was cared for less.

It was on a street like this that they came to a metalcrafter's shop. Its sign showed a pair of crossed scimitars above a round shield. There was a man at a worktable within. Swords and daggers of all kinds hung on the walls. She took them in at a glance: nothing remarkable leaped to the eye. Tools of the trade, well-made but without embellishment. The man who greeted them was of an iron mien like his merchandise. Zahir murmured to him and motioned Lin to follow. The man didn't watch them go.

The back room of the shop held a variety of oddments: barrels, bales of cloth, chests. It was dim, lit only by whatever penetrated from the window at the front of the shop, and dusty. Zahir made for one especially large chest in the corner. It was nearly the length of a man, black, bound with iron. The Magician spread his hands. Uttered one word in Kahishian, low and clear. *"Dakhira."*

There was a click. For a moment nothing else happened. Then, as Lin watched, the lid of the chest began to rise: a smooth, oiled movement and without a sound. Though she'd been prepared for this, she was unsettled. Zahir went to prise the lid farther, expose what was inside.

Lin thought of the word used for the charm. It seemed an odd choice. "Memory?"

"It is an open door." His grin was wry. "Whether or not we'd have it so."

He climbed inside. Lin watched as Zahir descended the wooden ladder that extended down into the tunnel concealed by the false bottom of the chest. There was, at the very edge of the dark she could see below, a hint of light. At last, grateful for the trousers she wore, she climbed in after him.

On their way down the mountain Zahir had said, "In the capital, I go by another face, another name. I am an itinerant musician. I come bearing tales from the world over—of cities and sights far away. And I listen. I listen more than I speak, or sing."

They were passing, in that moment, between the rose hedges. Lin turned her face to one of their red faces. Its perfume like a sign from a world beyond betrayal, or death. She inhaled with closed eyes. Said, "And what else do you do?"

THE tunnel beneath the metalcrafter's shop was tidy and tiled with smooth stone on all sides, the floor. It could have been a wine cellar, and perhaps had been one once, long ago. Through the eyes of Edrien Letrell she knew how over years cities expanded, collapsed, relentlessly changed. The towers that rose and fell.

Ahead was the light she had seen earlier from the top of the ladder.

It was the warm glow of lamps. The chamber they came to was nearly bare, just a table, some chairs, and two men seated there. They sat erect, clearly on duty. Before them on the table was a *tabla* board, but they were not playing: the sound of the chest had alerted them and their eyes were trained on the door, knives in hand.

In a jovial tone Zahir wished them a good morning. Their faces had altered when he came into view, though crinkled with suspicion at the sight of Lin. Both men were young and fit, with daunting shoulders. Not people she would want to fight if she could avoid it.

One demanded, "You bring a newcomer, Haran? Here? Without permission?"

Zahir approached the table with a walk that Lin could only have described as a strut. His hands gripped his belt above the hips. "Shantar doesn't mind me bringing a lady, does he?" He glanced behind him at Lin, then turned back to the men. "We've been half around the world, but it's not enough for my mistress. She's begun to grow . . . restless. She's promised that if I show her some danger . . . there are rewards in store. A little knifeplay, even, if I play my cards right. You understand, don't you?"

Lin kept her face expressionless. Then realizing this might not be sufficient, she made her face like stone. While he'd briefed her on much of what she was to expect here, this had not been included. She suspected it had been a spur-of-the-moment invention. She did not know whether to be amused or annoyed.

The men were smirking and studiously avoiding looking her way. At last one of them said, "I don't know, Haran. Shantar would want to see you, but lately he's in a temper. There's some strangeness abroad. If he finds out you brought her here, not even blindfolded, I don't know what he'll do."

Lin thought this was the right time to join Zahir at the table. She'd removed the scarf when they entered the storage room, her hair tumbled about her shoulders. Zahir reached out his arm, without turning; she came forward and let him wrap it around her waist. Her eyes still hard as she looked from one to the other of the men. "I'm no snitch," she said. She grabbed Zahir's hair in a fistful and pulled, perhaps harder than necessary. Or perhaps not. "This one squeals more than I do."

"She has an accent," said one of the men, even as he was trying not to laugh. "She's very pale."

"From Eivar," she said curtly. "Haran here came to my town to sing. And then, later on . . . I made him sing."

"All right," said the man. Perhaps younger than she'd thought at first. "Go through, go. But later, Haran, you'd better tell us how you found this one. If they're all like that in Eivar, I'm overdue for a visit."

A massive door, crowded with boltlocks, opened from this antechamber to another room. This was the real sanctuary, Lin guessed: the flagstones were softened with a fine carpet, and there were satin cushions at the low tables. Light flickered from the lamps set on each table. There were men here, conversing in low voices when she entered. They looked up only briefly before carrying on their conversations—all but one man with red hair and powerful build who gave a shout. "You bastard!" He hurled himself at Zahir. Enormous arms wrapped around the Magician. "Where have you been hiding this time? And you bring a lady? You'd better have an explanation, friend. Or do I have to kill Samir and Kor for their negligence?"

When Zahir drew back, he was grinning. "I hope you don't. The fault is entirely mine—and that of my lady, who is most persuasive."

Lin returned the direct gaze of the large man. So this was Shantar Nir. In his rough-hewn way he was handsome, with a prominent jaw and a broken nose. His hazel eyes were shrewd. She thought she might have the measure of him. "*Gvir* Nir, we are here to request a favor," she said. "Haran has made clear to me that every favor has its price. And I am qualified, if necessary, to deliver."

Curiosity in the hazel eyes. "How, qualified?"

"Like Haran, I can sing," she said. "Moreover." She drew one of her smaller knives and flicked her wrist. There was a dartboard on the wall, stuck with darts. And now her knife quivered there, too, near enough to the heart as to make no difference. Not if the target had been a man.

Shantar lowered himself onto one of the cushions. He looked thoughtful. But then his gaze sharpened as it returned to Lin. "And who are you?"

"You may call me Miryan," she said.

"One of our flowers. I see."

"You like flowers, as I understand it," she said.

The man gestured dramatically around the room. His thick fingers were adorned with rings. "I have been remiss with the courtesies," he said, sardonic. "Welcome to the Jonquil Safehouse. Anyone trusted by this rapscallion is a friend to us. Sit, we'll drink. What is this favor you desire of me?"

As they sat, a man hurried over with a pewter pitcher and cups. The beer he poured out a rich brown. Zahir leaned across the table on his elbows. He waited until the serving man had gone before he said, "We seek the Fire Dancers, Shantar. Do you know the place they hide?"

The red-haired man looked at him askance. "Do I want to know what this is about?"

Zahir grinned, took a sip. Wiping his mouth with the back of his hand he shrugged. "Likely not."

"Hm." Shantar steepled his hands as he surveyed Zahir across the table. "You stay away for months—off west this time, if your friend's accent is an indication. And then you make a request like this. It's not your usual."

"Do I have a usual?" A faint smile was playing around Zahir's mouth.

The other man sighed. "I guess not. Bastard." Shantar took a long, savoring drag from his own cup. For the first time, Lin noticed that behind the other man's swagger was a discordant note. His eyes darted around to others in the room, but no one seemed to be listening. Nonetheless, Shantar leaned forward and spoke more quietly. "Since Nitzan, something has been happening in the city. Our people are . . . they're starting to disappear."

"Disappear?"

"They go on missions and don't return. Last night it was someone important . . . the chief of the Delphinium Safehouse. Old Raygar Shenk, if the name means anything to you. He was a captain in Yusuf Evrayad's army, long ago. No friend of mine—we had our differences—but nonetheless. The Brotherhood is on edge. And with war coming . . . things have taken a strange turn, Haran. You picked quite a time to show your face here. And now you want to speak with the Fire Dancers when we are about to be at war with them." He was watching Zahir's face.

"That's one way of looking at it," said Zahir. "But may I remind you—though none knows better than you: war never put an end to commerce and profit."

"So you seek them on business." This seemed to satisfy Shantar. "Very well. I know how you might find your friends. They are well-hidden, but you've come to the right place. Much as the Fire Dancers keep to themselves, they're not above dealings with the Brotherhood of Thieves." He stretched his legs on an adjoining cushion, let out a sigh. "It's just as well you're here—I have a confounding problem that you're about to help me solve. That is, if you're as interested in the Fire Dancers' lair as you say." Now the cast of his face had sharpened, from uncertainty to cunning. "There's a certain merchant prince I've had my eye on. He keeps a rare medicine under lock and key. Let's just say I have an interested buyer. This is a mixture that's *very* hard to procure. And now, with the turn of events in the city . . . we need more men. More resources. A tidy sum would go far for the Brotherhood at this time."

Zahir shrugged. "Like you need a reason to want money," he said. "Have you sent advance spies?"

"We've got everything. The plans to the house, the place where he keeps the medicine. But that's as far as I could go without arousing suspicion. What's needed is someone who can get close to the man—his name is Khadar Zuhalan—preferably of an evening when he's been softened by indulgences. And of course I thought of you. He is known for a fondness for overly pretty young men—that's right, you fey bastard. Moreover he is a connoisseur of music and holds entertainments in his home most nights. I can get you introduced to the people who scout fresh talent for him. I can get you in."

"Would I need to go to bed with him?" Zahir asked. He was inspecting his nails. "That would increase my fee."

"If that happens, I'll increase it. Though by all accounts he is gentle, and, ah, is not often the one actively participating." Shantar smirked. "You could close your eyes and pretend it's your whippet, here."

"You *really* want this medicine," said Zahir. His eyes were now intent on Shantar. "You will pay what I ask, on top of giving us the whereabouts of the Fire Dancers. I want that commitment from you in advance." He named a figure that made Lin suppress an incredulous stare in his direction. She was sure the thief would refuse.

Shantar looked resigned. "The Brotherhood keeps its word," he said. "You drive a hard bargain, Haran."

"We all have things we want," said Zahir. A velvet tone, satisfied, as at a seduction achieved.

* * *

THEY had dinner with Shantar Nir and his men that evening in the Jonquil Safehouse. The cuts of meat were fine, the wine plentiful. Majdara's Brotherhood of Thieves was, it seemed, a prosperous operation. In undertone, at one point in the meal when Shantar had left the table, Zahir explained to her that there were even city guards who cooperated with the Brotherhood. That the organization went back centuries, though it had grown and strengthened under the reign of Yusuf Evrayad, a result of expanded trade. Once there had been only three Brotherhood safehouses in Majdara. Now there were six. The Jonquil Safehouse was chief among them, which made Shantar Nir master of the Brotherhood.

"He may not look it," said Zahir, "but the man has been instrumental in more political and trade deals in this city than some of its grandees. He cultivates that common air to throw people off guard."

"Yet he gave in to you easily," she said. "Why?"

Zahir's new dark eyes were opaque. "He knows a job assigned to me will be done. I'm pleased—the money will go to Eldakar. To help offset the costs of this war."

"What other jobs have you done for him?"

He grinned. "That would be a very long story, my lady. Maybe someday we'll have the time."

When Shantar returned to the table, he fixed his attention for the first time on Lin. He seemed more relaxed, perhaps a combination of the effects of drink and his confidence that Zahir would get the task done. And besides, it was late. "Never, in all the time I've known Haran, have I known him to travel with a companion," said Shantar, gaze boring into Lin. "Always seemed a lone wolf sort to me. Ever since we met years ago. I was carrying out one of my first jobs, and terrified. And then this musician, out of nowhere, helped me."

"How did he do that?"

The thief's smile was distant. "I was to lift something from a house in the course of a party. I arrived in the guise of a guest. Later I was to discover it was a test—if I succeeded in the job I'd be promoted. If not . . . well, life is only worthwhile when the stakes are high. The Brotherhood believes in keeping them that way. A lost hand, a lost *head* . . . the possibility of these, hanging over us, is what gives us life." He was not smiling anymore. "At any rate. The item was kept in a safe in a room to which I gained access. A library. I knew the combination—it was a plan months in the making. But when I arrived, there browsing among the books was a woman. Beautiful, I recall. I couldn't carry out the job with her watching. Time was running short. Then Haran came in. He looked from one to the other of us, and introduced himself as a wandering singer."

"He charmed her, didn't he?" said Lin. Felt Zahir shift beside her, whether uneasily or with pride, she didn't know.

"Of course. He led her out to the garden. And I thought it coincidence, because—why not? She was beautiful. Everyone loves a handsome musician. There were many secluded parts of that garden, and I saw the look in her eyes. As sweet a triumph for him as for me. No one else arrived to disturb me—I was able to complete the job as arranged. But later on . . . before I left the party, there was that hand on my jacket collar," Shantar shook his head with disbelief. "I'm twice this bastard's size, and still he put his hand on me. He said, 'I've done you a good turn. Now you'll do one for me.' Turned out he was newly arrived to Majdara and wanted to be introduced to the chief of the Brotherhood. My predecessor. Well. The stolen item—a dagger, I well remember, a treasure of Almyria with a ruby pommel—was on my person, and we were still in the home of its owner. I could hardly refuse. Though it was a risk for Haran here. I could have deceived him, led him into an ambush."

"You were intrigued by me," said Zahir with a wicked grin. "Admit it."

"It's true," said Shantar, and drank. "I did want to see what kind of man would be so foolhardy as to actively seek out the Brotherhood. And I've regretted it ever since."

"Naturally," said Zahir. "One more drink and you'll confess your undying love."

"Perhaps I would," said Shantar. "But alas. It seems your heart is taken. By a woman whose real name you won't disclose."

Ah. Lin didn't visibly react. Nor did Zahir. Instead, he said, "Old friend, do you ever find it is wearying, in the depths of your soul, to be alone? And aren't you alone, always, even surrounded as you are by colleagues, even some friends? With them you must continuously mask yourself, dissemble, if you are to maintain control."

"I am not too drunk to murder you where you sit," said the thief with a roll of his eyes. "Bear that in mind."

Zahir laughed. But soon became earnest. "All I'm saying is—my lady and I—I believe we found one another for that reason. We were both alone, and profoundly weary. Above all, weary of masking ourselves as other than we are."

"And she's proficient with a knife."

"And music," said Zahir. He seemed mellowed by drink as well. Lin was sure he was about to expound upon the skills in which she was supposedly proficient, an encore of the lurid fiction they'd delivered to the men on guard. She awaited it, cynical and weary. But instead Zahir took a tone she recalled from the nights in the gardens. His eyes grown distant. "Music, the knife. Aren't these the things that matter for us, Shantar? People like us, who must keep to the shadows. At the center of our lives—of what *makes* us alive—the dance of blood. The violence of music."

"Now you sound like a Fire Dancer," Shantar drawled over his cup.

Lin smiled, more irony than mirth. "Or a poet."

THE yellow smoke, the drink, and above all the hypnotic performance of Zahir Alcavar in the guise of the wandering musician Haran had done their work. Father and son, both, had fallen into what appeared a trance. But especially the father, which was the point. At a lull in the music, Khadar Zuhalan had in a voice made husky by smoke and emotion invited the singer Haran to sit with them.

Zahir presented himself to the men with a deep bow. When he took his place at the table, Lin noted that his leg was not far from the other man's leg. He held the merchant's gaze as if they'd known one another all their lives. His final song had been one of passion, cried out with a ferocity that recalled to her his words to Shantar about the violence of music. Across the table, *Gvir* Zuhalan appeared transfixed. Here it was: her cue.

Sidling up to the son, she made her voice timid and deferential as she asked where she might attend to her needs. She already knew the tiled, scented room where she'd be directed—where she might splash herself with rosewater and make use of a garderobe—adjoined the room she sought. She had studied the floor plans of the house intently, late into the night before she and Zahir had slept. The Jonquil Safehouse extended some distance underground and included a number of rooms. In one of these was a large, soft bed where she and Zahir Alcavar had been invited to spend the night.

Beneath the silly gown she had a knife buckled between her breasts, another at her shoulder blade. Not ideally positioned, but still within reach. At the same time, Lin was acutely aware of the futility of these defenses. If she was caught, this man could summon a personal guard that would easily overpower her with swords and spears. A man did not keep such wealth in his home, and trade goods, without men-at-arms ready to hand. And the Zuhalan family was known for being cautious. For that reason the Brotherhood had been finding the house difficult to penetrate.

Yet here she was, carrying out this folly. Despite herself, she did trust the judgment of Zahir Alcavar.

The doors to the room that adjoined the purification chamber were heavy. She carried a vial of oil to apply to the door hinges. Her heart racing as she did so. The hallway was empty, but anyone might pass by at any moment.

Thankfully the oil did its job and soon she was inside without a noise. She closed the doors behind her. She was in a room that might have been the merchant's study: at its center was a splendid desk of cherry-wood where ledgers were piled in a stack, alongside an inkwell and pen. Shelves of books lined the walls. She felt a pang of anxiety at the sight of the window that looked out on the street, where someone might look in. In a brisk motion she advanced to the window, staying adjacent to it at all times, and closed the drapes.

On the desk, a lamp was burning, lending its illumination to Lin's purpose. There should not have been. This was undoubtedly the work of one of Shantar's people, though she didn't know how that was arranged. Perhaps one of the servants had been turned, or solicited for a favor about which they otherwise knew nothing.

The light of this lamp was reflected in a copper mirror, round and bronze-framed, that hung on the wall facing the desk. It was of an ancient style, its frame ornate with scenes of a siege battle, recalling the fallen empires of the south. Given *Gvir* Zuhalan's extensive travels, it might have been a relic of just such a place and time.

Lin went to the mirror and felt along its edge on the right side. She tried to avoid the sight of her own face, though caught a glimpse of herself in the vacuous makeup. One of Shantar's men was a professed expert and had applied himself to making her look, in her own estimation, like a whore. Her eyes were painted to appear larger and somewhat slanted. The Seer's mark concealed beneath a thick layer of powder.

She felt a catch on the side of the mirror. It came free. The mirror slid outward from the wall on concealed hinges. Behind was a groove cut into the wall, and inside it a brass jar, sealed with a stopper. It was small enough to conceal in the pocket sewn in the inside of her skirts, as had been the plan. She would secrete it there, return to the room of yellow smoke, and wait for the game of desire between Zahir and the merchant to run its course.

As her hands closed around the jar Lin felt a chill. She turned. There stood Zweir Zuhalan. Behind him a contingent of armed guards. They had entered soundlessly, thanks to her efficient work on the door hinges. So close and large they loomed that they blocked the light. Still she saw the glint of steel and steel and steel, everywhere she looked.

"Bind her with double knots," said the merchant's son. "These thieves are like eels that slide from your grasp at the slightest mistake. I will not tolerate mistakes." They were already there, all around her; two had pinioned her arms, another two her legs. Lin had to admit they were well-trained and fast. Just now she was too dazed to think anything else.

"Sir, what of her accomplice?" asked the man who led the guards.

Zweir's lip curled. "Soon," he said. "After my father is finished with him."

CHAPTER 23

THEY abused her body on the way down to the cellar. The gold head-dress fell off somewhere and her skirts rode up her legs. She knew it could have been worse; a squeeze of her breasts and between her legs was not as bad as what could have happened had they license to do as they pleased. They did not, however. Zweir had instructed the guards to leave her intact for his father's justice. They found and took away her knives.

As these things were happening, as they carried her down the corridor, groped and twisted and squeezed, sniggered among themselves, Lin felt her mind go to another place. As if she hovered somewhere above her body. She knew this place outside herself: it was where she'd gone many times, from childhood, when Rayen cornered her in various secluded parts of Vassilian. First, always, she'd fought back; then when his men held her down and Rayen did what he did, she would feel herself float away. Her body would break while she was preserved somewhere else.

It had been a long time since she'd been to that place. It was easy to return there.

Now she lay bound on the flagstones of a room without light. She began to return to her body. Inside and out she ached. She thought, first of all, that this was a stupid way to die. Better to have wasted away from Darien's spell than be executed as a thief. At least in the first was some semblance of honor.

She was still Amaristoth, she thought, and grimaced because she could not bring herself to laugh.

She thought of Zahir and then, truly, could not smile at all. Whatever was happening to him, it was taking too long.

Did he have a place to go, as she did?

She'd been avoiding thinking of the previous night, because it confused her. They'd shared that bed in the Jonquil Safehouse. Though she thought him decent enough, she'd steeled herself for possible drunken advances. She thought even the best of men might be given to these.

It was Darien who woke her in the night, as it happened. As so often happened. Weeping and nearer to her than ever before. She could now rest her hands in his hair where he knelt. In life she'd never touched it. She regretted this now. She murmured to him, *"Don't grieve. I'm ready."* Knowing it was a lie. But his anguish was too much for her. And then she remembered, at the edge of waking, that Valanir Ocune was dead, too.

She awoke blinking back tears in a quiet room. She sat up. Beside her, Zahir had stirred. In the absolute darkness here beneath the streets of Majdara she could not see his false face.

"What is it tortures you?" he said. "I felt it even in my dreams." He shifted beside her in the bed. "It was like a cry that woke me."

"You already know," she said. "I've told you everything."

She heard him swallow hard. A pause, that seemed to stretch for a long time. They lay in the dark and all she heard was his breathing, in and out. She thought perhaps he'd fallen asleep. Until he spoke again. "Will you let me hold you? That's all I would do."

She wanted to refuse but tears were tracking down her cheeks. She didn't know where they came from. Whatever inward cry had woken him, it was something that had become commonplace to her. It was all the terrain she knew. "All right," she whispered. She lay with her back to him. His arms came around her. They were warm and smelled of him. He did not press himself against her. Once he did lift a hand to brush at a tear on her cheek. "Try to rest," he said. "I would take on your burdens if I could."

It seemed hours that Lin had lain in the cellar that the door upstairs opened and Zahir was flung inside. He was bound, too. Lin tried to maneuver herself so she could get a look at him. "Are you all right?" she said. "Did he hurt you?"

He lay back on the flagstones, staring upward. Shockingly to her, he laughed. "Of course you ask that. All I feel is hatred, of myself, that I let this happen to you."

"I'm all right," she said. "It's just bruises."

"I know what men like that are. It's not all right. It's another sin weighed against me in the balance. And, my dear one, I have so many."

She decided not to ask what had happened to him upstairs with Khadar Zuhalan. Not now, anyway. She knew something of self-hatred in the wake of violation and did not want to make it worse. "I don't care," she said. "We are none of us without sin. Now all we must do is plan our escape."

"He'll turn us over to the magistrate at first light," said Zahir. "He told me. I can try to summon the Ifreet to come to our aid, but that would require time, concentration. I don't know how much of either we'll have in this place. My guess is, they'll be coming soon for us. I'm so sorry. This is not the honorable end owed to you."

"The lives of your people . . ."

He winced. "I have failed them, too."

"What if you revert your disguise?" she said. "Reveal you're the First Magician? I know it's the last resort, but—"

"That transformation would take time as well," he said. "And I'd need use of my hands."

At that moment the door opened at the top of the stairs. Lin caught her breath. They heard footsteps, but not heavy ones. Then saw a shadow take the shape of a man. One man, alone. Zweir Zuhalan stood over them, carrying a torch. Carefully, he set the torch in a wall sconce. He said, "I am about to untie your bonds. If either of you makes so much as a hiccough, I'll call the guards."

There was no danger of either of them doing such a thing. Not even when he drew a knife, the sight of which made Lin shiver involuntarily. But he made short work of untying them, starting with her. As she painfully drew herself to a sitting position, rubbing the life back into her wrists, she saw the way Zahir instinctively curled inward as Zweir approached, as if to shield himself. She felt a grief like she had in her dream the night before. For something irrevocably lost.

But Zahir was impassive as he drew himself upright. He even

attempted a smile. Whatever was happening, perhaps he'd already guessed.

"I will explain this quickly," said Zweir Zuhalan in a dry, curt tone. As much, if not more than his father, he was a businessman. "You were betrayed. Someone in this city works against the Brotherhood of Thieves and told us to be ready for you. So we were. You may want to look into that. But it's not my concern." From his cloak he drew an object. By light of the torch, a gleam of brass.

"As it happens, our goals are aligned. My father needs this medicine in order to live. I don't particularly want my father to live. And so. If I allow you to steal it, I dispose of him and remain above suspicion. You slipped your bonds, of course. I'll have to execute the guards who tied you. Messy, but a small price to pay for my inheritance and freedom." He handed the jar to Lin. "Here you are, dear. Try not to lose it this time." He leered at her. "Give the Brotherhood my compliments."

As they staggered out into an alley behind the merchant's house, bent in the cover of shadow in the hours before dawn, Lin felt a tug of conscience. She did, despite whatever had been done to Zahir Alcavar. They'd been given no advance knowledge that their mission would—however indirectly—lead to a man's death. She hesitated, knowing that. But knew the arguments against such hesitation. They acted now for many lives, for thousands. And besides, Khadar Zuhalan had proven himself a cruel man. Nonetheless she felt soiled, more so than before, when she'd imagined it a simple theft. And that had been bad enough.

She uttered none of this to Zahir. They didn't exchange much by way of words after leaving the merchant's house. He seemed to have retreated from her in his mind. Every so often, he muttered directions. When to turn a corner. Where to stand, motionless and alert, as the city guard went by. Zweir had returned to them their weapons, clearly desirous of the success of their mission. The theft of the medicine would take it deep into the network of the Brotherhood and beyond his father's reach. They kept to the side streets and alleyways on the way to the Jonquil Safehouse.

They entered the metalcrafter's shop through a back door, as the front was kept locked at night. As they made their way to the storage room Zahir finally did speak, low and urgent. "Not a word to Shantar about . . .

about me," he said. "The guilt would never leave him. All he need know is there was betrayal. I fear he's in danger."

When they reached the storage room he made a sound she'd never heard, like he was being strangled. It took Lin a moment to see why. Peering into the shadowed corner of the room, she saw the chest hung open.

Zahir ran to the chest and looked down. He tilted his head above the opening, as if to listen. Nothing.

Lin found herself afraid to speak. She drew her knife and kept it drawn, however it hampered her climb, as they clambered down the ladder. Keeping silent, both of them, moving with the stealth of snakes. She a hunter, and he . . . well, he had once fled for his life. A skill that perhaps he'd kept.

As it turned out, there was no need for silence. In all the rooms of the Jonquil Safehouse they found no enemies. They found only dead. The two young men who'd been awed by Zahir's hints of her sexual prowess were sprawled beside the *tabla* board on the floor where it lay upside down. Their throats were cut.

In the next room they found Shantar Nir. He had fought, it was clear. His torso pierced with multiple wounds. He had been, at the last, like a great tree in the felling. All around lay his men. Most with slit throats—work brutal and quick.

After they'd searched the safehouse and determined they were alone with the dead, Zahir turned to Lin with a face like death. "This isn't the city I know," he said. "It is falling."

THAT night she didn't dream. She knew the difference, after all this time; a dream was something that, good or ill, belonged to her. This was not her body that she wore, not her smile as she faced the people arrayed before her. Edrien Letrell held his harp in the curve of his arm. The people he faced were dressed distinctly, as if for a festival: the men in brocade vests, the women in long, gathered skirts of bright colors and with flowers in their loosened hair. One in particular caught his eye, a dark-eyed beauty in a dress of yellow and crimson. He held her gaze more than a moment before he returned his attention to the crowd.

"Why will you not show me your ritual dance?" he implored. A tone light, wheedling. He had pretended to drink a great quantity of the fiery liquor they'd given him, so they'd think him intoxicated. That would excuse him, at least somewhat, if he inadvertently transgressed on their customs. "I make a study of such things for my work. You like my work, don't you?"

A woman came forward, hands on her hips. "We admire your work, Seer. That does not mean we give up our secrets. It was no small thing that we allowed you entry here. May I remind you." She was older than he was, with grey-streaked hair and snapping eyes. She wore a man's blouse and trousers, with an ornate vest and satin sash, through which was stuck a dagger sheathed in red leather. The thin blouse showed intriguing curves. Though not as lovely as the woman nearer his age who had initially caught his interest, Edrien began to think this person, in fact, might be the more memorable company if he was sufficiently persuasive. By the look of her it would not be easy. That was, of course, part of the appeal.

They stood in a large windowless space lit by tall braziers that emitted the scent of incense. The floor was of a white marble that shone like glass. Marble, too, were the balustrades that flanked a pool at the center of the floor. It made a perfect circle and unlike the floors was oddly unreflective, the water dark as a hole in the earth.

Edrien swept a bow. "I am honored to be here, in your secret space," he said. "I had only wished to see the wonders of which I'd heard. In my country there is a traveling people, like yours, in the mountains to the north. They, too, possess a tradition of dance. I have long studied them and made music dedicated to their glory. Such is what I would do for you." He became solemn. "It is music that will live after I am dead. Of that I am certain, or as certain as any man can be of his art. Your tribute would resound down the ages, for as long as people play music, or sing. And it would travel the world—with me, and after I am gone."

A silence in the crowd surrounding the circle of water. A sea of flat dark eyes regarding him. And then, at last, a sound: a laugh that rang within the room of stone.

It was the woman, of course. Hands on hips, head flung back. Her hair, black and silver and long as a banner. She was perhaps twenty years older than Edrien but her neck was smooth and supple beneath the gold chains she wore. "Whatever you learned of these people in your land, it taught you nothing about us," she said. "We who worship the moon goddess, ever-changing in her form and phase, take no interest in that which is inscribed on paper or engraved in stone. That which takes permanent form, which is fixed . . . is dead."

"You have no books," said Edrien. "I know this."

"No books," she confirmed. "No songs that are written. No choreography which is written. Our dances are ever-changing as flame and once they are done . . . they are done."

"Such is your life," he said.

She nodded. "Such are our lives."

He grinned, then, unexpectedly gratified. "Countess Sitara, you have given me more than you know. And taught me much."

She smiled back, then. As women in his presence often did. Even, sometimes, powerful women like this. "There is more I might teach you, singer," she murmured, and the breath caught in his throat. He had no doubt it was true. As Edrien Letrell approached her, he noticed carved along the walls surrounding them a pattern of scrollwork: a series of winged horses. A reminder of the city above, even as here underneath they worshiped a goddess. The space they used had been built by Ramadians, by those who ruled in the capital. Winged horses stood for death.

These thoughts drifted through Edrien's mind, then evaporated as he found himself dancing with the woman he knew as Countess Sitara, though he doubted it was the name she went by with her people. Someone was playing a lute. Others were dancing, too. It was a tame, measured start, but there was a hint that it would build to more. Much more. In the corner of his mind, beside his reverie of what this woman would teach him when she drew him later to the scented chambers beyond this one, he was thinking that all his life he'd sought two things: fame for himself, permanence for his art. And now here was transience at its extreme, and he'd make music of that, too—music he believed would endure. A paradox that made him smile as he danced, as he let the woman guide him close and into a heated moment in time.

WHEN Lin came awake it was still night. They were in a fetid inn on the edge of the city where none might find them, in a rough bed that stank of countless bodies. Zahir had thought it vital, after what had happened to the Brotherhood, to distance himself from all his old contacts, all the haunts where he'd taken succor in the past. It meant a retreat to one of the worst parts of the city. It was a miracle that either of them had slept, given the stench of the place and the horrors they'd seen, the various ways in which they were injured; yet they had. Zahir slept restlessly, she saw; he tossed and muttered. Lin touched his arm, said his name. And again. He came awake slowly, as if emerging from deep water. He met her eyes and smiled. "I was in a dark dream. You saved me. A Seer's insight?"

"Not that," she said. "The Fire Dancers. I think I know where they are."

CROUCHING outside the door of the sickroom, Nameir heard singing. In the course of days, anguish had weakened her, so it seemed natural to be prostrate, on her knees. For so long she'd directed each breath, each painful inch forward through the hills, to reaching the palace and safety. Bringing her prince to safety. Now they were here and he lay abed, attended by the king's physicians. But there was nothing they could tell her; nothing. His condition was grave. They could only minister to him, and wait.

That was what it boiled down to, what they'd told her. *Wait. Wait and see if he wakes.*

She was not his guard anymore. She'd been relieved of that duty, of all duties; her job was to recover and rest. In a ceremony she could hardly remember Eldakar had awarded her an estate near the eastern border for her devoted service to the land, to his brother. She did not care. She would stay here and wait. At this door. The guards at the door pretended not to see her, as if to spare her dignity. As if she cared for her dignity.

Now Eldakar was within and he was singing. It was deep night. The song sounded, to her ears, like a lullaby. Perhaps one the brothers had shared as children? She didn't know. Mansur never spoke of his childhood. It was irrelevant to him. All that mattered was the cut and thrust of present achievements, of bloodstained triumphs attained. Vagaries of the nursery were relegated to the past.

She knew, of course, that Eldakar had recently suffered losses. His queen had deserted and humiliated him in the worst way possible. The defeat of Almyria reflected on him, his leadership. She'd have expected him to appear broken, after all that. He did not seem broken to her. But there was an otherworldly quality to him, as if he'd detached himself. The cool dignity with which he comported himself was appropriate for a monarch but it was also, perhaps, *too* calm in light of recent events.

As if thoughts of him were a summons, Eldakar opened the door. He said, "Nameir, come in. I don't know if he can hear us, but he'd want you here."

"You can't know that," she said, bleak. "He was more interested in your queen, as it happens."

"Everyone was interested in her," he said, unperturbed. "Maybe she used that with him. Maybe not. It doesn't matter. I know he cares for you, too."

It took her a moment to realize that she had, without thinking, possibly revealed herself. And that the king did not seem surprised or to care.

"Forgive me," she said, standing. "I spoke . . . I spoke with great insolence to your grace."

Eldakar hugged her. Nameir, stiff and shocked, did not respond and he backed away. He said, "Commander Hazan, it matters not. Not now. Don't you see? We who care for him must put aside whatever . . . whatever else he is or did. I love him and so do you. Come sit with us."

So she let him lead her by the hand, and took her place in a chair by the bed. The room was lit in the faintest outlines from scant moonlight. Eldakar sat by his brother and held his hand. He began again to sing. A simple air such as a nurse might have sung to them, once. Or their mother. Now Nameir heard the words.

> *When the moon climbs*
> *When the owl cries*
> *When the fire wanes*
> *I think of you.*
> *You and only you.*
> *You and only you.*

It was on her sixth day in the palace, when she'd allowed herself to leave the prince's room, that Nameir encountered a phantom.

She froze. It was not the place where one would expect to see a figure from her nightmares. The day was a splendor of sunlight such as one might expect of a Kahishian spring. In the courtyard, orange trees dripped tender blossoms. Beauty that made mockery of her sadness, but also, just then, of the shock at what she was seeing.

It was a man with a darkly furred jaw, a man who looked just a little bit like a wolf. Greying hair, trim figure but solidly built. He wore a ruby earring in one ear which gave him an attractive, rakish look.

She stared. He crossed the courtyard with the easeful arrogance of a fighting man. He glanced her way only briefly, assessing a potential threat, deemed her a part of the scenery. So she was, she supposed; drained by grief, and besides, loyal to Eldakar. She'd never initiate a fight within these walls. But what the appearance of this man stirred in her began as an inward tremble that spread to every inch of her flesh.

She saw things she thought she had forgotten. She had remembered blood puddled on the floor of her childhood home and scraped along the threshold. Now she remembered that the threshold looked that way after her mother had dragged herself across it. And now Nameir began to recall what she'd seen before that. It was like a box she had kept bound with iron and chain because to open it would eviscerate her. The sight of this man in the courtyard brought it all back.

All this in moments. With a jaunty step the man vanished through the double doors that led inside the palace. She was alone again under the orange trees. Their scent like a heaven from which she was barred.

He wore the red and black of the Tamryllin guard. So he was one of theirs now. He hadn't been, not on the night he broke into her parents' home. That time he'd been with one of the viziers, back when the provinces were continuously at war. The community of Galicians had made for an easy, if predictable, scapegoat on that day. The raid had been joined not only by those under the command of the vizier but even by residents of the town under attack.

Nameir had been playing hide-and-seek with her younger sister. She'd been hiding under a table. She was small and—at the end—evaded notice. The men hadn't stayed long—there was little in the home to steal. They'd found her family. They'd found the copper shrine, which could be melted down. They had, of course, burned the books. Burning Galician books, wherever they were found, was a popular pastime during raids.

What they'd done to her parents, to her sister, was inside the box in her mind. It had to stay there. She had fought battles in Kahishi and overseas, waded through blood, to keep that box sealed tight.

She thought she might lose her mind so she began to walk. She did not have an idea where she was going. Leaving the Zahra was out of the question—she'd sworn fealty to the king. She only needed to walk. To leave behind what she'd seen, if such a thing could be done.

Her steps carried her into the gardens, to an area dense with trees. Not flower trees; these had broad leaves, in the shape of small hands. They left the ground thickly shaded, offered pockets of dark. She entered these as if toward an embrace. It was cool in the shade, and quiet. The only sound was of birds. Nameir was still. Another sound came through: a rush of water. Of course. These trees might appear wild, but they were part of a plan. That plan included the Zahra's famous fountains.

The undergrowth was springy beneath her feet and smelled of sweetness and earth. She was grateful for that. She was grateful for the birds calling in the upper branches. Anything that might help her forget.

In time she came to a stream banked with smooth white stone. The sound of water was louder here. If she followed it, she reasoned, she'd arrive at the fountain. It seemed as credible a goal as any, just now. Soon she would return to her vigil beside Mansur's door. The thought of him gave her an uneasy tug; she ought to have been there just now. But first she would do this. She would follow the water, with its rushing sigh, that sparkled in the sun. The way it both made her think of her sister, yet also let her forget.

The water was clear and green. She followed it. The number of trees thickened, then thinned out again. Looking back once, she saw she had somehow covered a significant distance. She might have walked for an hour for all she knew. From here the palace was soaring, graceful, all archways and pillars at the foot of the hill. There was a subtle upward slope here that she was climbing.

Lilies clustered beside the water, a reminder of something—what was it? She recalled they were symbolic of various things. Purity. Virginity. Oh yes, another: death.

But there were purple irises, too, and these had no unpleasant traditions bound to them of which she was aware. She lingered to admire their contrast to the green water; their hearts of gold. No wonder there was a tale, Nameir recalled now, of a princess who commanded her seamstresses to create a gown fashioned after the iris. It was one of those children's tales—one to do with flowers and magic. Maybe she did have a piece, here or there, of Mansur's childhood that he'd shared with her. She'd never have been raised on such stories, herself.

There were so many reasons to live. She had come here to remember.

The sound of the water grew louder. She had come to a great rock wall grown over with tiny white flowers and moss, fashioned into a grotto. The fountain burst within: at its center, the figure of a woman, arms outspread. A goddess, perhaps. Her eyes were bits of blue glass, but her hair flowed in a manner that was lifelike. So, too, did her dress. Still there was something cold to Nameir about the figure, unsettling in the lifelessness of the eyes. She shivered a little even there, under the sun.

That was before she saw something in the fountain. She drew nearer for a look. First thing she saw was a stretch of silver that was like, yet unlike the water. Then that legs protruded from beneath this, the heels of satin shoes. It took a moment for Nameir to register that what she was seeing was a man, facedown in the water.

The corpse she hauled from the fountain had been there for some time. And Nameir knew the significance of the silver cloak.

Tarik Ibn-Mor, Second Magician of the Tower of Glass, had not run off with the queen after all.

THE Magician followed her in silence, though it was a long trek to the western edge of Majdara. Lin hadn't explained herself and though she could see he wondered, he didn't ask for details. As if he trusted her word. Even though it was clear she'd lied about at least one thing: she had not told him everything, as she had claimed that night in the Jonquil Safehouse. She had not told him, or anyone, about her dreams of Darien. More to the point, she had said nothing of Edrien's presence within her.

Zahir knew what the words of the wizard had been. *A body cannot give shelter to the dead, even for a little time, and still live.* She had left him free to extrapolate from there. As First Magician of the Tower of Glass, she assumed he had theories.

Now she led him through streets Lin Amaristoth had never trod, that she could not have known. Not only that. With each step her certainty of their surroundings increased; scarcely did she glance about to orient herself or take stock of where they were. He had to have wondered about that. But he said nothing.

He trusts me, she thought, sometime during that long walk in the cool morning. *He shouldn't.* She felt that she was not stable, not to be relied upon. Not only because her soul could fly from her at any time. What had overtaken her in the Tower of the Winds, that had made her bleed on the page, was with her still. She felt herself a poison dart of rage. Not far, in the end, from where she'd come.

She recalled Zahir's smile when she'd woken him. Open and trusting as a child. *I was in a dark dream. You saved me.*

A deliberate hardening of herself, not to break a little from this. Sometimes it seemed as if various such moments in her life broke something in her, one piece at a time. No matter how she hardened herself.

With time, streets gave way to dirt road and fallow fields. They had not exited the city walls but had come to a place less populous, with only the occasional hut or farmhouse. The road wound upward. From here they could see that in the course of their walk, they'd been climbing a hill which was incremental, not steep; and by now, they could look across the rooftops of the city to the mountain where the Zahra and its piled gardens were. Here on this hill were wrought-iron gates and a place that seemed deserted. But it was, in its own way, occupied.

"City of the dead," Zahir murmured as they passed through the gates. They saw no one else about. Crypts dominated the hill in neat rows, as far as they could see. The place was overgrown with trees and even, nearby, blue morning glories that had twined about the pillars of a great tomb. Some crypts were the size of small homes, were varied in their architectural styles as the eras represented.

This was not the sort of place to which many in the city would come. Only the very wealthy and, most often, the nobility were buried here. Gold was insufficient to buy entry—one must also possess the right bloodlines. Families whose ancestry predated the Alfinian conquest reserved plots in Majdara's ancient cemetery. Some graves, Lin knew, were old as the city itself.

"Let me help," said Zahir, hushed. Perhaps out of respect for the dead. "What are we looking for?"

She shook her head. "I wish I knew." Then shook her head again, this time at her own obtuseness. "Wait. Give me a moment." Standing in the path between rows of crypts, Lin shut her eyes.

When she opened them, she began immediately to stride forward. "Of *course*," she muttered, forgetting a moment that to Zahir she'd seem mad. "It had to be from that time, and it had to be someone who had sympathies with . . . with them." She did not want to name the Jitana here. Some superstition, or something more, held her back. The place was so quiet. Lin knew how fluid was the boundary between the living and dead. More than most people, she knew.

"Take me to the tombs of the Acazrian kings," she said.

He nodded, assenting. She could have led them there but it seemed more fitting, now, to be led by the First Magician to the king.

The crypts of the Acazrian dynasty were masterworks whose architects had held nothing back, whether in materials or workmanship. Their reign was a period of flourishing for the city, made possible by a lull between wars. The winged horses that adorned these crypts were gilded. One crypt, grander than most, boasted a winged horse sculpture of porphyry before its entrance. Structures like these would house not only a king, but his queens, concubines, and heirs. Names were engraved along the sides of some of these, long lists. Many stillborn children, Lin guessed.

The winged horse sculpture was distinctive; it caught her eye as a possibility. But only a moment. "Not this one," she said. "No. But . . ."

And there it was, without fanfare, with nothing more than some instinct that made her glance up. Up at the tomb they had come to that was less splendid than some, though graceful with its rose-colored columns, a copper-tiled roof long since gone to green.

"Here?" said Zahir.

"Look," she said. She felt something almost like joy. She indicated one of the steps to the tomb, where at a corner—so remotely placed one might well miss it—was a symbol worked in gold.

"The ibis," he breathed, as if he, too, feared to disturb the peace.

"It will be sealed against tomb-robbers," she said. "There must be some secret way in. Let me think . . ."

"I suspect," he said with a grin, "what you're doing is not exactly thinking."

"Hush," she said. She turned inward to the depths of her mind. To

Edrien. It was a process less smooth, this time; as if the nearer she came to her desire, the more the Seer withdrew. Perhaps he wanted to protect these people. From her? From Zahir? Though she and the Seer were intertwined, nearly as one, she could not always read his intent.

She had come to it now: a wall between her and the Seer, such as the time he had shielded her from her knowledge of how to access the Path.

Just in case, she marched up the steps that led to the tomb doors, and tried them. As she expected, they were sealed.

"I need your help," she confessed. "I feel sure—I *am* sure—that the ibis signifies what we believe it does. There must be another entrance. Those who use it must have a key. Is it possible—with your magic, would it be possible to make our own key?"

Zahir was examining the sign of the ibis in the stair. He had cleared away the dirt and debris that dulled it. Its gilding caught the sun. "I know one charm," he said. "With the help of . . . of my friend. It is . . . complex, and will leave me weakened for a time." He smiled at her. "I trust you will not take advantage of me in that state."

She thought it was a forced smile. She said, "Never."

"Cities are their own mystery," he said. "Each one. Especially the old ones. And a city of the dead . . . it is where dimensions of the world meet and mesh. There are forces here that, with great effort, I may harness."

"Your . . . friend will help you."

"As ever he does. There is one condition, though." Zahir took hold of her arms, set his gaze firmly to hers. "You must look away. If you don't, I can't shield you from what may come."

"Zahir, is this dangerous?"

He smiled again, as if at a secret joke. "Magic is always dangerous," he said. "Don't let anyone tell you otherwise. Oh . . . but you know that better than anyone, don't you? I'm sorry." His smile died. "Yes, there is danger. No more than I've dealt with in the past. Just be patient with me after, my dear one. I will, for a time, have the strength of an old man or a child when this is done. There are risks in that . . . in being vulnerable like that. But this needs be done, so look away now. Look away."

She turned, gripping her arms against her body. She felt cold and knew it was her fear.

"Remember," he said. "No matter what happens . . . no matter what you hear . . . don't turn." His tone became pleading. "Don't add your death to the tally of my sins."

"All right," she said. "I won't turn. I promise."

"No matter what you hear."

"No matter what I hear."

He sighed, as if at a task accomplished. She stood very still. He had begun to mutter under his breath. Harsh, guttural sounds. Just barely she could hear him as winds stole away the words. *Winds.* That, in fact, was strange. It was a mild day, the sky without clouds. But she heard what sounded like a thundering above them. The wind picked up. Lin's hair whipped at her face.

Zahir's voice had grown stronger, resonant in the wind. He hissed, hurling imprecations at something unseen. As if whatever he worked was fashioned not of the serene enchantments she'd glimpsed in the Tower, but of some elemental rage.

But of course, she thought—the Ifreet was no "friend." Not to him nor to anyone.

There was no mistaking his rage as he gnashed out words in a language she didn't know. She wondered if it was a tongue spoken anywhere on earth. She thought of him as a boy, bereft of parents and a home, resolving to turn this dark force to his purpose.

Lin gripped her arms tighter to try to keep still.

Another thunder strike, this time directly above their heads. Then another sound. What began to tear from Zahir was a scream. As if he were being flayed alive. Again the thunder struck; he did not even pause for breath. It was agony, unmistakable. Lin was shaking uncontrollably now, her eyes screwed tight. It took every particle of her strength not to turn.

It seemed to go on for hours. Later she'd come to realize it had been only a matter of moments. But the memory of that cry was something she knew she'd carry with her all her days, because while she did not know what manner of magic Zahir had worked, she was certain of one thing: the price he'd paid for it was real, and lasting.

After he'd fallen silent, after the thunder, when all was quiet again, Lin found that her heart had slowed to its accustomed rhythm. She wanted to weep. She wanted to rage, as well, at the Magician for failing to warn her sufficiently. But when at last he said, "You can look now,

Lin," it was with satisfaction. He looked exhausted, yes, and drenched in perspiration; but predominantly seemed pleased with himself.

"You're all right," she said, half relief, half irritation.

"Yes, yes," he said impatiently. *"Look."* He was pointing at the crypt. The front door was still shut as before. But between ornamental columns that flanked the side wall, a door had opened into the tomb.

He grinned wide, with obvious delight. "There was an enchantment in the ibis sign," he said. "I managed to . . . shall we say, activate it. Though everything in it fought me. It is meant as a protection against enemies."

"All right, that's very impressive," she said, still shaken and, therefore, annoyed. "Let's go inside, shall we?"

"Yes," he said. "Just one thing. I'll need to lean on your arm, if you'd be so kind."

The stairs that led down inside the crypt were lit with candles. So someone was here. Lin dearly hoped whoever was here would not be hostile to them, for Zahir was clearly not in fighting condition. He leaned hard on her arm and breathed heavily even though they were descending. They made slow progress, and once or twice she had to catch his arm when he slipped. She began to realize that much of his insouciance after the enchantment might have been for her benefit—whether as a masculine pose, or to reassure her, she didn't know.

The room they came to was identical to that which she'd seen through Edrien's eyes. Nothing changed. Lit braziers surrounded the round, deep pool on a floor like glass. But this time the room was not filled with people. Their footsteps rang too loudly as they arrived at the foot of the stairs.

A voice, cold but instantly familiar. "So it's you."

It was Aleira Suzehn, looking haggard and thin. Her clothing the worse for wear. "And you bring a Tower Magician," she said. "It is as well that the people have gone. I wouldn't trust any Magician of that palace."

Lin's heart sank. "They've gone."

"Of course. They couldn't stay. Not with what is coming to Majdara. And just as well, since you bring the enemy to our door. To our sanctuary."

Lin shook her head. "You must understand . . . we only want peace. I found your letter about the prophecy. I vouched for you and King Eldakar believes you. We want to speak terms of truce, to fight what comes."

Aleira shrugged. "If that is true, I shall let her be the judge," she said. That was when Lin caught sight of another figure in the room with them.

She was seated in shadow, upright, thinner even than Aleira. A purple gown, regal in cut, clad her slight frame and was belted with gold. Her hair pure white. "This is the Mistress of the city," said Aleira. "Queen of the Jitana underground. She alone stayed behind." Looking more closely, Lin saw the woman's eyes matched her hair: filmed over white. "If the Mistress judges you worthy, you will be allowed to leave this place alive. And if there is any way you may serve as allies . . ." Here Aleira's voice trembled, until again it held. "It is not usually our way, to associate thus with enemies. But perhaps now it is time."

LIN and Zahir knelt at the pool's edge. The floor cut into her knees. She knew better than to move. This had been the old woman's command, spoken in a voice that was reedy yet implacable with resolve.

Beside her, Zahir was teetering slightly, still weak. He had uttered few words since their arrival. Lin didn't know what Aleira had meant by allowing them to leave alive; she was confident she could take on both women if need be, if it came to weapons. It would be stupidly easy, in fact, and she couldn't possibly harm an old woman. But Aleira was clever, so Lin suspected she had meant something else altogether. Some other, unspoken threat.

Up close, the water swirled. It was indigo in color, like ink, and reflected none of the light.

The woman Aleira had called Mistress was seated across from them in her chair. Aleira stood behind her, a hand on her shoulder. The older woman spoke. "I believe we need not fear these strangers, Aleira Suzehn. Each is capable of great harm. Each has done, or will do, terrible acts. It is hard to see which—past and future are, to my sight, much interlinked. But they intend no harm to us." She went silent. They heard her breathing, a labored wheeze. The filmed eyes fixed on Lin, then Zahir. Again she spoke. "They are both so interesting. Each is beset with a dark rider."

Aleira stared at Lin, perhaps accusingly. "Really."

"Calm yourself, child," said the old woman with a note of derision. "As I said, we are not the ones who need fear these two. They speak truth about their intentions here." For the first time she smiled, as if charmed by a discovery. "The man wears a face not his own. *His* rider gives cover to him."

Up close, Lin could see her seamed lips, the strong line of a jaw that would once, she was sure, have been beautiful. She wore earrings of emerald and pearl. She appeared unspeakably old. Yet also, in some way, familiar.

Lin saw her opening to speak. "Mistress, if we have your trust, we are grateful. It is why we are here."

The woman laughed. "You are here because I permitted you entry," she said. "Otherwise, that spell outside? You, Magician, would have perished of it. As it was, you almost did."

Zahir met her blind gaze steadily. He looked numb, like an animal caught in a trap. Lin had never thought to see him thus.

When the woman sat back in her chair, it was with a changed expression. "And the idea of that—that I could have killed you—that terrifies you. Doesn't it, Magician? But not for your own sake. There are voices added to yours. A multitude, if I listen. As if their lives are tied to you, and your death would damn them. Again, interesting. I have not had a puzzle like this in so long. But that's not why I allowed you here. Magician, hear me. I know you work in prophecies."

Zahir nodded. In a flat voice said, "Yes, Mistress."

"We Jitana do not. Not exactly. But through the years a few prophecies have acted as our guideposts, handed down by the goddess Eret through her messenger. Cambias, who led us from the desert lands with the promise of home. Some of the prophecies have come to pass. Some have not. One, in particular, speaks of a time of darkness from the west." Her face turned to Lin. "Your people. Seers. They work evil on us here. In my dreams it takes the form of a tower, where they are, on an island swept with cold."

Lin kept her voice neutral as she could. "How does your prophecy say to stop them, Mistress?"

With a quick motion, the woman tossed something into the pool. It was powder, a sprinkling of what looked like gold. As it fell on the water it was submerged instantly, disappeared. "There must be a dance," said the woman. In the water, an image was gathering. A flare, as if flames burned beneath the water's surface. As the image sharpened and took shape, Lin saw it was fire, indeed. In the silence of the chamber they could even hear its crackling, smell its smoke. "It will be a true Fire Dance like that of old. Like has not been seen in some years."

Aleira made a sound, an indrawn breath. "I thought those were myth."

"You hoped," said the woman. "As we all hope such things will never be. But here, look." She threw another handful of powder into the water. It sank again. The water began to brighten and they saw, emerging against that brightness, the outline of a figure. Then it came into focus. A pale woman with long hair, clad in a dark dress. It looked to Lin like a painting. Clasped between her white hands, pointed downward, a sword nearly of her own height. There were symbols etched in the blade.

"The Queen of Swords," said the Mistress. "A woman of power and intelligence. She has strong passions which she holds in check. Wielding the blade for justice."

The figure dissolved. Once again the pool was dark. The woman tossed in another handful of powder. Another figure surfaced. This was a man, clad in a crimson cloak, a tunic belted with gold, presiding over a table. The table held a jeweled chalice, a scroll, and a grinning skull. "The Magician," said the Mistress. "This can be a man or a woman. A person with great power, too, employed with lighthearted wit. Someone versed in the world's dimensions."

The image had changed: the Queen of Swords and the Magician now shared the space of the pool, though did not touch. The Mistress said, "These two will be central to the Fire Dance. That is the prophecy. What falls from there, I cannot say. It is a single flaring in the dark. What comes to pass after will be determined by the acts of many—not only by us and our dance. But do you want to know how *you* may act, Lin Amaristoth? This is all I may tell you."

"I have one more question," said Lin. "You said, before, that we hope such things—such as the Fire Dance—will never be. Why?"

Sometime in the dialogue Zahir had taken her hand. Lin didn't know why, but did not withdraw. She watched, as she knew he did, as the image of the Queen of Swords and the Magician faded, until the pool was lifeless again. She continued to stare into that water. She almost expected the words to come, as if she had dreamed them once before.

They were a long time coming. The silence stretched. At last Lin glanced up at the Mistress and saw the woman gazed down at them with what seemed a look, for the first time, of compassion. "Every dance is, at its heart, a transformation. This one more than most. For a shadow to be vanquished, there must be sacrifice."

Aleira choked. Lin saw there were tears on the woman's cheeks, though she kept her lips pressed tight. The older woman squeezed Aleira's hand where it rested on her shoulder, the first sign of softness from her Lin had seen. But her face showed no emotion.

"I cannot say whether it is the Queen or the Magician who will meet their end," said the Mistress. "Or I should say, meet the final transformation, which is death. That is the prophecy: Two enter into the dance. One survives."

⁂

ON the third day that Garon Senn was in custody for the murder of Tarik Ibn-Mor, Nameir descended to the dungeons to see him. For three days she had postponed what felt to her like a queasy, unavoidable obligation. Suspicion had fallen upon him after her discovery of the Magician's body, since Garon had been seen so often in his company. Or, as one servant put it, "creeping about" in Tarik's vicinity. Garon had confessed to spying on the Second Magician on behalf of Lin Amaristoth but that was, he'd insisted, as far as it went. Tarik had been in the process of betraying his king, brokering a deal with Ramadus. This was documented; Eldakar already had been informed of it by the Court Poet. It had been unsurprising that a man engaged in such treasonous activities should flee.

But some of the more grizzled of the palace guard testified, one after another, of the brutish nature of Garon Senn. Murder was nothing to a man like him. What remained a mystery was motive. What had Garon Senn, commander of the Court Poet's personal guard, to gain from the murder of the Second Magician? It made no sense.

Such were the thoughts Nameir shouldered as she made her way down the winding stair through the part of the palace—perhaps the only part—that was devoid of beauty. It was lightless, dank, and polished tile gave way to slabs of granite. The delicate scents of the palace—ambergris, incense, orange blossoms—drowned here with the stench of fecal waste.

Nameir had seen and smelled far worse. These were not what made her feel as if the ground dropped from beneath her as she viewed the man through the bars of the cell door. Mostly what she could see were his eyes, sullen whites agleam in a slant of light from above. "What do you want?" he said.

An easy answer for that. She said, "I want my family back, but that's neither here nor there."

Now she saw something other than his eyes; the baring of teeth. "Are you here for revenge, commander? I'd thought you were more the obedient type. Not the sort to enact your own justice."

"You thought right." The bile had risen in her throat. To be talking to this man. It felt like betrayal. "I am here for the king. He doesn't know I'm here, but it is in his service. I wanted to hear for myself what you had to say. There's a false ring to this story and while I don't mind the idea of your execution, I want to make sure my . . . my people are not in danger. Someone who murdered the Second Magician might kill again."

Again that unnerving grin. She could imagine, with dizziness bordering on nausea, that that grin might have been the last thing her mother saw. "You're right to worry," said Garon Senn. "I don't know who killed Tarik, but it wasn't me. Why would I do it? I was doing well in my career. Lin Amaristoth had promised to raise me up, reward me with lands for my service to her. For what possible reason would I go out of my way, risk everything, to turn all that to shit?"

"What if Tarik knew something about you . . . something you wanted hidden?" *Like, for example, that you're a monster.*

He laughed. A sound that made her shudder. "Everyone knows about me," he said.

Everyone. A thought that caught her in the belly like she'd been kicked. The people of the Zahra knew what Garon Senn was . . . what he'd done. The Court Poet of Eivar knew. And it didn't matter, because the world had moved on. Because his skills were indispensable in war.

He said, "If I'm not executed before we're attacked, mark my words, commander, I will be freed. Your king needs me in this fight. It's a mistake, keeping me here. I led his father's troops to victory and could do the same for him."

The world had moved on, indeed, from the small house with its copper shrine that she could hardly, no matter how she might try, conjure in its details anymore. It had moved on from deeds too awful to be spoken of or even recall. Worst of all was that she understood. She had spent too many years with a sword in hand, with fighting men in her charge, to delude herself about the exigencies of war. And its horrors.

She had no further words for the man who had slain her family and violated her mother. But as she took the stairs, leaving behind the over-powering smell and tomblike murk, Nameir thought what she would say to Eldakar Evrayad, the ruler to whom she'd sworn allegiance. Who even now massed his troops for war in the north, when he was not attending to his brother.

She closed her eyes on this thought. Mansur had still not shown signs of waking.

She imagined meeting privately with the king and telling him that the man in the cell, a man who had demolished countless lives, was most likely guiltless of this particular crime. And that while she'd gladly have seen him dead, what she wanted was irrelevant. The question of justice too ambiguous to pursue. What mattered was that the murderer was still loose. Someone in the palace who had seen fit to murder one of its high-est officials. Who had succeeded in doing so despite all Tarik's powers and protections.

Someone who might therefore strike again.

THEY headed for the gate of the cemetery, hand in hand. Dusk was falling and the shadows of the crypts had lengthened. The paths be-tween them shaded as the sun set.

"I won't do something that could mean your death," he said.

"That's silly," she said. "I'm to die anyway. Remember? But it might be you. And . . . I don't think I can bear that."

"So we find ourselves at an impasse." Zahir kept walking. When she looked at him, she thought she saw hints of his true face in the lines of cheekbone and jaw. She recalled the earlier engagement with Jitana magic, that which had nearly cost his life, and wondered if it had worn this particular charm away.

"I don't know what to do," he confessed. Yes, he was back: the eyes he turned to her turquoise instead of black.

"We go north," she said. "We treat with them. Maybe there'll be no need of that dance at all. Maybe," she added, feeling inspired, "the old woman is mad and the prophecy nonsense. Or a malicious lie to frighten us." Now that she said it, she wondered why it hadn't occurred to her earlier. They had no reason to trust that woman, nor any of the Fire Dancers. And why this sudden mention of a Fire Dancer prophecy, when she'd never heard of them having prophecies before? Most of their lore was kept secret and never written, but still, it seemed convenient. What's more, Aleira had made no mention of them.

Aleira, who had stayed behind, looking bereft. Lin was moved to embrace her before they departed. And then they had taken the stairs back to the light above. The enchanted door closing behind them and leaving no trace, not even a seam in the stone.

"I refuse to believe you will die," said Zahir. "You are made of diamond and ivory and will last forever."

She laughed. "Believe what you will. So long as we go north."

He gave her hand a squeeze. "We go north. We'll meet with the self-styled King of the North. And you'll use that Amaristoth charm I've heard so much about."

And so, improbably, they were both laughing as they made their way between tombs, out through the wrought iron gates and back to the main road. As if whatever had taken place in the subterranean room beside that pool possessed no more substance than a fog that, as they walked and laughed, was already lifting.

CHAPTER 25

IT was impossible to say how long they'd been in the desert. It could not have been a long while: they didn't burn in the sun, nor grow thirsty from the punishing heat. Yet to Julien it seemed interminable. The presence of the woman floating ahead cast a pall, the heaviness from her almost palpable. It meant Julien and Dorn felt compelled to hold their silence, except for the most perfunctory exchanges.

It was Dorn who first noticed the change on the horizon. He exclaimed, nudged Julien's arm. Then lifting his voice said, "Where do you take us?"

"I told you." The woman's voice carried back. Cold, emotionless. "The city."

"You think there's nothing strange about it," said Dorn.

She turned, eyed him with a gaze chill as her voice. "There is everything strange about it."

They were in the scathing glare of afternoon. For some hours, had been walking thus, or so it felt to Julien. Yet now, hanging like a curtain over the landscape ahead was a night sky, shot through with stars and a full moon. There was also, from what she could see, a terrain of short grass and climbing hedges that grew low to the ground, rather than desert sand.

"So it's into the dark, now," said Dorn Arrin under his breath. Julien didn't say anything. She was thinking. There was something familiar to her about this, even the abrupt transition from day to night. It was a portal of sorts, she thought, and though she did not understand portals yet . . . some part of her did, a little.

And she thought, as they crossed the boundary from sand to grasses, from day to dark, that the constellations showed clear and bright in a way she'd never seen. Not even when lying in the bed of moss observing the night sky beside Sendara.

"There is something about that sky," said Julien in a hushed voice to Dorn. She didn't want their guide to hear. "In the configuration of the stars. As if it comes together for a purpose."

Crickets chirped from the scant trees about them. They were on a hill. From here, they could see the desert as a pinpoint of light in the distance, something already left behind. Soon it was gone, folded in on itself until it might have become one of the stars.

Downhill, not far below, the dark outline of what looked to Julien like enormous broken teeth. But that couldn't be right. Another thing that was strange: there were no lights. The black of what she could see, the mass down the hill, seemed a void where light could not reflect; could only disappear.

She neared their guide. "Is that the city?"

"Yes."

"But—"

The woman turned to face her. "We're at the end of the story. That story." She motioned a graceful arm to what looked to be a clump of trees. "And also a beginning." Julien had the sense, in that moment, that if this woman were capable of weeping, she would; but they would be tears of blood. An image that once conjured, she could not shake away.

A new voice, a man's. "It is done. You have your bargain."

The voice came from the trees the woman had indicated. There was a spark, a torch was lit. The man came into view. He was bearded, attired in a cloak of scarlet with a shine like oil. A strong, handsome face in middle age. Something about him made Julien's skin shiver on her bones.

"If that is so, where are the men-at-arms that were promised?" Another man's voice, younger. When he emerged into the light Julien saw he was fine-featured, slender.

A laugh from the older man. "You'll find them. They'll be drawn to you now that you've made the sacrifice of ten thousand. Well, give or take. There may have been more than ten thousand souls in Vesperia. Enough to seal a pact with the deep worlds. Which is where they remain now, indefinitely. Those souls. Trapped between life and death. Will that weigh on your conscience, Yusuf Evrayad?"

Julien heard Dorn's breath catch beside her. The name struck a chord of recognition in her, but barely.

The young man drew himself up. "Who are you to speak of conscience, Magician? You've proven you have none. You want only gold."

"Which you've promised," said the older man in a hiss. "And of which you'll have plenty, now that you're set to conquer. That is what will happen from this night, Yusuf. You'll build a great dynasty, a legacy, on the souls of the ten thousand. They will never be freed—not unless that legacy of yours is destroyed."

"And that will never be," said Yusuf. "Because none shall know." A flash in the moonlight. A blade, catching a slant of light as it arced and fell. The Magician now lay sprawled facedown on the ground. It had happened quickly, soundlessly.

They watched as the young man built a fire. A pyre where he cast the body of the Magician. He stood watching the flames for a time. In the light they cast, the dark at the base of the hill looked even more forbidding and strange. Towers that should have been upright were warped, aslant as broken bones. The gem of a moon, its attendant stars, in contrast seemed a mockery.

When at last the young man—Yusuf Evrayad, the Magician had said—turned away from the fire and began striding off into the trees, Dorn began to follow him. The woman, surprisingly, caught his arm. Her first time touching either of them. "No," she whispered. "The story is here."

They waited, on a moonlit hilltop where the corpse of the Magician still burned. Julien wondered why she felt no revulsion at the sounds, the smell of burning flesh. She felt distant from events as that receding pinpoint of desert light.

In Dorn's expression she read less detachment, however. There was something that drew him to this scene, even though he likely knew as little about it as she did. She said to him, "What's happening?"

"I don't know," he said. He seemed to struggle for words. "I feel as if, just now, everything we know—everything that's happened—whirls about us, while we remain fixed at the center. Do you understand me?"

"Not really," she said, but just then the woman, their guide, made a strange sound. Like a tearing of paper, but in the throat.

A figure had stepped out from the concealment of trees. By light of the moon they saw a boy. As he drew near the pyre of the Magician, where the figure of the man had nearly shriveled to cinders, the light caught his eyes. They were wide, his expression reminding Julien of a figure in a painting: those of men struck by a mortal blow. From his face, there might have been an arrow in his heart. Or a spear through his side, as in a hunting accident. But he stepped forward, nearer the fire, clearly unharmed. The color of his eyes apparent even in that uncertain light. Recognizable to Julien by now: the same color eyes as those of the woman who was their guide. A shade of turquoise, neither blue nor green.

MANSUR Evrayad had awakened finally, early one morning. Eldakar drowsed beside him in a chair. Rumor had it that the prince's first words, uttered with irritation, were, "Damn it. Bring me a sword!" But this seemed like it might be an affectionate tale, concocted by those who rejoiced to see their prince awake.

Nameir didn't know what to believe, but it hardly mattered. She had shown little emotion when she first saw him, leaning on the arm of his brother in the courtyard of orange trees. He was pale and weak but spoiling for a fight. He used a slew of colorful slurs in reference to their anticipated attackers, such that at first it was hard to discern a coherent narrative. But at last, "They're coming here," he said. "I saw it in my dreams. A gathering force. Guided by a man with bright hair. They ready themselves to attack us as they did Almyria. For them the Zahra is the ultimate prize."

"As we suspected," said Eldakar. "It's why I've been . . . hesitant . . . to allow my troops to march northward."

"Good. That was good," said Mansur. He seemed feverish. The bandage on his head was concealed with a scarf—red and gold, the colors of House Evrayad. "I will need to become strong again. Nameir. You must help me. I must walk the grounds every day."

"Of course, my prince," she said. "We'll spar, too, when you're ready."

He looked haunted. "Eldakar says . . . word is you risked yourself to save me. Idiocy, Hazan. You're too valuable for such heroics."

"We all make mistakes in the heat of battle, my prince," she said, and took his other arm. Between them she and Eldakar helped Mansur cross the courtyard, through the slant of light from the trees and out to the gardens. There he would be tested by sloping footpaths, the stairs.

A man with bright hair. Nameir recalled her own dreams the night the Fire Dancer had approached their camp. That now, it seemed, was likely not a Fire Dancer at all, but some illusion sent by this enemy.

Her conversation with Eldakar about freeing Garon Senn had been less complicated than she'd expected. But more unsettling.

"You're right," he had said, when she had come to tell him she thought Garon was innocent of the murder of Tarik Ibn-Mor. "I've known for some time, but . . . I think I deny it to myself. The truth—I don't think I can withstand the truth."

"What do you mean?"

"Tarik was one of our strongest Magicians," said Eldakar. They were in his private chambers. He stood at the window, his face turned partly away from Nameir. "It seems unlikely that someone without magic, however skilled with weapons, could have taken him unawares. Therefore the most reasonable supposition is that Tarik was killed by another Magician. One of the Six? But which? And which would be powerful enough to go against the man who made most of them what they are? They are young and not nearly as skilled as he was."

He turned to her and what she saw in his face was familiar. She saw in it the still shock of a corpse on the battlefield. It was worse than grief. Yet when he spoke it was in an even tone, calm. "Do you see my dilemma, Nameir Hazan? Perhaps not. But I have freed Garon Senn in the meantime and put him in command of a battalion. So that is done."

She swallowed. "My king, if we are attacked . . . if things go as they should not . . ."

"Go ahead, Nameir," he said with gentleness. "It's all right."

She nodded. "It's crucial to preserve you. It is you who unites the people. Mansur once mentioned . . . a means of escape from the palace. A secret known only to the royal heirs. And to me."

"So I would be not only the weakling king," he mused. "Weakling, cuckold, fool. Atop all that . . . the king who flees?"

"*No.* You'd be the one who rallies to save House Evrayad. The house that has kept this land united all the years, and made us prosper."

"You are kind to say that," he said, and looked away again to the window.

THERE was an advantage to traveling with a Magician so well acquainted with portals. When Lin first suggested they'd need horses for the ride north, Zahir laughed. Soon she found out why. For of course this was how he'd so swiftly navigated the hillsides and northlands on scouting missions. And this was how Valanir Ocune had once, that memorable night she was to become a Seer, whisked her from Tamryllin to the Tower of the Winds.

It meant there was a sense of unreality to their days and nights, a disorientation. Scarcely had they departed the walls of the city when, all at once, they were in a forest beside a creek of sweet water. The sheltering of aspen and birch trees had made the place feel remote, and through openings in the bracken she caught glimpses of mountain slopes. "This is one of my favorite places," Zahir had told her, a hint of mischief in his eye. "Keep it between us, or the next royal hunt will be here."

There was something about his smile, these days, that left her feeling disoriented, too. He seemed genuinely mirthful, pleased to be in her company; but underneath that was something else. She didn't know when it had begun—whether it was with the Ifreet or with the night of Nitzan or their time in Majdara—but it was like a hook that caught at her from behind the merriment, made her look twice. The second time, often, the smile was gone.

Another night—for these travels were invariably done in dark— he brought them to a meadow where flowers stirred gently among long grasses. At daybreak, Lin awoke to see Zahir kneeling at a stone slab. It was smooth, black, with a shine to it. It was the tomb of the Magician he had mentioned earlier, now a key to their travels here. She gathered that Zahir paid his respects to the dead. So they were in Vizier Miuwiyah's province. It would be the only time, until they reached the marches, that Lin would have some orientation as to where they were.

"How long until we are there?" she asked him once, tersely, thinking of Eldakar and the Zahra and the attack they awaited.

"Three days," he said. "I know what you're thinking. I wish it were faster, too."

The day before they were to reach the fortress of the Fire Dancers, they saw smoke. It rose from between mountain peaks as if the rock itself spat it out. But Lin did not need Zahir to say, "Almyria," to know it was what they saw.

"What hope do we have?" she said. "Even allied with the Jitana, if they'll have us. How can we fight something like this?"

"They are Magicians," he said. "This enemy. In that case, what we need is magic. That of the Jitana joined to ours. Take heart. Your idea was right the first time."

But something was awry with their plan. She didn't know how she knew, or what it was. That lack of certainty accompanied her when she lay down for the night, curled in blankets on the rough grass of the foothills south of Hariya, the highest mountain.

It was that night a girl came to her. They were camped outside, overlooking the mountain range at night. The stars above Hariya abundant and clear. Zahir was asleep, lying flat on his back to face the stars. So when the girl arrived, it was only Lin that saw her.

The girl was of small stature so it was hard to tell her age. She wore a prim, dark blue dress with lace at the collar and cuffs. A child, unremarkable, though with a cast of seriousness in her eyes.

Her eyes. Her right eye, in particular. The moon showed it clear.

Lin drew a sharp breath. "The sign," she said. The girl nodded. She appeared sad, but could not seem yet to speak. Lin said, incredulous, "*His* sign. I know it. I . . . feel it. Who are you?"

"No one important," said the girl. "I'm a student. Not even really a poet. When Valanir Ocune made me Seer—when he gave me his sign—he had no choice, as he saw it. It was to save you. He . . . he died trying to save you." Her face crumpled, no doubt at Lin's expression. "I'm sorry. He would not have wanted you to know that. But I have to tell you because . . . because it's important. I'm here to show you something." She beckoned, looked commanding beyond her years yet still sad. "Come."

A doorway had opened before them in the air. It was black, blacker even than the night sky. The girl walked through and vanished. Lin followed her.

They were on the street of a city at night. So it appeared at first. Then Lin noticed that it was not a city, but a ruin. All around them were crushed walls, towers collapsed in pieces.

There was a full moon, merciless in its glare. In that glare a boy was hunched, picking through rubble. Scrabbling. His hands dark with blood where stone had cut into the skin. He had clearly been doing this for some time. His movements frantic like a rat. The low whimper he made, every so often, recalled an animal, too.

Finally he rose and faced her. It was clear he could not see her, but she knew him. Despite that he was a boy, she knew his face.

He was scratched and bloodied, coated with dirt. Clothes frayed to rags. In his eyes there was nothing left. What he recited seemed rote. As if he'd already said it many times, perhaps in the course of his long search in the stones. For in all that broken city, Lin knew, was not one living soul.

"I swear vengeance," he said. "On my mother, my father . . . all Vesperia. I swear it." He had done with weeping. Tears had made streaks in the filth. But his eyes now were dry. In a voice that could have belonged to someone much older he said, "All that you build, Yusuf Evrayad, I will destroy."

THEY were in a *khave* house; Lin knew by the sweet aroma. The men seated within at tables engaged in rowdy banter. No one showed any awareness that a pair of unaccompanied women—generally off-limits in Kahishian *khave* houses—had entered.

The girl beside Lin stood silently. She raised her arm, pointed to a table. Lin followed the direction of her hand.

Smoking a pipe, his lute beside him on the table, sat Zahir in the guise given him by the Ifreet, when he went by the name of Haran. There was less silver in his hair, Lin saw, though he was otherwise unchanged. He looked wary.

Seated across from him was a man uncommonly handsome, with wild red-gold hair. Though not visible in the light of the *khave* house,

Lin knew immediately that this man had the mark of a Seer. "I appreciate your meeting me here," he said, and Lin was stirred, even amid the noise, by the resonance of his voice. "I believe we share a common interest."

Zahir, as Haran, leaned back in his chair. "I'd tell you it was dangerous to send me that message, but I believe you know all too well. I assume you are armed in your own ways."

The other man nodded appreciatively. "You assume correctly. While the enchantments of my land are . . . dormant, for now . . . I have been relentless in pursuit of other skills. I've traveled the world in search of what my own land could not provide. On one of these journeys, I discovered a site of astonishing power. The villagers nearby made a sign of the Evil Eye when it was mentioned, told me there was a penalty of death for any who entered. I believe you already know its name. A great ruin in Ramadus, of which it is forbidden even to speak. I made it my personal mission to uncover all I could about the place . . . how it came to be destroyed, the manner of dark magic that hangs upon it. I followed the threads for some time. These led, at last, to you."

"And who are you?" said Zahir. "If I am to speak further with you of such matters—of things forbidden—perhaps I should know your name. It's clear that you are a Seer."

"A reasonable question," said the other man with a laugh. "My name is Elissan Diar. A Seer, yes, though it's been a long, long time since I was at the Isle." He leaned forward, spoke in a lower voice. "I know your purpose. The salvation of your people, of your city, can come only with the destruction of the ruling house in Majdara. Of the palace itself . . . its very walls built on blood. Am I right?"

When Zahir didn't answer, Elissan said, "Here is my proposal. Very soon, the Seer Valanir Ocune will approach you for help in unlocking the enchantments of Eivar. Perhaps he already has. I see in your face that the latter is most likely the case. All I ask is that you continue to help him. Not difficult, is it? But know this—in helping him, you cement your own plan. It is only with combined powers—yours, and ours—that we might bring about the fall of House Evrayad."

"And what is that to you?"

"I have plans of my own, for Eivar," said Elissan. "You have plans here.

You see what I am suggesting? That in time, we may work together towards common goals. Your magic, joined to mine."

LIN was crouched in the grass. Her head in her hands. When she looked up, she saw the girl stood over her so that now, at least, she appeared the taller. Her mark of the Seer radiated by light of the moon. The peaks of the northern mountains outlined silver.

Beside her, undisturbed, Zahir slumbered on.

Lin stared at him, then back to the girl. "Who are you?"

"I am Julien Imara," said the girl. She reached out a hand. "I am nothing like you, Court Poet. I am no one. But we share a maker in Valanir Ocune. I'm here as his messenger. His gift to you beyond death."

Lin reached out her hand, joined her fingers with that of the girl. "Don't say you are no one," she said. "Never say that, Julien Imara. You've done important work today. I expect you will again. Keep yourself safe."

The girl bowed her head. The next instant she was gone. Lin was alone with Zahir on the hill. Faced now, for the first time in what seemed a while, with a clear task.

She crept like a shadow, like an Amaristoth. She hunkered astride the Magician's waist, set her blade to his throat. Said, "Wake up." His eyes fluttered open instantly. He appeared unsurprised. As if he'd expected this. It unnerved her, though not enough to make her withdraw the blade. "Tell me the truth," she said, "or I'll carve out your eyes." Her vision blurred; she blinked violently. *Tell me what you did,* she commanded. "All of it."

His eyes were like the mountain pools by which once she'd hunted, glass-still and calm. "I killed Valanir," he said. "You already know."

chapter 26

"THIS was all your plan."

"No," he said. "Not all. I didn't expect a lot of things."

He was looking up at her. Her knife still poised at his throat. His neck bare and smooth. It would be easy to finish him, right here. He seemed to intend no resistance. Did not even seem to feel fear. There was no increase in heartbeat that she could detect, no speeding of the pulse. They were so close she could feel his breath on her face. She would have felt a change in his heart.

"What didn't you expect?" she said at last.

"First, there was Eldakar," he said. "It began as you'd think. I was using him, and it was easy. Until it became more, and then I knew I had to let him go. For his sake. He reached my heart at the end. The first time anyone had. I had come to the Zahra with so much hate in me, particularly for all things Evrayad. Hate fueled me from childhood, through my university days, through everything. Even in the midst of parties, when I made jests to make people laugh—secretly I hated those people. And then I met this man who loved music and wanted nothing more than to make a better world. Eldakar became my weakness. Until then, I thought goodness could not truly exist. That it was a sham, a ploy people used to get what they want. And maybe that is often true . . . but it is not always true. He taught me that. When I killed Tarik Ibn-Mor during Nitzan, it was one last gift to Eldakar. I knew Tarik worked against him."

"Eldakar will be killed. Because of you."

"No." The first trace of emotion so far. "He can escape. Even if the palace falls. Yusuf was wily in that, as he was in all things. Under the palace is an elaborate system of tunnels, for irrigation. One of these tunnels, cleverly concealed, is unlike the rest. It leads outside the city walls. Yusuf was nearly assassinated in his youth and was not about to let it happen again. He'd prepared for every eventuality."

"Did Yusuf ever find out who you are?"

"No. I grieved when he died. Truly grieved. Because I would never have the chance to make him suffer. The damned magic was too impenetrable, politics too slow-moving towards my goal."

"To destroy the Zahra." She recalled what Elissan Diar had said: *Its walls are built on blood.*

"The Zahra had to fall, Lin, if I was to free the ten thousand. That is the rule, the first I learned. From childhood I set out to destroy a kingdom. Not knowing, then, what it would make me do. What I'd become."

She felt cold. "You knew. You knew you'd be a traitor."

"Perhaps some part of me knew," he acknowledged. "When I began to plot against Rihab Bet-Sorr, knowing how that would weaken the court from the inside . . . that was an incredible ugliness. I was betraying the only person in the world who mattered to me. But then when I became complicit in murder, on a monstrous scale . . . everything that had led up to it seemed a game. The deaths . . . those posed the great question that kept me awake at nights. If I had foreseen that, would I have ever begun? When I recall my mother's eyes, my father's face . . . Lin, what ought I to have done? I have asked myself this question countless times through the years. What are the souls of thousands of Kahishians weighed against thousands of mine?"

"I don't know," she said. The only truth she had.

"You haven't asked why I killed Valanir," he said. A flare in the calm of his eyes. "He saw a way to release you from Darien's spell. That night, he tried to free you. I had to stop him." A pause, as if he couldn't believe it himself. "I killed my friend."

Her eyes were blurring again. *"Why?"*

Zahir closed his eyes as if her pain was his. "We still have time. Just for this."

"What?"

"I want to show you."

The world vanished around Lin. When she tried to cry out, it was soundless. When sensation returned, she saw two things. One was that Zahir was at her side. Another was that they were wrapped in sky, black and bejeweled. Only this time was not like the Tower of Glass. This time, there was no barrier between them and the lowest heaven. They floated free.

When Zahir turned to her, it was with a smile almost sweet. "Fear not, lady," he said. "This is illusion. In reality, I am at your mercy, still, on that hilltop. You can still kill me."

"And I will," she said, thinking of Valanir. She had the image of him, carrying her as if she were a bird, that kept repeating itself in her mind. And now would have nothing more.

So many lost. Darien, Hassen, and now Valanir. Her chest felt it would burst from the hurt.

"Take me away from here," she said. "This adds insult to what you've done."

"There was something Valanir didn't know," said Zahir. His eyes sought hers and she, despite herself, could not look away. "I helped him bring back the enchantments because of a prophecy. That prophecy showed you. From the start . . . years ago . . . I saw you."

"You saw me." Lin remembered, years ago, Valanir saying the same words. She felt sick.

"Yes. Running through the woods in winter, branches clawing your face. I saw one day you would be a Seer under a curse of death. I saw the one who would save Vesperia. With me. Your ties to the Underworld would help me, with the magic of the Ifreet. Together we would free the souls of my city. Release them to their final rest."

"So that was your plan," she said. "To use me."

"Yes," he said. "And then to save you. If you came with me to the other side . . . joined with me in your power . . . I could purge you of Darien's spell. My life would still be shortened by the Ifreet, but not yours. You would live—forever, if I had my way." Again that smile. "I can show you how it would be," he said. "And believe I do not control these matters. This is only what I have seen. One possible path."

In the heavens appeared what seemed a window. It showed the Zahra on its mountain. Lin let out a cry. The palace, the entire mountain, was engulfed in flames. Smoke made a spume of black clouds around and about, and to the sky.

"The price," said Zahir Alcavar. "One I shall mourn for always. But Eldakar will live. I take comfort from that." He pointed. "And there we are." Lin watched, dazed, and saw within that image, on a hill that overlooked Majdara, their two figures, she and Zahir Alcavar. Their hands were joined. She watched as a dark opening appeared in the air before them, these other selves. Watched as they two stepped through. "That is our descent," he said. "To the Underworld. With Edrien's help, and yours. We go there and harrow the place to its foundations for the souls trapped there. My parents. My people. They never deserved such a fate."

"And after?" she said, despite herself. She was hypnotized by what she was seeing. The two of them, their hands joined as if they belonged thus. Upright as they descended to the dark world. She herself, with a queenly posture and flowing cape, confident that what she did was right. Perhaps she always appeared that way, Lin thought. A lie told by her face to the world, continuously.

"After," he said, "you would be Court Poet, and I a Magician in your service. I would swear fealty to Tamryllin, and you. My life is shortened, but we would have some time."

Another image now, and this time she didn't see herself. This time she was there. She was in a chamber where the stars outside were a furious glow, unreal. A night that was unreal. She was standing at the window, but turned when she heard the door. And what she saw, when she looked at him, was the face of a man who had all his life trekked through a desert and now, at last, found a spring.

"You'd save me?" she murmured. "Or I you?"

"Both," he said, and was in her arms. "For as long as I live. I will pay for my misdeeds, my love. I loved you so long, from afar. I will give all I can to you before I'm gone."

And she thought, as she held him and lost her breath to that warmth, that perhaps Valanir would have given her his blessing. That he would understand why such things, such very difficult things, needed to be done. And after all, she further reasoned, before her senses were overpowered, Zahir would pay. He was soon to die, having given his life for the Ifreet's magic. He would pay. There was justice in this. Wasn't there?

She was astride him on a bed lit by the moon. They moved together violently, with purpose. She traced his face with her hands as the unbearable surge came, again and again. And didn't stop. She was weeping, they both were, as if all they had aimed for in life was right here.

"I will never stop loving you," he said, "whatever you choose."

They were back on the hilltop with her knife at his throat. Her hand had not stirred in all that time. Nothing was changed. She was breathing hard, that was all. No: she was weeping still.

"You know what I must choose," she said. "If you love me you must know me, too."

"We may have hope, past what we know," he said. But it came out hoarse, and he was pale.

Through her tears she almost laughed. A bitter laugh, that she had let desire obscure, even for a moment, what she knew to be true. "I can't betray Valanir," she said. "Nor all those others you killed."

"Even if it means you will die."

"Even then."

"Does the fate of my city not move your heart, Lin?" He was drained, appearing already as if she had killed him.

"You know it does," she said. It was difficult, now, to hold that knife in place. "But you asked a question. What are the souls of thousands of Kahishians weighed against thousands of yours? The soul of Valanir, against theirs? And for that . . . I have no answer. I can't be the one to decide. Certainly not to save myself."

Zahir lay back on the ground, looking spent. He forced a weak smile. "I should have known better," he said, "than to argue with an Amaristoth. That is where I went wrong." The smile faded, and in its place a hard look, one of resolve. "So that is your answer?"

"Yes."

"Then there is only one thing to be done."

Her hand tightened on the knife hilt. "What's that?"

"Elissan Diar is attacking the Zahra tonight," said Zahir. "Please, Lin. Let me kill him."

FOR days Nameir had drilled the men in preparation for the events to come; on a battle to be fought inside the walls. What she did not share

with them was her dread. Most of these men had not seen Almyria:
she had.

They had moments' warning, thanks to the Magicians stationed in
the Tower of Glass. But without their leaders, the Magicians were severely depleted. Zahir and Tarik had been the glue that held together the
Seven. With one away and the other dead, the Tower was in disarray at
precisely the time it was needed most. It occurred to Nameir, more than
once in the intervening days, to wonder why Zahir Alcavar had left at
such an inopportune time, and why the king had permitted it.

In the moments before the attack Mansur was with her. The red scarf
around his head hung askew. They stood back-to-back in the throne
room, which they'd been alerted would be a focal point of attack. In one
hand held a sword, in the other, a dagger. She said, "It's been an honor,
my lord."

"Shut up, Nameir," he said.

And then the white-clad ones fell upon them.

HE had never asked to be Chosen. This was a recurring thought for
Layne Durren all through that spring. As a fourth-year student, he was
among the younger ones, so he had even less of a say in what they did
than anyone, if you thought about it. If, as was whispered in corners late
some nights, their magic was really killing people, not just some warped
illusion or game . . . who were they to disobey an Archmaster? If Elissan Diar ordered it, there had to be some rationale that they, mere
novices, could not see.

At nights, as they gathered around and bathed in his melodious voice,
Elissan spoke of the importance of what they were doing. The Chosen
were warriors, he explained. He spoke of the original poets, before
Davyd Dreamweaver had excised the enchantments from Eivar. Before
that fatal excision—one that had doomed poets to servitude for
centuries—poets had used enchantments to fight the workings of evil.
Now that the enchantments had returned, it was time to take up the
cause anew. In this case, to engage in battle with a faceless foe in a place
beyond. With demons, Elissan said.

Layne knew his body was changing. That he had grown thinner, more
susceptible to chills and fever. He woke several times in the night,

restless. These changes were, Elissan made clear, the cost of enchantments. But it was to achieve something larger, something that would
enrich them all in the future, bring them and the Academy a greater
glory.

With great passion Elissan Diar said once, "It is not for us to remain
isolated on this Isle. Our powers were given us by Kiara to illuminate the
world. This is the way. Those who do not join with us will be left behind."
And those last words, *left behind*, like a cold draft from a door left open.

There were students who couldn't bear the strain of the enchantments. Who were sent home. Most recently it was Dorn Arrin, which
was strange: unlike the rest who had had to be sent away, Dorn was
not among the Chosen. And sometimes in his dreams Layne saw images from the night of Manaia that in daylight he surely could not
credit. It was impossible that Archmasters—that he, and the other
students—would have thrown someone to the fires. Whatever he saw
some nights, of himself and other boys carrying the tall final-year in
their arms towards the flames . . . that had to be the workings of his
imagination.

The atmosphere of the Isle these days lent itself to strange imaginings.
Boys who ventured into the woods kept getting lost. Some returned
with stories and a distant look that never faded. No one knew what to
believe. Lingering with them was the memory of the boy who had tried
to kill himself in the cook's storage room.

But these thoughts were not appropriate to the moment as he and the
other Chosen, led by Elissan Diar and his second-in-command Etherell
Lyr, stood at the lakeside that night. It was Layne's task, tonight, to concentrate on their goal, which Archmaster Diar had assured them was
their greatest yet. "Tonight," he'd said in the dining hall, "we will ascend
to heights never reached by any generation of Seers. Not even in the time
of the enchantments. This will be a new order, lads, and those of you that
I've chosen will be granted a high seat."

Beside him stood Etherell Lyr, who every day appeared more like an
anointed prince. At his side Sendara Diar, with a smile perpetual and
tremulous, as if she were already a bride. Everyone knew that Etherell
and the Archmaster's daughter were as good as promised to one another; the idea of such gratification haunted their adolescent dreams.
Her beauty in the past summer had come to full flower, as if to taunt

them. Everyone wanted to *be* Etherell Lyr and in consequence, obeyed him. Though another reason was his eyes. He never used threats as Maric had, but without words conveyed the impression that disobedience would be met with consequences much, much worse.

Layne could barely remember Maric Antrell and his time as Elissan's second-in-command, as if a fog hung over that time. That fog hung most thickly over the night of Manaia. He had awakened the next morning in his bed without any recollection of how he'd gotten there. He was aching in every limb and shivering with a fever. This was true for all the students. By the time their sickness had dissipated, so had all memory of Manaia been eradicated, though there was evidence—the piles of desiccated wood and ash in the courtyard—that the rite had been carried out.

The night at the lakeside, named the apex of what they aimed to achieve, began like all such nights. The students made a circle, with Elissan Diar at the center. Standing beside him—flanking to either side—High Master Lian and Etherell Lyr. The High Master's participation was a recent development, one much noted though not discussed. You never knew, after all, who might listen and report. It was better to keep speculation to oneself.

The moon was low and full that night, and tinged red, like a fruit ripe for picking. Some memories of past nights like this surfaced in Layne's mind. Perhaps recalled by the red. He stilled his hands, which were trembling.

I came here to make music, he thought. And then stifled the thought. At this he'd become adept.

The rituals *did* involve music. Their singing combined in ways that would in time carry them away from this place, even from their bodies where they stood at the shore of the lake. They had become accustomed to this. To being transported, through whatever power of their music under the influence of Archmaster Diar, to a place where they faced shadowy figures. Where they gripped swords and axes in hand which they swept at opponents. These enemies were shadow-people, without faces. There was no sound in this other place; if there were screams, they were silenced.

From boys who had been chosen earlier, Layne had heard that lately it was not so easy as it had been in the beginning. At first they'd faced opponents without weapons, or barely, who'd collapsed like stalks of wheat. But then came the first skirmishes with armed combatants. Then came the great city, after which two more boys had been sent home. Elissan Diar had replenished his Chosen after that, hastily training additional and younger boys to take their place. These had been selected by Etherell, who seemed to have an eye for talent, or perhaps for a quality of cold-bloodedness. It was hard to say.

After all this time, Layne wasn't sure what sort of talent was called for, here. He had come to the Academy to sing. At this he had, from boyhood, excelled. It seemed apropos for a younger son of a noble house with a talent for music to study at the Academy. He had not counted on the resurfacing of the enchantments, on being pulled into acts that felt wrong and gave him twisted dreams. But there was that high seat promised by Elissan Diar. There was that coldness in Etherell's eyes. Layne did as he was told, as did all the Chosen.

That night when their ritual song had reached its peak, they entered a place of battle once again. They faced armed opponents. Layne had the hazy impression, after stumbling down a staircase, of finding himself in a place of grass and trees. That was all he had time to notice, however; for everywhere they looked were more combatants who had clearly been stationed at the ready.

Not that it mattered. The Chosen had a significant advantage against their faceless enemy: they couldn't be killed. If one fell, he'd arise immediately in a new body. In that way it was like a game.

THE fight had taken Nameir and Mansur from the throne room to the gardens. So many bodies lay already under the moon, so much blood poisoning the soil, that Nameir wondered if they could be named gardens anymore.

Mansur turned to her with battle-crazed eyes. "You're sure Eldakar got out?"

They were crouched behind a willow, a momentary lull. Nearby a man's head rested on the ground on its side, staring at them. Nameir thought she recognized the man and turned her eyes away. "I forced him," she said. It had almost been a physical act, the night before the attack: she had escorted the king to the tunnel entrance nearly by force of arms. "Mansur wants this," she had said pointedly, when he had looked on the verge of refusing.

"Nameir," he said. "How is this not cowardice?"

"You'll return," she said. "When this is over. Your people need you."

Now, observing the carnage of the garden, she couldn't imagine that anyone would return to this place, where blood was soaking into the ground, where the marble fountains ran a rusted brown. Forever tainted, she thought, these works that had been the pride of Yusuf Evrayad.

"My prince," Nameir said now, "I see no option but to stall them for as long as we can. Until dawn." Dawn, when their powers would lose their hold and they'd vanish, leaving corpses behind.

He clasped her hand hard. "Let's to it, then."

IT was like a dash of cold water in his face when Layne found himself, gasping, pulled from the place of battle. He was back, abruptly, on the lakeside. This was not normally how these events would go.

There was a disturbance in the center of the circle. The boys all backed away reflexively, as if to make more space for what was to come. There was, growing before them, a greenish glow that, as they watched, took the shape of a man. Stupefied, they stared as the figure of light took on features, became defined. A man with dark hair and clothes markedly different from their own, who stood across from Elissan Diar and the two who flanked him to either side.

Elissan said, contemptuously, "What is this? Has she gotten to you?"

"I'd expect a more courteous greeting from a colleague," said the man. "Even if I intend to kill you."

Elissan waved his companions away. "Let me attend to this," he said curtly. He stepped forward, towards the man who glowed. When he spoke it was in a smooth, honeyed tone. "So, Zahir Alcavar. You'll doom all you love . . . for a woman?"

The other man smiled, though it was more a baring of teeth. "Not exactly. It seems no matter what I do, I doom those I love. Either way." He stepped nearer the other man, the space between them rapidly narrowing. "With no good choices, ridding the world of something monstrous seems the least I can do."

"And by that you mean me," said Elissan. "Despite all you have done."

"Not despite. Not at all," said Zahir Alcavar. "When I look at you, I see myself." He barked an incantation, his hands together. A rent appeared in the air before them. That was how it appeared to Layne—as if the world itself was torn. What began as a streak of black grew wider, longer. It emitted a strange wind, hot and sulphur-smelling. "With the help of my companion," said Zahir, "I can open portals to the lower depths. This seems an appropriate fate for you."

The wind became stronger, more insistent. Elissan was being drawn to it, inexorably. For the first time, Layne saw fear on the man's face, a sight he'd have thought impossible.

"It cannot be closed," hissed the man who glowed, "unless it is fed. And it wants you."

What happened next was too quick for Layne to register. Elissan was leaping forward with a cry, of terror and rage. The next moment, another cry: this a scream of pure terror. High Master Lian, gripped in Elissan's burly arms. His arms waved, his hands scrabbled at the air. It was useless. Elissan flung the older man with all his strength. The High Master tumbled through the black portal, headfirst. His scream cut off abruptly as the opening closed.

"I have always wished for control of an Ifreet," said Elissan. He was breathing hard. "How fortunate you've been, Magician. In so many ways. As I admit, I, too, have been fortunate. But your luck ends tonight."

The other man looked weary now, but stood his ground. "So we're to fight, then," he said. There were strange markings on his arms, Layne saw, that burned through his sleeves: black serpents, edged in flame. Up and down they coiled, as if of their own accord. "You with your weapons, and I with mine."

Elissan laughed. "Shall we take a wager, then," he said. "Glass against the Winds."

THE gardens were quiet. It had happened suddenly. One instant the enemy warriors were there, the next they had vanished. Mansur's force was in disarray, confused. Nameir shouted to them. "Regroup!" she called. "Assume your positions." Nameir looked to Mansur, who seemed as bewildered as she. She did not trust this sudden reprieve. "Until dawn, we must assume they will return," she cried to the men. "Be ready."

*   *   *

ON the hill by moonlight Lin sat and stared at Zahir. He had entered into a trance, his eyes closed. She knew this might be some elaborate scheme, a final betrayal. But if there was even a chance it was true . . .

She had taken a risk. But she still had her knife to his throat. She remained in that position, dropped to her knees beside him where he sat cross-legged in the grass. She and Rayen, when hunting, had adapted to assuming such stances for long periods. If you stirred even an inch, you might alert the prey.

He had taken on the signs of the Ifreet: the green glow of his skin, the serpentine markings on his arms. His eyes were closed and he remained expressionless, but the markings writhed. As she watched, the glow seemed to fade, then grow stronger again. Lin was filled with dread for no reason she could have put into words. She felt relief, then, when he opened his eyes.

Then he spoke. But it was barely a whisper. "Lin." She leaned nearer to hear him. "I injured him. It may . . . it may have stopped the attack. May have . . . may have saved the Zahra, at least. It's all I could do." Black trickled from the corner of his mouth. As if from a wound inside. *"Miryan, I'm sorry."*

His eyes began to change as she watched. They were turning to pools of black, until the whites were obliterated. And then his lips stretched in a long, lazy smile. "Lady Amaristoth," he said. This was not Zahir's voice. It was a voice she'd heard once before, in the vision of the *khave* house that Julien Imara had shown her. The voice of the bright-haired Seer—Elissan Diar. "I'm pleased to make your acquaintance," he drawled. "You have, after all, played a fascinating part in this story. A part that is, I'm afraid, soon to come to an end."

She held the knife tight to his throat. "You seem sure of that."

He laughed. The next moment had flung her back, as with the force of a wind. She went flying, landed on her back. She immediately leaped up; he was still laughing. "Silly woman, do you think Zahir was ever in your grasp? He could have called upon the Ifreet for aid. He chose not to. In the end he was weak—too weak to take the reins of power as a man must, and do what must be done." He stood tall now, and possessed of the green glow. He looked at her with the strange black-filled eyes and laughed again. "I have no need to fight you. You're dead already, Court

Poet—it's clear in your eyes. Death was written into you with Darien's spell. I have only one task here before I'm done." His voice sank deep. "The Ifreet does Zahir's bidding. And now he does mine."

Lin leaped forward with a shout, but it was too late. Zahir had drawn his dagger and, before she could stop him, plunged it into his own heart.

As he tottered on the grass, tumbled back, she thought she saw a return to his features of the man she knew. But she was never to know.

Lin kept watch that night beside the body as the stars faded above Hariya, and a new, cold wind blew from the west. The winds of home.

At some point a deep tiredness such as Lin had never before felt came over her. As if every part of her were weighed down with stone. When she slept, she found herself riding a pearl-grey horse through the hills that overlooked the mountain range of Hariya. It was dawn and the air was sweet. Before her in the saddle rode a man, and she clung to him about the waist; she knew, without knowing how she knew, that it was Zahir Alcavar. The horse glided at an impossible speed, swifter than a gallop. She realized then: it was flying. A winged horse.

WHEN Lin awoke she was bound hand and foot and slung across a mule. "She's waking up," said a man's voice. "Just as well. We'll need her awake."

She tried to turn her head towards the voice. Still so tired she could barely form words. "What . . . ?"

"We got word you'd be here," said the man. "The orders are to bring you north. It is time for the Fire Dance."

CHAPTER
27

JULIEN and Dorn spent the night on the hill overlooking the ruined city. Their guide had long since gone. Before leaving, the woman had had one more thing to say. The chill in her eyes intensified to hate. "Magic compelled me to bring you here," she said. "To betray my son."

And then she was gone, and Julien had known at once what she needed to do. What at the very last Valanir Ocune had given her, and the use for which it was intended. She could not have said how it came to her, only that the new tatters of her had begun to take on a shape. That shape given clarity with the words of their guide and even the hate in her eyes.

The mark of the Seer guided Julien Imara to the only other person walking the earth who bore the same mark. The person Valanir Ocune had desired her to find. She had ended up joining hands, briefly, with the Court Poet. Had felt a kinship deeper than she had with even her own sister. At the same time, the cold knowledge that this was someone on the edge of death.

The weight of that knowledge was with her when she rejoined Dorn Arrin at the overlook above the ruin. He'd been waiting. They sat side by side under the trees. Below, the blackness of the ruin, the teeth of its towers, no longer seemed menacing. Now it seemed forlorn. A place of mourning.

"You seem to know how to get us home," he said.

She leaned on his shoulder. The knowledge she'd brought back seemed too heavy to carry alone. "I think so," she said. "But Dorn, if we do . . . we are walking into danger."

"Etherell . . ."

"We can't trust him, either. You know that."

He put an arm around her, sensing, perhaps, that she was chilly. He tried to make light of it. "Well, you're the Seer. You'll see a way for us."

She laughed shakily. "Maybe. In the morning, we'll see."

THEY had come to an open field. A bowl of a valley spread between the foothills and northern mountains, flooded in its entirety with grass and tall-growing wildflowers. An assemblage was gathered there. Lin recalled the scene in the crypt that she'd witnessed through Edrien's eyes: the men in their fine clothes, the women in skirts vibrant as flame.

There was a focus to the gathering. Her gaze was drawn immediately to it. A pile of logs with a long pole driven into it. She thought of Aleira's grief in the place beneath the crypt; how Lin and Zahir had laughed together afterward. Making light of an old woman's prophecy.

For a shadow to be vanquished, there must be sacrifice.

And Lin Amaristoth, who had known for some time that she was to die, now knew the means by which it would occur.

At the center of the colorful assemblage was a man, imposing, wearing a long fur-lined cape and chain of gold links. A gold pendant hung from this chain in the shape of the ibis. His hair and trim beard were frosted grey. His face rugged, the dark blue of his eyes—so unusual as to be nearly violet—an answer to a question Lin had not even known she harbored. *Ah.* As she was dragged forward, still bound, Lin said, "This is hardly how a king greets a Court Poet of Eivar." She risked a small smile. "I may not, in this manner, make proper obeisance."

"None is needed," said the man. He appeared sober, even weary. "This gives me no pleasure. But it is what the Mistress has foretold."

"She saw two would go to the flames," said Lin. "But the Magician is dead."

"Indeed. Perhaps the shadow overtakes even what prophecy requires. For I understand it is that which slew the man." He drew nearer to Lin. She'd been raised to stand erect; they met at eye level. Though the men who held her were unyielding, they were not rough with her. This was not, indeed, the way heads of state ought to meet; she had a sense that the Renegade might have wished it otherwise. "As I understand it, the prophecy requires only one sacrifice," he said. "I must do as the Mistress dictates, Court Poet. I'm sorry."

A murmur through the crowd. Lin could not tell if it was sympathy or excitement. She felt as if this were all unreal. But then, she had never been this sure of her own end as she was now. One could call it an interesting experience, she thought. She had lived so long with the expectation, almost she could see it that way.

"How can you be so sure of this prophecy?" Lin asked—one last card, though a weak one.

"I am sure of the decrees of the goddess Eret," said King Sicaro, heavily. "The Mistress speaks with her voice. Understand, this rite has not been performed in centuries. Some believe it was never performed at all. We would not do this if not expressly commanded."

He barked an order over his shoulder. A man, likely a servant, came forward bearing a silver cup. As he neared Lin, she saw it was a boy, who looked awed and frightened at the sight of her.

"Drink," said the Renegade. "This way you won't feel pain. We aren't monsters."

Lin allowed the boy to hold the cup to her lips and tilt its contents into her mouth. He was clumsy but patient. He let her take her time, so the liquid would go down smooth. It tasted of honey and cloves. "I had not imagined death would be this palatable," she quipped. She already felt a slight tingling in all her limbs. She was entering a detached state, as once she had with Rayen. This was happening somewhere else, to someone else. It was from a distance she watched as the men tied her to the stake driven into the log pile.

Evening fell as they began the dance. It comprised five men and five women. Their air was sombre, and they were dressed in white. In this they contrasted with the brightly colored attire of the onlookers.

Each dancer carried a torch.

There were no musical instruments for this dance. There was only song. The dancers cried fiercely as if in mourning. As if already they grieved her death. They whirled about the pyre in perfect rhythm, caromed in circles as if they flew, each time landing without sound. All this as they bore torches and sang in torn lament. The fire made circles with them, a spectacular sight as evening deepened over the valley.

Some time passed, and it might have been just that—a spectacle. Until one dancer, with a cry raw from the throat, tossed his torch onto the bier. Lin watched, with that same detachment, as the flame began to catch on the logs beneath her.

He was the first. As each dancer reached that spot they would, with a similar cry, fling their torch. It would spin through the air, a whirling sphere, before it came to land at Lin's feet. By this time the flames engulfed the logs and had begun to catch on her clothes. On her skin. The potion worked: Lin felt no pain. Only a warming sensation that was almost pleasant. She had been cold for so long, it seemed. Now it would soon be over.

She thought of Aleira, her tears, and wanted to tell the Galician woman that she forgave her. She wasn't certain why. But if there was one thing Lin had learned in her time on earth, it was that one often missed opportunities to say what most needed saying. This was another.

She thought of the world to which she journeyed, the world beyond this, and wondered if there would be others to meet her there. Or if it was a void into which one tumbled, as into sleep. A mystery Edrien Letrell had never unveiled to her. Perhaps such revelations were forbidden even to the dead.

Valanir had died trying to save her. If she had a chance to thank him, or ask forgiveness, that would be something.

It should have been you, she'd said to him after Darien died. So coldly. At the time she'd seen the shaft sink home, by the look in his eyes. She did not doubt he'd remembered those words, carried them. If not for that, would Valanir Ocune still be alive?

Lin stiffened against the stake, against the cut of the ropes, as the flames encircled. Remarkable that regret could torment her even now, at the end of everything.

Or perhaps, now that she looked at the shape her life had taken—an arc completed—she could not help but see where it was flawed. Where she had failed.

The flames rose higher. Lin became aware that in all the valley she— the fire she fueled—was the only source of light. Otherwise it had grown completely dark. Here, then, was her task.

Vanquish a shadow.

The song around her gathered force. Still it sounded like cries of grief. More so as time passed. Building almost to rage, if mourning could be called thus. Her death was to be sacrifice and a weapon—both at once.

It was hard to imagine that beyond the portal were any she loved. Such was the most desperate desire of man poured in prayer to all the gods. That yearning for continuity. But desires and reality were not akin—a thing life and even the people she'd loved had taught her again and again.

Smoke surrounded her, shortened her breath. It would not be long.

Nearly done. Nearly done, at the last.

She was in a hall of columns. It was cool here. She wondered if her body had given out, if she'd fainted or suffocated and was now in a dream. The singing was still audible, but less, as though it came from a great distance. This was a place of peace, where she glimpsed a pool just beyond the colonnade. Its surface like a mirror.

And there beside her was Edrien Letrell, looking fit and handsome as he had in his youth. His youth, which she knew so well; had practically inhabited. How much she was attached to, understood, admired, loved, envied, hated this man. How often had she not been sure where the revered Seer ended and she began. And now he stood beside her. Separate. Resplendent in blue and gold, as if for some occasion. The famed gold harp at his side.

The singing was pitched higher now, she could hear. As if the Fire Dancers emptied their voices, themselves, of all they had.

Edrien's gaze was full of humor. "That numskull brought me back, not knowing what it would do. To me, or to you."

"Darien? He was well-intentioned," she said. "What's more, he has paid."

He reached out and traced the mark above her eye. "This should be yours. Yours alone." He laughed. "There are many worlds," he said. "I never thought to learn more than I had already discovered in the realm of death. But now there is so much more I know, having lived through your eyes. Yet never will I be able to translate it to music. A loss I must accept." He took her hand, set it to his lips. "Safe travels, always," he said, with sparkling eyes.

Lin was kneeling in a pile of ash and dirt, back in the open field. Her clothes had burned away. So had her bonds. She looked down at herself, at her arms and legs. Ash made a grey film on her skin. But beneath this, there were markings. Delicate lines spiraling around all her limbs, that shone through the patina of ash. Markings like gold.

"The sacrifice is done." Sicaro, coming forward. He sounded awed. "Bring the Court Poet something to cover herself."

Lin found herself wrapped in white, a soft cloak. Her thoughts were descending back to the reality of where she was; she didn't understand. "The sacrifice? But . . ."

"You're alive," said Sicaro. "I wouldn't question the goddess in this matter. But if I could suggest something . . ."

She stared up at him. Hugging the cloak tight around herself. Wonderingly she stared at her own hand, that at various angles shimmered gold. *Two enter into the dance. One survives.* "The Magician," she said. Murmured to herself. As if in answer, from the depths of her mind where once had been another voice, was silence.

"You weren't alone," he said.

"No," she agreed. She strode to the heap of ash, not caring what they thought or what they might see of her body when the cloak shifted. Knelt before the pyre that had earlier been a tower of flame. That had been some time ago; the night nearly done. She wasn't certain what she searched for, but she found it in the remains of the fire. A round, smooth stone. Black, yet a splendor of many colors. Seemingly every color in the world showed in it as it caught the light.

She cupped it in her hands. This was what remained of him. Of the Seer Edrien Letrell. And she was certain as she had ever been that he'd meant it for her. A black opal, such as had never been before in an Academy ring.

Nor had there ever before been a poet quite like her.

The stone was warm from the pyre. She strode back towards the king of the Jitana. "It's true—I was not alone when I came here," she said. "I am now."

SHE was bathed, gently, by women in a tent. Clothed in a dress of her choosing, soft linen, but grey. She wanted nothing just now of colors. Her thoughts were with the dead. The women respected her wish for silence.

Later that day, a horseman rode into camp with tidings. "They battled all through the night," said the man to King Sicaro. "No use. Though Majdara is intact, yet. We believe the shadow was halted, perhaps even sustained damage, before it could reach the capital. But . . ."

"What news of the Zahra?" said Lin.

He looked at her, then at Sicaro. The king nodded, granting permission. The horseman said, "It is burning."

EPILOGUE

WHEN they dragged him into the underground chamber Ned was already considering the ways he could ensure a good death for himself, if nothing else. The room was shadowy, lit with torches, but he could see it was furnished like a tavern. That matched the description he'd expected. The Brotherhood of Thieves had become familiar to him in the past weeks, as first he'd stalked various of their members, looked for an opening. Ever-nearer to his target.

What he had not expected was that they might find him first.

The men who held Ned between them were enormous and armed with knives; there was no use struggling. They threw him down, hands rough in his hair, which had grown shaggy, as had his beard. Gripping his hair, they pulled his face up to the light. One said, "We found him, Master. What are your orders?"

A figure came forward. Looked down upon Ned. He stared up at the figure, clad in breeches and a dashing red cloak, but still familiar. A sword was buckled to her side. "It seems I found you, Rihab," he said. "Or perhaps you found me. Was I a loose end?"

She approached, set a hand on his head. "Raise him up," she told the men. They did so, and Ned straightened, loosened his shoulders. Now he could look into her eyes, though this was no help; they were unreadable as ever. "I knew you sought me," she said. "I know everything that happens in this city, Ned."

"So it's you who took over the Brotherhood," he said.

She smiled. "I've always valued your intelligence. Even if you never did beat me at chess. Yes, I took over the Brotherhood."

"You killed the Safehouse chiefs."

She nodded. "Men I admired greatly, but they had to die. There was no other way. You understand, Ned. That is the game."

"What I don't understand," he said, "is what you want. Being what you are. What do you play at here?"

Her expression was gentle. "Ned, I lied to you. But I also told you the truth. It's true I am a Fire Dancer. I am the daughter of King Sicaro, sent to the Zahra to seduce Eldakar and spy on him. My true name is not Rihab. It is Myrine. The name of a long-ago warrior queen, such as my father hoped I'd become."

Ned cleared his throat, which had grown hoarse. "Yet you say you told the truth."

"Yes. I wanted you to know, Ned, because there was something in you I thought I could trust. What I told you the night in the garden was true. I came to the Zahra to conquer and was, myself, conquered." She smiled. "I am, I'm afraid, a disappointment to my people in that regard. I love Eldakar and will do anything to protect him. But was powerless to do so in the Zahra. Was a liability to him there, with the politics in play. But here in the city is a force that has always been organized, well-trained, strong. All they need is a new purpose. And leader."

Ned's jaw dropped. "You can't mean . . ."

She smiled. "I see you've got it. Eldakar escaped the invasion and will try to rally the provinces. This fight will continue, that is certain. He will need help. And here, in Majdara, is a force at the ready."

"Which you will lead."

"Which I lead."

Ned breathed deep to still the rattling of his heart. He wanted to go bravely. "Now that you've told me all, I imagine I am indeed a loose end for you—Myrine. Will you do one thing for me? I would get word to my wife. I'd have her know . . . that she is free. So she won't have to wonder what happened to me."

The queen—for so he could not help thinking of her—laughed. "Ever the honorable knight. Still unaware of how the pieces upon our battleground interact—the acts that *must* be carried out. Not those executed by caprice, or worse—in error." Her fingers trailed down the back of his head, through his hair. Sending a chill all through him. Coming to rest, at last, at the back of his neck. "Kill you?" she said. "I'd hoped, rather, that you would join with me."

Acknowledgments

I received invaluable feedback on the final draft of *Fire Dance* from Batya Ungar-Sargon, Scott Hawkins, and Seth Dickinson.

These books would not exist without the encouragement and stead-fast support of my agent, John Silbersack, and my editor at Tor, Marco Palmieri. I especially appreciate their patience as I took time to wrestle this book into what I needed it to be.

Most of all I am grateful for my life partner, Jack Reichert, who is a source of light in this world.